JULIANA

LAUREN ROYAL

DEVON ROYAL

June 2021 Edition

SWEET CHASE BRIDES: THE REGENCY

JULIANA by Lauren Royal & Devon Royal

Published by Novelty Books, a division of Novelty Publishers, LLC, 205 Avenida Del Mar #275, San Clemente, CA 92674

June 2021 Edition

Cover by Kimberly Killion

Learn more about the authors and their books at www.LaurenandDevonRoyal.com.

ISBN: 978-1-63469-173-4

~

SWEET CHASE BRIDES

The Earl's Unsuitable Bride

The Marquess's Scottish Bride

The Laird's Fairytale Bride

The Duke's Reluctant Bride

The Viscount's Wallflower Bride

The Baron's Inconvenient Bride

The Gentleman's Scandalous Bride

The Cavalier's Christmas Bride

A Chase Brides Christmas

SWEET CHASE BRIDES: THE REGENCY

Alexandra

Juliana

Corinna

SWEET CHASE BRIDES: THE RENAISSANCE

Alice Betrothed (coming soon)

For our Chase Family Readers Group

With our everlasting thanks for all of your support!

ONE

The Foundling Hospital, London
Saturday, June 8, 1816

LADY JULIANA Chase's sisters often accused her of looking for trouble. Of sticking her nose where it didn't belong. Of exaggerating—if not outright imagining—other people's problems and sorrows and miseries.

But she would swear she'd never seen anything quite so sad in her life.

Upstairs in the Foundling Hospital's picture gallery, she stared through the window down into the courtyard. There, arranged in six neat, regimented lines, a hundred or more young girls performed calisthenics, resignation written on their faces. In all of her seventeen years, Juliana couldn't remember ever feeling that grim.

"William Hogarth was a genius."

Sighing, she turned from the window to see her younger sister scrutinizing the art on the gallery's pale green walls. "I thought you preferred the Dutch masters."

"I do," Corinna said. "But look at the characters in this painting."

The work was titled *The March of the Guards to Finchley*, and the people depicted were, indeed, characters. Humor, rowdiness, and disorder abounded. "The drummer looks quite amused," Juliana said, swiveling back to the window.

The painting seemed a striking counterpoint to the figures outside.

Miss Emily Neville, Juliana's eight-year-old next-door neighbor, stood beside her, gazing upon the same scene. "The girls don't appear to be ill. So why are they in hospital?"

"*Hospital* is an old word that originally meant 'guesthouse,'" Miss Strickland, the battle-axe of a woman assigned to shepherd visitors through the orphanage, explained in her no-nonsense way. "This is a charitable institution for children whose mothers couldn't keep them."

"My mother died." Still gazing outdoors, Emily absentmindedly raised a hand to stroke her beloved pet, Herman, whom she always carried on her shoulder—or rather, draped around her shoulders. "May I play with the girls?"

Ranging in age from about five to perhaps fourteen, the children all had identical haircuts and wore aprons of stiff, unbleached linen over brown serge dresses. Juliana smoothed her palms over her own soft yellow skirts. "I'm afraid your pet might scare them."

"The girls aren't playing." Miss Strickland crossed her arms. "They're exercising. Outdoor exercise is advocated for maximum health. And you couldn't play with them in any case, young lady, with or without that horrid creature."

"Herman isn't horrid," Emily said, turning to the older woman. "He's quite friendly, and he couldn't hurt a soul, I assure you. See the black bars along his sides and the yellow collar behind his head?" She lifted Herman's head to show Miss Strickland. "He's just a harmless, common—"

"Get it away!" the woman shrieked.

Juliana hid a smile. Not long ago, she'd received the very same lecture from her young neighbor. For a child of eight, the girl spoke with impressive eloquence and conviction. Not to mention persistence.

Still, her pet snake would have to go.

Emily was Juliana's latest project, and Juliana was sure that with a bit of patience she could turn the child into a perfect little lady. A young lady of good grace and courtesy—most especially the courtesy to leave one's reptile at home. A few more outings like this one ought to convince her that Herman would never be welcome in public.

She took Emily's hand and gave it a squeeze, then looked back to Miss Strickland. "Do the girls *ever* play?"

"Of course they do," Miss Strickland said. "For an hour every Sunday." As though suddenly remembering her duty—principally to encourage donations—she stretched her lips into an unnatural smile. "Are you ladies enjoying your visit to the gallery?"

"Very much." Corinna moved to view the next painting. "George Lambert," she breathed. An artist herself, she'd suggested this day's outing to the Foundling Hospital's gallery. "What a lovely scene."

Mr. Lambert's picture *was* lovely, but Juliana couldn't peruse the painted people for long. Not when there were real people— disadvantaged children—to consider.

"What do the foundlings do all day?" she asked. "If they don't play?"

Miss Strickland began reciting by rote. "They rise at six and prepare for the day, the older girls dressing the younger children, the boys pumping water and such. At half past seven they breakfast, and at half past eight they begin school. At one o'clock they dine and return to school from two until dusk." She paused for a much-needed breath. "After supper, those not employed about the buildings are instructed in singing the Foundling Hymns and anthems, and in their catechism. At eight they go to bed."

What a life. Thinking about her own days and nights filled

with parties and shopping and dancing, Juliana swallowed a lump in her throat. Still, the children looked healthy, warmly clothed, and well fed—which she supposed was more than could be said for much of London's youth.

"Is there anything I can do to help?" she asked.

"Certainly, my lady. We are always pleased to accept monetary donations."

Juliana knew that was one of the purposes of the gallery. Popular artists donated paintings and sculpture, a scheme that not only earned favorable publicity for the artists, but brought the Hospital wealthy and aristocratic visitors—exactly the sort of people who might commission works of art for themselves and be persuaded to become patrons of the Hospital. It was a most satisfactory arrangement for all concerned.

But Juliana hadn't the option to become a patroness just yet. While she had a substantial dowry and wasn't in any way deprived—quite the opposite, in fact—as an unmarried girl she had no money of her own, other than a small allowance granted by her brother, Griffin. "I cannot donate significant funds," she said apologetically.

Miss Strickland aimed a rather disbelieving look down her knife-edged nose, pointedly skimming her gaze over Juliana's fashionable dress.

"I cannot," Juliana repeated firmly. "But I should like to do something." She could ask Griffin to donate, of course—and she would. But she wanted to contribute herself. "Perhaps I could make clothing for the children." Her allowance was surely enough to cover the fabric.

"The children have no need of clothing. They wear uniforms, as you've seen."

Juliana had seen the boys eating luncheon in their dining room, all wearing white linen shirts with military-style suits made of the same brown serge as the girls' dresses. "But someone has to *make* the uniforms."

"The girls make and repair them during their sewing lessons."

"Then perhaps I can make treats," she suggested. "The ladies in my family are rather renowned for our sweets."

"The children are all fed a plain, wholesome diet. Sweets aren't allowed except on very special occasions. However, food does account for a large proportion of the Hospital's budget, so your monetary donation would be much appreciated." Before Juliana could repeat that she had no money to give, Miss Strickland continued. "This is a reception day. Perhaps looking upon the infants might persuade you."

Though Juliana knew nothing could change her mind, she adored tiny babies. "We should very much like to see the infants," she said, drawing Emily toward the door.

"I'm not finished looking," Corinna said, finally moving to view the next painting.

The battle-axe cast her a speculative glance. "Well, then, the horrid snake can stay with you."

"Herman isn't horrid!" Emily said, pulling her hand from Juliana's. "If Herman stays, I shall stay." She marched over to take Corinna's hand instead. "There's an infant right here in this picture."

Corinna nodded her dark head. "It's Andrea Casali's *Adoration of the Magi*."

Juliana would never understand how anyone could stare at a single painting for so long. Two minutes with any painting, and she was finished. But then, she'd never been as interested in things as she'd been in people. "What's a reception day?" she asked, trailing the battle-axe out of the room.

Miss Strickland led her down a corridor. "On the second Saturday of every month, mothers are invited to bring their babies for possible admission."

"Possible?"

"They must meet specific criteria. An acceptable candidate

must be under twelve months of age, the mother's first child, and healthy, so as not to risk infecting other children. In addition, although only illegitimate offspring are admitted, the mother must establish her good character. A secondary purpose of the Hospital, you see, is the restoration of the mother to work and a life of virtue. Most petitions come from women who were seduced with promises of marriage and then deserted when they became pregnant. In such cases, many mothers can avoid disgrace and find employment only if they give up their children."

"How awful!" Juliana felt a twinge in her chest. She couldn't begin to imagine the heartbreak of having a baby and then needing to give it up. She certainly wasn't exaggerating *these* mothers' sorrows and miseries.

Miss Strickland opened a door. "The Committee Room," she whispered.

Inside the elegant chamber, a queue of young mothers clutched their infants tightly, the expressions on their faces a mixture of anguish and hope. Their simple cloaks and aprons were a poignant contrast to the silk gowns of the fashionable lady patronesses who'd come to observe the spectacle.

And what a spectacle it was. Juliana's chest began to ache.

As she watched, a mother about her age was invited to the front, where a well-dressed man held out a cloth bag. Shifting her baby, the mother reached a trembling hand into the bag and pulled out a little red ball. She swallowed hard and, gripping the ball in her white-knuckled fist, stepped off to join a small group of mothers and babies huddled at one side.

Abandoning the battle-axe, Juliana walked over to join the other spectators. "What does the ball mean?" she asked in a whisper.

A tall, middle-aged woman answered in kindly tones. "The system is called balloting. These mothers have already been screened and deemed acceptable. But the Governors can accept only ten infants at a time. Balloting is the fairest method of allocating places."

As she finished her explanation, another young woman drew a ball—a black one—and let it fall to the floor, tears spilling down her cheeks as she ran from the room, taking her baby with her.

"Black is bad?" Juliana asked.

"Mothers who draw black balls are immediately turned out of the Hospital. A white ball means the baby will be examined and admitted if it is healthy. Mothers who draw red balls are invited to wait and see whether any babies are refused admittance, in which case they are given a second chance to enter the lottery."

An agonizing lottery. Juliana watched as two more mothers drew black balls and one lucky woman nabbed a white one. "How many mothers are hoping for placement today?"

"About a hundred, which is typical."

And only ten would see their babies admitted. The fortunate woman with the white ball was ushered toward a corner, where a doctor waited to evaluate her child—a girl, if Juliana could judge by the scrap of ribbon crookedly tied in the baby's sparse hair.

During the short examination, a dozen more mothers drew balls—nine chose black, one red, and two ecstatic women got white. When the first baby was declared healthy, the mothers waiting with red balls visibly drooped, gripping their infants even tighter. The lucky mother—if one could call her that—was given a numbered document that certified the Hospital's acceptance of her baby, and a lead tag with a corresponding number was threaded onto a chain and placed around the child's neck.

Juliana's heart squeezed as she watched the tearful parting, the mother kissing her baby girl over and over before regretfully surrendering her to a Hospital employee. "Is she given that paper so she can reclaim her child?"

"Partly. The babies are baptized with Hospital names—the child is never told the identity of the mother, and the mother won't know her child's new name. But if at a later date she can convince the Governors of her reformed character and improved circumstances, the paper and matching tag will ensure she collects the right child."

"But you said *partly*," Juliana prompted.

The woman sighed. "Truthfully, that seldom happens. She's more likely to use the paper for her own defense; if she's accused of having disposed of her baby by murder, the certificate might save her from the gallows."

"Faith." None of the mothers looked like criminals—they were just women in dreadful circumstances. "I saw no infants in either the girls' building or the boys'. Have the babies lodgings of their own?"

"The babies aren't kept at the Hospital. They'll be baptized with their new names at Sunday services tomorrow and then placed with wet nurses in the countryside on Monday. The nurses receive a monthly wage and keep the children until they are five years or thereabouts, at which time they return to live here."

Juliana watched as the infant was carried off. "Does anyone make sure the babies are treated well?"

"Oh, yes. Inspectors visit regularly. They're responsible for the nurse's pay and the child's medical fees, and for purchasing clothes for the infants—"

"Purchasing clothes?"

"Baby clothes. Babies are sent to their new homes with frocks and caps and clouts and coats and blankets—"

"Don't the girls make these in their sewing lessons?"

"The baby clothes aren't uniforms—"

"Then I can provide them!"

"Pardon?"

"I can make them. I can make baby clothes and donate them to the Hospital."

The kindly woman blinked at her. "I don't know about that. I don't believe they've ever received any donations of a non-monetary sort."

Juliana watched another mother draw a red ball and, trembling, take her infant to join the small group of hopefuls. She imagined having to wish someone else's baby proved ill so her own baby could have a chance at a decent life. Or at least she tried to imagine it. The very thought was enough to break her heart clear in two.

Perhaps providing baby clothing could free enough funds for the Governors to accept another child or two. She wouldn't let them refuse her donation.

She turned back to the lady patroness beside her. "There's a first time for everything, isn't there?"

TWO

SPICE CAKES

Take three scoops of Flower and put into it a Spoon of ale-barm, crushed cloves, mace, and a goode deal of cinnamon. To a halfe Pound of sweet Butter add a goode deal of Sugar and mixe together. Stir in three Eggs and work until good and stiff, then add a little cold Rosewater and knead well. Knead again, pull it all in Pieces and bake your Cakes in a warm oven.

I've heard tell that should you eat one of these before a gathering where you are likely to meet available men, their spiciness will clear your head and allow you to choose wisely. This did not, however, work when I baked them for my daughter. In any case, they are delicious.

—Amethyst, Countess of Greystone, 1690

"**H**OW MANY BABY clothes do you need to make?"

"A lot." In her bedroom at the Chase town house in Berkeley Square early that evening, Juliana set down her little pot of lip pomade and picked up the list the Governors had given her. "Three frocks, three caps, three nightshirts, one mantle, one coat, one petticoat, two blankets, and ten clouts. And that's *per* child. There will be ten babies."

Emily bit into one of the spice cakes she and Juliana had baked after returning from the Foundling Hospital. "So you need to make thirty frocks?"

"Yes." The girl was articulate *and* good with arithmetic. "And thirty caps, thirty nightshirts, ten mantles, ten coats, ten petticoats, twenty blankets, and a *hundred* clouts. All within a month, before the next reception day."

Juliana set the list on her dressing table. Upside down, so it would stop taunting her. Whatever had she got herself into? She'd been thrilled when the Governors accepted her offer to provide clothing for the next intake of infants—until she'd realized just how *many* clothes she'd need to make.

She wasn't worried about the cost of the materials, because she could easily cajole Griffin into paying for whatever her allowance wouldn't cover. But the mere idea of making so many items was daunting. "You'll help me, won't you?"

Emily frowned. "I'm not very good with a needle."

"You can hem blankets and sew clouts. That's not difficult, and it will be good practice." Reaching over the girl's snake, Juliana wiped a few spice cake crumbs off her delicate chin. "I'm going to invite my sisters to help, too. We'll have a lovely sewing party." She dipped a finger into the lip pomade. "But I think you'll need to leave Herman at home."

"I told you, he's not dangerous."

"His danger, or lack thereof," she told the child, watching her in the dressing table's mirror as she slicked pomade on her lips, "is not the point. Ladies do not keep company with snakes."

Emily's chin went into the air. "I do." She adjusted the reptile's position around her neck, the better to reach for another spice cake. "What are these cakes supposed to do again?"

"Help me choose the right gentleman to wed."

"All the gentlemen will want to wed you. You always look beautiful," Emily said with a wistful sigh.

Juliana lifted a pot of rouge. "You'll look beautiful when you're grown up."

It was true. Other than her unfortunate taste in neckwear, the child was a model of femininity. She always wore pink. Her cascading blond hair and large, luminous gray eyes held much promise, and she was tall for her age. Since Juliana was small in stature, Emily was nearly her height already.

"I'm certain you'll be wildly popular," she assured the girl, "if only you'll get rid of the snake."

"I'll not give him up. Mama would be so disappointed."

Juliana sighed. When Emily was four years old, she and her mother had stumbled upon baby Herman while playing in their garden. Her mother had suggested they keep the critter and watch him grow; then, the very next day, she took ill, and she'd faded away very quickly. Emily had clung to Herman ever since.

Having lost her own mother less than three years prior, Juliana felt for the girl deeply. But she also felt that her pretty little neighbor's alarming companion was beginning to cause a disturbance, especially among those who would turn their noses up at such unconventional behavior.

Thank goodness Juliana was here to take the situation in hand.

"Your mother would understand," she told her gently. "Surely she only intended to keep Herman while he was small. Why, he must be three feet long now, much too big to stay cooped up inside the house all day—much less carried about on your shoulders. Don't you think the poor creature would be happier outside?"

"Herman isn't a creature. He's a *pet*."

"A cuddly kitten is a pet. A rambunctious dog is a pet. A snake is a—"

"Are you ready yet?" Corinna arrived in the doorway and smirked. "A Lady of Distinction doesn't hold with wearing rouge."

Juliana threw a sour glance to the book on her bedside table, *The Mirror of the Graces* by A Lady of Distinction. Their brother had given each of his sisters a copy, hoping that learning fashionable manners would help them secure husbands.

"A Lady of Distinction can keep her sallow cheeks," Juliana said. "I'll keep the admiration of the gentlemen." To emphasize her point, she brushed on more color before rising. "Yes, I'm ready. Have a spice cake while I deliver Emily home."

"You'd best hurry." Corinna took one. "Aunt Frances is already waiting in the carriage."

Much to Corinna's and Juliana's delight, their kindly Aunt Frances was acting as their sponsor and chaperone for the season. Not only was she a dear, she was also sensationally oblivious, meaning her young charges could more or less do as they pleased.

Juliana took Emily by the hand and led her downstairs, Corinna following in their wake.

It was raining when Juliana led Emily outside—it seemed to rain every day lately—but a quick dash brought them safely next door to the lifeless Neville house. Emily had two older brothers, products of two earlier marriages, but one was married and the other was away at Cambridge most of the year, so she usually shared her home with only her father and a collection of aging servants.

Their gaunt butler, who must have been eighty if he were a day, swung the door open as they arrived.

Emily stepped inside. "When shall I see you again, Lady Juliana?"

Who could deny that precious, pleading face, even if it *was* framed by a snake? "Monday," she promised the girl. Rain peppered her parasol and puddled at her feet. "I'm sure your father is looking forward to being with you tomorrow, but on Monday we shall visit the shops and choose fabric for the baby clothes."

"Will Lady Corinna come, too?"

"I believe she'll prefer to paint." Corinna always preferred to paint. "I shall see you Monday," Juliana promised and headed through the drizzle to the carriage.

Inside, Corinna waited with Aunt Frances, their matching deep-blue eyes impatient. The ladies' eyes, however, were their only similarity. Aunt Frances's peered from behind round spectacles in a face surrounded by clouds of soft gray hair, though she was only forty. Sixteen-year-old Corinna's hair was a swing of wavy brown, her face fresh and blooming. She had no need of rouge.

Juliana, on the other hand, figured she needed all the help she could get. Due to the untimely deaths of her parents and eldest brother—God rest their souls—she'd been in mourning nearly the whole of her fifteenth and sixteenth years. Thus, at seventeen, she was enjoying her *first* London season. And with the dratted season already half over, she was no closer to securing a husband than on the day she'd arrived.

Much to her brother's vexation.

Griffin was waiting at the ball when they arrived, surveying the crop of gentlemen in a businesslike manner. After weeks of events, Juliana feared she had already met more or less everyone there was to meet. The *ton* comprised all the people who mattered in society, but that was a limited social group, after all. Yet her brother had already managed to line up candidates for her first three dances and was keeping an eye out for more.

He'd become a matchmaking mama of the finest caliber.

Juliana wasn't sure she appreciated her brother's efforts, but she knew his heart was in the right place. And she did enjoy dancing, so she dutifully stood up with all three young men, smiling and chatting agreeably.

Lord Henderson was far too tall; petite Juliana spent the whole of the dance conversing with his cravat. Lord Barkely didn't laugh at her witticisms—not a single one!—though she deployed several of her best just to make certain he was truly devoid of humor. And Mr. Farringdon was kind but more than a little dim.

The spice cakes weren't going to help her choose wisely, she thought with an internal sigh, if no acceptable men bothered to attend this ball.

THREE

JAMES TREVOR, the young Earl of Stafford, hadn't been to a ball in ages. And he hadn't particularly wanted to attend this one, either.

However, being a good-natured sort of fellow, he'd chosen to regard tonight as an opportunity for renewing a number of neglected acquaintances. Among these was Griffin Chase, now the Marquess of Cainewood.

But his old schoolmate was looking rather sullen. James approached with caution.

"At whom are you glaring, Cainewood?"

"My sister." Cainewood's frown deepened. "She's not dancing."

James's gaze followed his across the ballroom. He lifted his quizzing glass and squinted through it. "The little blond one?"

"The girl in yellow, yes. That would be Juliana, wasting precious time."

"She appears to be agreeably engaged."

"With our sister. But Juliana is *supposed* to be meeting gentlemen. I despair of ever finding her a husband."

James chuckled at that. Lowering the quizzing glass to dangle on its long silver chain, he refocused on Cainewood. He hadn't seen his old friend since their time at Oxford, and he'd never met his family, but still he sensed an easy familiarity between them. He felt well within his rights to laugh at the fellow's consternation.

"Juliana is seventeen," Cainewood added as though that explained everything.

"That doesn't sound particularly old."

"No, but I'll still have Corinna to settle after her." He gestured toward his other sister, a pretty brown-haired girl. "I'd hoped to get them both married off this season, but Juliana is overparticular. And unfortunately, I believe she's already met everyone here…" His green gaze narrowed on James. "Except, perhaps, you."

"Me?"

"You. Won't you at least suffer an introduction? You're an earl now, are you not?" He flashed a crooked grin. "An earl in need of a wife."

An earl in need of a wife—the exact same words James's mother had used to describe him earlier this evening as she'd all but dragged him from the carriage into this house.

But although James had inherited the title more than two years ago, he still had a hard time thinking of himself as an earl, let alone *an earl in need of a wife*.

His older brother was supposed to have been the Earl of Stafford.

Straight out of Oxford, James had been perfectly content with his parents' plan for him to be a captain in the cavalry. Good-natured as he was, contentment was his natural state, and, in fact, he'd been pleased when his father bought him the commission. Unfortunately, less than a week into active duty, a wound ended his laughably short stint in the army.

He shifted and flexed his left knee, which always ached in this type of cold, wet weather. On days of this sort he still walked with a slight limp, which made him feel conspicuous and much older than twenty-five. But he was profoundly grateful the army surgeons had managed to save his leg rather than amputating it. So grateful that, needing a new occupation after his recovery, he'd decided to become a physician.

He hadn't been long in medical school before he'd realized he'd found his calling. For the first time in his memory, James had been more than just content with his life—he'd been truly happy. Especially after he fell in love.

Then everything fell apart.

His brother had died first, leaving James shaken by grief and the realization that he'd someday inherit. He didn't *want* to be an earl—he *liked* being a physician. He liked helping people, and he liked feeling that he made a difference. Every day was surprising and challenging, and there were always successes to balance the disappointments. Managing an earldom seemed tedious and superficial in comparison.

Then, while he was still reeling from the loss of his brother, his father's heart had stopped, and suddenly James *was* the earl.

After that came a dark, miserable blur. It was some time—he knew not how long—before the cloud began to dissipate. He simply found himself awakened one morning, not by the paralysis of grief or the weight of obligation, but by the sun. Gradually he began to feel that his despair was subsiding—by, say, a thimbleful per day—and he was growing used to his new role. His work *could* make a difference in the lives of his tenants and in the stodgy House of Lords. And his lovely new bride, whose resilience had kept him afloat, showed him that he didn't have to do as society expected—he could be an earl *and* a physician.

Harnessing the vast Stafford fortune, James had opened a facility in London where those who were too poor to afford doctors could get smallpox vaccinations, an endeavor dear to his heart. At last, he saw true happiness peeking over the horizon. Life was looking good again.

Then Anne died in childbirth, and their baby, born too early, died along with her.

No physician, himself included, had been able to make a

shred of difference. And James was certain he'd never be truly happy again.

A year later, he'd regained some measure of his old contentment. But his mother was pressuring him to take a new wife, and, while the idea pained him, he knew it was an earl's duty to sire heirs. Though he couldn't love another girl, he might as well at least consider making his mother happy. So he'd allowed her to drag him to this ball, and, by the same token, he would allow Cainewood to introduce him to his sister.

"Yes, I'd be delighted to meet Lady Juliana."

Cainewood wasted no time marching him across the ballroom and introducing him to both of his sisters. It had been so long since any girl made an impression on James that he was surprised to find his gaze locked on Lady Juliana's as he bowed over her hand. Her eyes were so full of life. He felt drawn to her energy.

And that felt incredibly wrong.

But Cainewood's sister was a pretty thing, and he couldn't seem to wrench his gaze from those eyes. Green eyes. No, blue. He couldn't decide. They seemed to change as he watched.

"Will you honor me with a dance?"

He wasn't sure whether he'd asked out of impulse or obligation, but he was glad when she responded with, "It would be my pleasure."

She let him lead her out onto the floor. He hadn't danced since Anne died. He felt a wave of panic—what if he didn't remember how? But there was a waltz playing, and Lady Juliana fairly melted into his arms.

He remembered.

"What color are your eyes?" he asked.

She gave a merry, tinkling laugh, a laugh that matched her eyes. "Hazel. Why?"

"I couldn't tell. They looked green at first, but now they look blue."

"Well, they're hazel," Juliana repeated, wishing he would

stop staring into them. It seemed almost as though he saw right through them into her head, as though he could guess exactly what she was thinking and feeling. And that was unnerving, no matter that she had nothing to hide.

She glanced away, her gaze landing on her older sister. Alexandra had come to town for the season while her new husband claimed his seat in the House of Lords. How happy they looked dancing together, Alexandra's dark eyes locked on Tristan's steady gray ones. Their road to wedded bliss had been a rocky one, but they'd been fated to be together from the first— as Juliana had known, of course.

Where was *her* great love? Was fate taking a protracted holiday?

Still feeling Lord Stafford's gaze on her, she met his stare dead on, daring him to look away. He didn't. His eyes were a warm brown, reminding her of chocolate. She loved chocolate. But she had to look up to see those eyes. Way up.

She could get a crick in her neck dancing with such a gentleman.

"I haven't seen you at any other balls," she observed. "You must take your duty to Parliament seriously."

The corners of those warm eyes crinkled when he smiled. "That and my profession."

"Your profession?"

"I'm a physician."

"I thought you were an earl," she said.

One of his dark brows went up. "Can I not be both?"

"Of course you can," she said quickly, although she'd never heard of an earl-physician. "What do you do, exactly? Have you many patients?"

"Some, although I'm not taking on any new ones. Most of my time is spent at my facility, the New Hope Institute."

"New Hope," she mused. "I've heard of that. Something to do with smallpox?"

"I provide vaccinations, yes. Mostly to London's poor."

"That sounds like very important work," she allowed. He was a most unusual young man. And an excellent dancer. Having noticed a slight limp as he'd initially approached her, she wouldn't have thought he'd move so nimbly.

Still, much as she loved dancing, finding a gentleman who excelled at it wasn't her priority. After all, it wasn't as though she had a shortage of dance partners—she danced her feet off at every ball, with or without Griffin flinging every eligible bachelor her way. She had no problem meeting young men; the problem was finding one she considered husband material. And Lord Stafford was definitely not what she had in mind.

When the music came to an end, he led her by the hand off the dance floor. "It was a pleasure, Lady Juliana."

His voice was warm like his eyes, low and smooth, reminding her again of rich chocolate. "Thank you," she said.

The musicians struck up a country dance, and as he was still holding her hand, she half expected him to lead her straight back to the dance floor. Instead, he raised her fingers and, rather than kiss the air above her hand, he actually pressed his lips to her glove.

Scandalous! Equal parts appalled and amused, she hardly knew how to arrange her face. *What* an unusual young man.

She could have sworn she felt the kiss—a tingly sensation—through the white silk.

"Thank you," she repeated more faintly.

"Thank *you*," he echoed with a vague smile.

She couldn't help wondering if he was dazed or just bored.

No sooner had he turned to leave than Griffin descended. "Well?"

She watched Lord Stafford walk away. The cut of his tailcoat emphasized broad shoulders. Dark, tousled waves grazed his velvet collar. Many fashionable men achieved a similar look with pomade and curl papers, but his coiffure looked *genuinely* tousled. Like he was too busy to bother with it.

"His hair is too dark," she said.

"Pardon?"

"You know I prefer golden-haired gentlemen. And he's entirely too tall—I felt like a child dancing with him."

Griffin looked down on her, both literally and figuratively. "Face it, Juliana—you're short."

As though she hadn't noticed. "He works," she said. "He has a *profession*."

"And you find this unacceptable?"

"He wouldn't have any time for me." She wanted a grand love, like Alexandra and Tristan's; she wanted a husband who loved her to distraction. She wanted special outings and thoughtful surprises and long, lingering, endless hours together. And faith, *this* fellow couldn't even find a few minutes to comb his hair. "I'm sorry, but he just won't do."

The fact that Lord Stafford's work was important made him admirable, but no more suitable—and the fact that she *may* have enjoyed his chocolate eyes and his impertinent kiss had no bearing whatsoever. Even if she could fall for a too-tall, too-dark earl-physician, their attachment could only end in tears.

Griffin released a long-suffering sigh. "I shall keep looking."

"You do that," she said, patting his arm and silently wishing him luck. The spice cakes had clearly been a waste. Poor Griffin. "In the meantime, I must speak with Alexandra."

She scanned the ballroom and finally found her married sister talking to Aunt Frances.

"Who was that you were dancing with?" Alexandra asked as she approached.

"Lord Stafford."

"He's very handsome."

"His hair is too dark. Can you come to the Berkeley Square house this Wednesday afternoon?"

"I expect so. Why?"

"I need help making clothes for the Foundling Hospital babies."

"Your newest project, I take it?" Alexandra's brown eyes

gleamed with mischief. "What have you got yourself into this time?"

If only she knew. "Corinna wanted to see the Hospital's art gallery, but oh, the poor foundlings were heartbreaking. And their mothers." Just thinking back on the balloting, Juliana wanted to cry. "I *must* do something to help them."

"Of course you must," Aunt Frances said. "With you, it's always something."

That much was true; Juliana wouldn't deny it. "And what does that make me?" she wondered. "Impulsive? Interfering? Overwrought, overdramatic, overbearing?" She stopped there, knowing she was all of those and more.

Which was why she wanted to hug Alexandra when she said, "No, that makes you compassionate, giving, hopeful. Good-hearted and unselfish and sensitive. And lovable—that's what it makes you most."

Juliana *did* hug her sister. Her perfect, responsible, *married* sister, who always managed to summon the right words to fix everything.

But a small part of her couldn't help wondering…if she was so lovable, why couldn't she find someone to love?

FOUR

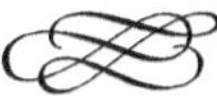

"**T**HIS PINK IS pretty," Emily said Monday at Grafton House, a draper's shop in New Bond Street.

"It is," Juliana agreed, watching a snooty woman give the girl and her ever-present snake a wide berth. "But silk isn't sturdy enough for babies. And pink won't do." She stroked a length of thick white wool. "The Governors want white, so all the clothes will suit both girls and boys."

Emily cocked her golden head. "Won't the babies be overly warm in frocks made of that?"

"I'm considering this for the blankets. We'll buy linsey for the frocks."

"I'll look for linsey, then," Emily said and walked away.

Juliana nodded absently, deciding the wool would do fine. She was about to ask the price when she heard a little shriek and a familiar voice. "Gracious me, Miss Neville! Are you *still* carrying that varmint everywhere?"

Juliana turned, surprised to see another Berkeley Square neighbor, Lady Amanda Wolverston.

Young Emily looked more affronted than surprised. "Herman isn't a varmint," she protested, returning to slip her hand into Juliana's. "He's a pet."

"Not a very proper one," Lady Amanda said.

Although she agreed, Juliana squeezed Emily's hand. Amanda could sometimes be a bit *too* proper. But she and Amanda had grown up as neighbors and played together as children, so Juliana considered her a good friend.

"I'm so glad you've come to town," she told her with a smile. "I've invited my sisters to a little sewing party on Wednesday afternoon, to make some clothing for the Foundling Hospital babies. I do hope you'll join us."

Amanda didn't answer. Juliana's tall blond friend was slouching—a habitual posture for her. But she seemed to be slouching even more than normal, and she looked unusually pale.

Blinking, Juliana peered up at Amanda's wan face. "Where have you been hiding all season?"

"In the countryside. My father is *still* excavating the Roman ruins he found on the estate." Amanda gestured toward a chair in a corner of the shop, where her aunt sat primly. "Aunt Mabel came with me, which was very kind. She didn't want to come to town this year at all."

A slight, pinch-faced woman in an ill-fitting gown, the poor lady was as pink-cheeked as Amanda was pale. She seemed to be wheezing slightly. "I know she suffers from asthma," Juliana said sympathetically, absently musing that Amanda must have inherited her aunt's fashion sense—or rather, lack thereof. "And the London air has never agreed with her. However did you persuade her to come?"

"Father persuaded her. Or rather, he ordered her." Amanda took a deep breath. "Because..." Her gaze slid to Emily and back, wordlessly telling Juliana she had something to confide.

Dying to hear the news, Juliana squeezed the little girl's hand again. "Could you do me an important favor, sweetheart, and see if you can find that linsey?"

"All right," Emily said, happily wandering off.

"Well?" Juliana asked when Emily was out of earshot.

Amanda's voice dropped to a whisper. "Father has arranged my marriage. He sent me and Aunt Mabel to put together a trousseau, which is why I'm here at Grafton Hou—"

"He's arranged your marriage?" Juliana interrupted. "To whom?"

Amanda closed her blue-gray eyes for a moment and released a slow, dramatic breath before she reopened them. "Lord Malmsey."

"Lord *Malmsey*?"

Juliana was vaguely acquainted with the man, who was skinny and meek and shorter than her friend. But what stuck in her mind was an image of his forehead. His large, age-lined forehead, prominent and proud and still gaining ground over his poor, defenseless hairline.

"Why, he must be forty, at least!"

"Forty-two," Amanda corrected. Well more than twice her age. She was a year older than Juliana, which made her all of eighteen. "I met with him last evening—not that either of us had much to say to each other. We're to be married four weeks from Saturday, in a private ceremony by special license."

The same day as the next Foundling Hospital intake, when Juliana had to have all the baby clothes ready. Amanda looked to be in the dismals, which was no wonder. "Can you refuse to wed him?"

She shook her head. "Father has made it clear that if I fail to go through with this wedding, he'll disinherit me—which would leave me slim chances of ever wedding at all."

A denial was on the tip of Juliana's tongue, but she wasn't one to lie—not outright, anyway. In three seasons, no one else had offered for Amanda, and without her substantial inheritance, it was unlikely any gentleman ever would.

"I'm miserable," Amanda added unnecessarily.

One thing Juliana was sure of: Griffin would never expect her to wed other than where her heart led her. For that, she was grateful. "Have you told your father how you feel?"

"Countless times. But nothing I can say will make him breach a contract. His honor is more important to him than my happiness."

Juliana had always thought Lord Wolverston rather cold, but this was downright cruel. "There's no honor in putting his reputation before his own daughter. He should want to see you in love."

"He believes that when it comes to marriage, there are more important matters to consider."

Juliana couldn't disagree more. Her parents had wed for practical reasons, and Mama had suffered for it the rest of her days. Eighteen was much too young to resign oneself to such a future. Perhaps any age was too young. Look at dear Aunt Frances, soldiering bravely on into her forties.

Amanda slouched even more. "He's pleased beyond belief to have an offer for my hand at all, let alone one from a baron. I suppose I *am* lucky that Lord Malmsey is willing to marry me."

"Amanda!"

"Gentlemen never look at girls like me, Juliana."

Amanda *was* a bit plain, but Juliana rather thought that was because her mother had died giving birth to her. Much like little Emily, she'd grown up without anyone to offer guidance. Her Aunt Mabel was certainly no help. Amanda wore shapeless clothes in all the wrong colors, her brows were too heavy, her blond hair was pulled back into a frightfully tight braided bun, and she never met anyone's eyes—not even Juliana's now. Her blue-gray gaze was focused in the vicinity of her unsightly footwear.

In short, Amanda was a project just waiting to be tackled.

"Who else knows about your engagement?" Juliana asked.

"We arrived only yesterday. You're the first one I've told."

"Excellent." The secret should be safe with Lord Malmsey as well. Although he was a fixture at society gatherings, Juliana couldn't remember ever hearing more than half a dozen words leave his mouth. "Don't tell anyone else. We shall save you from this dismal fate."

The older girl glanced up. "How? Do you truly believe it possible?"

"Without a doubt." Juliana had never been one to disregard a friend in need. Or a stranger in need, come to that. "Let me think on the matter."

"Look here, Lady Juliana!" Emily returned, brandishing an armful of white fabric with Herman coiled on top.

"That's perfect, sweetheart." Juliana hoped the clerk wouldn't faint when she asked for a length to be cut. Or maybe she hoped the clerk *would* faint, because that might convince Emily, once and for all, that carrying a snake around was a bad idea. She looked back to Amanda. "You'll come to the sewing party Wednesday, won't you? One o'clock. By the time you arrive, I'm certain to have a solution."

FIVE

"WHERE IS Amanda?" Juliana said Wednesday afternoon in the drawing room.

Rain pattered outside the windows. "You've asked that more times than Emily's pricked herself," Alexandra observed as she patiently knotted a thread.

Her sister could afford to be patient, Juliana thought, stitching a tiny frock with more speed than care. Alexandra wasn't the one who'd promised to deliver twenty dozen articles of baby clothing in one short month. "Amanda said she'd be here."

"No, she didn't," Emily pointed out, rearranging the snake on her shoulders. Alas, the clerk at Grafton House hadn't fainted. She'd only glared, which had upset the girl, making her cling to Herman all the more. "You invited her, but she never actually said she would come."

"Perhaps not in so many words. But she'll come." Amanda *had* to come. Juliana had devised a plan. An excellent plan, which she couldn't wait to explain—

"Ouch!" Emily hollered, sticking her pricked finger in her mouth. She really *wasn't* very good with a needle. "This blanket is turning out dreadful."

Juliana leaned over to inspect the girl's handiwork. "It isn't that bad." The hem was rather uneven, but it wasn't *dreadful*. Luckily, infants couldn't criticize. "The blanket will keep a baby warm no matter what it looks like."

"But I want it to look *good*."

"With more practice, it will," Corinna said. "You need to practice to become good at anything." She pointed her needle toward an easel set up by the large picture window. Even in the dim rainy-day light, the scene on the canvas—a man pushing a laughing lady on a swing by a gleaming lake—conveyed movement, vibrancy, a sense of life. "My first painting didn't look like that."

Still patiently working her own needle into the little cap she was making, Alexandra smiled. "As I recall, your first painting was a willow tree that looked more like a haystack."

"We're none of us expert seamstresses, Miss Emily." Aunt Frances squinted at her own handiwork through her spectacles. "I've only ever done samplers and embroidery. After a few more practice blankets—"

"This isn't practice," Juliana interrupted. "Every single item will be used." If she was lucky, today's efforts would produce five or six finished garments. And she needed two hundred and forty! Although it was a bit early to panic, she realized already, less than an hour into her first sewing party, that she was going to have to host many more of them than she'd anticipated. "Where is Amanda?"

Just then the knocker sounded in the foyer.

"That must be her!" The tiny frock fell to the floor as Juliana jumped up and rushed from the room.

Though their butler, Adamson, was nearly as short as she, he always managed to look dignified. "Good afternoon, Lady Amanda," he intoned as he opened the door.

"Good afternoon, Adamson," Amanda replied formally.

"Where on earth have you been?" Juliana asked.

"Playing chess with Aunt Mabel. I couldn't leave in the middle of such an exciting game."

"Exciting?" Juliana could think of little she found less exciting than chess. Even sewing was more fun. "Come into the library."

Amanda peeked through the open door across the way. "Isn't everyone in the drawing room?"

"Yes. That's exactly the point." Juliana took her in the opposite direction, closing the door behind them and ushering her friend toward two leather wingback chairs. "We must keep your engagement a secret. I've devised a plan to break it."

Amanda sat and clasped her hands in her lap, suddenly looking nervous. She blew out a breath. "All right. What's the plan?"

Picturing her sisters listening at the door—after all, she herself had instituted the practice—Juliana lowered her voice. "We shall arrange to have you compromised by a nice, eligible young man. Once the public has seen you together in a compromising position, your father will be forced to let the two of you wed."

"A compromising position?" Amanda's laugh, an awful guffaw like a donkey braying, made Juliana wince. "I've never even been kissed!"

"I haven't been kissed, either," Juliana said. "I've always warded them off." She wished for her first kiss to be with someone she cared for, and so far, nobody had been up to snuff.

"Well, no one's even tried with me," Amanda said mournfully. "There's no chance of a suitable gentleman compromising me. Not willingly, anyway."

"I didn't mean *unwillingly*—perish the thought!" Anyhow, such a thing wouldn't be necessary. When she was finished with Amanda, gentlemen would be falling all over themselves trying to compromise her. "Don't fret on that matter." She leaned closer to squeeze her hand. "Are you free tomorrow and the day after?"

"To be compromised?"

"To be fitted for a few ball gowns. You'll require a new wardrobe, among other things. We'll need to visit a seamstress and comb the shops."

Amanda appeared both dubious and hopeful, which was an impressive feat. "My father did give me leave to assemble a trousseau."

"Excellent." There was little Juliana relished more than transforming an ugly duckling into a lovely swan. "We have a lot of work to do before Lady Hammersmithe's ball on Saturday."

"I cannot attend Lady Hammersmithe's ball."

"Of course you can. I shall summon Madame Bellefleur to trim your hair—"

"My hair has never been cut." Amanda's hands went protectively to her head. "And I cannot attend—"

"Ouuuccch!" The howl was so piercing, it shot from the drawing room, across the foyer, and through the library's closed door.

Juliana bolted from her chair. Lifting her skirts, she dashed out the door. "Emily!" she shouted, running through the foyer and bursting into the drawing room. "Emily, what's happened?"

And there she stopped, a sudden sickness in her middle, her head suddenly swimming.

Emily was *bleeding*.

"It *hurts*," the girl wailed, bent over her hand. Tiny red spots dotted her pink skirts. Although the injury clearly wasn't serious —they were just *tiny* spots—Juliana knew she should hurry to help. To comfort. To make everything all better.

But she couldn't. Because the sight of those red spots seemed to make it hard to breathe.

Thank goodness everyone *else* was helping. Well, maybe not helping, precisely, but at least they weren't riveted in place. In the scant seconds Juliana stood there—because that's all the time it was, really—her sisters and Aunt Frances leapt up and surrounded Emily, making assorted clucking, compassionate noises.

Thankfully, that hid the sight of Emily's wound. But all the sympathy seemed to make her sob harder. "M-my needle s-slipped. It-it didn't just poke me this time, it caught—"

"For goodness' sake!" Amanda snapped, pushing past Juliana and into the little cluster of females. "It's just a little blood. Here, someone take the snake." While Corinna moved to do so, Amanda reached for some linsey and tore off a strip, then drew Emily to her feet. "Let's clean it up and bandage it, shall we?" she said, leading her from the room.

Juliana collapsed into a chair, her knees giving out. Which was absurd, as she well knew. Corinna teased her mercilessly on this point. How silly it was for any woman past puberty to find the sight of blood distressing. But her own monthlies never bothered her. That sort of bleeding was natural; other bleeding wasn't.

Fortunately, Corinna and the others hadn't seemed to notice her foolishness.

Corinna held Herman at arm's length, looking almost as ridiculous as Juliana felt. "Why didn't you bring Amanda straight in here?" she asked.

"I wanted to talk to her about Lady Hammersmithe's ball on Saturday. Talk her into attending, I mean."

"Why wouldn't she?" Alexandra asked.

Juliana shrugged—casually, she hoped. "She's rather shy around young men. I'm helping her with a new wardrobe, which I hope will raise her confidence."

"That's kind of you," Alexandra said.

Corinna looked suspicious. Or perhaps just wary of the snake. "Whyever did you feel the need to talk privately? We could have assisted in persuading her—"

"Here she is, all repaired," Amanda announced, returning with Emily.

Emily sported a neat little linsey bandage wrapped around

her finger. When she reached for Herman, Corinna didn't hesitate to hand him over. Juliana's sister still looked wary, though. Or suspicious.

Drat.

"Shall we get back to work?" Juliana asked cheerfully.

Emily shook her head. "I'm not sewing anymore."

"You can start cutting the clouts," Juliana suggested, handing her a bundle of cotton fabric, a pair of scissors, and a simple pattern. She hoped that when the cut rectangles were folded and sewn, they would turn out the right size to cover a baby's bottom. Refusing to even *think* about doing that a hundred times, she gave Emily's half-finished blanket to Amanda. "Here. This is almost done."

It wasn't, of course, and Amanda proved to be no handier with a needle than the rest of them. Not only was Juliana going to have to host more sewing parties, she would also need to invite more friends—ideally some who had sewn more than samplers. "I hope you'll all help me recruit more ladies at Almack's tonight."

"I'm not attending," Alexandra said. "Since Parliament isn't sitting, Tristan wants to stay home, just the two of us."

Juliana was looking forward to dancing, of course, but still, she envied her sister. Since Almack's was essentially a matrimonial bazaar, Alexandra could afford to skip the mayhem and spend a pleasant evening at home instead. At the rate Juliana *wasn't* finding a husband, she began to wonder if she'd ever have that luxury.

Corinna looked up from the petticoat she was stitching. Suspiciously. "Amanda, you'll be attending Almack's, won't you?"

"No," Amanda said. Juliana held her breath, half expecting her to blurt out the news of her engagement. Instead, Amanda added, "Aunt Mabel isn't feeling up to chaperoning me these days."

"Is it the asthma again?" Aunt Frances sighed. "Poor Lady Mabel. I shall have to pay her a call."

"She'd appreciate that very much," Amanda said, hemming her blanket almost as crookedly as Emily.

If anything, Corinna looked even more suspicious. "But Juliana said you're going to Lady Hammersmithe's ball."

"As I tried to explain to her, I don't expect Aunt Mabel will be well enough by Saturday, either. The London air—"

"Aunt Frances can chaperone you along with us," Juliana said.

Amanda's needle slowed—not that it had been moving especially quickly in the first place. "There's no point in going. No one will ask me to dance anyway."

"Oh, yes, they will." Alexandra smiled down at her handiwork. "Juliana will teach you *the look.*"

Now Amanda's needle stopped. "What look?"

"Allow me to demonstrate." Juliana looked up from her little frock. "First you choose a fellow you wish to entice—"

"Entice?" Amanda's cheeks were pink.

"Enticement is the objective of *the look.* Trust me, should you do it properly, men are guaranteed to fall at your feet."

"Are they?"

"Positively," Alexandra declared.

Amanda looked from one sister to the other. "I'm listening."

"Excellent. First you choose a fellow and command his gaze." Juliana focused on Amanda, a beguiling look in her eyes.

The older girl swallowed hard. "And then?"

"Glance down, bowing your head a little to display your lashes against your cheeks. Then sweep your eyelids up, gaze at him full on again, and slowly—very slowly—curve your lips in a smile."

Amanda's forehead crinkled. "Show me again."

"Watch closely." Juliana took her time with the second demonstration.

Corinna snickered, but Amanda and Emily both sighed. "Can I learn, too?" Emily asked.

"It's never too early to begin practicing. Amanda, give it a try."

Amanda stared hard at Juliana, closed her eyes, popped them open, and stretched her mouth into a wide grin.

Juliana suppressed a sigh of her own. This was going to be harder than she'd thought.

SIX

"**I REALLY MUST** be on my way, Aunt Aurelia." James gave a forced smile. "You're healthy as the day you were born."

"My heart was paining me so." Plump but elegant nonetheless, Aurelia reclined on her peach-draped bed. Her entire house was decorated in peach. In fact, sometimes when James found himself here—which he did far too often—he felt he was *in* a peach. "I tell you I could barely breathe," she continued. "Won't you check it with that ingenious instrument of yours?"

"If you insist." Suppressing a sigh, he opened his black leather bag and drew out the ingenious instrument, which was simply a foot-long cylinder of wood. One end had a hole to place against the ear, and the inside was hollowed out in the shape of a cone. This past March, a young French physician named Laennec had invented the instrument and christened it the stethoscope, derived from the Greek words for "I see" and "the chest."

James placed the wider end of the cone over his aunt's heart. Her scent, an unappealing combination of camphor and gardenias, wafted over him, and he gained a sudden appreciation for Laennec, Frenchman though he was. Without the stethoscope,

James would have had to press his ear directly against Aunt Aurelia's over-perfumed bosom.

Her heartbeat sounded strong through the tube, the thump-*thump* clear and distinct. "Regular as Grandmother's clock," he assured her.

"You're certain?" She shook her coiffed gray head in disbelief. "And my lungs?"

"Sit up, if you will." Bracing a hand on the headboard, he applied the stethoscope to her corseted back. "Breathe in," he said as patiently as he could. "Out. In. Perfect. As I said, you're healthy as a newborn babe." He dropped the instrument back in his bag and fastened the clasp. "Now I really must leave, Aunty."

She climbed from her bed and accompanied him downstairs. "You're expected in Parliament?"

"Not today. It's Wednesday." The House of Lords sat on Mondays, Tuesdays, Thursdays, and Fridays. "But I was expected at the Institute hours ago. Only one other doctor volunteered for the early shift today."

"I do appreciate your visit." She squeezed his hand, and James squeezed back. Aunt Aurelia was a sweetheart, even if she was exasperating. In the foyer, she glanced at Grandmother's tall-case clock. "Such a shame that Bedelia hasn't returned. She'll surely want to see you, too. She had a horrid case of the putrid sore throat this morning."

Bedelia, his mother's other sister, shared the house with Aurelia. Two childless over-anxious widows living inside a peach. It could be a nursery rhyme.

"Tell Aunt Bedelia to gargle with salted water. I'm certain that will cure her."

"Do you expect so?" Aurelia's blue eyes looked dubious.

"Absolutely." James doubted Bedelia's throat was putrid; if her throat hurt her at all, it was likely due to nothing more serious than excessive chatter. "I'll see you again soon," he added, escaping to his carriage before Aurelia could ask him what he meant by *soon*. If she had her way, *soon* would be tomorrow—if not an hour from now.

On the way to New Hope Institute, he scribbled more notes for a speech—his first—he planned to deliver in Parliament. Immersed in his work, he arrived in front of the Institute before noticing all the people queued in a line that stretched down the street.

Way down the street.

Mothers shivered in the cold, damp air. Babies cried. Small children whined, and restless older children taunted one another. Rather than wait, people were giving up and leaving, walking away from the Institute.

For the second time this month.

Without waiting for the steps to be lowered, James vaulted from the carriage and hurried through the drizzle into the building. In the reception area, more babies wailed on impatient mothers' laps. Two boys playing tag raced around the room, bumping into people's knees.

Slipping off his tailcoat, James looked to the counter for help. No one was behind it. He untied his cravat as he pushed through the door into the back.

His private office was tiny—not much more than a desk and chair, since he preferred to do paperwork in his study at home. He tossed his coat and cravat onto the chair, then poked his head into the first of three treatment rooms, finding it empty although the next patient should be waiting there. The second room held one harried-looking physician along with a mother and her tearful three-year-old.

Unfastening the top button of his shirt, James frowned. The vaccination procedure went more smoothly with a calm patient, and candy—a real treat for a poor child—usually did the trick. "Where are the sugar sticks?" he asked.

Dr. Hanley shrugged, setting aside the ivory lancet he'd used to inoculate the little girl. "I haven't a clue where...what is that new assistant's name?"

"Miss Chumford."

"Right. " He tied a fresh bandage around the girl's arm. "I haven't a clue where Miss Chumford keeps the sugar sticks. I cannot seem to locate anything on those shelves. I consider myself lucky to have found a supply of the vaccine."

"Where *is* Miss Chumford?"

"In the next room. Crying her eyes out. And I don't expect a sugar stick will help." Dr. Hanley stood the sniffling child on her feet. "There you go, little miss. If you want a sugar stick, follow Lord Stafford."

"Dr. Trevor," James reminded him. He preferred not to be called *Lord* at the Institute—it intimidated the patients. As did his aristocratic clothing, which was why he always shed the more formal items. "I'll send in the next patient," he added as he ushered the girl toward the reception area. "Did Dr. Hanley tell you what to expect?" he asked her mother.

Clearly overawed by his presence, the woman answered shyly. "Yes, my lord. A big blister but no pox."

"That's correct. It may take some weeks for the blister to heal, and it will leave a scar. But your daughter will be spared from the smallpox."

"Thank you," she murmured, lifting the little girl onto her hip. "If I could pay, I would."

Noting the telltale pox scars on her face, he knew she meant it. He usually encouraged parents to be vaccinated along with their children, but that was obviously unnecessary in her case.

"Thank *you*," he returned, "for doing your part. We don't need your money, but please tell your friends and neighbors about the Institute. If everyone stands together, we can rid ourselves of this dreadful scourge once and for all."

Well said, he thought, then excused himself and pulled out his notes on the spot. That was going in the speech.

It was his belief that if only everyone everywhere were vaccinated, smallpox could be wiped off the face of the earth. It was a formidable project, he knew, but one had to start somewhere.

Unfortunately, London wasn't particularly cooperative. Many were uninformed and skeptical, and some churchmen preached that vaccination interfered with the will of God, convinced that smallpox was sent to chasten the population. James disagreed, believing He had provided the vaccine as a mercy. None who'd come face to face with a poor, ailing child could but wish to prevent her suffering.

In addition, the Institute could handle only a certain number of people per day. But James hired men to visit the poorer parishes—whose congregations were most vulnerable to disease—and talk people into bringing their children. Which made it all the more frustrating when those who agreed were forced to stand out in the cold and rain.

He found a box of sugar sticks and sent the girl and her mother on their way, then settled the next patients in the two vacant treatment rooms and knocked on the door to the third room. "Miss Chumford?"

An emphatic sniffle was the only answer.

"Miss Chumford, may I come in?"

"It's your Institute," she called out in a ragged voice.

Yes, it was. He opened the door. Then closed it again at the sight of Miss Chumford's splotchy, red face.

There were few things James feared more than a crying girl. Crying from heartache, that was—as a doctor, he'd learned to console tears of physical pain and discomfort. But the other sort of tears…he just couldn't think what to do. Anne hadn't been the emotional type.

With an effort of will, he reopened the door. Now she looked a bit resentful, which was an improvement, to his mind. Resentment he could cope with. "There's a queue outside," he said gently, "and if it grows any longer it's likely to reach all the way to Surrey."

"I'm sorry," she whimpered.

"What is amiss?"

Both of her hands pressed to her middle, she looked at him with brimming eyes and said nothing.

He shifted uncomfortably, torn between sympathy and dismay. He had the Institute to run. People in need. He'd employed her to keep the physicians well supplied and make sure the patients were seen to quickly and efficiently. A simple job, really, but a necessary one. And she was the second assistant within a month to—

He looked back to her hands, still clutched at her middle. She couldn't be more than seventeen or eighteen, and her stomach was flat, but he had a sinking feeling...

"Are you with child?"

She nodded miserably, with the longest, most pitiful sniffle yet.

Good gracious, his last assistant had left for the same reason! Was there something in the water?

"And you're not wed?" he asked. After all, she was *Miss* Chumford.

She nodded again, and words began tumbling from her mouth. "Papa will k-kill me, or at least throw me out of the house. Harry, my...the f-father of my child, cannot afford a home of his own. We shall have to live with his p-parents, and his mother hates me, and his father—"

"Your Harry is willing to marry you?" James interrupted. "And do right by the child?"

She nodded around fresh bawls. "H-Harry is a good man, m-my lord, and a hard worker. B-but—"

"Wait here, Miss Chumford." He ducked out, relieved to escape momentarily. He knew one way to stop the flood for certain. It had worked last time, anyway.

He had a small safe in his private office, from which he withdrew fifty pounds. A pittance to him, but enough to cover a small family's rent and food for two years or more. It would provide Miss Chumford and her soon-to-be husband with a new start, and should Harry be as decent and hardworking as she claimed, James prayed the couple would find their way.

After Miss Chumford left—sobbing her thanks—he shook his head and lettered a HELP WANTED sign, propped it in the Institute's front window, and settled down behind the counter for what he knew from recent experience would be many hours spent interviewing candidates. Surveying the throng of people waiting for treatment, he felt overwhelmed by responsibility. He wished his father were here to guide him.

Well, at least his mother wouldn't be able to drag him to Almack's tonight.

SEVEN

TRIFLE

Take yokes of four egges and a pinte of thicke Creame, and season it with Sugar and Ginger and Rosewater, so stirre it as you would then have it and make it warme on a chafing dishe and coales, and after put it into a Silver piece or a Bowle, and so serve it to the board.

Extra-strong Rosewater will put Roses into your cheeks.

—Lady Jewel Chase, 1687

O VER THE NEXT two days, Juliana helped Amanda order an entire new wardrobe. They shopped for cosmetics, hats, shoes, hosiery, and other assorted fripperies. They practiced posture and walking, devised new flirtatious smiles, and perfected *the look*. Juliana taught Amanda how to apply the cosmetics so skillfully that no one would notice she was wearing any. She plucked Amanda's heavy brows, doing her best to ignore her friend's squeals of pain and protest—after all, all but the luckiest of girls suffered for their beauty.

With each hour, Amanda's confidence grew, as did Juliana's confidence in her scheme.

At last, Saturday dawned.

Juliana dragged Corinna out of bed early—at noon—to help

her make trifle before Amanda arrived to dress for Lady Hammersmithe's ball. But Corinna was hopeless in the kitchen on the best of days, and considering she'd stayed up painting until seven o'clock in the morning, this day wasn't her best.

"My arm hurts," she grumbled. "And I'm tired."

"Just keep beating until the eggs are creamy, please." Juliana added two more handfuls of rose petals to the water she had boiled. She was determined to make sure Amanda's cheeks would be nice and rosy. "I cannot understand why you won't go to bed at a reasonable hour."

"I'm not a reasonable person—I'm an artist," Corinna said dramatically. "*I* cannot understand why you won't ask a kitchen maid to beat these eggs."

Juliana consulted their family's heirloom cookbook, an ancient volume to which each lady in the family had tradition-ally added a recipe every Christmas since the seventeenth century. Many of the sweets were thought to be magic charms. She poured the rosewater into a pot of cream and sprinkled it with a bit of ginger. "How many times have you been told that the Chase family recipes must be made by Chase family members if they're to work?"

Corinna rolled her eyes. "Alexandra has turned your head. You don't truly believe such nonsense, do you?"

"It hurts no one to try."

"On the contrary, it hurts me and my arm!"

"You won't be complaining once you've tasted the trifle—you'll have some, won't you? If you and I and Amanda all have rosy cheeks tonight, perhaps we'll all find husbands."

"If rosy cheeks are all you're after, a rouge pot would be more effective." Corinna grated sugar into the eggs. "I won't tell A Lady of Distinction if you don't," she added dryly.

"I'll take no chances with Amanda," Juliana said, stirring tire-lessly. "She shall have rouge *and* trifle. Her gown will be exquisite, her complexion flawless. I've summoned a hairdresser—"

"Just don't make Amanda so beautiful she steals your own suitors."

"That's an ungenerous thought." Juliana snatched the sugar loaf from her sister before she could add too much as usual; Corinna had a legendary sweet tooth and no concept of the proper amount of any ingredient. "I've no suitors worth safeguarding anyway," she added with a sigh.

"You're trying too hard," Corinna said. "Just relax and enjoy all the attention."

Relax? Juliana nearly burst out laughing. With the season drawing to a close, Griffin beginning to panic, the baby clothes' due date looming, and Amanda's future at stake, the last thing she could do was relax.

"There, it's creamy." Corinna banged the bowl onto the big wooden table and rubbed her arm. "Am I finished? Assuming I can still hold a brush, I'd like to varnish my painting."

"Varnish away," Juliana said and watched her sister leave the kitchen.

Corinna seemed happy with her life, as though her paints and her solitude were all she required. Juliana was proud and pleased for her, but lately Corinna was so often immersed in her work. And Griffin was the same—between running the estate and ferreting out eligible bachelors, he hadn't a moment to spare.

The thought of returning to Cainewood, of facing another year in the country with naught but her siblings for company— including Alexandra's frequent letters overflowing with marital bliss—was the primary reason Juliana couldn't afford to relax.

She stirred faster.

EIGHT

HE TRIFLE WAS chilled in its silver bowl by the time Amanda arrived with two footmen carrying boxes. The French hairdresser was waiting, and less than an hour later, Amanda's once knee-length hair reached only the middle of her back. She watched in Juliana's dressing table mirror as her golden tresses fluttered to the floor, her face white as linsey, her eyes wide and apprehensive.

Juliana scooped trifle into a cup, thinking it might distract her friend. "Eat this. It will make your cheeks rosy."

"What is it?" Emily asked, stroking Herman on her shoulder. "May I have some?"

"It's trifle, and yes, you may."

The girl cocked her blond head. "Our cook's trifle has cake and fruit."

"This is a very old recipe."

"Our cook is probably older," Emily said, then spooned the sweet into her mouth and smiled. "It's good. Your hair looks pretty, Lady Amanda."

Amanda drew a sharp breath. "Do you truly think so, Miss Neville?"

"Absolutely," Juliana answered for the girl. "Shorter hair is the thing. I cannot imagine why you hid those gorgeous curls in that plait." Juliana had always despaired of her own stick-straight hair, but at least she didn't scrape it all back into a plait so tight it looked plastered to her head.

Amanda grimaced at another snip.

"Hold your head still, if you will." Madame Bellefleur clipped off a final inch. "*Parfait.*"

"It's trifle," Emily corrected. "Not a parfait."

"In French," Juliana told her, "*parfait* means 'perfect.' That length will be so much lighter and easier to put up."

Madame smiled and nodded. "Now, some shorter tendrils around the face, *oui?*"

"Brilliant." Juliana resumed unpacking the boxes, admiring all the dresses they'd ordered. The seamstress had sent only one of the ball gowns, but promised the rest would be ready next week. "Your hair will be stunning," she assured Amanda.

Amanda responded with a truly bizarre sound, which Juliana interpreted as strangled laughter. She recognized the donkey bray.

She put Amanda's dresses aside. "You must practice a new laugh. An enchanting laugh, like tinkling bells."

"Like this?" Amanda attempted a girlish giggle—and even Herman recoiled.

By the time they'd perfected the new laugh, Madame Bellefleur had experimented with different hairstyles, ulti-mately choosing one in which Amanda's blond mane was loosely gathered, twisted up, and pinned, with the remaining curls arranged artistically on top of her head. The hairdresser left, and Juliana swept the ball gown off her bed.

Amanda looked from the lavender silk dress to Emily and Herman, then back to Juliana. "I'd prefer not to disrobe in front of a snake," she said stiffly.

"So that's why you refused to undress in order to be measured." Juliana seized on the potential lesson, turning to

Emily. "The seamstress, Mrs. Huntley, was also distressed by Herman's presence. Many find his company unwelcome."

"I don't care," Emily said.

Juliana called her maid and asked her to walk Emily home. But after Juliana and Amanda were alone, it turned out Amanda didn't want to undress in front of *her*, either.

"Turn around," the older girl instructed.

"It's just me."

"Turn around."

Sighing, Juliana did so.

Much rustling followed as Amanda grappled with her garments. Finally it seemed she'd successfully clothed herself when she exclaimed, "I cannot wear this!"

Juliana spun around. "Of course you can. You look beautiful." She could hardly wait to see society's reaction to the new Amanda. "Turn around and let me button you up. Once you see the dress properly fastened, you'll love it."

But turning around brought Amanda face-to-face with the looking glass. Her hands flew up to cover her collarbone. "The neckline is too low! I must change into something else."

"You have nothing else suitable. Besides this gown, Mrs. Huntley sent only day dresses. The rest won't be ready until next week."

Amanda yanked up on the bodice. "I'm certain the example Mrs. Huntley showed me had a much higher neckline."

Of course it had, else Amanda would never have approved the order. But that was before Juliana gave Mrs. Huntley her instructions, which, thankfully, the seamstress had followed to the letter.

Amanda had always appeared rather round, but clothing of the proper size showed a surprisingly charming figure—which Juliana intended to use to her friend's advantage. If Amanda hoped to secure a husband on a tight schedule, she'd need to create a bit of a stir. Anyhow, the gown was cut quite modestly compared to some of the latest fashions.

"It's not too low," Juliana said, reaching around to tug the bodice back into place.

"It is so." Amanda jerked it higher.

Watching her friend in the mirror, Juliana had to laugh. "Look at yourself!"

Amanda's neckline was indeed at her neck—which meant the ribbon sash that was supposed to circle the empire waistline was perched above her bosom. Her mouth quirked, then spread into a reluctant smile, followed by a nervous titter.

"Tinkling bells," Juliana reminded her, and Amanda responded with her new, polished laugh.

"Much better." Juliana reached once more to adjust the bodice, but she mistakenly pulled it too low and revealed a birthmark near Amanda's breastbone. It was shaped like a fleur-de-lis. "How pretty!"

Amanda quickly tugged the lace-trimmed bodice up to cover it. "You weren't supposed to see that!"

"Whyever not? It's quite lovely."

"Lovely?" Amanda blushed. "It's *private*."

As she tied the sash, Juliana hoped that her improvements would be enough to compensate for Amanda's shy and stand-offish manner. At least her blushing brought out the roses in her cheeks.

She gave her more trifle, just in case. And brushed on a little extra rouge. As she completed the finishing touches, she drilled Amanda over and over again. "Let me see your smiles one more time. And you must practice *the look* again before we leave."

All of this preparation was *not* going to be for nothing.

NINE

"**THERE HE IS,**" Amanda said grimly as they stepped into Lady Hammersmithe's ballroom.

"There's who?" Juliana asked.

"Lord Malmsey." A frown marred Amanda's perfectly done-up face. She turned to her surrogate chaperone. "Should I dance with him, Lady Frances?"

It seemed she was already losing heart. Juliana wouldn't stand for it.

Unaware of Amanda's engagement, Aunt Frances patted her hand. "I expect someone younger would suit you better, my dear. But if you've already been introduced, of course you should dance with him if he asks."

Juliana doubted he would ask, although if she could judge by his pained expression, he was attempting to screw up his courage. Excellent—here was a perfect opportunity to strengthen Amanda's resolve. "You definitely should dance with him," Juliana declared, laying a gentle hand on her friend's back to steer her toward Lord Malmsey. "It would be the polite thing."

She figured ten seconds in his aging arms would have Amanda *begging* for introductions to other men.

Lord Malmsey's eyes widened as they approached, and

Juliana saw him swallow hard. Taking pity on the poor fellow, she smiled when they drew near. "Good evening, my lord. Lady Amanda was just telling me she hoped you'd ask her to dance."

"Very well," he said.

Amanda said nothing.

The strains of a waltz rose into the air, and the two of them walked off.

Or rather, they shuffled off.

Aunt Frances joined Juliana and watched them dance. "They don't seem a proper match."

"No, they don't," Juliana agreed. She'd never seen a more awkward couple. Due to Amanda's height, her eyes came level with his expansive forehead. Neither of them spoke or looked at each other. Lord Malmsey radiated apprehension, Amanda pure misery.

Juliana could not have been more pleased.

On the other side of the ballroom, she spotted Lord Neville ambling out of the refreshment room. "Wait here," she told Aunt Frances. "I must speak with Viscount Neville, and he's sure to leave the ball early." Having no plans to take a fourth wife, Emily's father preferred to spend his evenings gambling at his club. "I'll return momentarily."

Aunt Frances nodded absently, smiling at the dancers whirling past. Juliana patted her dear shoulder and went off to intercept the viscount.

"Lord Neville, if I may speak with you for a moment?"

"Ah, yes, my dear, of course." Emily's father was blond and gray-eyed like his daughter, tall and a bit hefty. As he seemed to overindulge in everything, Juliana wasn't surprised to see a heaping plate in his hand. He popped a grape into his mouth. "What can I do to help you?"

"It's about Emily—"

"Ah, yes. I do appreciate the interest you've taken in my girl."

"She's a delight." Juliana watched him choose a biscuit and

devour nearly half in a single bite. "But I'm wondering if I can prevail on you to discourage her from taking Herman out in public. It's not the thing for a young lady to carry a snake."

"Ah, yes," he repeated, plucking three more grapes off the bunch. "But my Emily is very attached to Herman. She and her mother found him in the garden just before my wife died."

"I'm aware of that, sir. But earlier this week when we visited the shops, a patron at Grafton House fainted dead away at the sight of Emily's snake." While that wasn't precisely true, it *could* have been true. "If only you'd heard the shrieks of terror, Lord Neville. It wasn't the sort of scene a young lady should inspire."

Apparently the viscount found that more amusing than distressing, because he guffawed.

And then he stopped.

In fact, not only had he stopped laughing, it looked as though he'd stopped breathing. The plate dropped from his hand, shattering on the parquet floor as he clutched at his throat and chest. His mouth was open, but he seemed unable to speak. His skin was turning blue.

"Faith!" Juliana exclaimed loudly enough to make the people nearby look over. "Lord Neville, are you all right?"

Clearly he wasn't.

"Help!" she yelled, moving to thump him on the back, the way people did when someone swallowed the wrong way and went into a coughing fit. But it seemed he couldn't even cough. His eyes bugged out in his blue face, panicked.

Just then, Griffin ran up with his friend Lord Stafford in tow. "A chair," Lord Stafford instructed. "Now."

Griffin rushed to do his bidding. In the meantime, Lord Stafford very quickly—and very calmly, under the circumstances—untied the viscount's cravat and loosened the buttons at his throat. All the while, he murmured soothing words in his smooth, chocolatey voice.

But Lord Neville didn't look soothed. In fact, Juliana feared he was running out of time. Lord Stafford didn't seem to think so, though. Decidedly *un*panicked, he continued to murmur calmly while he waited for Griffin to return.

She couldn't imagine why Lord Stafford wanted a chair, but when it appeared a moment later, he plunked it down in front of the viscount and shoved the man's big body to lean over the back. Forcefully, again and again. After several thrusts, an intact red grape shot out of Lord Neville's mouth and landed at Juliana's feet.

The viscount took several gasping, gulping breaths while Lord Stafford moved the chair around and helped the man lower himself onto it. Lord Neville slumped there, the color returning to his face while he breathed deeply, as though the simple act of drawing air was the most satisfying thing he'd ever done.

Juliana released a long sigh of relief, as did the audience that had gathered to view the drama.

"You saved his life," she marveled, watching Lord Stafford in awe. After all, she tried to help people as best she could, but she'd never done something like *that*.

Lord Stafford merely shrugged. Turning his back on Juliana, he crouched down by his patient and asked to have a look in the man's throat.

The audience began to disperse.

Since her discussion with Emily's father was obviously over for now, Juliana turned to see how Amanda was faring on the dance floor. But apparently the waltz had ended sometime during the commotion. A quadrille was playing instead, and Amanda was nowhere to be seen.

"I told you Lord Stafford was a good man," Griffin said beside her.

Juliana glanced back at the man in question, who was now examining Lord Neville's throat through a silver quizzing glass attached to a chain around his neck. His dark hair was as tousled as ever.

"He saved the viscount's life," Griffin added.

"That's his job," she retorted. Lord Stafford's heroism didn't erase his shortcomings. He still was *not* what she wanted in a husband. "Where in heaven's name is Amanda?"

"Right there," Griffin said, gesturing toward a cluster of gentlemen across the room.

If Juliana hadn't recognized the blond curls piled atop her friend's head, she'd never have believed it was Amanda at the center of the cluster. Why, she was literally surrounded by suitors!

The trifle was clearly doing its job.

Juliana swooped in for a closer look. Maddeningly, she was too short to see around the crowd of black-clad shoulders. Would it be unladylike to worm her way in amongst the gentlemen? While trying to decide, she noticed Lord Malmsey hovering nearby, looking more than a little perturbed.

A delicate laugh like tinkling bells carried over the crowd.

Her mind made up, Juliana charged into the clutch of admirers. Many of whom, she noted, were quite young and handsome. Never mind that she'd already met and rejected every one of them—Amanda was sure to have different tastes and requirements. Juliana's heart swelled as she realized her friend might fall in love with someone this very night! And when she finally reached her protégé, statuesque and radiant and smiling one of the smiles Juliana had made her practice over and over, she thought her heart might burst with pride.

She touched Amanda on the arm and whispered, *"The look."* Amanda startled and gazed down at her in confusion. Then her expression cleared, and she quickly chose a young man and took aim, lowering her newly darkened lashes.

"Would you honor me with a dance?" he asked immediately.

"With pleasure, my lord," Amanda said, just as Juliana had taught her. As she went off on the gentleman's arm, she cast her friend a look of wonder. "It works!" she mouthed silently.

Of course it did. Hadn't Juliana told her so?

Without Amanda at the center of it, the group slowly dispersed. But Lord Malmsey remained in place, gazing toward the dance floor dejectedly. Although Juliana didn't know him well, he seemed a kindly man. And aside from his small stature and vast forehead, he was pleasant-looking for an older fellow. But his pale green eyes seemed troubled.

Quite suddenly, Juliana realized there was a flaw in her perfect plan. In seeing to Amanda's happiness, she was making Lord Malmsey *un*happy. And that would never do.

"What are you plotting now, Juliana?"

She looked over to see Corinna and Alexandra approaching. "Nothing," she told them both.

"I recognize that look on your face," Alexandra said.

Juliana never had been able to fool her older sister. "Oh, very well," she admitted, and led them a safe distance from her target. "I'm trying to find a match for Lord Malmsey."

"Holy Hannah," Corinna groaned, "whatever put that thought into your head?"

Juliana pressed her lips together, maintaining her silence.

"Something is going on." Corinna narrowed her eyes. "Something to do with Amanda."

Juliana sighed. She should have known Corinna would weasel the truth out of her one way or another. "Can you keep a secret?"

"Of course we can," Alexandra said, looking a little hurt. "Have we broken a confidence ever?"

Well, no, neither of them had. Not to Juliana's knowledge, anyway. She leaned in closer and lowered her voice. "Amanda's father has betrothed her against her will to Lord Malmsey."

"I knew it!" Corinna exclaimed at the same time Alexandra said, "That's dreadful!"

"Quite. Lord Wolverston is deaf to her protests. He's told her that if she refuses to go through with the wedding, he'll disinherit her."

Corinna gasped. "Then no one else will *ever* offer for her."

Of the three of them, she always *had* been the most blunt.

"Precisely," Juliana said. "Which is why I'm working to help

Amanda charm a more suitable man, in the hopes that he'll offer for her before it's too late." While that wasn't exactly the plan, it was close enough. She dared not mention the compromising position in front of her sisters, who rarely approved of her schemes. "But I cannot find love for Amanda at Lord Malmsey's expense. That would be terribly unfair."

"Juliana always wants to see *everyone* happy," Alexandra teased affectionately.

"In all his many years," Corinna pointed out, "Lord Malmsey has never proposed to anyone before Amanda. He's too shy to approach another lady."

"Then a shy spinster will be a perfect match." Juliana's gaze wandered the ballroom. Miss Hartshorn was too old; Lady Sarah Ballister was too young; Miss Ashton was too outgoing. She scanned past her chaperone, then back. "Aunt Frances," she said, nodding to herself with more than a little satisfaction.

"Aunt Frances?" Corinna's brilliant blue eyes widened. "You're thinking to match *Aunt Frances* with Lord Malmsey?"

Alexandra frowned toward their aunt, no doubt considering her spectacles and unstylish gray hair. "I've never seen Aunt Frances show romantic interest in a gentleman."

"That's only because no one has shown an interest in her," Juliana said. "And that will all change when she receives Lord Malmsey's love letter."

"What love letter?" Alexandra and Corinna asked in unison.

Juliana shook her head. "The one I'm going to write, of course."

Her sisters had no imagination.

She spotted one of their cousins, looking aimless. "Rachael!" she called with a merry wave, starting toward her.

Corinna grabbed her arm. "Are you plotting something else now?"

"Of course not," Juliana said, although she was indeed plotting to get her brother to dance with her cousin. Lately, Rachael seemed withdrawn or absent from most events, which had hampered Juliana's ongoing efforts to match her with Griffin.

She put on her most innocent smile and added, "I intend to invite Rachael, Claire, and Elizabeth to my next sewing party." Which, in point of fact, *was* precisely true.

It just wasn't her only intention.

ARY OF Juliana's grin, Griffin watched her heading his way with their cousin in tow. "Oh, there you are," she said. "Rachael would love to dance with you."

Rachael's gorgeous sky blue eyes narrowed in obvious annoyance. An awkward moment passed while Griffin shifted uncomfortably. But there was nothing for it—no way to duck out of this situation gracefully.

"I would be honored, Lady Rachael," he said at last, "if you would join me for the next dance."

"Splendid," Juliana said, beaming as the musicians struck up a waltz. "Please excuse me." She waved them toward the dance floor. "I must speak with Alexandra."

Griffin was already concocting his revenge. See if Juliana still thought this a fun game after being forced to dance with—

"Griffin!"

"Pardon?" Blinking at Rachael, he realized they were waltzing. She felt so natural in his arms that he hadn't noticed she was there—except now that he'd noticed, he couldn't *stop* noticing.

She looked amused. "Do you always allow your sisters to run roughshod over you?" she asked in a conversational tone.

"Only Juliana," he told her lightly.

"Balderdash," she said. Rachael could curse like a sailor, but he considered that part of her charm. "Alexandra and Corinna know how to play you just as well."

Since he couldn't really argue, he twirled her and changed the subject. "You've been hiding this season."

Her good humor suddenly vanished. Even the chestnut tendrils around her face seemed to droop. "I haven't felt much like mingling."

She didn't have to say why. Griffin knew—although his sisters didn't—that Rachael had been dealt a blow several months earlier when she'd learned the man she'd called "Papa" since birth hadn't actually been her father. He was dismayed, though not surprised, to find her still brooding on the subject.

"It doesn't signify," he said quietly.

"It signifies to me. I feel like my life has been a lie."

"Has something changed at home? Is Noah treating you differently? Or Claire or Elizabeth?"

"No. Not at all. But I feel as though they should."

"You all shared a mother. They're still your brother and sisters."

"I know." Her eyes grew suspiciously damp, and her chin— her adorable, dented chin—began to tremble. He could see her straining to maintain composure. She was too dignified to fall to pieces in a crowded ballroom.

And Griffin cared about her too much to just stand by and watch—yet what could *he* do? In truth, the matter was none of his concern. Besides which, he had plenty of his own concerns to be getting on with.

But he couldn't bear to see Rachael like this. She was young, lovely, intelligent, strong. And she'd already endured more than enough grief. She should be trying new things, enjoying herself, falling in love. Instead, she was hiding.

"Have you considered searching for your true father?" he asked.

"Of course not. He's dead."

Dead or not, he wanted to say, learning her father's identity might help. But the music ended, and she drew back and dipped a curtsy.

"Thank you, Lord Cainewood," she said without meeting his eyes. And then she walked away.

Given their shared childhood, her curtsy and address had both been too formal. But Griffin decided it was for the best. He shouldn't be getting involved—spending more time with Rachael would only complicate his life.

As he made his way from the dance floor, the Duke of Castleton walked up. "When are you going to sell me Velocity?"

Grateful for the distraction, Griffin laughed. "Never. When are you going to give up asking?"

"Never." Although Castleton gave a determined nod, not a hair on his carefully coiffed blond head moved. "I heard he made a good showing at Ascot."

"A pity you missed the meet," Griffin said, remembering Juliana preferred fair men. "You've a fine stable, Castleton."

"It would be finer with Velocity."

"Velocity—as I've told you at least a dozen times—isn't for sale." Considering the subject closed, Griffin gestured across the room. "I say, would you care to meet my sister?"

Revenge against Juliana might have to wait until *after* he found her a decent husband.

EVERYONE WHO was anyone was at Lady Hammersmithe's ball. Including James's mother, Cornelia—the Dowager Countess of Stafford—and her older sisters, Aurelia and Bedelia.

In the refreshment room, James handed them all glasses of champagne. "How is your throat, Aunt Bedelia?"

"Better. But my chest has been paining me." She put a narrow hand to her flat chest—Aunt Bedelia was as skinny as a rail. "Perhaps you should stop by Monday morning and have a listen."

Doing his best to appear concerned, James sipped champagne. "Perhaps I'll do that."

"Certainly you will," his mother said, but she softened the rebuke with a smile that reached her brown eyes.

Besides sharing James's eyes, she had the same dark hair, and a trim figure for a woman of her years. Aurelia might be a mite plump, and Bedelia a bit too thin, but Cornelia was perfectly in between.

"Have you enjoyed the dancing this evening?" she asked her son pointedly.

"Am I supposed to?" he retorted. "I thought marriage was the object, not enjoyment."

"Grandchildren are the object," Aunt Aurelia put in. "And grandnephews and grandnieces."

"Aha, the truth emerges," James said dryly.

He wondered if his older brother had had to endure this sort of pressure. Probably not, else he would have taken a wife long before he passed away. Mother was a master of killing with kindness—she always got what she wanted in the end. She would get the grandchildren she wanted, too.

Eventually.

But for now, James would continue to sidestep her pointed questions, because the answers would only disappoint her. Of the handful of girls he'd danced with this night—and the dozens of girls he'd met this last year—he couldn't imagine marrying a single one of them. Try as he might, he couldn't seem to imagine marrying again at all.

The problem was, he'd had love and marriage once. So now one without the other—marriage without the love—just seemed plain…impossible. But a loveless marriage was the best he could do, because loving a girl who wasn't Anne was unthinkable. Even the idea of it felt wrong, as though he was desecrating her memory.

Not that she would have objected. She was a generous and understanding person, and she wouldn't have wanted him to be unhappy or lonely. If he'd asked her permission—which he hadn't, of course—she would definitely have said he could fall in love with someone else after she was gone.

But that wasn't going to happen. No matter which girls he danced with, all he could see was Anne's pretty, loyal face shimmering before his eyes.

"I only want you to be happy," his mother said.

"I know." He also knew that she understood how he felt. Or at least she should. She'd also lost her life's love, after all. "Why aren't *you* dancing, Mother?"

"Me?"

Perhaps if he turned the tables, she'd realize she was pushing too hard. That he wasn't ready. "Yes, you. "

Aunts Aurelia and Bedelia both tittered into their champagne.

"What?" he said, turning to challenge them. "Father has been gone longer than Anne. And *your* husbands have been gone even longer. All three of you should be dancing."

The sisters exchanged startled glances. "We're too old," Aunt Aurelia said for all of them.

"Nonsense." His aunts were not yet sixty, and his mother was only fifty-two. He put down his champagne, then took their three glasses and set them down, too. "Come along," he said, taking Mother's elbow and trusting her sisters to follow.

"Where are you taking me?" she asked.

"To the ballroom, of course." He grinned at her obvious dismay. "You're not going to find a new husband while standing around the refreshment table."

TWELVE

HILE AMANDA was off dancing with her fourth or fifth potential suitor, and Juliana was inviting —well, perhaps begging—Rachael's two sisters to attend her little sewing party tomorrow, Griffin brought a strange man to meet her.

Not that he was actually *strange*. But he was definitely a stranger. Which Juliana found intriguing, because, honestly, she'd thought she'd already met every eligible young man who'd bothered to come to town this season.

"My sister," Griffin said by way of introduction. "Lady Juliana."

The man was handsome, fair-haired, and not too tall. Juliana smiled and curtsied.

"Juliana, I'd be pleased for you to meet the Duke of Castleton."

A duke! Handsome, fair-haired, not too tall, *and* a duke! Juliana's heart fluttered with excitement as the duke bowed over her hand. "Would you honor me with a dance, Lady Juliana?"

"It would be my pleasure," she said and let him lead her onto the floor.

The duke's dress and bearing were both impeccable, and he

proved to be an excellent dancer. "Where have you been all season?" she asked.

"Abroad, seeing to some of my interests now that the war with France has come to an end."

"Ah." Though he wasn't holding her very closely, she could smell his costly eau de cologne. "All your many interests keep you busy, then?"

"Not usually." He had calm, pale blue eyes. "It's been years since I've been overseas. I much prefer to stay here in town and fill my life with amusements."

No profession, nothing to keep him from spending lots of time with her. His blond hair was neatly groomed—unlike tousled Lord Stafford, he obviously had time to tend to it. He was sounding better and better.

Perfect, as a matter of fact.

"I adore being amused," she told him and gave him *the look*.

Unfortunately, he didn't fall at her feet. In fact, he appeared rather taken aback, until he quickly schooled his face back into a neutral expression. "It was cold on the Continent," he said as though nothing had happened.

So he was proper and reserved. She could admire that. He was sure to be the very soul of gentlemanly behavior. "As cold as it's been here?"

"Not quite. And certainly not as rainy."

"It *snowed* this month. In June!"

"Amazing, isn't it?"

"Yes, amazing."

They both fell silent.

Juliana could admit: scintillating conversation, it was not. But then, they didn't know each other yet. There would be plenty of time later to speak of deeper things.

When the dance ended, the duke quite properly delivered her back to her brother.

"Well?" Griffin asked after the young man had bowed and walked away. "I suppose you want me to keep looking?"

"To the contrary," she said. "I expect it's likely no more introductions will be necessary. How old is the duke? Do you know?" He didn't *look* terribly old, but most of the dukes she knew were downright ancient.

"You're not dismissing him out of hand?" Griffin looked vastly surprised—and pleased, not to mention relieved. "I believe he's twenty-eight."

While she'd prefer someone a bit closer to her own age, twenty-eight wasn't *so* very old. After all, she was a quite mature seventeen, wasn't she? "You didn't mention his given name."

"It's David. His family name is Harcourt."

Harcourt—an elegant surname for her children. And his title, Castleton, sounded rather romantic, did it not? And he was a *duke*.

Could he *be* more perfect?

A deep voice interrupted her musings. "Good evening, Lady Juliana."

She glanced up to see Lord Stafford. Way up. "Good evening."

"Cainewood," he said, addressing her brother, "you wouldn't happen to know any aging widowers, would you?"

The odd question drew a bark of laughter from Griffin. " Looking for more patients, Stafford? Old ones, with many ailments?"

"No." He gestured toward three mature women standing in a tight cluster. Was it Juliana's imagination, or did they look a bit petrified? "I'm looking for dance partners for my mother and her sisters, Lady Avonleigh and Lady Balmforth."

"Dance partners?" Juliana asked, her interest piqued. "Or possible suitors?"

"My sister fancies herself a matchmaker," Griffin explained.

"I do not," she retorted. "I just like helping people find happiness."

"A noble pursuit," Lord Stafford said grandly. "However, I'm *not* looking for suitors. Dance partners will do."

Lord Malmsey came to mind, but although he was too old for Amanda, he was too young for Lord Stafford's mother. And besides, she'd already decided he belonged with Aunt Frances.

"May I borrow your quizzing glass?" she asked.

Instead of taking it off, Lord Stafford handed it to her with the long chain still around his neck. She leaned closer to raise it to her left eye. He smelled not of costly eau de cologne but of soap and something vaguely spicy.

A quick scan of the room through the quizzing glass revealed several likely dance partners for his relations, and she wasted no time corralling and introducing them to the three women. Not five minutes later, she stood hip to hip with Lord Stafford, the two of them watching his mother and aunts perform a quadrille.

Or at least they would have been hip to hip had he not been so overly tall.

"That," Lord Stafford said, looking a little stunned, "was remarkable."

Juliana shrugged, much the same as he had when she'd remarked that he'd saved Lord Neville's life. "I'm good at what I do."

"You certainly are." The musicians finished the quadrille and struck up a lilting waltz. "May I have this dance?" he suddenly asked.

Although she would rather have danced again with the duke, it wouldn't be seemly to refuse. So she said, "It would be my pleasure."

As he spun her around the floor, a flutter sprung up in her middle. That had nothing to do with Lord Stafford, of course— she was simply dizzy from the dance and from the evening's happy successes. She'd found the duke, and Amanda had her pick of young suitors, and Lord Malmsey was going to fall head over heels for Aunt Frances. She might even be able to match Lord Stafford's mother and aunts with eligible widowers this season, no matter that he only meant for them to dance. All of her projects were beginning to come together.

She glanced up to find Lord Stafford staring at her again, like he had the first time they'd danced. And again she found it unnerving. He seemed a very intense young man. Much too intense for high-spirited Juliana, but perhaps he'd make a good match for Amanda, who was a serious sort of girl. In fact, they might just be ideally suited! He was a doctor, after all, and Amanda had quite competently tended Emily's wound. She would make an excellent doctor's wife. And Amanda was tall, so the two of them would look wonderful together.

And meanwhile, she, Juliana, would be a duchess! She could already picture herself walking down the aisle with the duke.

But now wasn't the time for daydreams—it was the time for making polite chitchat with one's dance partner. So she forced herself to meet Lord Stafford's intense gaze with a gracious, not-at-all-unnerved smile. "I missed you at Almack's last Wednesday."

His raised an eyebrow. "You missed me?"

She hadn't meant it like that. "You weren't there. Do you not like Almack's?"

James abhorred the very idea of the place—it was little more than a hunting ground for young girls and their scheming mamas to ensnare eligible bachelors. But he wouldn't say that to Juliana. "My mother obtained a voucher for me," he said instead, which was entirely true, "but there was trouble at the Institute that night, so I was unable to attend."

That was likewise entirely true. Although another truth was that he'd have found a different excuse if that one hadn't presented itself.

"How unfortunate," she said. "I hope the trouble wasn't too dreadful."

"A shortage of staff. I had to fill in myself, as well as interview new candidates."

"What sort of staff were you looking for? Did you find anyone?"

Given her talent for matching people, he wouldn't be

surprised if she offered to find someone for him. "I needed an assistant. To coordinate supplies and greet patients. And yes, I found someone. I wouldn't be here tonight if I hadn't."

Her blue-green eyes narrowed. "You would work on a Saturday evening?"

"I work often on Saturday evenings. Many patients who are working people cannot visit during normal working hours. When I'm in town, New Hope is open from ten o'clock in the morning until ten o'clock at night, every day except Sunday."

Most shops kept the same hours, so he wondered why she looked so disapproving. And he wished she didn't. Because the more he saw of her, the more he liked her. She was so full of good intentions and liveliness. Liveliness that suddenly seemed missing from his life.

All at once, he realized that Anne's face wasn't shimmering before his eyes. In fact, he hadn't thought about Anne at all while dancing with Juliana. Not for the barest moment. Probably because the two of them couldn't be more different—where Anne had been tall, brunette, and restrained, Juliana was small, blond, and spritely. Marriage to her would never be boring.

But it wouldn't be love.

And it wouldn't be right for James. Juliana was quite appealing, and certainly "good at what she did." She would make a fun, charming wife—for someone else. Someone who had time for such frivolity. He didn't; not if he hoped to accomplish his goals.

But as long as he was stuck at this ball, he might as well enjoy her company. He liked the way she danced on tiptoe, as if she had so much energy she could scarcely keep her feet fastened to the floor. Or perhaps she was merely reaching as high as she could because he was so much taller. From his height, he could look down at the top of her blond head, which gleamed beneath the chandeliers. Her hair was an intriguing mix of pale gold and light brown and every shade in between. And when she looked up, those blue-green-hazel eyes...he couldn't quit gazing into them, trying to figure out what color they were.

As the dance came to an end, she said, "I have someone I'd like you to meet."

He didn't want to meet anyone. He wanted to go home to Stafford House. Without his mother. Maybe she'd sleep at her sisters' town house tonight, the three of them giggling like young girls discussing their latest conquests. A fellow could hope.

But no, she'd come home as always, probably vexed with him for making her dance. That had been the whole idea, hadn't it? To give her a taste of her own medicine?

"You don't mind, do you?" Juliana's eager voice snapped him back to attention. "Lady Amanda is really quite lovely."

Oh, yes, she wanted him to meet someone. Lady Amanda. Right. "I don't mind at all," he lied. "Where is this lovely lady?"

She shot him an unreadable glance before starting across the ballroom. "Follow me, Lord Stafford."

"James."

"Pardon?"

He watched her graceful, springy steps as he followed her. "My given name is James."

She slowed down until he caught up. "We barely know each other, Lord Stafford."

True. But he'd been thinking of her as Juliana since the first moment he'd glimpsed her here tonight. Not Lady Juliana, just Juliana.

Odd, that.

"We've danced together twice," he pointed out.

"That hardly makes us intimates."

Intimates. To his very great surprise, the word made his face heat. What was wrong with him? He felt like a bashful schoolboy. "Just call me James," he snapped.

"Very well." She huffed out an impatient sigh and came to a

stop before a clutch of gentlemen. "Come along," she said and pushed in.

A blond girl was at the center. A lovely blond girl.

Juliana tapped her on the shoulder. "Amanda, this is Lord Stafford. Lord Stafford—James—meet Lady Amanda Wolverston."

"Lady Amanda," he said with a proper bow. He wasn't tempted to call her just Amanda. Or even think of her as just Amanda. She was Lady Amanda through and through.

But Juliana was just Juliana.

This entire evening was proving most troubling.

"Lord Stafford," Lady Amanda returned formally. "I'm delighted to meet you."

She was lovely and delighted. Being a gentleman, he had to do the polite thing. "May I have the honor of the next dance?"

Lady Amanda smiled a lovely smile, though it looked a tad forced. "With pleasure, my lord," she said, sounding much less pleased than she claimed.

Juliana shot them both a grin.

At least *someone* was happy.

Lady Amanda was a fine dancer. Although not as animated as Juliana, she chatted amiably enough. And she *was* quite lovely. But when the dance ended he wasn't sorry.

Another gentleman claimed her immediately. James's mother sidled up to him, out of breath. "What a lovely girl."

"Quite. Did you enjoy your dance?" he asked, expecting to hear that she hadn't. That she wasn't ready to consider getting close to someone new. That she was sorry for pressuring him when he clearly wasn't ready, either.

"They were delightful," she said instead.

"They?"

"The dances. All three of them. And all three men. Aurelia and Bedelia thought one dance quite enough, so I danced with their men, too." She took both his hands in hers. "Thank you, my dear. I'll admit I thought the very idea was daft, but it's high time I resumed a social life, and I appreciate your little push."

He groaned inwardly.

"I'm going to spend the night with Aurelia and Bedelia," she added, looking happier than he'd seen her in ages. "Good evening, dear. I'll see you tomorrow."

At least she was happy, he thought as she walked off. And he'd have an evening at home alone, like he'd hoped.

Now, if only he could unclench his jaw.

"Well, Stafford, you've certainly danced with your share of the ladies."

He turned to see Cainewood. "I'm finished," he said. But he wasn't ready to go home yet—suddenly *home alone* sounded lonely. "Can I interest you in a game of chess?"

"Chess? Haven't touched a board since I left the army." Cainewood sipped from a nearly empty glass. "Sure. For how much?"

"You want to wager?"

"Afraid you're going to lose?" Grinning crookedly, he finished his drink. "Ten guineas."

"Deal." The stake was high—much more than they'd ever bet in their schooldays—but James returned the grin. "Follow me," he said, leading his friend toward the card room.

He didn't expect he'd lose. Cainewood was looking a bit foxed.

THIRTEEN

"*I* SAY, Cainewood. You're looking a bit foxed."

Griffin looked up from the chessboard where he and Stafford were playing, to find Castleton standing over them. "I'm quite sober, I assure you," he told the duke, fascinated to hear a bit of a slur in his own voice. Just a bit, because he was just a bit foxed. Which was perfectly reasonable, since he'd had much to celebrate this evening.

Juliana had finally—*finally*—found a gentleman she wanted.

This gentleman right here.

He took another sip of Regent's Punch, an inspired mix of six different spirits. "What do you think of my sister, Castleton?"

The duke shrugged. "She's lively."

"Yes, isn't that nice? Nothing like a lively young lady." Griffin blinked. Castleton looked a bit stiff. And a bit blurred.

He wondered what his sister saw in the fellow.

Castleton was a keen judge of horseflesh—a fine recommendation, to Griffin's mind—but surely Juliana didn't care about that. She could sit a mount and enjoyed riding up and down Rotten Row in Hyde Park, the fashionable place to see and be seen, but she'd never been a particularly horsey sort of girl.

Griffin supposed, however, that a lady might find Castleton

handsome. In a pale sort of way. And, oh, yes, he was a duke. There was *that*.

Besides, did it matter *why* Juliana wanted him? The fact that she did was good enough for Griffin.

"It's your turn," Stafford said.

"So it is." Griffin focused on the board—or at least he tried to focus. He was losing, but he didn't care. Life was too good at the moment to worry overmuch about a chess game or a few guineas.

Pondering his strategy, he took another celebratory sip. He'd never tried Regent's Punch before tonight. It was astonishingly good stuff.

He moved a rook and looked back up at Castleton. "I suppose you've come over to ask for permission to call on my sister?"

"Not really. I was just sitting over there playing cards and noticed you looked foxed."

Castleton sounded disapproving. And quite pompous. Why again did Juliana like him? Oh, yes, he was a duke. And her reason didn't matter. Griffin wanted his sister to be happy—he wanted all of his sisters to be happy. If Juliana had her heart set on Castleton, he'd do whatever it would take to see them married.

"Did you know," he said, noticing that slur again in a detached, amused sort of way, "that Velocity is part of Juliana's dowry?"

The horse wasn't, of course. Until now.

"You don't say," Castleton mused, suddenly looking much more lively himself. "I hadn't heard that."

FOURTEEN

SHREWSBURY CAKES

Beat half a pound of Butter to a fine cream, and put in the same weight of Flour, one Egg, a measure of grated loaf Sugar, and small spoons of Nutmeg and Cinnamon. Mix them into a paste, roll them thin, and cut them with a small glass or little tins, prick them, lay them on sheets of tin, and bake them in a slow oven. Serve spread with raspberry Jam if you wish.

Should you wish to convince someone of something, these cakes will do the trick.

—Helena, Countess of Greystone, 1784

*D*ESPITE HAVING persuaded her cousins to attend her party, Juliana had no more ladies sewing than last week. Corinna, while present today in the drawing room, was "involved" with her latest painting and refused to pick up a needle. Aunt Frances was at Amanda's house, visiting with Lady Mabel. And Sunday was the one day of the week Emily's father made sure to spend time with her.

Luckily, Rachael's mother had been artistic and had taught her girls to sew. Since Rachael, Claire, and Elizabeth were sewing much faster—not to mention better—than last week's crew, Juliana's panic subsided. And since Aunt Frances and Emily were missing, she took advantage of their absence to explain Amanda's situation to her cousins.

After hearing of Amanda's woes, Rachael sighed. But then her smile made Juliana hopeful she was growing a bit cheerier. "Well, you certainly were last night's Incomparable, Lady Amanda." Her needle flew in and out of the miniature coat she was making. "Were you enthralled by any particular gentleman?"

"Lord Stafford," Juliana answered for Amanda. "He's absolutely perfect."

"I'm not certain." Seated on the drawing room sofa between Juliana and Alexandra, Amanda stitched as slowly and clumsily as ever. Juliana doubted she'd ever progress beyond blankets. Perhaps *this* blanket. "Lord Stafford *is* handsome," Amanda admitted.

"He's gorgeous," Corinna corrected from where she was painting by the picture window.

"Quite," Juliana agreed, reaching toward the platter of Shrewsbury cakes. She might not personally prefer James's dark looks, she thought as she spread raspberry jam on one of the sweets, but she couldn't argue with her sister's assessment.

"But I'm not struck by love," Amanda said, her stitches getting shakier.

Fearing her friend might stab herself and bleed, Juliana pulled the needle from her hand and put the cake into it instead. "It might take a while," she said gently.

"Not everyone marries for love," Claire pointed out, her unusual amethyst eyes fixed on her expert handiwork.

Elizabeth reached for a spool of white thread. "Your parents didn't marry for love, did they, Juliana?"

"No, they didn't. And that was a big mistake."

"Don't listen to Juliana," Corinna told her cousins. "Her head is full of *romantic* notions. Our family was perfectly happy."

"Not Mama. She loved Father desperately, and he never returned her feelings." As Juliana had grown older and more aware, she'd found Mama's unrequited love painful to watch.

"Her children made her happy," Alexandra put in.

"Yes, but that didn't erase her hurt. All she wanted was for him to notice her, spend time with her, make her part of his life. But he couldn't be bothered."

Juliana wouldn't let that happen to her. Until she found someone she loved madly—someone she knew loved her madly in return—she meant to remain unwed.

"Mama's life wasn't that tragic," Corinna argued. "Besides, Amanda cannot afford to wait to fall deeply in love."

Juliana shook her head. "Love is *always* worth waiting for," she said stubbornly.

"But Amanda's wedding is quickly approaching," Claire said. "Better to take a chance on a suitable young man she *might* come to love, than to face certain doom on the arm of Lord Malmsey."

Perhaps they were right. Unfortunately, Amanda didn't have enough time to get to know Lord Stafford well. Juliana squeezed her friend's hand. "You might have to find someone you like a lot and marry him, then be struck by love later."

Amanda swallowed her mouthful of cake before speaking. "Grow into love, you mean?"

"Exactly," Juliana said. "Lord Stafford isn't just handsome, he's also young and well-off."

"What are you looking for in a husband?" Alexandra asked Amanda. "Besides appearance and status, that is. Looks fade, after all. Shared values and interests are much more important."

"Very true," Elizabeth said deferentially.

They all deferred to Alexandra on the topic of marriage.

Amanda seemed to consider that question for a minute. "I would like a husband who is interested in Roman antiquities."

Juliana nearly dropped her jam knife in surprise. "Since when are *you* interested in Roman antiquities?"

"Since my father found the ruins on our property. It's a fascinating subject."

"Hmm," Juliana said.

She suspected Amanda's fascination had begun as a hopeless attempt to please her father, but it might have grown into a real interest. One sometimes had to go to extremes, Juliana knew, to amuse oneself in the countryside.

However, she sincerely doubted James shared her friend's passion for Roman antiquities. How could he have time to pursue a hobby when he couldn't even find a few minutes to comb his hair?

"What else are you looking for in a husband?" she asked.

Amanda pondered a moment more. "I would like for him to play chess. If I'm to live away from Aunt Mabel, I'd like someone with whom to play chess."

Juliana doubted James had time for chess, either. So she was surprised when Rachael said, "Lord Stafford definitely plays chess."

"However do you know that?" she asked.

Having finished sewing the coat, Rachael knotted the thread. "When Griffin came out of the card room last night, I overheard him saying he'd lost thirty guineas to Lord Stafford playing chess."

"Thirty guineas!" Now Juliana *did* drop her knife. Surely that sort of money could be better spent elsewhere—donated to the Foundling Hospital, for instance. "I had no idea Griffin gambled such high stakes."

"He usually doesn't, I expect," Rachael said, looking amused. "He seemed a bit foxed, which isn't usual for him, either. In any case"—she smiled at Amanda—"Lord Stafford does enjoy chess."

Juliana jumped on that positive attribute. "See, there's more to him than appearance and wealth..." She trailed off as she noticed a smear of jam on the little frock in her lap. Drat. She pulled out her handkerchief

"He's also a physician," Claire reminded her.

"That, too. Which means he's well-educated and he cares for people."

"He limps," Amanda pointed out.

"Only slightly. And does it signify?"

"Indeed, it shouldn't." Corinna looked up from her easel. "You make him sound ideal, Juliana. Why don't *you* marry him?"

"Don't be a goose. I have a duke courting me."

She wetted a corner of her handkerchief and scrubbed at the stain, thinking that only yesterday she'd despaired of ever finding a husband. How quickly her life had turned around! Not only had the duke danced with her *twice* at Lady Hammersmithe's ball—raising eyebrows and sparking rumors—but toward the end of the evening he'd very kindly asked if he might pay her a call tomorrow afternoon.

She'd accepted, of course. She wasn't an idiot.

"By the end of the season," she said dreamily, "I may be the Duchess of Castleton."

Amanda's mouth dropped open. "You'd marry the Duke of Castleton?"

"Wouldn't you?"

"No!" She looked horrified. "He's a by-blow."

Juliana quit scrubbing. "What do you mean?"

"It's an open secret," Rachael explained. "The previous duke was away many years ago, looking after his interests on the Continent, when his wife conceived a child here in London. To this day, no one knows who fathered the child. It really doesn't signify, though, since the last duke arrived home before the current duke was born and acknowledged him as his son."

"It signifies to me," Amanda said. "Marriage to a known by-blow would taint my family."

"It *is* shocking," Juliana mused. "But on the other hand…he's a *duke*. His parentage hasn't affected his standing in society. And it plainly isn't his fault."

"I'd never be certain of my children's true heritage. For all we know, the duke could have been fathered by a footman!"

"I cannot see why that makes a difference," Rachael said, "considering the last duke claimed him for a son."

"I'd never trust him to be faithful to me."

"Why shouldn't you trust him?" Juliana wondered. "I'd guess the last thing he wants to do is subject his own children to the shame he's had to live with."

Amanda raised one of her newly plucked brows. "You know what they say: like father, like son."

"In this case, don't you mean: like mother, like son?" Corinna chimed in.

"They also say the sins of the father—or mother—shouldn't be visited on the child." Juliana felt sorry the duke had been forced to grow up under this cloud. "He was a victim, not to blame. You're being unfairly judgmental."

Amanda just shrugged and returned to her atrocious blanket. But Juliana could tell that her straitlaced friend would never change her mind. Of course, that didn't matter, since it was Juliana who intended to marry the duke. Amanda belonged with Lord Stafford.

Juliana passed her a second Shrewsbury cake, hoping it would help convince her that James was right for her. That was why she'd risen at dawn this morning to bake them, after all— they were supposed to help convince people. "Did you meet a young man you liked better than Lord Stafford?"

"No," Amanda said. "But there are many more to meet."

"Not this season. They seem to be staying home." Juliana recommenced scrubbing. "I wonder if it's because of all the cold and wet."

"Now *you're* being a goose." Corinna swirled her brush in green paint. "I'm having a marvelous time this season—there are plenty of young men."

Of course she was having a marvelous time. It was her first season, and Griffin wasn't pressing her to marry. Not yet, anyway. Juliana was supposed to wed first. "Don't tell me you've fallen in love."

"I'm not in any hurry." Corinna dabbed at her canvas, creating a grassy field out of nothing.

Juliana would never figure out how she did that. Giving up on the stain, she rose and wandered closer to inspect the scene. A gentleman and a lady walked hand in hand over rolling hills. Corinna never used to paint people—only landscapes and still lifes. But this past year she'd been adding people to her paintings more and more often.

And not just any people. Couples. Maybe she *was* falling in love. "Are you sure?" Juliana asked.

"I don't have time to fall in love right now." Corinna added a dab of white to the green paint on her palette. "My art is more important. Next year, I plan to submit to the Royal Academy."

"You do? I'd no idea there were women in the Royal Academy."

"There aren't. No woman has been admitted in almost fifty years." Corinna mixed the colors together, creating a lighter shade of green. "But there's no rule banning us, though there *is* a minimum age requirement. In a few years, I'll be old enough to campaign for admittance. And in preparation for that, my first objective is to have one of my paintings selected for next year's Summer Exhibition."

Juliana was a bit stunned. Of course, it was just like her sister to formulate an elaborate, ambitious plan without talking to anyone, even her own family. Corinna went her own way, always. And maybe it was just the Shrewsbury cakes, but Juliana found herself convinced—her little sister would soon make history.

Meanwhile, Juliana herself couldn't even make a batch of baby clothes.

Though she knew she should get back to work, she stepped to the window and gazed out at the unceasing rain. Not only was her sewing project in jeopardy, her scheme to match Amanda and James was at a standstill. Amanda seemed, at best, unsure about her feelings for him, and *he* was making no effort to persuade her. The trouble was, there was only so much Juliana could do to prod them along.

Or was there?

Suppose James's problem wasn't apathy, but inexperience? He spent all his time doctoring—had he ever even courted before? Did he know how to woo *any* lady, let alone a proper, prissy one like Amanda? Considering what Juliana had seen of him so far—the odd staring, the lack of careful grooming—she'd wager that he was entirely clueless about women.

Maybe she'd even put thirty guineas on it.

There was only one solution: Juliana would have to instruct him. Of course, convincing him of the necessity of such training was sure to be a delicate matter. She'd visit him at the New Hope Institute tomorrow, she decided, since it was closed on Sundays. And she'd have the cook package up some Shrewsbury cakes to take along.

She returned to her chair and the jam-stained frock. It seemed all her scrubbing had only served to spread the pink splotch further and ruin her handkerchief in the process. But this was only the third of thirty frocks she had to make, and she'd already poured hours of work into it.

While no one was looking, she turned the garment inside out —now the stain would be hidden inside the lining—and continued sewing.

FIFTEEN

"**W**HAT DO YOU think of this dress, dear?" Sitting across from James at the breakfast table Monday morning, Mother held up her copy of *La Belle Assemblée*, open to one of the hand-colored fashion plates. "Shall I order something like it for the next ball?"

"It's lovely, Mother." Given that his mother hadn't shown any interest in clothes since his father passed away, James knew he should be pleased to see her enjoying life again. But instead he was still annoyed that his plot to convince her to quit pressuring him had failed so miserably.

"I had a wonderful time dancing," she said for at least the dozenth time since the ball.

His only relief had been the few hours she'd spent overnight with her sisters. She'd enjoyed that, too. His aunts' peach-ridden town house was near Oxford Street with all its shops. A perfect distance from his own mansion in St. James's Place—close enough for an easy visit, but far enough that he didn't see his aunts every time he stepped out the door.

He folded the *Morning Chronicle* and set it carefully by his plate. "I have an idea, Mother."

"Hmm?" She flipped a page of her magazine.

"Why don't you move back in with your sisters? You could help them redecorate and get rid of some of that horrendous peach. I'm sure you'd enjoy that more than living here with me."

Mother hadn't always lived with him. Once he'd finished medical school and wed Anne, he'd established his own household. After his father's death, when James inherited Stafford House and the country estate that went along with his title, his mother had moved in with her sisters, not wishing to intrude on his life with his wife. But then Anne died, and Mother came running back home to "help" him.

And here she'd stayed. For too long. He loved her dearly, but a grown man was entitled to some privacy and autonomy. He'd truly appreciated her "help" while he'd needed it, but he'd long since recovered some semblance of a life, even if he didn't feel ready to marry.

"Don't be foolish, James. Should my sisters ever decide to redecorate, I can help them from here. Who would run this household if I abandoned you? Stafford House is one of the largest homes in London."

One thing he wasn't lacking was money. "I have a staff. And I can hire more people should I need to."

"That's not the same as having family oversee matters." She flipped another page, tilting her head to peruse the dress pictured. "I wouldn't think of moving out until you have a wife."

Yet another reason to marry. James took a big gulp of tea to settle his churning stomach.

"Very well, then," he said, setting down the cup. He knew she wouldn't budge on this matter. "I must be off." He pushed back from the table and rose. "I wish you a pleasant day."

She looked up. "I trust you haven't forgotten that Bedelia is expecting you this morning?"

Blast it. He had. His mind had been on other things. Especially a hazel-eyed sprite he had no business thinking about.

"I haven't time, I'm afraid." He shrugged into the tailcoat a footman held out. "Only one doctor volunteered today, so I must fill the other spot," he said, buttoning the coat. "I'm expected at the Institute by ten."

"The people can wait a little longer for their vaccinations. Bedelia has been suffering with chest pains."

"Aunt Bedelia is fine, Mother."

"I'm sure you're right." She paused for a sip of her tea. "But what if she isn't?"

She always got her way in the end.

SIXTEEN

"**T**HIS DOESN'T look like a nice neighborhood," Aunt Frances said with a worried frown.

"It's perfectly safe, I assure you." Reaching over the basket of Shrewsbury cakes on her lap, Juliana pulled the carriage's curtains closed.

"Herman doesn't like the dark," Emily said, reopening them.

"Then Herman should have stayed home," Juliana told her. Aunt Frances was peering out the window again, looking even more nervous, so Juliana dug into her reticule for something to distract her. "Here, Aunty. I forgot to give you this letter. It arrived in the morning mail."

Emily stroked Herman's olive green scales, for all the world like he was a real pet. "I never get letters."

"I never get letters, either." Eyes wide behind her spectacles, Aunt Frances broke the seal and held the paper up to the light. As she scanned the single page, she sucked in a breath. "Goodness gracious!"

Juliana stifled a smile. "What does it say, Aunty?"

Her aunt's cheeks were suddenly so rosy, she looked like she'd eaten an entire bowl of trifle. "It's a poem."

"A poem? Does it rhyme?"

Aunt Frances nodded violently.

"Who is it from?"

"I'm not at all certain. He didn't sign his name."

"How do you know it's a *he*, then?" Emily asked. "It might be from a girl."

The older woman raised a hand to pat her modestly covered bosom. "He signed it"—her voice dropped conspiratorially—*"Your Secret Admirer."*

"Oh, Aunt Frances! That's so romantic!" Juliana sneaked a glance out the window, wondering how much longer she could distract her. "Whoever he is, he must have been at Lady Hammersmithe's ball Saturday night and seen you in that beautiful fawn dress."

Aunt Frances looked doubtful. "I've worn that dress dozens of times."

"Well, then, we must order you new ones, don't you think? Before next Saturday's ball."

Though she hadn't bought a new dress all season—probably all decade—her aunt nodded. "I suppose we must."

Juliana toyed with the handle of her basket, fighting off a self-satisfied grin, until the carriage drew to a stop before a small, neat building with a sign that said NEW HOPE INSTITUTE.

The neighborhood hadn't improved, but her aunt no longer seemed to care. When a footman lowered the steps, Aunt Frances all but floated down to the street. Carrying the basket, Juliana climbed out after her, and Emily and Herman followed.

The door to the Institute opened, and a woman came out and down the steps, holding two children by the hand. Aunt Frances nearly collided with them, but her niece managed to yank her out of the way in time. "What color dresses shall we order?" she asked Juliana.

"Pastels will look best with your golden-brown hair."

On the Institute's steps, Emily turned and frowned. "Her hair isn't brown."

Juliana smiled. "It will be after I summon Madame Bellefleur to dye it."

They all went inside. The reception area looked very new and clean, though it was noisy and crowded with people in ragged clothing. "A snake!" a boy exclaimed, and several grimy children ran over to cluster around Emily and Herman.

A young woman with an air of authority walked out from behind a counter. She was dressed a little better than the patients. "Twenty-three!" she called.

A mother stood up with a baby and followed her through a door into the back.

When the young woman returned to the counter and began adding some rather scary-looking supplies to the jumble already on the shelves, Juliana went over to her. She handed Juliana a worn square of paper with a big black *36* written on it. "You're number thirty-six," she said very slowly and clearly, as though Juliana couldn't read it for herself. "Please be seated. I'll call you when it's your turn."

Juliana put the paper in her basket. "I wish to have a word with Lord Stafford, if I may."

"Lord Stafford?" The woman blinked. "Oh, you mean Dr. Trevor. He isn't here, milady."

Drat! Juliana hadn't even considered the possibility. "Do you know when he's expected?"

"I'm sorry, milady, but I don't. Only one doctor volunteered for today, so he should be here to vaccinate the other half of the patients. But his note said only that he'd be delayed—"

Just then the door opened, and in walked James, his coat and cravat draped over one arm. Even though he was scandalously undressed, Juliana couldn't have been more delighted. "Lord Stafford!" she exclaimed. "I'm so glad to see you!"

He looked shocked—and maybe pleased. "I'm glad to see you, too."

She hadn't meant it like that. "I thought you'd be here, but you weren't."

"I was examining my Aunt Bedelia. She's been suffering imaginary chest pains."

"The poor, sweet lady." She paused, just realizing what he'd said. "Imaginary?"

"Aunt Bedelia is the healthiest woman I know. Except possibly my other aunt, Aurelia." Unfastening the top button of his shirt, he cleared his throat. "What can I do for you?"

Aunt Frances suddenly turned to her. "I was wondering that myself. Why *are* we here, Juliana?"

She had no answer, so instead she said, "Aunt Frances, have you met Lord Stafford?"

James offered a bow. "Good afternoon, Lady Frances."

"Good afternoon, my lord." She looked at him sharply. "Did I see you at Lady Hammersmithe's ball?"

"I had the pleasure of attending, yes."

Aunt Frances's gaze grew more focused. At first Juliana assumed she was staring at the little V of exposed skin where James's shirt was unbuttoned, which Juliana found rather fascinating herself. Other than her brothers'—and they hardly counted—she'd never seen any part of a man's chest. But then she realized her aunt was actually looking at James's face, and her blue eyes had turned speculative behind their lenses. Juliana had never seen her look at a gentleman like that before…

Faith! Middle-aged, gray-haired, half-insensible Aunt Frances was wondering if *James* was her secret admirer! Juliana pressed a gloved fist to her mouth, but couldn't quite manage to hold back the mirth that was bubbling up inside her. She covered it with a cough.

She'd have to write another love letter from Lord Malmsey and sign his name to it this time—before Aunt Frances set her hopes on someone much younger and better-looking.

James's gasp interrupted her thoughts. "Is that a *snake* in my reception room?"

Across the room, the children were still gathered around

Herman, enthralled, while Emily, in her glory, proudly lectured them on his care and allowed them turns to touch.

Juliana smiled. "That's Viscount Neville's daughter, Miss Emily Neville, and—"

"Get it out of here."

"No need to worry." The light in here was odd; James was looking rather pale. "It's perfectly harmless, Lord Stafford."

"James," he corrected distractedly. "And I want it out. It's frightening the children."

It was doing no such thing, but Juliana wasn't about to argue. She had much more important matters to discuss with him. "Aunt Frances, would you please take Emily and Herman outside?"

Her aunt was still scrutinizing James. "It's dreadfully cold out there," she said without taking her eyes off him.

"You can wait inside the carriage. I won't be long, I promise."

"The neighborhood—"

"The coachman and three footmen are there for your protection." Juliana took her aunt's arm and began easing her toward Emily. "You'll be safe. I'll be out in five minutes."

Her gaze no longer focused on James, Aunt Frances consulted the little watch pinned to her dress. "You'd better not take any more time. The Duke of Castleton is calling at half past two."

Following a short negotiation, Juliana finally shut the door behind Aunt Frances, Emily, Herman, and several children who refused to stay inside when there was a snake outside to play with. "Now, if I could have just a few moments of your time, Lord Stafford—"

"James," he interrupted.

"James." She looked around. "Is there someplace private we could speak?"

SEVENTEEN

ONDERING WHAT Juliana wanted of him, James led her to an empty treatment room. He also wondered why the thought of Castleton calling on her irritated him so. Perhaps because Castleton was so very wrong for her. The duke was a prig; she was much too lively for such a stuffy fellow.

Not to mention the prig wanted her only because she came with a fancy racehorse.

The treatment room held nothing but a chair and a table spread with medical supplies, but Juliana glanced around as though she found it interesting. She was wearing a dress made of a thin, soft yellow material that did nothing to hide her curves.

Well, in truth the dress's fabric wasn't any finer or thinner than the dresses other young ladies of her class wore—thin, fine fabric must be in fashion, he supposed—but James wasn't used to seeing women in fashionable dresses at the Institute. The women who came to the Institute generally wore drab, practical clothes made of warm, sturdy fabrics. He wouldn't have noticed Juliana's thin dress at a ball, but here at the Institute it made him suddenly—uncomfortably—aware that he was alone in a room with an unchaperoned young lady.

An unchaperoned young lady he found way too appealing.

He left the door open.

"That child doesn't sound happy," she said, referring to the sobbing girl in the next room.

"Dr. Hanley will give her a sugar stick."

Sure enough, the sobbing stopped. Juliana smiled. "I love sweets." She handed him the small basket she was carrying. "I brought you these."

He lifted the number 36 on top and peered underneath. Appetizing scents of cinnamon and raspberry wafted out.

"They're Shrewsbury cakes," she said. "Chase ladies always bring sweets when we pay calls."

"People don't generally *call* at the Institute."

"It's not in a very nice neighborhood," she allowed. "Why is that?"

"Those who live in nice neighborhoods are vaccinated by their own doctors. The patients we serve cannot afford to take a hackney coach to Mayfair."

"Oh," she said, looking chastened. "That does make perfect sense."

He smiled, trying to put her at ease. "Have you been vaccinated?"

She glanced warily toward the instruments. "Actually, I was variolated shortly after birth, before Dr. Jenner's vaccination method became known."

Variolation was an older procedure, a method of taking pus from the pocks of someone suffering from smallpox and inoculating healthy people with it. James was surprised and impressed that she knew the difference. Perhaps she wasn't *entirely* frivolous. "Where did you learn about Edward Jenner?"

"I do know how to read—and not only ladies' fashion magazines." She spoke archly, but with a nervous edge. James guessed why when she glanced toward the instruments again.

"You don't need to be vaccinated," he assured her, "not if you've been variolated."

She instantly relaxed.

He grinned and went on, "Smallpox variolation grants life-long immunity. You're lucky you lived through it, though." The technique usually caused only a mild case of smallpox, but about two patients in a hundred developed a severe case and died. That was much better odds than the thirty percent risk of death from naturally-caught smallpox, but the newer vaccination method was safer. Jenner had discovered that giving people cowpox would keep them from getting smallpox, too.

"Were you variolated as a child?" Juliana asked.

"No, but I was vaccinated while in the army. My commanding officer didn't want his men dying of smallpox." He set the basket on the table. "So, what was it you were wanting to speak of?"

"Try a Shrewsbury cake." She waited while he chose one and took a bite. "I was wondering what you thought of Lady Amanda."

He hadn't thought of Lady Amanda even once since Saturday's ball. "She's lovely," he said tactfully.

Juliana beamed. "I'm so glad you think so."

He didn't like where this was leading. "The cake is delicious," he said, polishing it off.

"Have another." She reached into the basket and put one into his hand. "Do you expect you might wish to marry Lady Amanda?"

He promptly had a violent coughing fit.

She waited patiently while he recovered, her expression a mixture of amusement and concern. "Do you feel quite all right, Lord Stafford?"

"James," he choked out between deep breaths. "And yes, I do, thank you."

"You *do* wish to marry Lady Amanda, you mean?"

She was absolutely incorrigible. He took several more breaths before pointing out, "I've only danced with her once."

"Very true. I expect you'll want to court her for a while before making such a decision."

He didn't want to court Lady Amanda in the slightest. But it would be rude to say so out loud, so instead he said, "Yes, one doesn't come to such a decision lightly."

The *yes* was a mistake. Juliana's lips curved in a delighted smile. "I'm so happy to hear that! I hope you'll accept my offer of assistance."

"Assistance with what?"

"Wooing Lady Amanda, of course."

James couldn't have heard correctly. "Wooing, did you say?"

"Precisely. She's a very particular girl, besides which, I gather you've been too busy to court many ladies"—James opened his mouth to protest, though it was no less than the truth, but she headed him off —"not that there's anything wrong with that! I think it quite adorable, in fact."

Adorable? Didn't girls realize that the worst thing they could possibly call a fellow was *adorable?* A flush seemed to be rising in his cheeks, which only doubled his mortification.

"Have another Shrewsbury cake, will you?" She pushed the basket toward him and kept talking. "I'm thinking you could simply accompany me on a few occasions, such as to the theater. I could show you the proper seats to purchase and what sort of refreshments to fetch Lady Amanda during the intermission. And if we went riding in Hyde Park, I could point out the popular places and you could practice being gallant. And perhaps I could make a few suggestions regarding your hair—"

What was wrong with his *hair?*

Seeing his thunderous expression, she quickly backtracked. "Or rather, just one suggestion: don't change a thing. It's perfect as it is!" Since he hadn't taken a third cake, she selected one and shoved it into his hand.

He stared at her, holding the cake, utterly torn between insult and amusement. What on earth was this girl on about? Gallantry practice? Lessons in wooing? Without question, it was the most absurd—and rudest—offer he'd ever heard. But her heart seemed in the right place, so he'd refuse her gently.

"While I appreciate the offer, my schedule—"

"I won't take up much of your time, I assure you," she said earnestly. "After all, if our outings fill *my* schedule, I won't be available for the duke to pay court to me."

The duke. By whom she meant the prig, Castleton, didn't she? James felt a resurgence of irritation.

He bit into the cake and chewed slowly. Juliana was clearly a lunatic, but she was also kind—she'd come all the way across town just to try and do him a favor—and she didn't deserve to spend the rest of her life in an unhappy marriage. If agreeing to a few harmless outings might save her from Castleton, how could James refuse? What kind of a man would let her throw her life away instead of trying to help?

He did like helping people. It was very gallant.

His mind made up, he swallowed the cake. "Very well," he said. "Shall we start tomorrow?"

EIGHTEEN

BEFORE THE duke left on Monday afternoon, he'd asked if he might pay Juliana another call on Tuesday. Two calls in two days! Since she already had plans at one o'clock —helping James pick out some suitable gifts for Amanda—she'd suggested the duke call at noon.

Which is how it happened that, on Tuesday, as the duke was leaving and James was arriving, they crossed paths.

"Castleton," James said with a curt nod.

"Stafford," the duke returned. And with a stiff little bow, he left.

As the butler closed the door behind him, Juliana turned to James. "Do you not like the duke?"

He shrugged. "I don't know him very well. But he seems a bit stuffy."

She was about to disagree when Aunt Frances came down the stairs, her footfalls so light she seemed almost to be skipping. A piece of paper fluttered in one of her hands. "Juliana! You'll never *believe* what arrived in the morning mail!"

"What is it, Aunty?"

"Another love letter from my secret admirer! Only"—as she

reached the foyer, she paused for dramatic effect—"his name is no longer a secret."

"Who is he?" Juliana crossed her fingers behind her back. "Is he anyone I know?"

"Oh, yes," Aunt Frances said. "It's Lord—"

She cut off, finally noticing James.

Who looked more than a little intrigued.

Two rosy spots appearing on her cheeks, her aunt clutched the letter to her bosom. "Good afternoon, Lord Stafford."

"Good afternoon, Lady Frances."

Juliana reached out to squeeze her hand. "Who's your admirer, Aunty? Lord Stafford will keep your secret."

James nodded. "My lips are sealed."

Though Aunt Frances hesitated a moment more, it was obvious she was dying to tell. She leaned closer to Juliana. "It's Lord Malmsey," she whispered, her face lit up with excitement. She looked ten years younger.

"Aunt Frances, how wonderful!"

"Isn't it, though?" Clearly Frances didn't mind Lord Malmsey's age or appearance. In fact, by her reaction, one would think she'd been pining after the man all her life. "I'm so glad you made plans to visit the shops this afternoon. I must order a few new dresses, and at least one must be ready by Saturday. Lord Malmsey indicated in his letter that he will be attending Lady Partridge's ball."

James cleared his throat.

"Yes?" Juliana asked.

"I thought we were going to just quickly choose a gift?"

"Several gifts," she corrected.

"Several?"

"You'll want an assortment so that you can give one to Lady Amanda every few days over the next two weeks."

"What happens after two weeks?" He didn't look happy.

Juliana hated seeing anyone unhappy. "We'll cross that bridge when we come to it, all right?"

When Juliana had suggested he court Amanda for a while before proposing, she'd been entirely sincere—it was just that, in this *particular* case, by 'a while' she'd meant two weeks. Which might not seem like much time, but it was all the time they had, and a lot could happen in a fortnight! James would see. Once he fell in love with Amanda, he'd want to secure her hand right away. And until then, Juliana saw no reason to cause the fellow undue stress by telling him about the time constraint.

Or the part where he'd have to publicly compromise his future bride. He might have difficulty swallowing that requirement.

But the power of true love would conquer all, in the end. She was sure of it.

Juliana flashed him her most ingratiating smile. "It shouldn't take long for Aunt Frances to order a few dresses as well. You won't mind, will you? She'll be coming along in any case, to chaperone." Though this outing with James wasn't romantic in any sense, it wouldn't do for the two of them to gad about town together unescorted.

Before James could answer, a knock came at the door. The butler opened it. On the other side stood young Emily with a footman in Neville livery. And Herman, of course.

Emily twirled her pink parasol. "Is it time to leave, Lady Juliana?"

James took a step back. "Don't tell me *she's* coming, too."

"I'm giving her lessons as well," Juliana explained. "In being more ladylike. An outing like this can be very instructional."

His jaw looked rigid. "Surely she won't be taking that snake."

Emily stopped twirling. "If Herman doesn't go, I don't go."

"That's fine by me," James said.

He seemed more unhappy than ever. Concerned, Juliana laid a hand on his arm and lowered her voice. "James, do you not like children?"

When he glanced down at her hand, she gasped and

snatched it away, surprised at herself. Though she wore gloves, and his arm was sleeved, it wasn't proper to be touching him.

But the look on his face was troubling. Amanda definitely wanted children—children *not* fathered by a by-blow, to be precise—and surely her partner should want them, too.

"Of course I like children," James said. "I vaccinate children every day at the Institute."

"Of course," she echoed, relieved. She should have realized that. "Amanda is good with children," she told him, remembering how well Amanda had handled Emily that day she'd bled.

Motioning for him to follow, she stepped farther away from the little girl.

"I know you're worried that some patrons of the shops might be upset by Emily's snake," she said quietly. "But that's the whole idea, don't you see? She needs to learn that it's not lady-like to carry a snake, and the only way to teach her is by demonstration. Once she's convinced that Herman's presence causes trouble, she'll realize she should leave him at home."

"I see," he said tightly.

They headed outside to where James's carriage was waiting. It was splendid—all polished rosewood and rich green velvet—and the pair of matched bays drawing it were gorgeous animals.

Juliana meant to sit beside Aunt Frances, but somehow she ended up beside James instead. Aunt Frances sat opposite James, with Emily next to her. When he squished himself into the corner, as far away from Juliana as possible, she supposed that was to make sure he wouldn't touch her inadvertently.

But then somehow he kept touching her anyway.

During the drive to Pall Mall, he touched her three times on the arm, in the bare area between where her short puffed sleeve ended and her short white glove began. The touches were all accidental and innocent, of course, but the little jolt she felt every time was...well, not bothersome exactly, but distracting. Or invigorating in an odd sort of way.

She simply wasn't used to being touched by young men. Mourning had kept her and her sisters hidden away so long, Juliana was probably the oldest unkissed girl in all of England.

Well, except for Amanda. And maybe Aunt Frances.

In any case, the sensation was new and intriguing, most especially because it was James doing the touching. If she found it this exciting to be touched by *James*, how must it feel with someone she actually cared for? Why, being touched by the duke must be twice as thrilling! Ten times, even! He was, after all, her ideal match.

But despite two social calls in two days, the duke hadn't touched her since they'd danced at the ball. Which didn't count, because he hadn't touched her bare skin. He hadn't even kissed her gloved hand. He respected her too much to do any such thing. He was as proper and reserved as Amanda.

But he definitely wasn't stuffy.

Aunt Frances was so anxious to order her dresses, Juliana decided they should do that first. Mrs. Huntley sighed when she saw Emily and her snake again, but after all, Juliana and Amanda had ordered a *lot* of dresses, and no shopkeeper would turn away that sort of business. So she pressed her thin lips together and pulled out her measuring tape.

"Sit over there, Emily," Juliana instructed, waving her toward where two chairs sat against a wall. "And James, you sit beside her. When you visit the shops with a lady, you must wait patiently until she's finished."

"I'll wait outside," he said.

"You shouldn't do that if you wish to please Lady Amanda. A man should appear interested in a lady's purchases."

"I'll keep that in mind," he said, heading toward the door.

"It's raining out there," she reminded him.

"I won't melt."

True to his word, James didn't melt. It took so long to order Aunt Frances's dresses that it had stopped raining by the time the ladies joined him outside. And he certainly didn't look melted—in fact, he looked frozen solid.

"Where to now?" he asked grimly.

"I believe you should send Lady Amanda some flowers." Juliana indicated a florist's shop across the street, and they all started toward it.

"Send red roses," Emily suggested beside him. "My mother loved red roses."

"Red roses it is, then." He crossed to Juliana's other side and took her left arm. When she glanced up at him, startled, he said, "A gentleman should escort a lady across the street."

"Excellent," she said, pleased with his progress. "That's very gallant. But I don't think red roses would be appropriate. They symbolize love, and it's a little too soon for that. You wouldn't want to appear too forward. Pink or yellow would be perfect."

James's arm felt solid beneath hers, and she was aware of their contact all the way into the shop. When they entered, a woman shrieked and ran past them out the door. Three other patrons left directly, muttering to one another.

The florist was a tall, thin man with a long, narrow nose and eyes that glared at Emily. "Take that snake outside, miss."

Emily stroked Herman. "Snakes don't eat flowers, Mr. Flower-Man. Only frogs and mice."

Aunt Frances took Emily outside, and James ordered an arrangement of two dozen pink roses. Quickly.

Back outdoors, the people walking along Pall Mall were giving Emily and Herman a wide berth, and there was a lot of "Well!" and "I never!" to be heard.

"She should have left that snake at home," James said.

"She will next time, I'm sure." Juliana offered him her left arm again, thinking some more practice in escorting ladies might be appropriate.

"Where are we going now?" Emily asked beside him.

He crossed to Juliana's other side and took her right arm instead.

Juliana suspected he was impatient. "Harding, Howell and Company," she decided. Down the street just a bit, Harding, Howell & Company was a big department store that took up all the floors of an old mansion that used to be called Schomberg House. Perhaps James would be happier if they could find the rest of Amanda's presents all in one place. "You don't enjoy shops very much, do you?" she asked as they began walking.

He shrugged. "I'm a man."

She'd noticed. She'd walked arm in arm with other ladies before, but this felt entirely different. It wasn't like the jolts she'd experienced when he'd touched her arm in the carriage, but more of a tingly awareness all over her body. It rather stole one's breath. Amanda was going to love it.

Aunt Frances and Emily walked in front of them, the two of them getting farther and farther ahead. People were crossing the street to avoid them. "We should catch up," Juliana said.

James didn't change his pace. "I believe a gentleman should walk leisurely with a lady, to accommodate her shorter stride."

"That's considerate," she allowed. "You really are quite an apt pupil, James."

He tipped his hat to her.

"I'm famished," Emily announced the moment they stepped through Harding, Howell & Company's grand mahogany double doors. "May we visit Mr. Cosway's Breakfast Room?"

"It's not breakfast time," James said. "In fact, it's past luncheon."

Juliana laughed. "Mr. Cosway's Breakfast Room serves refreshments all day long." Located on the floor above, the restaurant offered wines, teas, coffee, and sweetmeats. "Have you never been here before, James?"

"I'm a man," he said.

The department store *was* patronized mostly by women. Juliana hadn't ever noticed that before, but she did now. Especially because a good number of the women were emitting little squeals and hiding behind the delicate pieces of furniture that were on display.

Emily started up the wide staircase with Herman and Aunt Frances. When Juliana went to follow them, James held her back. "She really should leave that snake at home," he said once Emily was out of earshot.

Juliana was getting a bit tired of hearing that. "Are you hungry?" she asked.

"I'm a man," he said again, and she laughed.

Upstairs, Mr. Cosway's Breakfast Room had a glorious view over St. James's Park to Westminster and the Surrey hills beyond. Aunt Frances and Emily were already seated across from each other at a table for four. Juliana slid into the chair beside Aunt Frances, but James just stood there, more frozen than the ice cream in the restaurant's glass display case.

And that's when Juliana realized the truth: he didn't want to sit beside Emily. Or walk beside Emily. Or have anything to do with Emily—at least not while she was holding a snake.

Though it wasn't very kind or ladylike, Juliana couldn't help herself. A little smile quirked her lips. A snigger escaped. And finally—inevitably—she burst into laughter.

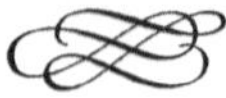

NINETEEN

"**Y**OU-YOU-YOU'RE afraid of Herman!" Juliana hiccuped from laughing so hard. "Don't tell me you're not."

James felt heat creep up his neck and into his face. He'd never seen a lady *quite* so consumed by hilarity. Especially at his expense.

Every diner in Mr. Cosway's Breakfast Room was staring at them, and he wasn't sure whether that was because of Emily's snake or Juliana's hiccups. Either way, it was embarrassing, possibly the most embarrassing moment of his life.

Juliana thought him laughable.

But he couldn't deny her accusation. "Deathly afraid," he confirmed with as much dignity as he could muster. "I was bitten by an adder at the age of seven."

"Oh, my," Juliana said, covering her mouth. "That must have been dreadful."

"Very. It was quite painful, and my ankle swelled up horribly, and I was consumed by fever." He had also cast up his accounts several times, but he wouldn't say so in the presence of ladies. "I should never want to encounter such a thing again," he added, scowling at the *thing* around Emily's shoulders.

"But Herman isn't an adder," Emily said, lifting the loathsome, scaly body over her head and holding it up, evidently to give James a better look. "He's a grass snake. He doesn't have any poison, and he doesn't bite."

James was well aware of that—'know thy enemy,' after all. He knew that adders were the only venomous snakes found in England, and that this specimen was quite obviously not an adder. It was too long and slender and had different markings. James's fear of it was completely irrational, and he'd be the first to acknowledge that fact.

But that didn't mean he was going anywhere near the blasted thing.

Even now, though he stood a good six feet away, the sight of it made his pulse feel thready and his insides clench. If Emily came any closer, he feared he might cast up his accounts right here in Harding, Howell & Company's froufrou little restaurant.

He glanced over to see that Juliana was no longer laughing, but instead was watching him closely. So closely he had a funny feeling she was peering right through his skin to glimpse his churning stomach and his pounding heart. To glimpse just how pathetic he was. Too weak to conquer his ridiculous fear of a child's harmless pet.

"He's very nice," the child was saying. She made to rise from her chair. "You can pet him…"

James meant to move away, but his stomach began to rebel—

Suddenly Juliana pushed back from the table, making a loud *screech*. "I've just realized I'm not hungry," she announced.

"But I am!" Emily plopped back onto her chair.

Juliana turned to her with a bright smile. "You can stay here with Aunt Frances while Lord Stafford and I finish our shopping."

Lady Frances frowned. "Shouldn't I accompany the two of you?"

"No, Aunty, you can stay with Emily. We're in a public place, surrounded by dozens of people, and we shan't be gone long."

With that, Juliana placed her arm in James's and marched him away. He looked back to see Lady Frances humming to herself while one of her charges left alone with an unmarried man and the other cradled a reptilian menace.

As he walked, James was taking deep, slow breaths to calm his stomach. He wasn't certain, but he thought Juliana might have just saved him from utter humiliation and infamy.

"Thank you," he said quietly as they headed down the staircase. "You must think me a coward."

"Don't be silly. We all have our fears."

He doubted that. "What's yours, then?"

"Blood," she said without hesitation. "I would make a terrible doctor. And unlike you, I don't have a legitimate reason for my fear. No traumatizing bloody events in my childhood."

She laughed, but this time it was at herself, not him. Which made all the difference.

Which made him like her even more.

"Lady Amanda isn't afraid of blood," she informed him. "I should think you'd be pleased to know that, since I expect it's an important attribute for a physician's wife."

"I don't think that really matters," he told her. It certainly wasn't on his list of wifely requirements. Not that he was looking for a wife, anyway. He tightened his grip on Juliana's arm, and she leaned closer to him. Even though it was cold and rainy outside, she seemed to smell of sunshine and flowers.

"I think Lady Amanda would like a fan," she said, guiding him past the glazed mahogany partition that separated the fur and fan departments.

He didn't want to buy Lady Amanda a fan, but he didn't want to disappoint Juliana, either. And he especially didn't want her to give up on their "lessons," because she really *was* too good for stuffy Castleton. After the way she'd just come to James's rescue, he felt even more strongly that he must spend as much time with her as possible—to keep her away from the duke, of course.

So he bought a fan.

"I think Lady Amanda would like gloves," she said next. And although he didn't want to buy gloves for Lady Amanda—although he didn't want to buy *anything* for Lady Amanda—he dutifully paid for the lace pair she picked out.

She thought Lady Amanda would like perfume, so they stopped by the perfumery department. She thought Lady Amanda would like candy, so they visited the confectioners. Soon he was burdened with bags and boxes.

He'd always hated shopping, and he'd been extremely displeased when she'd chosen the shops for their first outing. But—besides the unfortunate snake incident—this day wasn't turning out as badly as he'd anticipated. He rather enjoyed being gallant and saving Juliana from stuffy Castleton.

Seeing that prig at her house earlier had made him grit his teeth.

They were buying some fancy writing paper when Lady Frances and Emily sought them out. "Lady Juliana," Emily said, "you are taking *forever*."

Looking startled, Juliana turned from the stationery counter. And the next thing she did was immediately move to put herself between Emily and James. He could have kissed her for that.

Not that he'd actually kiss her, of course—that would be highly improper.

But he wanted to.

He did?

He did. What did *that* mean?

Perhaps it was just that he'd been without female companionship a long while. After all, he only wanted to *kiss* Juliana. It wasn't as if he wanted to marry her. Even if he couldn't remember wanting to kiss anyone since...well...

Anyhow, it was a perfectly natural urge. It didn't have to mean anything.

"Goodness, Emily," Juliana was saying, "you're right. We *have* taken forever. In fact, we've taken so long that Lord Stafford is going to be late for Parliament. We'll have to take a hackney coach home so he can go there straightaway."

James might have been a coward, but he wasn't a fool. He knew she'd said that to save him from riding with the *thing* in his carriage.

He could have kissed her for that, too.

TWENTY

ALMOND MACAROONS

Beat Whites of Eggs with salt until stiff, then add Almonds ground fine, Sugar and a bit of ground Rice. Put in little mounds and make flat on Paper, then add an Almond in each middle before baking in your oven.

When I wish to see my husband amorous, I feed him these macaroons. They've never failed me yet.

—Katherine, Countess of Greystone, 1763

*J*ULIANA PLACED little mounds of dough on a paper-lined baking tin, spacing them carefully while she hid a yawn. She'd been up since dawn. After spending the morning with Emily—who *still* refused to relinquish Herman—now she was making almond macaroons with Amanda.

According to Chase family legend, the macaroons were supposed to make one—Juliana blushed to even think the word —*amorous*. Juliana planned to give some to James and tell him to eat them tomorrow, hoping they would make him act warmly toward Amanda at Lady Partridge's ball later that evening. Since she wasn't certain whether the macaroons needed to be made by the woman seeking attention—her grandmother, who'd penned the recipe, hadn't been clear—she'd decided to ask for Amanda's help just in case.

"Put an almond in the center of each macaroon," she said through another yawn.

"That's the third time you've yawned," Amanda observed, plopping the nuts on top rather haphazardly. "Are you sleepy?"

Juliana's fourth yawn seemed to echo off the basement kitchen's walls. "This week has been exhausting."

She'd been very busy since Monday's visit to the Institute and Tuesday's jaunt to the shops. Not only had she hosted another sewing party and spent all her free time stitching, but the duke had called on her every single day—though their visits were always brief, as she was forever running off to outings with James. The duke had danced with her twice at Almack's on Wednesday night, and he said the nicest things to her. His attentiveness was encouraging, and she was certain it was only a matter of time before he asked for her hand. A perfect gentleman, he remained careful not to touch her, demonstrating the respect due a lady.

James, on the other hand, seemed to touch her so often she was beginning to think the accidents might not all be accidental.

On Wednesday afternoon, when she and James had taken advantage of a few glorious dry hours to go riding in Hyde Park, he'd helped her on and off her horse on six different occasions— to buy refreshments from a stand, to look at some flowers, to take a stroll by the Serpentine—and she didn't think she'd imagined the way his hands rested on her waist longer and longer each time.

James had skipped Almack's again Wednesday night—more trouble at the Institute, apparently—but Thursday evening, when they'd attended the theater, he'd set his chair so close to hers in the box that his leg was against her skirts during much of the performance. In the intermission, he'd brought her a syllabub and then claimed twice that she had cream on her lip and wiped it away with his handkerchief.

"Did I tell you I received another gift from Lord Stafford?" Amanda flattened a macaroon and stuck a piece of almond in it. "Three gifts in one week!"

"Use the whole almonds, Amanda. You want the macaroons to look pretty, don't you?" Juliana picked out the broken nut and replaced it with a perfect one, thinking Amanda was almost as hopeless at cooking as Corinna. It was a good thing that earl's wives weren't expected to set foot in the kitchen. "What did he send you this time?" she asked.

"The most elegant lace gloves. I'm not sure Aunt Mabel would approve of something so personal. Fortunately she was having a lie-down when the package arrived. I suggested maybe she should return to the countryside, since Lady Frances is doing such a fine job as chaperone."

Juliana choked back an unladylike snort. A fine chaperone, indeed—for *her* purposes, anyway. "I'm glad Lady Mabel doesn't mind Aunt Frances filling in for her." Mostly because it would be difficult to carry out their plan if Amanda were under anything like competent supervision. "Still, I hope she isn't feeling poorly enough to leave London. I enjoyed her company at Wednesday's sewing party."

"She surely enjoyed attending, too. It was much less strenuous than going on outings. Why, she hardly even wheezed."

And she'd proved a much better seamstress than her niece, completing four blankets in two hours. Unfortunately, even with Lady Mabel's help, Juliana had so far collected only thirty-three of the two hundred forty items she needed. And she had just three weeks left—the same three weeks Amanda had to find a new fiancé before she was forced to marry Lord Malmsey. "You're planning to keep the gloves, then?"

"I wouldn't dream of returning them. They're stunning. The pink roses he sent were beautiful, too. And I adore the painted fan." Amanda placed another almond off-center. "Lord Stafford has exquisite taste, don't you think? Especially for a young man."

Juliana was glad she'd taken it upon herself to have each of James's gifts delivered rather than trusting him to remember. Tomorrow evening, she would make sure Amanda wore the gloves and carried the fan, which should please him. She could scarcely wait until the ball, when he'd dance again with Amanda and ask for permission to court her. She was certain Amanda would agree.

Everything was going perfectly.

Hearing the tall-case clock chime upstairs, she hurried to place the last almonds. She had only half an hour to ready herself before James arrived for today's excursion to the Egyptian Hall. "Thank you for your help," she told Amanda as she shoved the pans into the oven. "I'll have a footman deliver half the macaroons to your house as soon as they're finished."

Not usually one to show affection, Amanda wrapped Juliana in a timid, awkward embrace. "Thank *you*," she said. "I had no idea that macaroons make one's eyes sparkle, but I appreciate your telling me and letting me help bake them."

"You're very welcome," Juliana murmured, feeling a bit guilty about misleading her. But only a bit. Honestly, she'd had no choice. Amanda would be scandalized if she knew they were baking *amorous* macaroons for her suitor—and herself, of course, as Juliana saw no harm in warming up Amanda's demeanor as well.

After her friend took her leave, Juliana went upstairs to change her dress and put on a little rouge and lip salve. She was on her way back down when she heard the knocker bang. As she arrived in the foyer, expecting to see James, Adamson opened the door to reveal a deliveryman holding an enormous arrangement of red roses.

"Holy Hannah!" Paintbrush in hand, Corinna came in from the drawing room. "There must be five dozen!"

Aunt Frances came in from the library. "Goodness gracious, I can smell them from here. And just look at that gorgeous silver vase!"

"Do you expect they're from the duke?" Corinna asked.

"They must be," Juliana breathed, setting the gloves she was carrying on the marble-topped hall table. *Red* roses. The duke must be in love with her already!

Fragrance filled the foyer. After tipping the deliveryman, the butler put the arrangement on the table. She plucked the card from it with shaking hands.

"A small token in comparison to the great love I hold in my heart," she read aloud, her pulse pounding harder with each precious word. "And it's signed—"

Her mouth gaped open.

"Who signed it?" Corinna demanded. "Are the flowers not from the duke?"

Juliana closed her mouth and held the card out to Aunt Frances. "They're from Lord Malmsey. They're for you."

Aunt Frances's hand flew to her heart. She looked as if she might swoon for a moment, but in the end she just said, "For me?" in a squeaky little voice.

"For you," Juliana repeated, beaming with pride—her project was working! And she was thrilled for Aunt Frances, too, of course. She eased the swaying woman onto a striped satin chair by the table. "Are you all right, Aunty?"

Still clutching her chest, Frances blew out a breath. "Heavens, child, I've never been better." Her eyes looked misty behind their lenses. "But I do feel just a bit faint."

A kitchen maid came up from the basement and handed Juliana a small basket covered with a lace doily. "Your macaroons, my lady. A dozen, as you requested."

"Thank you," Juliana said and set the basket beside the flowers.

"May I speak with you a moment?" Corinna took her by the arm. "In the drawing room."

They left Frances gazing at her roses.

"Do you not think," Corinna said once they were behind closed doors, "that this is going a little too far?"

"What?" Juliana asked, feeling bewildered.

"Sending Aunt Frances flowers and claiming they're from Lord Malmsey. Really, Juliana, what do you think is going to happen tomorrow at the ball when she thanks him for flowers he didn't send?"

"He *did* send them to her," Juliana said.

"He didn't."

"Well, who did, then? Because it wasn't me. I had nothing to do with those flowers."

Corinna eyed her skeptically. "He's engaged to marry Amanda. Why would he send flowers to Aunt Frances? What would make him think she'd want to receive flowers from him?"

"The love letters he received from her."

"*What* love letters?"

"The ones I sent, of course." Honestly, had Corinna stayed up all night again? She seemed a bit on the slow side today. "It wouldn't do to have Aunt Frances be the only one getting letters. A true love must be two-sided."

Juliana had never written so many sappy letters in her life. In a week of incessant activity, Aunt Frances's romance had proved to be her most exhausting project.

Besides writing all the letters, she'd had to take Frances shopping for shoes, bonnets, and accessories to match all of her new dresses; buy cosmetics and practice applying them; and hire a dancing master to teach Frances all the new steps. And Frances's hair—oh, her hair! Madame Bellefleur had had to visit not once, but twice—the first time to dye Frances's hair with henna and walnuts, and the second to trim it and tinker with various styles.

But it was all worth it. Aunt Frances was going to look beautiful tomorrow night. And Lord Malmsey was already in love with her.

He'd sent *red* roses.

"You sent fake letters to both of them?" Corinna pointed the paintbrush she was still holding at her. "What if they compare notes?"

"They won't," Juliana said confidently. "They're both far too shy, and too grateful to question their good fortune." The knocker sounded again. "Excuse me. That will be Lord Stafford."

She returned to the foyer, but it wasn't James at the door. It was another deliveryman with flowers. White roses, and there were only a dozen, but they were in a beautiful crystal vase.

"What does the card say?" Corinna asked behind her.

Not assuming anything this time, Juliana pulled it from the arrangement. "The Duke of Castleton," she read with some relief.

And happiness, of course.

"That's it? No message?"

"The flowers say it all, do they not?" She gestured grandly toward the arrangement, which, in truth, looked rather paltry next to the extravagant one Lord Malmsey had sent. But the duke wasn't an extravagant man. He was restrained and refined and everything that was tasteful and proper. "I don't *need* a written message," she said. "I know perfectly well how he feels."

"How who feels?" James asked, entering through the still-open door.

"The Duke of Castleton," Corinna informed him. "He sent flowers to Juliana."

"Did he?" James scanned the foyer, blinking as his gaze landed on the hall table. "That's a *lot* of roses. *Red* roses."

His tone implied he found something objectionable about the roses, although Juliana wasn't sure whether it was the amount of them or their color. Or both. And why would he care, anyway?

Aunt Frances's hand was still over her heart. "They're mine," she said, sounding awed.

Corinna nodded. "The *other* arrangement is from the duke."

"White," James said with a raised brow. He turned to Juliana. "He must think you're very virtuous."

What on earth did he mean by that? She *was* virtuous. She'd never even been kissed!

Though not entirely by her own choice.

She swept the little basket off the table and thrust it at him. "Here," she said rather ungraciously. "I baked macaroons for you."

"Why?" he asked, looking nonplussed.

She hadn't anticipated that question. She didn't want him to think she'd made them as a gift, because he might take that the wrong way. But she couldn't very well tell him she hoped they'd make him amorous.

Or that they'd make his eyes sparkle.

"I thought you'd want to eat them tomorrow. They're supposed to provide extra energy."

That brow went up again. "Energy of what sort?"

How many sorts were there? "The *extra* sort," she said firmly.

"I see." The corner of his mouth twitched, as though he were trying not to laugh. "But pray tell, why should I need extra energy tomorrow?"

"For the dancing," she said. "At the ball. You're not accustomed to hours on your feet."

"Ah," he said. Just *ah*. But something about the way he said it told her he was well aware she was making all of this up as she went along. "In all the time I've studied medicine," he drawled, "I've never heard macaroons prescribed to increase energy. I shall have to pass this wisdom along to my colleagues."

"You do that," she said, snatching up her parasol and turning to Aunt Frances. "Are you ready to leave, Aunty?"

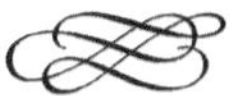

TWENTY-ONE

*A*S JAMES'S carriage crawled toward the Egyptian Hall through the miserable London traffic, he smiled to himself. Juliana might claim their outings were for his benefit, but she wasn't fooling him. She liked him, whether she was willing to say so out loud or not.

The proof? She'd baked him macaroons.

He lifted the froufrou doily atop the basket and pulled one out.

"No!" Juliana cried. "You're supposed to save them for tomorrow."

"There are plenty of them," he said, depositing the macaroon into his mouth. It all but melted on his tongue. He'd never heard of a girl of the *ton* making sweets—or setting foot in a kitchen, for that matter—but given Juliana's talents, he heartily approved. "These are delicious," he told her and chose another.

"Please don't eat them today!" She looked concerned…quite concerned. Certainly much more concerned than was warranted. They were just macaroons, after all, and he knew she'd invented that ludicrous 'extra energy' story—probably to conceal the obvious truth that she'd baked for him because she liked him. So why should it matter whether he ate them today or tomorrow?

He reached for a third.

"I'd prefer you save them," she said firmly, taking the basket right out of his hands. She set it on the seat beside her, scooting closer to him in order to do so.

Which he didn't mind in the least, though it was highly improper. She was all but sitting in his lap. As he finished the third macaroon, he eyed Lady Frances, thinking she'd have to object. But instead she just gazed out the window, her eyes glassy behind her spectacles.

Really, if he didn't know any better, he might have thought she had a touch of dementia.

Once again, although it was a rainy, gray day, Juliana smelled like sunshine. And flowers. It made him want to slip his arm around her shoulders and pull her even closer. But he wouldn't. At least not with Juliana's chaperone watching, even if her aunt was by far the most oblivious chaperone he'd ever encountered.

Maybe Lady Frances would conveniently fall asleep.

Since that day in Harding, Howell & Company, he'd been thinking quite a bit about Juliana. Or more specifically, about kissing Juliana. Though the idea had seemed appalling at first, it didn't any longer, because in the interim—during the hours he'd spent riding with her and accompanying her to the theater— he'd come to realize something else: He was no longer going on these outings to prevent her from wasting her time with Castleton.

Not that he *wanted* her to spend time with Castleton. Seeing her with that vase of white roses had made him want to scream. Perhaps even scream something like, "The prig is only courting you for a horse!" He wished he'd told her as much in the beginning, but he hadn't wanted to hurt her feelings. And he was even more reluctant to hurt her now. She was clever; she'd realize Castleton was wrong for her before it was too late. Or the duke himself might come to his senses and end the charade.

But even if Castleton did the right thing in the end, it

wouldn't improve James's opinion of him. He was worse than a prig. He was…

What was worse than a prig?

He was a *turd.*

Anyhow, James was no longer going on these outings to save her from the turd—or at least not *only* to save her from the turd. He liked her company. She was bright and charming, and she cared about people. She'd cared about *him* when he'd feared a stupid snake. And, all right, she was very pretty. But he couldn't help noticing *that*—it was simply an objective fact.

All of which pointed to another fact: He fancied Juliana Chase.

He didn't love her, of course—he wouldn't, couldn't love her or anyone else. But fancying a girl was very different from loving her. And it wasn't a betrayal of Anne, because it wasn't long-lasting or meaningful. James had fancied other girls before he met Anne, and it had always taken the same course: They danced. They flirted. They went on outings. They stole a kiss or two. Then their interest waned and they went their separate ways.

It would be the same with Juliana, he thought with a contented yawn. And today she had baked him macaroons, which meant he was one step closer to kissing her.

He was very much looking forward to that part of the course.

She followed his yawn with one of her own and tried to cover it with a hand.

"I saw that," he said.

"I'm not bored, I promise."

"I didn't think so," he assured her. "It's a medical fact that yawns are contagious."

She smiled, making him smile, too. He appreciated a girl who appreciated his attempts at humor.

"Are you as short on sleep as I?" she asked.

"I'm afraid I am. I was up half the night finishing the speech I'm delivering this evening in the House of Lords."

"A speech?" She looked dubious.

"Your confidence in me is an inspiration," he said dryly.

"It's not that!" she said, chastened. "I was just…surprised. I've always pictured parliamentary speeches being given by aging lords in grey wigs. Not someone like you."

"Someone with hair?"

She swatted his arm. "Someone *young*."

He nodded his understanding. As one of the youngest members of the House, he *was* being rather bold. He shouldn't have brought up the speech—now his nerves had returned.

"What is your speech about?"

"A bill I've put forth to publicly fund smallpox vaccinations and make them compulsory for infants."

"Compulsory?" Her blue-green-hazel eyes widened. "I've never heard of such an idea."

"I'm not surprised. England is quite behind the times on this matter. Vaccinations were made compulsory in Bavaria in 1807, Denmark in 1810, Norway in 1811, Bohemia and Russia in 1812, and now this year in Sweden." He hoped he had all those dates right; he'd had to memorize them for the speech. "If we're to defeat this scourge, everyone must cooperate."

She seemed to mull that over for a minute. "This is very important to you, isn't it?"

"Yes, it's very important."

"Why is that?"

"Must there be a reason? Can't it just be for the good of humanity?"

"I think not," she said. "Not when you're so passionate about the subject."

He mentally added *perceptive* to the list of her assets. "My brother died of smallpox."

"Oh," she said quietly. "I'm sorry."

"There was nothing I could do to help him. Nothing I could do but watch him die. Have you ever seen someone suffering with it?"

She shook her head. "No, I don't think so. At least not in the final stages."

"I hope you never will. The pain is excruciating, and the pocks—well, never mind." He wouldn't sicken her by describing the way they'd spread until Philip had seemed to be little more than one huge, oozing pustule. "Suffice it to say I'm hoping someday no one will ever suffer with it again. And I plan to do my part to make that happen."

Her gaze was full of admiration. "You're a good person, James."

Her praise made his spirits soar, but she didn't need to know that. So he shrugged. "We cannot afford to ignore this chance. Vaccination has given mankind an opportunity we've never had before—to wipe a horrific disease off the face of the earth. Forever."

"I hope you can convince Parliament, then," she said and reached to take his hand.

She was holding his hand. He was afraid to react, for fear she might notice and snatch hers away. Keeping himself still, he glanced toward her chaperone, but Lady Frances was still gazing out the window, humming softly to herself.

He looked down at their joined hands. Juliana wasn't wearing gloves. Prior to flouncing out to the carriage, she'd grabbed her umbrella but left a pair of white gloves sitting on the marble-topped table. Lady Frances hadn't noticed—shocking!—and James hadn't thought to remind Juliana to take them.

Or maybe he hadn't wanted her to.

Her hand felt small in his, her palm smooth and warm. He couldn't remember ever being so aware of anyone touching him before. Well, it *had* been over a year, he supposed, since he'd held a girl's hand.

"I see now," she said. "Your brother's death is why you became a physician. I've been wondering what would compel an earl to take up doctoring," she added, squeezing his fingers with compassion.

He tried not to squeeze back, lest she realize what she was doing. "That's sound reasoning, but not the way it happened. Philip was my older brother—he was supposed to be the earl. I became a physician before his death, not after, because, as a second son, I needed a profession. I was at his bedside as his physician when he died."

"You don't blame yourself for his death, do you?" Sympathy flooded her eyes. "Just because you're a doctor—"

"Good gracious, no!" What an active imagination she had. Even in James's darkest days, he'd never tortured himself with *that*. "He had the severe form of smallpox—variola major— which defies treatment. There is nothing a physician can do but keep the patient as comfortable as possible and hope for the best."

"So doctors do nothing?"

"Oh, there are things they *try*, but they generally involve bleeding, emetics, and purgatives—methods I don't favor. I've found they weaken a patient more than they strengthen him." He shook his head. It was difficult talking about this, but it seemed important, somehow, that Juliana understand his point of view. "I don't blame myself for his death. But I *would* blame myself if I allowed smallpox to continue destroying lives without doing everything in my power to stop it."

She nodded. Her eyes looked blue now, a blue softened by kindness and concern. "I'm truly sorry you lost your brother to such a devastating disease."

"You must have lost a brother, too," he realized suddenly. "Else Griffin wouldn't be the marquess. He wasn't meant to be, was he? After Oxford, he joined the military, same as I did."

"Our brother Charles died of consumption," she said. "A few months after our mother succumbed to it first."

They called consumption a "gentle death," but James knew better. Its victims might fade away rather slowly and gracefully, but watching a loved one die was never easy. And Juliana had suffered through that twice.

"Consumption seems to descend upon certain families," he told her. "Probably because it's not easily transmitted like smallpox, but after weeks and months in the same home—"

"I thought it wasn't contagious." She looked shocked. "We all cared for my mother and brother with no concern of risking our own health. The doctors told us consumption is caused by the patient's own constitution and runs in families only because relations are so often alike."

"That may be the prevailing wisdom, but I don't believe it. And I'm not alone. More than two thousand years ago, Hippocrates himself warned doctors to be wary of contracting it from patients. And early in the last century, Benjamin Marten wrote a paper theorizing that consumption is caused by 'wonderfully minute living creatures' that can pass from one person to another, although rarely without extended periods of contact." His explanation didn't seem to be making her rest any easier, so he tried a different approach. "I don't expect you need to worry about catching it now if you haven't already. Nor should your sisters or Griffin. Whatever 'minute creatures' might have been in your home are long gone, I'm certain, and you needn't fret that you were all born with constitutions that will cause you to develop it, either."

"So Charles caught it from our mother, but none of the rest of us did." She drew and released a breath. "I've always wondered if the rest of us might succumb eventually. Is it wicked of me to be relieved?"

"It's natural to be relieved," he said. "And I could be wrong. Most physicians wouldn't agree with me."

"*I* don't think you're wrong," she said. "I think you're a man who thinks for himself, who looks for his own answers instead of blindly accepting what others claim. We need your sort of people. You're the people who discover things that make the world better for all of us."

She would never know how much her words meant to him. He faced a lot of scorn from respected doctors—some of them even his own mentors—who sneered at his adoption of new, unconventional practices like refusing to bleed patients and believing cleanliness helped prevent infection. He wasn't the only physician who embraced such ideas, but he was definitely in the minority. Sometimes the pressure made James question his own judgement. But he never quite lost his faith that they—doctors—could do better. They could do more than offer old wisdom. They could provide *cures*.

And Juliana's faith in *him* made the pressure that much more bearable.

"Thank you," he said, squeezing her hand.

A mistake. Looking startled, she pulled it away. "So." She cleared her throat. "Tomorrow evening at the ball…just how are you planning to ask Lady Amanda if you might court her?"

His jaw dropped. The sudden turnabout made him feel as if his brain had just fallen off a cliff. How did she do that? How had Juliana gone from holding his hand to assuming he was still planning to court Lady Amanda?

Well, he wasn't. He'd decided instead to court Juliana. Or rather, to complete the sequence of this odd, sort-of courtship they'd already begun.

Put simply, he'd decided to kiss her so he could get on with his life.

But he didn't quite know how to answer her question, because she hadn't asked him *if* he was planning to court Lady Amanda. She'd asked *how* he was planning to ask for permission.

When he didn't immediately respond, she added, "Perhaps I can help you devise some particularly gallant method."

"Like what? Shall I ride into the ball on a charger, dressed in armor?"

"Really, now, James, be serious."

He *was* serious. Serious about wanting to kiss Juliana.

"James?" Juliana asked. "Why are you looking at me like that?"

Lucky for him, just then the carriage rolled to a halt in front of the Egyptian Hall, saving him from another question he couldn't answer.

TWENTY-TWO

THE EXTERIOR of the museum at Number Twenty-two Piccadilly bore a vague resemblance to an Egyptian temple. A very vague resemblance. In fact, it would look rather Palladian, Juliana thought, were it not for the ankhs along the cornice and the two full-length statues that flanked a window above the entrance.

"Are those sculptures supposed to be Egyptian?" Aunt Frances asked.

"An Egyptian god and goddess." James gestured toward the figures. "That's Isis on the left, and her brother and husband, Osiris, on the right."

Juliana wondered how he'd come to know such things. "Shall we have a look inside?"

James gave the doorman three shillings for their admission, took a guidebook and handed it to Juliana, then ushered her and her aunt into the museum.

"So many people," Aunt Frances said, looking dazed as they jostled their way down a corridor.

"They've all come to see Napoleon's carriage," Juliana told her. "And Captain Cook's artifacts. And," she added, reading off the cover of the guidebook, "'the Collection of Fifteen Thousand

Natural and Foreign Curiosities, Antiques, and Productions of the Fine Arts.'"

"I'm feeling faint," Aunt Frances said.

"We don't have to look at all of them, Aunty. Listen to this." Pausing in the first of the exhibition rooms, Juliana quoted from the introduction. "'The museum's owner, William Bullock, formed his collection during seventeen years of arduous research at a cost of thirty thousand pounds.'"

"Thirty thousand pounds," James said in wonder. "Just think how many vaccinations all that money could have provided."

Or how many foundlings it could have fed, Juliana thought. But there were other good uses for money. "Widening the public's horizons is also a worthy cause. Don't you agree, Aunt Frances?" She glanced around. "Aunt Frances?"

"There she is." James pointed toward an exhibit of stuffed African animals. "On that bench, by the rail."

Juliana wove through the crowd to sit beside her, beneath the raised trunk of a massive gray elephant. "Are you unwell, Aunty?"

"I'm fine, child. I thought I'd sit here a while and rest." Aunt Frances patted her chest with a happy sigh, and Juliana knew she was thinking about Lord Malmsey and his red roses. "You young people go ahead and start looking. I'll join you in a few minutes."

"We cannot just leave you here," Juliana said.

"Of course we can," James disagreed. "You wouldn't want to risk your aunt's health by taxing her, would you?"

"She doesn't look unhealthy to me. Her cheeks are rosier than I've ever seen them."

"Fever," James said succinctly.

Concerned, Juliana turned to feel her aunt's forehead. "She's not hot."

"Impending fever, then. She needs to rest as a preventative measure." When Juliana failed to rise, he reached for her hand

and pulled her from the bench. "Will you argue with a physician?"

"Go on," Aunt Frances put in, waving her gloved hand.

Juliana suddenly realized her own hand was bare, and pleasantly enveloped in James's larger one.

"Come along." He tugged on her hand. "Your aunt will be fine. I believe Captain Cook's artifacts are in the next room."

She pulled her fingers free. Holding her hand in the carriage was one thing—and no doubt the result of those macaroons—but she'd not allow it in public. "We haven't seen the things in this room yet."

"A bevy of stuffed animals," he said dismissively. Besides the African display in the center, the walls were lined from floor to ceiling with creatures in glass cases, stacked one on top of another. "What's so interesting about that?"

"There are hundreds of different species."

"You're too short to see most of them," he said. Then, apparently deciding the discussion was over, he draped an arm about her shoulders to guide her out of the room.

Shocked, she darted a glance to her aunt, but the woman was staring into space, a vague smile curving her lips. Daydreaming, no doubt. She certainly wouldn't be smiling if she'd seen James's arm around Juliana.

Unless, on second thought, seeing James's arm around her had struck Aunt Frances with a vision of Lord Malmsey holding *her* in the same fashion. Because Juliana had to admit that being tucked up under a gentleman's arm like this was quite a striking sensation.

But Amanda probably wouldn't like it, she decided. James was acting a bit more amorous than what she'd had in mind. She'd had no idea the macaroons would prove to be so potent.

The next chamber's walls were covered with historical arms and armor. Still attached to her, James walked slowly, admiring the collection as though nothing were out of the ordinary.

"James," she said quietly.

"Hmm?"

"You have your arm about my shoulders."

"I know. I'm practicing for wooing Lady Amanda."

Oh, dear, just as she'd feared. She'd known she shouldn't have let him eat those macaroons. "I don't think Lady Amanda would want you to do this."

"Why not? You like it, don't you?"

She couldn't argue with that, so she didn't.

"We fit together rather well," he added, studying a curved sword.

They *did* fit perfectly. She'd thought him too tall, but he was just the right height for her to fit perfectly under his arm. Not, of course, that that made it at all proper. And in any case, he wouldn't fit perfectly with Amanda, since Amanda was much taller.

"Um, James?"

"Hmm?"

"People are going to see us and assume you're courting me instead of Lady Amanda."

"We aren't acquainted with anyone here," he said easily, "so they're not going to assume anything." He looked up higher, to peruse a battered shield. "Fascinating, isn't it?"

She tried to wriggle away without looking conspicuous. "I cannot really see it. I'm too short. Perhaps we should go see Napoleon's carriage instead."

"Use my quizzing glass," he offered, handing it to her with a smile.

She really had no choice but to take it. Like at the ball, he'd left the long chain around his neck, so she had to lean yet closer to raise the glass to her eye. He smelled nice. Spicy. She couldn't seem to focus on the shield.

He dropped his arm and moved behind her, which was a relief. But then something—his fingers—brushed her neck, and a little shiver ran through her. She blinked through the lens at an ancient, pitted rifle. "What are you doing, James?"

"Just pinning up a strand of your hair that's fallen down."

Her hair was so straight it often slid right out of its pins. But she'd never had a gentleman fix it before. Studying the rusty edge of a cutlass, she wondered if she should stop him.

"I'd do the same thing for Lady Amanda," he said, apparently reading her mind. "It's very gallant, don't you think? I'm getting some excellent practice."

She switched to examine an old flintlock. "Are you finished yet?"

"Not quite."

That rich, chocolatey voice was making it difficult to pay attention, especially since it seemed to be coming from right behind her ear. "You're standing a bit close to me, James."

"You're holding my quizzing glass," he pointed out.

And whose idea had that been? "Do you expect Captain Cook used this pistol?"

"What pistol?" he asked, his hands leaving her hair to rest lightly on her shoulders.

She could feel his breath, warm on the back of her neck. "This pistol I'm looking at on the wall."

"That's part of Bullock's collection." His voice sounded even closer. "Captain Cook's artifacts are in a case to your right."

She turned her head to the right, and his lips met her nape.

They felt warm and soft. She inhaled sharply when the brief contact ended.

"You shouldn't do that," she whispered, scandalized—although, to be honest, she was mostly scandalized because it had felt so good. "I understand that you wish to practice, but you're taking things too far."

"What things?" James asked.

She dropped the quizzing glass and whirled to face him. "You kissed my neck."

"In public? I think not." His expression was one of studied innocence. "You have an active imagination, Juliana."

She'd been told that before, but she hadn't imagined *this*.

"You'd better not do that to Lady Amanda," she warned. "She wouldn't like it."

"I wouldn't presume to kiss Lady Amanda. She's rather stuffy, isn't she? Rather like Castleton."

"The duke is not stuffy!"

He shrugged and motioned toward a glass case with a few people standing before it. "Did you want to see Captain Cook's artifacts?"

"Yes," she said and made her way over.

She'd wanted for months to see Captain Cook's artifacts, ever since the *Morning Post* had printed an article about their arrival at the Egyptian Hall. But they weren't nearly as interesting as the newspaper had made them sound. As she stood before the glass case, her gaze wandering over yellowed shark's teeth and ugly specimens of cloth made from bark, she wondered how it would feel should the duke kiss her neck like James had.

Perhaps she ought to give the duke a few macaroons so she could find out.

"Do you expect those old bones are really from the grave of an ancient Hawaiian chief?" she asked.

"If Captain Cook said so, I'm sure they are."

She wondered if Amanda would find all of this more interesting. Probably, considering she was fascinated with crusty objects from ancient ruins. "Are there any Roman antiquities in this museum?"

"I haven't noticed any yet, but there might be." James slipped an arm around her waist. "Would you like to have a look around and see?"

"Not particularly." Remembering that he'd known the identities of the Egyptian statues outside, she asked, "Would you recognize Roman antiquities?"

"Most certainly," he said dryly. "My father and grandfather were both obsessed with the things."

"Really? Lady Amanda is, too." What an amazing coincidence. "Do you find Roman antiquities fascinating?"

"I wouldn't put it so strongly," he said, drawing her closer against his side. "Mildly interesting, perhaps."

Perfect. Amanda had said she wanted a husband who was interested in Roman antiquities. Her friend was going to love coming here with him—as long as he didn't eat so many macaroons first. "Shall we go see Napoleon's carriage now?" she suggested, sidestepping away.

He sidestepped with her. "Absolutely, if that's what you wish."

As they headed to the next room, he kept his arm firmly around her. Doing her best to ignore that, she opened the guidebook and read from it. "The Emperor's carriage was captured at Waterloo and later purchased from the Prince Regent for twenty-five hundred pounds," she reported. "And it's bulletproof."

"A wise precaution on Napoleon's part." He halted in the archway. "Good gracious, would you look at all those people?" The carriage was completely surrounded. "Perhaps it would be better to return another time."

She wouldn't be returning with him—his next visit here would be with Amanda. They would admire Roman antiquities together.

"I want to see the carriage now," she said, envisioning his arm around Amanda's waist instead of hers and wondering why that picture didn't look right to her. Probably because Amanda wouldn't approve, she decided as she broke away from him and he followed her to the front of the crowd.

"Pardon me," he kept saying in a tone that sounded half exasperated, half apologetic. "Excuse me. Pardon." Short as she was, she was very good at burrowing her way through a pack of people, but apparently he wasn't.

Up close, the vehicle was beautiful, painted a rich dark blue and ornamented in gold. She looked up and back at James, who had come to a stop behind her. "Even the wheels are gold," she said.

James examined it over her head. "It's such a crush in here," he complained.

"The newspaper reported that ten thousand a day are visiting just to see this carriage."

"There seem to be twenty thousand today." He bumped into her from behind, then placed his hands on her waist to steady her. "My apologies," he murmured by her ear. "These people have no manners."

Although nobody seemed to be jostling, she let him keep his hands there. Just in case. "There's a blanket inside, embroidered with the initials *NB*. Do you expect Napoleon actually slept in here?"

"That would have been wise, considering it's bulletproof." He wrapped his arms further around her. "There's a desk inside, too."

It was built in below the front window, with many compartments for maps and telescopes. "Very clever," she murmured, leaning back into him so no one would nudge her. He felt warm. His spicy scent swamped her again, making her curiously dizzy. She felt very cozy and safe.

"Do you think Lady Amanda would like this?" he whispered.

"The clever desk?"

"No, me. Holding her like this."

"Oh, yes," she breathed, followed by a horrified, "No!"

What had she been thinking? She could feel his quizzing glass against her spine, which she was certain Amanda would find quite uncomfortable. "Lady Amanda wouldn't like this at all," she said, twisting out of his embrace. "You're right. It's entirely too crowded here today." She pushed through the throng and began retracing their steps back to her aunt. "I believe we should fetch my aunt and leave. You cannot be late to Parliament if you're giving a speech tonight."

Aunt Frances was still sitting where they'd left her, gazing happily at nothing in particular.

"Come along, Aunty," Juliana said.

It took a few minutes for the coachman to bring James's carriage around—a few minutes during which she marveled that her macaroons had had such an astounding effect. No sooner had they climbed into the carriage than she burrowed into the basket to count how many macaroons were left.

"What are you doing?" James asked.

"I forgot to keep some for myself." She pulled a handkerchief out of her reticule. "I'm sure Aunt Frances will want some."

"I don't need any macaroons." Her aunt patted her newly golden-brown hair. "A lady should keep a trim figure."

Frances had never had a care for her figure before. "Corinna will want some, then," Juliana said, piling them onto her handkerchief. She couldn't leave all the macaroons for James. She needed some for the duke, and besides, the mere thought of James eating nine macaroons made her cringe. Nine! If three had made him this amorous, nine would be an utter catastrophe.

James took the basket and peeked inside. "One? You cannot leave me just one."

Maybe he was right. She *did* want him to act warmly toward Amanda tomorrow night—just not as warmly as in the museum. "Two, then." She put one back in the basket and folded the handkerchief around the remaining seven. "But don't eat them until right before the ball tomorrow," she instructed as she slipped the bundle into her reticule. "You're going to need extra energy, so you mustn't forget."

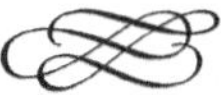

"**I CANNOT SEE,**" Aunt Frances complained. "I should never have let you talk me into taking off my spectacles."

"But you look beautiful, Aunty." Juliana patted her on the arm. "Just wait until Lord Malmsey gazes into your big blue eyes. You won't be sorry then."

Which *was* Juliana's main motive for making the suggestion. But she wasn't sorry that, without the spectacles, Aunt Frances couldn't see four feet beyond the end of her nose. Juliana could usually count on her chaperone's inattentiveness, but tonight she was taking no chances.

She spotted Lord Malmsey on the far end of the room. "There he is."

"Where?" Her aunt glanced around wildly. "I cannot see him."

"Right there, Aunty. Leaning on the mantel." Since it was quite cold for June, Lady Partridge had ordered the fireplaces lit on both ends of her impressive ballroom. "Come along. I'll take you to him."

Aunt Frances drew a deep breath and smoothed her soft

peach dress down her sides, eyeing her tasteful, lower-than-usual décolletage. "Do I look all right?"

"You look perfect," Juliana assured her, taking her arm as they started across the room. It was true. Aunt Frances looked much younger in a fashionable dress with her hair dyed and styled, and Juliana's skillful hand with the cosmetics had completed her transformation. She seemed to be trembling, but there was nothing Juliana could do to help that.

Standing in the glow of the fire, Lord Malmsey also looked nervous. More nervous than usual, that was. Which was no wonder, considering he was not only falling in love for the first time in his life, but doing so while betrothed to another lady—and while Juliana knew that would soon cease to be a problem, he didn't.

It was unfortunate a gentleman couldn't call off a wedding, because that would solve everything. He'd be free to marry Aunt Frances, and Amanda's father would have no grounds to disinherit her, leaving *her* free to find another suitor without so much pressure. But it just wasn't done. Although a lady could back out of an engagement—assuming she was willing to be labeled a jilt—a gentleman had no honorable way to withdraw an offer of marriage.

As Lord Malmsey noticed them approaching, a tentative smile spread on his face. While it didn't quite transform him—the regrettable forehead remained, after all—he did seem more handsome than Juliana remembered. Perhaps it was his stylish suit, which was obviously brand-new, or perhaps it was because what was left of his hair had been neatly trimmed. Or perhaps it was a glow that came from knowing a lady cared for him.

Love could change a person.

When they reached him, his anxious gaze met her aunt's. "Good evening, Lady Frances," he said shyly.

A youthful blush blossomed on Aunt Frances's cheeks. "Good evening, Lord Malmsey."

"Please," he said, gazing into her big blue eyes, "call me Theodore."

Aunt Frances stopped shaking, and her lips curved in a timid smile. "Call me Frances, then, please."

Lord Malmsey held out his arm. "Would you honor me with a dance...Frances?"

"My goodness, I'd love nothing more," she gushed, which sounded nothing like the formal words of acceptance Juliana had practiced with her. But it sounded better, more genuine, and made Lord Malmsey grin in response. Shooting her niece a disbelieving—and nearsighted—glance, Aunt Frances took his arm and sailed off with him.

Juliana sighed happily as she watched them drift toward the dance floor. A job well done.

"Did the macaroons work? Are my eyes sparkling?"

She turned to find Amanda standing beside her, wearing the dress Juliana had chosen for her because its gray-blue hue matched her eyes. Of course, those eyes weren't noticeably sparkling, but Amanda didn't have to know that.

"You look lovely," Juliana said instead. Amanda did look lovely, actually, whether her eyes sparkled or not. Juliana's hard work with her had certainly paid off. "Are you carrying your new fan?"

Amanda held it up. "And I'm wearing the gloves, like you told me to."

"Excellent. Have you seen James—I mean, Lord Stafford —yet?"

"No. I don't think he's arrived." Amanda's not-sparkling eyes looked apprehensive. "His gifts are wonderful, but what if I still don't like him particularly?"

"You will." How could anyone not like James? He was warm, intelligent, kind, and caring, and even though he didn't have time to go out much in society, Amanda shouldn't care a fig about that. It wasn't as though she was a social butterfly herself.

If anything, Juliana was more concerned about James liking

Amanda, mostly because he seemed much more affectionate than Amanda. But soon he would discover they had interests in common—chess and antiquities—and hopefully the macaroons would work to make Amanda warmer than usual. Or at least more receptive to *his* warmth.

Amanda frowned toward the dance floor. "Is Lord Malmsey waltzing with your aunt?"

"Yes. Isn't it wonderful?"

"He's engaged to *me*," she said.

Juliana narrowed her eyes. "You're planning to break that engagement, are you not? Really, you should be relieved to see him happy with another lady. Or is it your goal to devastate the poor man?"

Juliana wasn't finished scolding, but over her friend's shoulder she could see two young men approaching—as Rachael had said, Amanda looked to be this season's Incomparable. At least until her novelty wore off.

"Smile at the gentlemen, Amanda," Juliana instructed through a fixed smile of her own. "You're not engaged to Lord Stafford yet."

Before she turned her well-rehearsed smile on her potential suitors, Amanda at least had the grace to look chagrined. Which was a good thing, because given her earlier attitude, Juliana had been tempted to call the whole plan off. Except then Lord Malmsey would have to marry Amanda, which would hardly be fair to either him or Aunt Frances.

It was all becoming quite complicated.

As Amanda went off to dance with the luckier of the two young men, Juliana sensed a presence behind her and turned to see the Duke of Castleton. "Lady Juliana," he said, his tone reserved as ever, "may I beg the honor of your company for a dance?"

"By all means, your grace." She loved calling him *your grace* and thinking that someday—maybe someday soon—other people would say that to *her*. She took the duke's arm and headed toward the dance floor. "A waltz," she said happily, shooting him a smile. "Now you'll have an excuse to touch me."

She'd uttered the words in a flirtatious manner. But although she was an accomplished flirt, the duke didn't seem to take her hint. "You're looking beautiful tonight, my dear," he said, and then proceeded to hold her at a respectable distance. Throughout the entirety of the dance, he didn't touch her anywhere that wasn't absolutely necessary.

But none of that meant he wasn't enamored. He'd sent her flowers, after all. And he'd called her *my dear*. But all the same, Juliana wished for a more *physical* sign of his affection. Recent experience had shown her it was an essential component of courtship—physical closeness helped to breed emotional closeness. Which explained why she seemed to feel more comfortable and intimate with *James* than she did with her own future husband!

Luckily, she'd transferred the handkerchief-wrapped macaroons into the pretty yellow reticule that matched her dress. As the duke led her off the dance floor, she slid the beaded purse off her wrist and opened it.

"Thank you for the waltz, my dear," the duke said very formally.

"It was my pleasure." She pulled out the bundle and handed it to him. "I baked macaroons for you."

He looked startled. "In the kitchen?" he asked, as though there were somewhere else—someplace more acceptable—a proper lady might bake.

"Yes, in the kitchen. Chase ladies are known for making all sorts of sweets." Since he wasn't moving to do so, she unwrapped the macaroons for him. "Won't you try one?"

Looking pained, he selected an especially small one and slipped it into his mouth, then chewed and swallowed thoroughly before stating his opinion. "They're absolutely delicious," he said. "I can see why the Chase ladies are known for their sweets." He held forth the handkerchief with the rest of them.

She didn't take it. "I'm so glad they meet with your approval. I hope you'll enjoy *all* of them." Seven macaroons might seem a bit much, considering three had made James overly affectionate, but she feared it could take at least that many to ease a manner as reserved as the duke's. "Thank you for the dance," she added with a very proper curtsy. Then she took her leave, before he could try to return the sweets again.

Gentlemen didn't carry reticules—and the duke was entirely too fastidious to put a bundle of macaroons in his pocket.

He'd have no choice but to eat them.

TWENTY-FOUR

*I*T SEEMED lately people talked of nothing but the unusually cold weather, James reflected as he stood in a circle of gentlemen at Lady Partridge's ball.

"The sunspots are responsible for the cold," Lord Cravenhurst was saying. "Clearly there is something amiss with the universe."

Lord Davenport inclined his head sagely. "Nine groups of sunspots have been counted, plus several single ones scattered from the eastern to the western side of the sun. I fear they portend the end of the world. The sun is cooling off."

"I think not." Lord Hawkridge cut into the circle. "Sunspots are hardly new. Galileo noted them more than two hundred years ago. If you'll but examine the temperature records, you'll find Britain has seen both uncommonly cold and uncommonly warm summers since then, and such periods have nothing to do with sunspots."

James nodded. "Hawkridge makes a convincing argument." He didn't know Hawkridge terribly well, though he recalled the fellow as a particular friend of Cainewood's at Oxford. But James was glad to hear a voice of reason join the discussion.

Listening to these old crackpots for too long could melt one's brain.

"I agree with Hawkridge and Stafford," Lord Haversham announced. "Sunspots aren't responsible for the cold. The moon is to blame."

James groaned inwardly. "And how is that?"

Apparently not one for technical details, Haversham shrugged. "It's common knowledge that the cycles of the moon affect everything."

"Nonsense." Everyone turned to Lord Occlestone, a man who sadly—or fittingly, depending on one's point of view—resembled nothing so much as a pink-faced pig. "It's not the moon *or* sunspots," he declared loudly, spewing sputum on everyone else in the process. "It's the fault of those upstart Americans."

Hawkridge wiped his face. "How on earth can you blame this on the Americans?"

Occlestone had been another classmate at Oxford, though he'd *started* several years ahead of James and the others—a fact which always brought a smile to James's face, though he knew it was unkind to gloat. Occlestone was doing everything he could to block James's vaccination bill.

"North America is suffering even colder weather than ours," Hawkridge pointed out. "Their newspapers are predicting famine in the coming months due to crop failure."

"I've seen reports of famine in Switzerland as well," Lord Cavanaugh put in.

"Famine or not," Occlestone said, plainly indifferent to something so unlikely to affect him personally, "we can lay the blame at the feet of an American. Benjamin Franklin, to be precise."

"At the feet of Benjamin Franklin?" James blinked. "I expect Mr. Franklin's feet are decomposed by now, since he's been dead more than twenty-five years."

The others laughed, but Occlestone's porcine eyes narrowed. "Dead or not, he invented the lightning rod, didn't he? I'll have you know that the interior of the earth is hot due to electrical fluids circulating about beneath the surface. That heat is usually discharged into the air around us, but because of Franklin's lightning rods—which are now being installed all over not only his country but ours as well—the earth's process of releasing heat into the atmosphere has been interrupted."

"That's not how I've heard it explained," Cravenhurst said. "Quite the opposite, in fact. Since lightning is heat, the lightning rods have taken the heat from the air. Hence we shall never again see summer."

Davenport rubbed his balding pate. "Either way, Franklin would be responsible. But I still blame the sunspots."

James sighed. How could it be that *these* were the minds deciding the future of their country?

Hawkridge noticed the sigh. "You have a better explanation to offer, Stafford?" he asked, a twinkle in his eye.

James stiffened as the expectant gazes of all the men came to rest on him. They might be crackpots, but most of them were also older and more experienced than he. It had been harrowing enough trying to maintain an air of authority while delivering his speech on vaccination—a subject on which he actually *was* an authority. But if he hoped to make a difference in the House, he'd have to act like a man worth listening to.

He cleared his throat. "I've observed," he said carefully, "that there's been a haze overhead the last few months. I believe that haze is temporarily blocking the sun."

Occlestone crossed his arms. "A haze?"

"Yes, a haze. Or a fog, if you will, or perhaps it's some sort of dust, since it appears to be dry. Unlike the way the sun easily dissipates a moist fog, its warmth seems to have little effect on this haze. Therefore it reasonably follows that its rays aren't reaching the earth and warming the surface as usual."

"And to what do you attribute this haze?" Occlestone demanded.

"That I couldn't tell you. I'm a physician, not a meteorologist.

But I see no reason to jump to the conclusion that the condition will continue indefinitely." Out of the corner of his eye, he saw Hawkridge tilt his head, as if intrigued by the idea.

"Do you expect there's a haze above America as well? I think not." Occlestone's pinkish face was turning rather purple. "I was forced to listen to your two-hour speech in Parliament, Stafford, but I don't have to listen to you here." And with that, he stalked off, muttering so loudly he was audible halfway across the ballroom.

Brows raised all around, the group watched him go. Heat was crawling up James's neck.

Hawkridge broke the silence. "For heaven's sake," he crowed, thumping James companionably on the back. "It's no more absurd than the rest of your harebrained theories!"

The other men laughed, and after a moment of uncertainty James joined in.

"Good evening, Tristan," a familiar feminine voice said behind them.

James turned to see Juliana, dressed in such a cheerful bright yellow she seemed to make up for all the missing sunshine. But his sunny mood evaporated as he watched Hawkridge kiss her hand and she smiled. "You're looking lovely tonight, Juliana."

And they'd addressed each other by their given names. Just how familiar *were* these two?

They moved a short distance to confer together, and James couldn't hear what was said next. He turned away, telling himself he had no business caring what their relationship might be. Juliana was entitled to genuine suitors. And at least Hawkridge seemed far superior to the duke, being neither a prig nor a turd. In fact, they might be quite well suited—

"Are you all right, James?" Juliana asked.

He blinked. "Of course. Why shouldn't I be?"

"You just looked…odd."

He shrugged. "Hawkridge is a fine fellow, isn't he?"

"Yes, I think so, too. It's a shame Tristan was shunned by

society for so long. I'm so glad to see him finally receiving the respect he deserves. Thank goodness for Alexandra."

"Alexandra?"

"My older sister. His wife. She cleared his name of the scandal."

"Oh." Whatever scandal had afflicted Hawkridge, it must have happened while James was preoccupied by grief. Feeling an absurd rush of relief, it was all he could do to hold back a grin. Hawkridge wasn't Juliana's suitor—he was her *brother-in-law*. "I didn't realize he was married to your sister."

"I forgot you've met only Corinna. I shall have to introduce you to Alexandra." She caught sight of someone and frowned. "That man doesn't like you much, does he?"

James followed her gaze. "Occlestone?" He hadn't realized she'd overheard their conversation. "He's hated me since our school days. But I don't like him much, either, so we're even."

"Two hours," she said, looking impressed. "How was your speech received? Other than by Lord Occlestone, I mean."

He sighed. "I don't think the House of Lords is willing to spend more money fighting smallpox. They awarded two grants to fund Edward Jenner's research—in 1802 and again in 1806—and they consider that enough. And there are others who object to the very concept of mandatory vaccination. They believe forcing people to undergo the treatment is a violation of civil liberty."

"I never thought of it that way," she said.

He nodded. "It's not an unreasonable objection." It seemed very little in this world was black and white. "But I do wish there was more support for public funding to help eradicate the disease."

"Has your bill come to a vote?"

"Not yet, but I fear I know the outcome already." His two-hour speech had been followed by four hours of debate—mostly not in his favor. "I shall try again next year. Perhaps for the funding only."

"But will money alone help? You're already paying for other people's vaccinations."

"Only here in London. My income, after all, is generous but not unlimited. And government funds could pay for more than just doctors and supplies—they could also finance education. If everyone learned the benefits of immunization and decided to have their children vaccinated, the end result would be the same as if it were compulsory." Thinking this was quite a serious discussion for a ball, he smiled and changed the subject. "Are you enjoying the evening?"

"Of course. I didn't see you arrive."

"That's because you were dancing with Castleton." The turd had looked as stuffy as ever. "Can I convince you to dance with me instead?"

"You're here to dance with Lady Amanda," she reminded him. "Did you eat the macaroons before you came?"

"Absolutely. I assure you, I shall have enough energy to dance with you both."

"Very well," she said with a laugh. "We can talk about your strategy as we dance."

James didn't want to talk strategy. But he did want to get close to Juliana and hopefully make more progress toward kissing her. So he mumbled something that sounded like agreement and drew her toward the dance floor.

TWENTY-FIVE

"So," Juliana said to James as they waltzed, "have you decided how you're going to ask Lady Amanda's permission to court her?"

He pulled her closer. "I thought I'd start with 'May I have this dance?' and take it from there."

"That doesn't sound particularly gallant."

"I think it will work," he said dismissively. "After all, I bought her several gifts." He pulled her closer still, until their bodies were nearly touching, which seemed to spark an odd tingling sensation. "Have I sent her all of the gifts yet, or just some?"

"Only the fan and the gloves so far," she said, his hand trailing slowly down her back in a thoroughly distracting manner. "And the flowers, of course. You'll send the rest next week."

"You'll see to that, I presume," he said dryly as his hand slid back up. "Sending the gifts is a very gallant gesture, isn't it?"

"That's why I suggested them."

"Well, then," he said, his fingers skimming down again and making her feel lightheaded, "shouldn't that be enough? They do say that actions speak louder than words."

His actions spoke volumes—but in a language Juliana didn't understand. She couldn't imagine what he meant by touching her like this while they discussed his courtship of another girl. For that matter, she couldn't think what *she* meant by allowing it to continue.

But there was one thing she did know—if James asked Amanda to dance and touched her this way, made her feel this way, she was *sure* to accept his suit. Why, if it were Juliana in her friend's place, *she* might be tempted to propose to *him*.

What an absurd thought! Juliana nearly giggled aloud, but stopped herself, fearing laughter might lead to awkward questions from James. Hilarity aside, the important point was: her project was all but guaranteed to succeed!

As the waltz came to an end, she noticed her older sister conversing with Amanda. "There's Alexandra now," she said, maneuvering so that James would lead her off the dance floor in their direction. "Let me introduce you."

James told Alexandra he'd been delighted to learn Lord Hawkridge had wed—in fact, he seemed so delighted that Juliana supposed they must have been quite close friends at Oxford—and Alexandra was glad to meet the gentleman who'd been discussed so avidly at Juliana's sewing parties, although she didn't say so, of course.

After the introductions were complete, it was a simple matter to suggest that James and Amanda dance. Unfortunately, the musicians struck up a country tune, not a waltz, but the two of them headed off, looking as good together as ever. They were both tall, and James's dark handsomeness contrasted with Amanda's pale beauty. Anyone would agree they made a charming couple.

Juliana spotted James's mother gazing happily toward her son, clearly pleased to see him with a lady as lovely as Amanda. Lady Stafford looked different tonight—or younger, maybe— wearing a fashionable dress of deep rose with almond trim.

Juliana recalled seeing something similar in the latest issue of *La Belle Assemblée.* Remembering that James wanted his mother to dance, she looked around for an eligible gentleman and found one nearby.

"Lord Cavanaugh," she said, smiling when he shifted to face her. A dapper widower in his mid-fifties with a patrician nose and silver hair, he was ideal for Lady Stafford. "Are you enjoying the evening?"

He grinned down at her, looking surprised. Doubtless he wasn't used to being addressed by so young a lady. "Very much, Lady Juliana. And you?"

"Very much as well." She started edging toward James's mother. "Have you been dancing much tonight?"

"Not yet," he said, interpreting her question as an invitation, just as she'd intended. "But I'd be honored to—"

"Excellent," she said, walking him right up to Lady Stafford. "Good evening, Lady Stafford."

James's mother turned, the smile still on her face. "Good evening, Lady Juliana."

"Your dress is beautiful. Is it new?"

Her warm brown eyes, so like her son's, sparkled much more than Amanda's. She reached to touch Juliana's arm. "Why, thank you, and yes, it is."

"I believe you know Lord Cavanaugh?" Juliana smiled in the man's direction. "He would love to dance with you. I hope you'll enjoy yourselves," she added and sailed off.

Corinna stepped into her path. "Very smooth, Juliana."

Since she was so happy with the way everything was going, she ignored her sister's sarcasm. "Thank you."

"Has it ever occurred to you that some people might not appreciate your meddling?"

"I'm not meddling. I'm helping." She gestured toward the dance floor, where Lady Stafford was performing a quadrille with Lord Cavanaugh. "They're both smiling."

"They're being polite."

"They're happy. He's a wealthy widower; she's a lonely widow. Why shouldn't they be happy to dance together?"

"Maybe because you pushed them into it?"

"Some people need a little pushing." She eyed her sister, thinking she looked a bit lonely. "Shall I find a dance partner for you?"

"Holy Hannah," Corinna said and hurried off.

Juliana looked back to the dance floor. No matter what her sister said, it was obvious Lord Cavanaugh and James's mother were thoroughly enjoying their dance. And Lord Malmsey and Aunt Frances were dancing again, their eyes locked on each other in a way that made Juliana sigh with envy. If only the duke would look at her like that. Well, maybe he would now, having eaten the macaroons.

She was looking around for him when Amanda sidled up. "I talked to Lord Malmsey."

"About what?" Juliana demanded, picturing her giving him a piece of her mind about dancing with Aunt Frances.

But Amanda surprised her. "About our betrothal. You were right—I had no call to disapprove of him dancing with another woman. I told him that I understand his change of heart, and feel the same, and I'm going to find a way out of the marriage that will leave him with his honor intact."

Juliana slumped in relief. "You've decided to marry Lord Stafford, then."

Amanda shrugged. "I'm still not struck by love."

Impossible. "Did Lord Stafford touch you?" Juliana asked.

"Touch me? He touched my hand, of course, during the dance when we progressed."

"But nothing else? Nothing more…amorous?"

"Amorous?" Amanda's eyes widened. "I should hope not! It's not as though we're engaged."

They'd never *get* engaged if she didn't let him touch her!

"The plan was to find someone willing to compromise you," Juliana reminded her. "And some touching, after all, will be necessary in order to convince your father that you're compromised. Perhaps a little experimentation would be wise."

Amanda appeared to quail at the very idea. "It's too soon. I've yet to decide if Lord Stafford is the young man I wish to have compromise me."

"Well, your wedding is only three weeks off. You'd best make your decision quickly, or it will be Lord Malmsey touching you instead of someone of your own choosing."

The poor girl's face went white, and Juliana chided herself for the unfeeling remark. "We'll find someone," she soothed, reaching to squeeze Amanda's hand. "I'm just not sure it's realistic to expect to be struck by love in so little time."

Amanda bit her lip, looking more reserved than ever. "Perhaps you're right."

"If you'd allow Lord Stafford to touch you, that might help."

"He hasn't tried," Amanda said.

Surely the macaroons' effects hadn't worn off that quickly? "Perhaps if you were a bit more inviting."

"I'll try." Amanda fiddled with her fan. "Do you enjoy it when the duke touches you?"

"Very much," Juliana assured her, wishing the duke had actually touched her so she wouldn't have to fib. "Listen. The musicians are starting a waltz. That's an excellent dance for touching."

She took Amanda's arm and marched her to where James was talking to his mother. "Lady Amanda would love to waltz," she said.

When he didn't move, Lady Stafford nudged him. "Go on, James. We can finish this discussion at home."

"Very well," he said stiffly, offering Amanda his arm. "Shall we dance again?"

As the young couple walked off, Lady Stafford gave a happy

sigh and smiled at Juliana, looking as though she had something to say to her. Something nice. But just then, Lord Cavanaugh came up and smartly bowed before the older woman.

"Shall we dance again?" he asked.

Shooting Juliana an even wider smile over her shoulder, Lady Stafford went off with him.

Juliana looked around and spotted the duke exiting the card room. Aiming her best, perfected smile at him, she went up and tapped him on the arm. "Shall we dance again?"

The line had worked perfectly for everyone else, but the duke just looked startled. Juliana supposed it wasn't proper for a lady to do the asking, but she was dying to see how well the macaroons had worked, so she started toward the dance floor, knowing he would follow.

And he did follow, of course. But when they started to waltz, his arms were rigid, and he held her just as far away as ever.

"Who is that dancing with Stafford?" he asked. "Do you know her?"

"That's Lady Amanda Wolverston, and I know her very well. We grew up together as neighbors."

"I've never noticed her before."

Well, of course he hadn't. No one had noticed Amanda before Juliana took her in hand. "What did you think of Lord Stafford's controversial speech?"

"To which speech do you refer?"

"Yesterday's. In Parliament. Concerning smallpox vaccinations."

"How would you come to know of that?" he asked, but apparently the question was rhetorical, because he didn't wait for an answer. "I was at my club yesterday," he told her. "Playing cards."

She wondered why she found that irksome. After all, she wanted a husband who had plenty of time for her, and clearly he put pleasure before more serious pursuits. "Did you win?"

"Does it matter? It was an amusing way to pass the hours."

He smiled down on her indulgently. "I can afford to lose, I assure you. I have plenty of money to both gamble and buy flowers for a special lady."

She was glad he thought she was special, but if he had extra funds, perhaps they'd be better spent on something more meaningful. A worthy cause. The Foundling Hospital, perhaps, or smallpox vaccinations.

Once she knew him better, she'd make the suggestion. She wished he would loosen up so she could *get* to know him better. "Did you eat any more of my macaroons?" she asked, concluding he hadn't.

"All of them," he said, surprising her. "They tasted so wonderful, and I couldn't find anywhere to put them to save them for later."

That was as she'd expected. But why weren't they working? "I'm glad you enjoyed them."

"They were truly very good."

Apparently they weren't good enough. They didn't seem to be making him amorous at all. She moved a little bit closer, but he braced his arms until they were once more at a proper distance.

Lord Cavanaugh, she noticed, wasn't dancing nearly so properly with Lady Stafford. The two of them looked rather cozy. And Aunt Frances and Lord Malmsey were so close they were all but tromping on each other's toes. Amanda, however, was dancing at a proper distance from James.

She should have left James more macaroons, considering two had worn off too quickly and even seven hadn't affected the duke. What could make one so resistant to warmth and affection? She imagined the late duke might have acted distantly toward his son, knowing the boy was actually fathered by another. But a loving mother should have made up for that.

"Was your mother very affectionate?" she asked.

"Affectionate?" He looked taken aback by the mere question. "I wouldn't know. I never knew either of my parents."

Oh, how tragic! "Why was that?"

"They died when I was six months old. Drowned in a storm while crossing the Channel."

"I'm so sorry." Juliana had lost her parents at fourteen—she could hardly imagine growing up without parents altogether. Even motherless Emily and Amanda had fathers in their lives. "Who raised you, then?"

His handsome mouth compressed into a thin line. "My uncle and aunt—my father's brother and his wife. Did you know I was born in your house? The first thing they did as my guardians was sell that house to your father and then buy my current, more splendid house in Grosvenor Square. I was well satisfied to turn them out of it when I gained my majority."

She was happy to hear he had a splendid house, but she wondered at the bitterness in his tone. "Were they not nice to you?"

"Nice?" He laughed, but it was a laugh devoid of humor. "If I hadn't been born half a year before my parents died, my uncle and aunt would have been the duke and duchess. They never forgave me for robbing them of that."

He didn't offer any details, but Juliana could imagine them for herself. His uncle and aunt had been cold, cruel, and resentful. He'd received no hugs growing up, no physical affection.

No wonder he wasn't affectionate himself. No one had ever shown him how. "I'm so sorry you had a sad childhood," she told him.

"You're so caring, my dear," he said, giving her a fond smile.

She understood perfectly. No one had cared for him throughout his childhood, which was why he had a hard time getting close to others now. Like all people, he'd learned by example, and he needed a new example to learn by.

Human touch could go a long way. Once he learned to be more affectionate, he would also be more charitable. The poor man needed someone in his life to gently guide him, to help his softer side come to the fore.

He needed *her*. With her in his life, demonstrating warmth and generosity—

The dance came to an end. Before she could finish formulating her plan, he bowed formally and thanked her.

No sooner had he walked away than Lady Stafford walked up. "I must thank you for introducing me to Lord Cavanaugh."

"I thought you already knew him."

"Reintroducing me, then." She smiled, her kindly eyes reminding Juliana of her own mother. "I'm giving a little dinner party tomorrow evening at Stafford House, and Lord Cavanaugh has agreed to attend. My son will be there, too. Might I have the pleasure of your company as well?"

"I'd be delighted to attend." She liked Lady Stafford. The woman was very motherly, and Juliana missed her mother rather a lot. Plus the dinner would give her a chance to ask James how his courtship of Amanda was proceeding and remind him to invite her to visit the Egyptian Hall. Once Amanda discovered their shared interest in Roman antiquities, she might be struck by love quickly after all.

"I'm also going to ask the young lady with whom my son has been dancing." Lady Stafford's gaze slid to Amanda and back. "Shall I invite the Duke of Castleton to round out our party?"

"That would be lovely," Juliana said, mentally reshuffling her objectives for the evening.

That would be perfect, in fact. The duke never called on Sundays, so the dinner would give her an unexpected opportunity to begin helping him right away. She'd be able to direct the conversation to James's humanitarian work and show the duke the importance of charity. Perhaps she could even persuade him to contribute!

She hoped the duke would come to like James, and vice versa. Her fondest wish was that she and the duke would become fast friends with James and Amanda and have more dinner parties after both couples were married. That would be an ideal situation, because she'd come to enjoy James's company in the time they'd spent together.

"Eight o'clock, then?" the older woman asked. "Lady Amanda lives on your street, doesn't she? On the west side of Berkeley Square? I'll have the Stafford carriage sent round for you both."

TWENTY-SIX

APPLE AND ORANGE TART

Peel two Oranges and make into pieces, then peel some Apples into thin slices. Put in a bowle

with a smidgen of Flour, a cup of Sugar, some Cinnamon and Ginger. Put into your paste with

pieces of Butter all over. Cover with more paste and some Sugar and bake in your oven until

browne.

Excellent to take to a party with friends. As the apples and oranges in this tart go together, so

do the people who eat it.

—Eleanor, Marchioness of Cainewood, 1735

"*I*SN'T THIS A stunning carriage?" Juliana asked as she and Amanda neared Stafford House.

"Lord Stafford is an earl." Amanda absentmindedly ran a hand over the deep green velvet upholstery. "I'd expect him to have a nice carriage."

The well-sprung vehicle rocked, making Juliana tighten her grip on the tart she'd baked that afternoon. Was there nothing about James that would impress her friend? "He likes chess," she reminded her, and then, even though she'd meant to let Amanda discover they had more in common at the Egyptian Hall, she added, "And you might want to ask him if he's interested in Roman antiq—"

She cut off mid-word as the carriage came to a stop and the door opened, revealing a footman dressed in crimson livery trimmed in gold. "Welcome to Stafford House," he said, offering a gloved hand to help them down.

"Gracious me," Amanda breathed, her eyes widening as she stepped out and stood before the mansion. "I've noticed this house from Green Park, but I had no idea it belonged to Lord Stafford." It was three stories tall, the facade clad in brilliant white Portland stone. "Would you look at those statues on top of that Roman Doric portico? Bacchus, Flora, and Ceres."

Juliana hadn't a clue who Bacchus, Flora, and Ceres were, but she smiled all the same. "Lord Stafford can name ancient gods and goddesses, just like you."

A butler ushered them inside an impressive entrance hall with curved walls, a pale marble floor, and an arched window looking out on a resplendent central courtyard garden.

"Gracious me," Amanda repeated, staring up at a strip of decorations that ran around the room below the carved oval ceiling. "That frieze looks like the one in the Temple of Jupiter." Slowly, reverently, she walked toward a large marble bust that sat on a pedestal before the window. "This is amazing." She reached a hand as though to touch it, then stopped herself. "It must be priceless."

"He doesn't look like a god," Juliana said.

"He isn't. That's Emperor Lucius Verus, the adopted brother of Marcus Aurelius who ruled with him."

Juliana examined the haughty, bearded fellow. "He's very handsome."

"He was said to be weak and indulgent. I understand that his death was rather a relief to the Empire."

"How do you know such things?" Juliana asked.

"From books, of course. My father's library has grown by

leaps and bounds since he discovered the ruins on the property. Do you not read, too?"

"Most certainly." She glanced through the newspapers, because she liked to know what was happening elsewhere. Magazines by the dozen. Poetry and the latest novels discussed in polite company. And those discussed in whispers, such as the Minerva Press romance currently hidden beneath her pillow. But Roman history and mythology?

She'd had no idea that Amanda had grown so bookish.

After collecting their pelisses and umbrellas, the butler led them through a staircase hall. Or at least he *tried* to lead them through a staircase hall. Amanda stopped in her tracks, staring at a statue that was larger-than-life.

"It's a centaur," she said.

"Even I know that. My education isn't *totally* lacking." Juliana was rather fascinated by all the ridges on the creature's bare, toned chest. But Amanda had already moved on, kneeling down by a large fragment of carved stone that sat beneath an inlaid wooden side table.

"Part of a sarcophagus, I'd guess." She ran her fingers across the piece. "First century."

"How do you know?" Juliana wondered.

Amanda just shrugged as she rose, gesturing to two more carved stone pieces on either side of the table. "Funerary altars. Also first century. The flat surface was used for sacrificial ceremonies." She sighed expansively. "This house is just *full* of treasures."

The butler continued on, leading them down a corridor lined with gilt-framed paintings of Stafford ancestors, then turning into the most gorgeous room Juliana had ever seen. Between arched walls painted a soft pistachio green, gilded columns looked like golden palm trees, their fronds projecting high overhead. In the back of the room, a large alcove was crowned with a domed ceiling, divided into small gilt-edged squares alternately tinted green and pink.

Dressed in a burgundy gown with pink trim, Lady Stafford rose from where she faced Lord Cavanaugh across a chessboard and greeted them with a smile. "Good evening. I'm so pleased you could both come." She moved to take the dish Juliana was holding out. "What is this, my dear?"

"An apple and orange tart. The recipe was my great-grandmother's."

She lifted the lace doily that covered it. "Oh, my. It smells delicious."

"It's supposed to promote friendship," Amanda informed her, gazing down at the chess set.

"Lovely!" Lady Stafford set the tart on a marble side table. "We shall serve it after dinner."

"What a beautiful chess set," Juliana said, amused by Amanda's fascination. "Roman gladiators, aren't they? Do the pieces date back to that time?"

"No, they look much newer," Amanda said. "And besides, chess isn't that old. It wasn't invented until after the Empire fell."

"My father-in-law commissioned the set to be carved." Lady Stafford lifted a crystal decanter. "Would you care for some sherry?"

"Just a little, please." Juliana took the first glass she poured and perched herself on a pale green satin love seat with gilt palm tree legs that had obviously been designed to match the room. "Thank you so much for inviting us to your home."

"It's my pleasure, though this is my son's home, in truth," Lady Stafford said, handing Amanda another glass.

That son walked into the room with the duke, the two of them deep in conversation. Juliana was thrilled to see they were becoming friends already. She smoothed the skirts of her white dress, which she'd chosen hoping the duke would think it proper and ladylike.

Very virtuous, as James had said.

Sipping sherry, Amanda sat beside her. "He's so much taller," she whispered.

James *was* much taller than the duke. Which was why he and Amanda looked so good together.

"And darker," Amanda added.

Yes, James was dark. The duke looked pale in comparison. Pale and ashen-haired. But only in comparison. And Juliana preferred lighter hair.

"And *much* more handsome."

"It isn't polite to whisper," Juliana whispered back. She didn't want to think about James being much more handsome. And it wasn't true, anyway.

Was it?

"Good evening, ladies," James said in his low and chocolate-smooth voice.

"Good evening," the duke said in his perfectly normal voice. He smiled at Juliana. "It's lovely to see you again, my dear."

Well, why should a voice matter, anyway? The duke was a *duke*. And it was obvious he cared for her, even if he hadn't touched her. Yet.

A footman appeared in the doorway and announced dinner. Lord Cavanaugh offered Lady Stafford his arm. "Shall we?"

The rest of them followed the older couple into a large formal dining room. The extra leaves had been removed from the mahogany table to make it an oval for six. While a footman drew back Juliana's chair, she took a moment to look around. The dining room featured Roman-looking marble columns, a beautiful Turkey carpet, and a carved marble fireplace. But the most impressive thing was the ceiling, a scalloped design with round inset panels representing classical scenes, all decorated in gold.

"The ceiling is exquisite," she said as she sank onto her forest green velvet seat.

"My late husband's pride and joy." Lady Stafford sat, too. "It was based on a ceiling in the Baths of Augustus in Rome."

Gazing up at it, Amanda sighed. "This is the most magnificent house I've ever seen. Everything in it is absolutely splendid." She turned to James beside her. "You have wonderful taste, Lord Stafford."

His mother laughed. "The taste was his grandfather's. The man hired the venerable Henry Holland as his designer. Were it up to my son, he'd probably sell the whole lot and use the money to vaccinate every last soul in England."

James frowned. "The value of the house and its contents wouldn't begin to cover—"

"I was jesting," Lady Stafford broke in with fond exasperation. "I trust you not to sell off the family treasures."

Juliana saw an opportunity to segue into a matter she'd hoped to discuss. "If others would help with Lord Stafford's cause," she said as asparagus soup was served in porcelain bowls with gold Stafford crests on their crimson rims, "there would be no need to sell anything." Lifting her spoon, which was gold, too, she turned to the duke. "Eradicating smallpox is a worthy goal that all should contribute towards, don't you think?"

"All?" The duke raised his own gold spoon. "Worthy or not, I don't expect everyone can afford to donate."

"Certainly *you* can," she said sweetly.

She thought she heard choking sounds from James. Or maybe a muffled chortle.

Lord Cavanaugh took a sip of wine. "I'd be pleased to contribute."

"Thank you very much," James said with an expression of startled approval. "That would be greatly appreciated."

Lady Stafford looked quite delighted.

Amanda turned a smile on James. "I should like to contribute, too," she said prettily, "but alas, I shall need to ask my father for the funds."

Knowing Amanda's father, Juliana suspected he wouldn't donate a penny. And she was sure Amanda knew that, too.

"Time is also valuable," she said. "You could volunteer your assistance instead of money."

Amanda blinked and pressed a hand to her pale blue muslin bodice. "Are you suggesting I give smallpox vaccinations?"

"No, of course not. Doctors give the vaccinations. But I imagine there are other tasks you could do that would prove helpful."

"Certainly," James put in, setting down his spoon, which Juliana had decided was actually sterling plated in gold, because, really, solid gold spoons were a little much, even for people as rich as the Staffords. "There are always new supplies arriving that need to be unpacked and arranged on the shelves behind the counter, and schedules to be made out in a hand neater than mine, and treatment rooms to be cleaned, and—"

"You'd like me to clean rooms?" Amanda interrupted. She pinned Juliana with a pointed gaze. "Are you going to volunteer, too, then?"

In truth, Juliana hadn't a clue why she'd suggested Amanda volunteer in the first place. She certainly didn't expect her to clean treatment rooms—she doubted her friend had cleaned anything in her life, with the possible exception of her own teeth. But something about Amanda's disingenuous offer of money had rubbed her the wrong way.

And now she'd backed herself into a corner. "I'd be happy to volunteer," Juliana found herself saying. She lifted her chin. She did like helping people, and while she was quite busy sewing baby clothes, she imagined she could spare a little time. "As I said, it's a worthy cause."

"Capital!" James exclaimed so enthusiastically she half expected him to break into applause. "How about Wednesday at one o'clock?"

"She can't," Amanda said. "She has a sewing party every Wednesday at one."

Drat. "I'll move this week's party to tomorrow."

"Sewing party?" Lady Stafford asked.

"Lady Juliana supports many worthy causes," Amanda said. "She's making baby clothes for the Foundling Hospital."

Juliana had a sudden thought. "It might be a good idea," she suggested to James, "for you to vaccinate the foundlings."

"I already do," he said, which made her beam in approval. "I visit there twice every year."

Lady Stafford looked to Juliana. "Do you need more help sewing the baby clothes, dear? I'd be pleased to attend your party tomorrow."

"That would be wonderful," Juliana said.

And it was. But she spent the rest of dinner wondering how it happened that she'd ended up volunteering to help at the Institute when she'd suggested Amanda do so, and Lord Cavanaugh had ended up donating money when she'd asked that of the duke.

Maybe she was losing her touch.

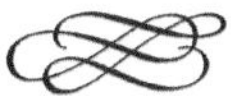

TWENTY-SEVEN

*A*FTER DINNER, when the ladies would usually have left the gentlemen alone with their port, Lady Stafford suggested they all adjourn to the Palm Room instead. While the men poured and Lady Stafford busied herself serving the apple and orange tart, Amanda drew Juliana into the alcove at the back of the room.

"Can you *believe* this house?" she whispered, her eyes sparkling at last. "Is it not the most amazing thing you've ever seen?"

Juliana's gaze wandered the gold palm fronds, the gold and crystal chandeliers, the gold-trimmed ceiling. "There's a lot of gold."

Smiling, Amanda nodded. "Even the silverware is gold."

"It's sterling plated in gold," Juliana informed her.

"Regardless. What's truly amazing is all the antiquities. They make the terracotta pots and glass flasks my father's uncovered look like so much rubbish." Her whisper dropped even lower. "I want to marry Lord Stafford."

The words Juliana had been waiting to hear. But her friend's sudden change of heart was...well, it was very sudden. "You cannot marry for antiquities," she whispered back, fearing

Amanda was making this decision for all the wrong reasons. "I would hope you would like the young man more than his possessions."

"Oh, I do. I've decided you're right. My wedding is drawing ever closer, and Lord Stafford and I suit well. We're compatible. He likes chess, and he's clearly interested in all things Roman. Maybe my father was right—maybe there are more important considerations than love. Besides, you said I will learn to love Lord Stafford, and I believe you."

Amanda *sounded* sincere, Juliana thought. Perhaps she should put aside her fears and just be relieved her friend was finally choosing an appropriate gentleman. They did share common interests, and they looked excellent together, and Amanda would make a good doctor's wife. It was unfortunate they hadn't the luxury to get to know each other leisurely, but the two of them had been destined to fall in love from the first. She'd said so all along, hadn't she?

She *was* relieved, she decided.

In fact, she was thrilled. How could she not be thrilled? With the possible exception of civilizing young Emily, all of her projects were progressing perfectly!

Lord Malmsey and Aunt Frances were getting along swimmingly. Indeed, at the ball last night, Juliana would swear she'd seen their aging eyes glittering with the fire of new love. Now that Lord Malmsey would no longer be obligated to wed Amanda, they would surely live happily ever after.

The duke seemed to be getting on with James and Amanda, which meant that after Juliana married him, she could remain friends with James. She and the duke would have to fall in love before marrying, of course—but maybe they were in love already! After all, how was a girl with her lack of experience supposed to know? And in any case, love was bound to happen soon. The duke cared for her, and he needed her. On the surface, he was perfect—everything she'd been looking for in a young man—but inside, he was hurt. With her help, he was going to learn to be affectionate and more charitable. And she was going to be a duchess! Her grace, Juliana, the Duchess of Castleton.

The name had a lovely ring to it, did it not?

And on top of all of that good news, it looked as though she'd managed to match Lady Stafford with Lord Cavanaugh, even though she'd only meant for them to enjoy a dance.

Clearly she wasn't losing her touch, after all.

Lady Stafford came into the alcove and handed Juliana and Amanda each a crested plate with a slice of the tart and a gold fork. "Your great-grandmother's recipe is delicious," she gushed. "Thank you so much for making and bringing it."

"You're very welcome," Juliana said, following her back to the main part of the room. Plate in hand, the duke wandered into the alcove and began chatting with Amanda. The tart was promoting new friendships already!

Lady Stafford seated herself on a chair covered in pale green satin with a palm tree design worked into the fabric. Lord Cavanaugh took the chair nearest hers. James was already sitting on the love seat, attacking a slice of tart. There were six more palm tree-decorated chairs and four matching stools, but Juliana sat on the love seat by James, even though she knew that place should be reserved for Amanda.

It would be for but a moment. She had something very important to discuss.

James didn't seem to find anything amiss with her sitting beside him. In fact, he shifted to face her, which put him rather too close. "This tart is excellent," he said. "Did you make it?"

"Of course," she said, trying to scoot a little to the side. Apparently the love seat was too small to share with a person of his size. "Your mother is getting along very well with Lord Cavanaugh, isn't she?"

"She seems to be, yes."

"They seem perfect for each other. His title even begins with C."

"C?"

"Like her sisters, don't you see? Aurelia is Lady Avonleigh, Bedelia is Lady Balmforth, and your mother would be—"

"Cornelia, Lady Cavanaugh. Yes, I see." Looking amused, he swallowed another bite. "But I should think there are more important things for a couple to share than matching names."

"Of course there are," she said, pleased to hear he agreed that couples should have things in common. "They should share interests—for example, chess and antiquities. And in your case especially, I should think you would want a wife who isn't disturbed by the presence of blood."

"I'm not a surgeon," he said patiently, "and I don't believe in bleeding patients. Nor would I expect a wife to assist me with my practice. So there's virtually no chance she would have to deal with blood."

That was a relief. For Amanda, of course—no lady should have to endure the sight of gore. "James…"

"You mentioned chess," he said. "Would you care for a game?"

"Lady Amanda adores chess." She really had something she needed to discuss. "I prefer playing cards, especially casino."

"I enjoy whist," he said. "Perhaps someday you can teach me casino. When is our next outing?" He reached for his glass of port, his arm brushing up against her in the process.

He should be touching Amanda instead. He should be making *her* shiver. Juliana leaned closer and lowered her voice. "You don't need any more lessons." She could smell his spicy scent.

"Oh." He took a sip and set down the glass, looking relieved. Or maybe disappointed.

No, relieved. For what reason could he be disappointed?

"Are you sure?" he asked.

"Quite. I've been thinking…"

"Yes?" Grazing her again, he forked up another bite.

Juliana lowered her voice. "We need to plan a way for you to publicly compromise Lady Amanda."

The fork clattered back to the plate. "Compromise Lady Amanda? Whyever would I do that?"

"In order to get her father to agree to your marrying her."

"What could make you think I'd do something so underhanded?" he hissed. Juliana couldn't tell whether he was more shocked or affronted. "And besides, why should her father reject me? It's not as though I'm a pauper."

That much was clear—a pauper didn't set his table with gold spoons. But if James reacted this way to the very idea of compromising Amanda, what would he do if he found out she was already engaged? What would he do if he realized that in order to marry her, he'd have to trick Lord Wolverston into breaking a contract with another man?

He'd refuse to marry her, that was what.

He was apparently too honorable to have anything to do with something as *underhanded* as what Juliana and Amanda had planned. But their plan wasn't underhanded—it was necessary. And under the circumstances, it was justified.

Lord Wolverston wasn't honorable—he was treating his daughter hideously—which meant dishonorable means were entirely justifiable to stop him.

But she knew James wouldn't see it that way. He was too good. Too good for his own good.

As Amanda and the duke stepped into the room from the alcove, Juliana sighed and moved to a chair so Amanda could sit beside James. But Amanda didn't, choosing another chair to sit upon instead, because, after all, she was a reserved sort of girl, and James's tall frame didn't leave very much room on the cozy love seat.

Heaven forbid Amanda should sit too close to a young man—even one she was planning on marrying.

Juliana rolled her eyes and took a bite of her tart, thinking that if James and Amanda weren't going to share the love seat, she should share it herself with the duke so she could start teaching him to be more affectionate. He'd chosen the chair beside her, unsurprisingly, but that wasn't close enough. Of course, before she could share the love seat with the duke, she'd have to get James to move off of it.

"Lord Stafford would like to pass some time playing chess," she told Amanda.

"Another time," James disagreed. "An evening is never long in good company."

"An ancient proverb," Amanda said with a small smile.

Whether it was a proverb or not, Juliana had failed to get James off the love seat. Oh, well, she thought with an internal sigh, she'd have to sit closer to the duke next time. And so she spent the evening being good company…all the while wracking her brains for a way to help a too-good person like James win the happiness he deserved.

And failing utterly to come up with anything.

~

"WHAT A LOVELY girl," Cornelia said after closing the door behind their guests.

James turned to her wearily. Spending time with Juliana—without being able to touch her—seemed to have worn him out. "Yes, Mother," he said. "Lady Amanda is quite lovely."

"Well, yes, she is, but I was speaking of Lady Juliana." She started up the wide, cantilevered stone staircase that led to the upper floors. "Lady Juliana is lovely on the inside, don't you think? Not that she isn't pretty, mind you—she's a darling little thing—but I think the way she tries so hard to help is lovely in itself. She really cares about people. She brought us all a sweet she made from her great-grandmother's recipe. She makes clothing for the Foundling Hospital. And she even volunteered to help at the New Hope Institute." Halfway up, she paused and turned to look back at him, her hand on the trompe l'oeil-painted metal balustrade. "A lady of the *ton*, helping at your Institute!"

James was quite aware that Juliana had mistakenly manipulated herself into that position, but he wouldn't say so to his mother. Because Cornelia was right. Juliana *was* lovely inside. She wasn't nearly as frivolous as he'd once thought. In fact, she wasn't frivolous at all.

"She's a treasure," his mother declared. "I think you should marry *her* instead of Lady Amanda."

"I never said I was marrying anyone!" James burst out in shock. The second time he'd been shocked this evening. Or rather, the third. The first had been when Juliana suggested he deliberately compromise Lady Amanda. The second had been when he nearly turned to her and replied, *What if I want to marry you instead?*

But he didn't want to marry her. He didn't want to marry anyone. He wasn't yet ready to face a loveless marriage. Least of all to a *treasure* like Juliana.

"Good night, Mother," he said, suddenly even wearier than before. But he took the steps two at a time so he could escape before his mother said anything more. "Sleep well," he called on the landing. Then he made his way down the corridor, ducked into the study, closed the door behind him, and dropped to the long leather sofa that sat before his father's big oak desk.

And there, without undressing—without even a thought of moving to his bedroom—he slept.

TWENTY-EIGHT

"**I** CANNOT believe you didn't tell me you'd talked to Lord Stafford," Amanda said the next afternoon. "What did he say, then?"

The day had dawned bright and sunny for a change, and if it wasn't exactly warm, at least it wasn't freezing. Following Juliana's rescheduled sewing party—after which, despite everyone's help, Emily had calculated that Juliana *still* needed a hundred and seventy-eight items of baby clothes—she'd taken Amanda across the street into Berkeley Square, where they sat on a bench beneath a plane tree, eating ices from Gunter's Tea Shop.

Or at least Juliana was eating hers.

"Do you know," she said, "this is the first ice I've had all summer." She scooped up the last spoonful and let it melt on her tongue. "Delicious. White currant is the best."

Amanda's strawberry ice sat in her dish untouched. "What did he say?" she repeated. "When does he think we should carry out our plan?"

Juliana sighed and licked her spoon. "He doesn't think we should carry out our plan at all. He called it *underhanded.*"

"Underhanded?"

"Yes. He wants to ask for your hand outright. He says there's no reason your father shouldn't agree."

"He doesn't know my father, then," Amanda said dejectedly. She poked her spoon at her melty pink ice, staring at the statue of King George in the middle of the square. "What did he say when you told him Father is too stubborn to break the agreement with Lord Malmsey?"

"I didn't tell him that. James—I mean, Lord Stafford—would never pursue you if he knew you're already engaged. He's too *honorable*." She spit out the last word.

"Like my father, putting his honor before my happiness."

"Lord Stafford isn't selfish, just principled. It's not the same."

"I don't see how it's different." Amanda slowly stirred what was now strawberry soup. "Why didn't you tell me this last night? On the way home in Lord Stafford's carriage?"

"I don't know," Juliana admitted. She shifted her gaze from Amanda's mopey face to the statue of their monarch. His Majesty was mounted on a horse, wearing some sort of draped garment she supposed was intended to be Greek or Roman. "I guess I was trying to figure out how to fix this."

"And what did you come up with?"

"Nothing."

"Nothing?" Amanda set the dish on the bench beside her. "You *always* have a plan."

"No, I don't." Juliana sighed. "I don't have a plan this time."

"Well, I do," Amanda declared.

Juliana couldn't have been more surprised if King George had suddenly come to life and danced a jig atop the horse. "You have a plan?"

"Yes. We shall trick Lord Stafford into compromising me."

"*We* shall do no such thing." Juliana wasn't sure which shocked her more: prissy Amanda suggesting such a plan or the thought of tricking someone who'd become her friend. "That would be reprehensible. Unethical. Completely disgraceful."

"Why? You said he wanted to marry me. If his supposed

honor is standing in the way, we'd be doing him a favor, wouldn't we?"

"No," Juliana said, and then, "Well, maybe. I don't know."

Amanda had a point. James *did* want to marry her. He'd said as much, hadn't he? He'd said Amanda was lovely—many times —and he'd said her father should accept his suit. He wouldn't *have* a suit if he wasn't wanting to marry her. Why else would he have bought her gifts and asked her to dance? More than once. At every ball, as a matter of fact. And he'd invited Amanda to his home.

Well, technically his mother had done the inviting. But it was his home, and surely she'd had his approval. "Do you enjoy playing whist?" she suddenly asked.

"Yes, but what does that have to do with anything?"

Amanda liked whist, as did James. And chess. And she wasn't sickened by blood. No wonder James loved her and wished to marry her. And the only way to make his wish come true was to...

Wasn't it?

"I think we should do it this Saturday," Amanda said, interrupting Juliana's line of reasoning. "At the Billingsgate ball."

Apparently Amanda had *destroyed* Juliana's line of reasoning, not just interrupted it. Because suddenly she wasn't sure everything quite made sense. "I don't know," she said again. "It just seems wrong somehow to plot behind Lord Stafford's back. It makes me feel guilty."

"Guilty? I think not." Juliana couldn't remember Amanda ever sounding so sure of herself. "I told you, we'll be doing him a *favor*."

There it was, that *we* again. That guilty-making *we*. "Maybe you should do this alone, Amanda."

"Why?" Amanda shifted to face her on the bench, her eyes not sparkling but pleading. "I cannot plan this alone. I need your help, Juliana—you're the bright one of us, after all."

Well, Amanda had *that* right. Bookish was not the same as bright.

"You cannot really feel guilty," Amanda added.

"Maybe just a bit."

"Well, you shouldn't."

Perhaps Amanda's arguments were valid. After all, James wanted to marry her. And Lord Malmsey certainly didn't. And Aunt Frances—dear, myopic Aunt Frances—would be devastated if Lord Malmsey left her for Amanda. The only person who would be happy if Amanda *didn't* trick James was her dratted, conniving father. Surely that would be the greater wrong.

That all sounded well justified, did it not?

Juliana's sisters often said that justification was one of her many talents.

"Well?" Amanda asked.

"All right. We'll make a plan."

TWENTY-NINE

ORANGE JUMBLES

Mix a cup of Flower with Almonds ground fine and Sugar, then add two spoones of grated

rinde of Oranges and Salt. Rub in some Butter and binde with beaten whites of two Egges.

When smooth, make into pieces and roll each out in the shape of an S. Bake on a greased tin

until browne and golden.

This receipt has been in our family for a very long time. They are a homely sort of biscuit, good

for taking to ailing villagers or anyone you like to make comfortable.

—Lady Diana Caldwell, 1689

JAMES HANDED the hopeful young woman a pencil and slid a piece of paper across the counter. "Write your name here, please, on line fourteen."

She squinted at the page.

"There," he elaborated, indicating the number *14.*

She bit her lip and wrote an awkward *X* beside it.

The eleventh *X* on the page.

"Thank you," he said, suppressing a sigh, "but I don't believe you will find this position suitable."

Her shoulders slumped as she turned, and he wished he could help. The introduction of new machinery was causing massive unemployment all over England, but his sympathy didn't change the fact that he required an assistant who could read and write.

As she plodded out of the New Hope Institute, Juliana danced in, gave a jaunty wave toward the Chase carriage outside, and stuck her umbrella in the stand by the door.

It was Wednesday, and—James checked his pocket watch—precisely one o'clock. Having not seen Juliana since the dinner at Stafford House on Sunday, he'd been wondering if she would actually show up. As she walked toward him, her smile seemed to brighten the whole reception room.

Though it was raining outside—of course—she was wearing a sunny yellow dress. A *thin,* sunny yellow dress.

"Good afternoon," he said. "No Lady Frances?"

"Oh, she'd be bored, and she doesn't care for this neighborhood. Besides, this is hardly a situation that requires a chaperone." She seemed to be peering at the area below his throat. "The carriage will return for me at four o'clock. Why are you out here?" Raising her gaze to his face, she placed the basket she was carrying on the counter between them. "Shouldn't you be in one of the treatment rooms, giving vaccinations?"

"I'm interviewing for a new assistant." He gestured toward the HELP WANTED sign he'd once again placed in the window. "And playing the part of assistant myself until I find one."

"I thought you'd already found a girl?"

"She left. This morning." The pouring rain had kept a queue from forming all the way to Surrey today, but that also meant potential new employees were staying home. Juliana seemed to be waiting for an explanation, so he added, "She found herself with child unexpectedly." Again. James half-believed there *was* something in the water.

"Unexpectedly? How can it be that a girl does what it takes to get a child without expecting to find herself with one?"

He was not at all interested in answering such an unseemly question. He was much more interested in *her* apparent interest in the bit of his skin that was exposed where he'd left his top button undone.

"She has no husband," he said, unfastening a second button just to see her reaction. "The father of her child cannot afford to support a wife."

"Oh." She looked a mite scandalized, but he wasn't sure whether it was due to the unbuttoning or to the news of his assistant's disgrace. "She must feel perfectly dreadful."

"Less dreadful, I expect, since I gave her fifty pounds and sent her off to get married."

Her entire face lit up. "Then she won't have to give her child to the Foundling Hospital. How sensationally kind of you, James!" The admiration in her voice made him want to kiss her.

All right, the mere sight of her made him want to kiss her.

He shifted uncomfortably, wishing they were someplace besides the Institute.

"I brought you orange jumbles," she said, lifting the cloth that covered the basket to reveal biscuits that smelled almost as good as she did. "They're supposed to be good for the ailing." She glanced around the crowded reception area. "Though I suppose these people aren't ailing, really, are they?"

"My aim is to *keep* them from ailing."

"Yes, of course. Well, the jumbles are supposed to help keep one comfortable as well. Try one."

As he took one of the sweets—wondering if it was so obvious that he was uncomfortable—a woman and her newly vaccinated son walked out, the youngster sucking a sugar stick.

"Excuse me," James said and stepped from behind the counter. "Number forty-three!"

Another woman and her two children rose and followed him into the back. Taking the biscuit with him, he showed them to a treatment room. The orange jumble was crisp and tasted sweet and citrusy, but it wasn't particularly comforting.

When he returned, Juliana was behind the counter, handing a number to a dripping family of four. "You're number fifty-seven," she said loudly and clearly. "Please be seated. Lord Stafford will call you when it's your turn."

James watched the family try and fail to find seats, then turned to Juliana. "I prefer to be called Dr. Trevor while I'm here. 'Lord Stafford' intimidates the patients."

"I'll try to remember that. There's a young man waiting to interview for the assistant position—I told him to sit until you were ready. Which of the treatment rooms shall I clean?"

"Pardon?"

"I came to clean treatment rooms, remember?" She pulled off her gloves. "I'm wearing my oldest dress."

He eyed her oldest dress. It looked no more shabby than the one she'd worn to his house for dinner, which meant, of course, that it didn't look shabby at all.

"What makes you think I would expect a lady to clean anything?" he asked. "The Stafford House maids take turns coming here to clean. Three times a week."

Her pretty brow creased. "Why did you tell Lady Amanda she could clean, then?"

He shrugged, remembering Lady Amanda's attitude at dinner. Very ladylike and rather snobbish. "I just wanted to see her reaction."

"Oh." Juliana looked thoughtful, or anxious—he wasn't sure which. "And what did you think of how she reacted?"

"Very much like a lady," he said, leaving out the word *snobbish*.

Now she looked relieved. "Amanda is very much a lovely lady," she said. "What shall you have me do if not clean treatment rooms?"

"You seem to make an excellent assistant. Why don't you keep doing that?"

She did prove to be an excellent assistant, which allowed him to vaccinate patients between interviewing candidates. Two hours later, the number of people in the reception room had dwindled to something approaching normal. The orange jumbles were all gone, and they'd indeed seemed to comfort some of the patients.

He'd talked to three more people who wanted the job, but none had been suitable.

"The tasks aren't very difficult," Juliana said during a rare lull. Her gaze flicked toward his open collar and back up. "Why haven't you been able to find an acceptable candidate?"

"My assistant must be able to read and write neatly."

"Is that all?" She handed him the box of sugar sticks he'd asked her to fetch. "I shall screen the applicants for you, then, and let you know if I find someone with those qualifications. You can keep giving vaccinations."

He wished he could find someone as efficient as Juliana. An hour later, she announced she'd found the perfect replacement, a young woman that Miss Smith, his last morning assistant, had apparently sent and recommended. All the supplies in the treatment rooms were restocked, the storage shelves were organized, Juliana had rewritten his scribbled July schedule in a tidy, legible hand, and—in part thanks to the rain—only five patients were waiting for vaccinations.

Even better, it was now four o'clock, which meant his second-shift assistant had arrived, as well as two fresh physicians. He was free, and it was Wednesday, so Parliament wasn't in session. Juliana's carriage was due to return any moment, but she had no chaperone, for once. Her curious gaze still rested where his shirt was unbuttoned whenever she thought he wasn't looking.

Most encouraging.

Maybe he could get her alone someplace where he could kiss her, he thought as he followed her toward the door. Maybe he could talk her into going somewhere besides home.

She pulled on her gloves. "Will I see you at Almack's tonight?"

Somewhere besides Almack's.

The door opened, admitting two new patients, a footman in

Chase livery, and a messenger boy. "Lord Stafford?" the messenger boy inquired.

"Yes." James took the note, broke the seal, and scanned the single page. "Blast it."

"Is it something dreadful?" Juliana asked, splaying a gloved hand over her bodice.

"No. Aunt Bedelia fears some ailment and wishes to see me."

"I hope she'll turn out to be well."

"She will, I assure you. But I'm afraid I won't make it to Almack's tonight."

"It's only four o'clock. How long can it take to examine her?"

"Very long," he fibbed. "I fear Aunt Aurelia will wish to be examined, too."

"How very unfortunate." She sighed prettily and pulled her umbrella out of the stand. "Shall I see you at the Billingsgate ball on Saturday, then?"

There was no way his mother would accept an excuse for not attending the Billingsgate ball. His aunts would be there, after all, so he could hardly claim that he must examine them again. "I'll be there," he promised.

It wasn't Almack's. And Juliana would be there, too. In another thin dress.

A pity he wouldn't be able to leave his top button undone.

THIRTY

THE **BILLINGSGATE** ball was in full swing, and music floated through the open door of Lord Billingsgate's library. "This will be perfect," Juliana said, glancing around. "It's close to the ballroom, so as soon as there's a commotion, plenty of people will come running to witness your disgrace."

Amanda tugged on the little puffed sleeves of the pale green dress Juliana had chosen for her. "Shall I have to kiss Lord Stafford for long?"

"I shouldn't think so. As soon as he starts kissing you, I shall fetch Lady Billingsgate to assure your ruin."

"What if he doesn't wish to kiss me?"

"Of course he wishes to kiss you! He's courting you, isn't he? Young men are always wishing to kiss ladies."

Except for the duke.

Juliana was beginning to wonder if she'd *ever* be kissed. The duke had been too busy to pay her any calls this week—doing what, she couldn't imagine—so she had yet to find an opportunity to start showing him how to be more affectionate. She knew he liked her more than ever, though, because he'd sent roses twice. That made three times he'd sent her roses! They were all white roses, of course, since he was proper and reserved. But he'd included notes these last two times—proper notes, very kind and complimentary—so she had high hopes he was falling deeper in love with her. After all, even Aunt Frances had received roses only once.

She turned her thoughts back to Amanda. "Remove your gloves so Lord Stafford can feel the warmth of your skin," she advised. "Drape yourself elegantly on the sofa. Before you lie down, douse two of the lamps. Low lighting is more romantic."

"Douse the lamps," Amanda repeated as though trying to memorize Juliana's instructions. "And take off my gloves." She tugged up the edge of her bodice.

"And stop playing with your dress." Juliana headed back to the ball, Amanda following at her heels. "It makes you look nervous."

"I *am* nervous." Entering the ballroom, Amanda paused. "Lord Stafford still isn't here. What if he doesn't come?"

"It's not even ten o'clock yet," Juliana said soothingly, scanning the glittering crush. James's mother wasn't here yet, either. Lord Cavanaugh was pacing like a caged animal waiting for food, looking as anxious to see Lady Stafford as Amanda was to see the lady's son. For different reasons, of course. "Stop worrying. Lord Stafford assured me he was attending."

"Then why isn't he here?" Amanda asked for the tenth time. Or maybe the twentieth.

Honestly, Juliana could hardly wait until midnight when James would compromise her friend, because even though tricking him still didn't sit quite right with her, it would be such a relief to have this whole business over and done with.

"Here comes the duke," Amanda said.

Juliana turned and smiled. She'd worn her most alluring dress, a pale rose confection with a wide neckline that hung just on the edge of her shoulders.

But he didn't look allured.

He did return her smile, though. "Good evening, my dear."

His gaze shifted to her friend. "Good evening, Lady Amanda," he added formally.

"Good evening, your grace," Amanda replied, sounding every bit as formal.

And that was when Juliana had a sudden bright idea.

She would encourage the duke to dance with Amanda. Seeing how tiresome it was to dance with someone so reserved might help him loosen up a bit. And in the meantime, while Amanda was dancing with him in a tiresome manner, Juliana would dance with other young men in her usual charming, vivacious way.

After all, she had no shortage of dance invitations. Perhaps a few less than normal, since she'd been dancing so often with the duke lately, but that hadn't stopped gentlemen from asking when the duke wasn't nearby to intimidate them. And there was another obvious benefit to accepting other invitations—it would also make the duke jealous and possessive!

"Lady Amanda would love to dance," she told him with a sweet smile. "Why don't you ask her for the next waltz?"

She didn't know who looked more startled, the duke or Amanda. But as the musicians struck up a waltz, he bowed to Amanda very properly—no surprise there—and escorted her to the dance floor.

Juliana turned, expecting to be inundated with invitations. Any moment, now. As soon as the other gentlemen noticed she was on her own.

Unfortunately, Corinna noticed first. "Is your duke courting Amanda?"

"Of course he isn't. Amanda would never consent to marry him—he's a by-blow, remember? But I thought it would be a good idea for them to get to know each other better, so I suggested they dance."

"If you wish to marry the fellow, you shouldn't shove him at other girls. What if he kisses her? He might decide he wants her instead, and Amanda could change her mind—"

"He's not going to kiss her," Juliana interrupted.

Corinna measured her a moment. "How can you be so sure?"

"He isn't interested in her—he doesn't call her *my dear*. And he's extremely reserved. He hasn't even kissed *me*."

"Then how on earth do you know you love him?" Corinna asked.

Juliana remained silent, wondering yet again how a girl who'd never been in love was supposed to *know* she was in love.

Her sister added, "And how do you know you want to marry him?"

"What do you mean, how do I know?" He was kind. He sent her flowers. He enjoyed amusements, fine horses, balls, and entertainments. He had wealth to support himself in style. He was classically handsome, as only an aristocratic Englishman could be. And he was a duke. "Who—besides Amanda—wouldn't want to marry him?"

"You really must kiss a young man before you marry him. In my experience, it makes all the difference."

"In your experience? What experience?"

"Kissing experience, of course."

"What?" Corinna was a year younger and far more interested in paint than men! How was it that she'd been kissed, while Juliana had scarcely even been touched?

"What?" Corinna blinked. "Have you not kissed anyone?"

"No!"

"Well, what have you been doing all season, then? Gentlemen don't all kiss the same, you know," her younger sister informed her with the surety of an experienced woman.

This was news to Juliana—how many different sorts of kissing were there?

Corinna crossed her arms. "How is a lady to know she's found her prince if she hasn't kissed a few frogs first?"

"Really, Corinna." The girl always *had* been a bit of a rebel, but this was quite beyond the pale. "I'd wager Aunt Frances—

your chaperone, in case you forgot?—wouldn't approve of you kissing gentlemen you've barely met."

"I don't let them kiss me when I've barely met them." Corinna's chin went into the air. "I make them wait at least a week."

"A week!" Juliana had known the duke *much* longer than a week.

"At least," Corinna repeated. "And as for Aunt Frances, she's known Lord Malmsey quite a bit longer than a week. Let's ask her if she's kissed him." She signaled to their aunt as she was coming off the dance floor.

Aunt Frances didn't notice. On Juliana's recommendation, she still wasn't wearing her spectacles. Which was a good thing, because such a question might make the poor spinster faint. "You cannot ask her that!"

"Why not?" Corinna said, marching toward her.

Juliana followed helplessly.

"Aunt Frances!" Corinna called.

"Yes?" Their aunt turned and squinted. "Oh, there you are, girls. Are you having a wonderful time?"

Corinna ignored her question, which was probably rhetorical anyway. "Aunt Frances, have you kissed Lord Malmsey?"

Two bright spots appeared on their aunt's cheeks. "Well…"

"Have you?" Corinna demanded.

Frances squared her shoulders and lowered her voice. "I'm not a green girl, you know. It's no great sin. A woman should kiss a man before she decides to marry him."

Faith! Aunt Frances had kissed Lord Malmsey!

And she wanted to marry him! Juliana was torn between jubilation at her project's success and shock at hearing that her shy, oblivious, spinster aunt had been kissed.

And *she* hadn't.

That made her officially the oldest unkissed woman in England.

Well, there was Amanda. But come midnight, when James

compromised her, even straitlaced Amanda would be kissed. Which meant Juliana would stand alone.

It was depressing beyond description.

"Aunt Frances!" Alexandra joined their circle with Tristan. "I've never seen you look so happy."

Aunt Frances kissed her on the cheek. "You look happy, too."

"I am, Aunty." Alexandra smiled up at Tristan. Love blazed in their eyes. "We are."

Splendid. Everyone was happy. Except Juliana.

James joined their circle next, squeezing in beside her. "Good evening, everyone."

While it was a relief that he'd finally arrived, Juliana was even more relieved to see he didn't look insanely happy. It was odd, because she usually wanted to see everybody happy. But honestly, right now the sight of one more blatantly happy person would likely make her gag.

"Are your aunts doing well?" she asked.

"They're fine. Not that they'd say the same—they're both convinced they're at death's door." He gestured toward the edge of the dance floor, where the two older ladies were talking to his mother. "They summoned me yet again this afternoon."

"They're keeping you from getting your important work done, aren't they?"

"Somewhat. But they're family." He shrugged philosophically. "What can I do?"

"There has to be something." She watched Lord Cavanaugh claim Lady Stafford for a dance. "Maybe they need suitors, like your mother. She's happy."

"I'm happy," Aunt Frances said with a nod of approval. "A suitor will do that for a lady."

"But I'm happy," Corinna pointed out, "and I don't have a suitor."

No, but she'd been kissed. Juliana glared at her.

Corinna glared back, then smiled sweetly. "Alexandra's happy, too."

"That's because she's with child," James said.

A little hush fell over their circle. Juliana swung to her older sister. "Is that true?"

"It is," Tristan confirmed. Beaming, he slid an arm around his wife's waist. "We're both thrilled."

James looked stricken. "My sincerest apologies. I didn't realize you hadn't told—"

He was drowned out by Corinna's and Aunt Frances's shrieks as they engulfed Tristan and Alexandra in a group hug.

Juliana took a step back. Corinna had been kissed, and Alexandra and Tristan were going to have a baby. She was happy for them. And for herself, for the whole family. She was pleased. Joyous. Jubilant. And something else. Something that made her fists clench at her sides.

"You're jealous," James said in her ear.

"I am not." Dismayed, she turned to him. "I'm happy for my sister. And for me. I'll have a niece or nephew to play with. How on earth did you know she was carrying a child?"

James shrugged. "I'm a physician."

With a huff she spun back around, intending to join the family celebration.

He stopped her with a hand on her arm. "Your turn will come," he said.

"Who said I wanted a turn?"

He shrugged again and removed his hand.

With her head held high, she strutted off to congratulate the beaming couple.

James left the Chases alone to enjoy a private family moment. He needed a drink.

Watching the scene had left an odd mix of emotions swirling inside him. Seeing Hawkridge's elation recalled his own happy memories, which recalled sad memories, all of which brought on a new and appalling realization.

He was jealous, too.

THIRTY-ONE

"**Y**OU'RE FOXED," Juliana told James later as they danced.

"Maybe." His thumb made its way beneath the edge of her glove and tickled the sensitive skin on the underside of her wrist. "Or maybe not."

"You are." She laughed, suppressing a shiver. "You've had three cups of punch tonight already."

"Four," he corrected. "Small cups. In two hours. And how would you come to know that, anyway? Are you watching me, Juliana?"

"Of course not," she said quickly, avoiding his eyes. Her gaze fell on his cravat, and she found herself picturing the golden skin she knew was behind it. And wondering what the rest of his chest might look like below it. Were men's chests truly all ridged and muscled like the centaur statue's had been? Or was that just artistic license?

It really wasn't fair how—in contrast to ladies' fashions— gentlemen's attire left *everything* to the imagination.

"Hmm," he said. A smug-sounding *hmm*. She looked up again to find him gazing at her in that way that made her fear he could read her mind. The pad of his thumb kept skimming her wrist.

It seemed liquor made him even more amorous than macaroons. Which was uncomfortable for Juliana, but also a good thing, because it meant Amanda would have an easier time getting herself compromised.

And poor, demure Amanda would need all the help she could get.

On the other side of the dance floor, Amanda was paired again with the duke, the both of them rigid as ever. In the two hours since Juliana suggested they dance together, she herself had danced with twelve other young men. Vivaciously and enthusiastically. But the duke hadn't seemed to take any note.

It hadn't helped that he'd spent more than half of those two hours in the card room.

Between Juliana's dozen dances, the duke had emerged and danced with her twice, but despite all her efforts to draw him out, she hadn't got him any closer to kissing her.

Still gazing at James's cravat, she tried to picture the duke's skin in the open V of a shirt. She imagined it would be ivory instead of golden. But he probably never loosened his collar, anyway. He probably went to bed fully dressed, with his shirt fastened up to his chin, a cravat knotted in layers to cover it, and a waistcoat and tailcoat besides. Both fully buttoned.

It was heartbreaking, really. He truly needed a girl like her in his life. She resolved to remain patient, to keep working toward his happiness, no matter how long the process took. After all, it had taken an entire childhood of cold treatment to turn him into the man he was today. She shouldn't be surprised if it took more than a few weeks of warmth to counteract that.

Thankfully, the rest of her projects were coming along nicely. Aunt Frances and Lord Malmsey had kissed. Lord Cavanaugh had danced three times with Lady Stafford, and they'd probably kissed as well. And Amanda and James would be kissing soon.

Every woman in London would be kissed tonight except for Juliana.

Unless…

Maneuvering the last few steps of the dance to end up by Amanda and the duke, she curtsied to James and then turned to them. "Shall we exchange partners?"

The duke looked so startled at her forwardness, she nearly lost her nerve. But she'd never been one to just stand by and let things happen—or in this case, not happen—so when the musicians resumed playing, she got the duke into position, steeled herself, and began surreptitiously inching him toward a potted palm.

At least she *tried* to be surreptitious. Unfortunately, the tune wasn't a waltz but a minuet—which meant the dancers moved back and forth rather than progressing in a particular direction.

"I'm supposed to lead, my dear," the duke gently chided. "Why are you taking larger steps towards the right than the left?"

She decided not to play coy. The duke never seemed to take a hint, so she'd best come out and say it. "I'm hoping to get you alone behind that potted palm."

"Pardon?"

"I'm hoping for a kiss."

He blinked. "Before marriage?"

She mentally rolled her eyes. "Yes, before marriage." And though she'd never expected to quote Aunt Frances regarding intimate matters, she found herself adding, "It's no great sin, you know."

"Perhaps not, my dear, but it also wouldn't be proper."

Her heart sank. "Don't you *want* to kiss me?" she asked. "You're courting me. You've sent me flowers three times. I thought you were falling in love with me."

The instant the words left her mouth she wished she could stuff them back in.

Until he said, "Oh, but I am."

Oh, but I am!

Her heart soared. The duke *was* falling in love with her! She'd swear she could hear birds singing. Or perhaps they were angels. Either way, it meant everything was marvelous! She and the duke would be married—just as soon as she finished falling in love with him. She'd be a duchess! People would call her *your grace!*

It was more than enough to make up for having to wait for her wedding day to be kissed.

As the dance ended, the clock struck midnight. Finally. After thanking the duke rather profusely, she hurried to meet Amanda.

"It's midnight."

"I know." Amanda looked paler than normal. Paler than the duke. Paler than Juliana suddenly felt.

Juliana didn't know how a person could *feel* pale, but somehow, despite her recent elation, she did. "Are you sure you want to go through with this?"

"I cannot marry Lord Malmsey."

Of course she couldn't. That would be a disaster for everyone involved. Especially dear Aunt Frances.

"You're going to have to kiss Lord Stafford," Juliana warned. The thought made her stomach turn. But only because she was about to be the only unkissed girl in England.

"Right." Amanda rolled her head about her neck, as if loosening up.

"And you're going to have to get close to him."

"I know." She was breathing deeply, in through her nose, out through her mouth.

Juliana's hands gripped both of Amanda's shoulders. She looked her friend dead in the eye and spoke very clearly. "A chaste, hands-off kiss won't be enough to guarantee a compromise."

The girl's fists clenched in determination. "I can do it."

With a decisive nod, Juliana let go and stepped back. Amanda was ready.

"All right, then. I'll bring Lord Stafford to the library. Remember to take off your gloves. And make your voice a little breathy."

Amanda marched off to do as she was told. Juliana watched her go, thinking she looked more like a soldier going into battle than a young woman about to get herself engaged to a rich, handsome, earl.

Juliana felt paler than ever.

But it was too late to call off the plan. If they delayed the compromise much longer, it might not happen at all. And it wouldn't be fair to deprive Amanda, James, Lord Malmsey, and Aunt Frances of their happiness just to save Juliana from a little distress.

Besides, she'd feel much better soon. There'd be a huge scandal following Amanda's compromise, which would make her overbearing father come running to London. He would demand that his daughter wed the culprit. It would all be over quickly. And then Amanda would be happily married. To James. She'd move into his grand, antiquity-filled house, and she'd go all tingly when he touched her, and...

And Juliana would feel better.

But right now she was feeling a little sick.

She found James standing in a group of men, sipping another drink while Lord Occlestone grumbled about unnecessary "reforms" that had been introduced in Parliament. She'd been planning to feign a troubled expression, but given her current mood, she didn't need to. She tapped James on the shoulder.

He turned and looked down at her. "Juliana."

She pulled him away from the group. "What an unpleasant man. His face suits his personality, don't you think? His nose is square just like a pig's."

"I've often thought that myself," James said, a tipsy smile curving his lips.

Excellent. She wanted him tipsy and amorous. "Lady Amanda is feeling ill."

"I was just dancing with her. She looked fine."

"Well, she's feeling ill now. She went to the library to lie down. Will you come and have a look at her?"

"Of course," he said, suddenly looking sober and concerned.

She led him to the library, where Amanda was draped elegantly on the sofa, emitting little moans of "pain." She'd followed Juliana's instructions exactly. Her gloves were on the desk, and the room was romantically lit, not too dark and not too light.

James set his drink and his own gloves beside Amanda's, then knelt by the sofa. "Lady Amanda, where does it hurt?"

"It's my heart," Amanda said breathily, laying a graceful bare hand on the skin exposed by her neckline. She was a surprisingly good actress. James didn't stand a chance.

"You're a mite young for heart trouble," he told her.

"But it aches," she insisted, implying it ached for him. "Won't you listen to it at least?"

"If you wish." He rose to his feet.

"You cannot listen from there." With a sultry pout, Amanda patted her chest and leaned toward him. Faith, she was practically falling off the sofa. "You need to press your ear to my heart."

"No, I don't." He walked over to the writing desk. "I can hear it better through a tube."

"Are you sure?" Amanda asked.

"I'm positive." He opened a couple of drawers, then found a piece of paper and rolled it up. "This won't work as well as my new stethoscope, but it should be better than listening without it."

Juliana was flabbergasted. James seemed completely oblivious to Amanda's shameless antics. Was he the thickest fellow who ever lived?

Crossing back to Amanda, he placed one end of the paper

tube on her chest and lowered his ear to the other. Except for Amanda's breathy sighs, the room was silent for a moment.

"A little fast," he reported at last. "But strong and steady."

Apparently at a loss, Amanda looked toward Juliana.

"Maybe Lady Amanda has a rash," she said. "James, I think you should loosen her clothes and have a look."

He eyed Amanda's bare arms and low décolletage in an altogether clinical manner. "I see no evidence of a rash." He smiled at his patient, but it was a kind smile, not romantic in the least. "This ball is quite a crush. If you've no symptoms to report other than a vague ache in your chest, perhaps sitting quietly for a few minutes might help."

Juliana didn't know what to think. Amanda was doing everything right, yet James appeared unmoved.

Then she suddenly realized why. "Please stay with her while she sits quietly, James. I'm going to fetch Lady Billingsgate."

She didn't, of course—there was no point in fetching Lady Billingsgate until James and her friend got into a compromising position. Which clearly wasn't going to happen with her in the room. Of course James wasn't going to kiss Amanda while another girl watched! Juliana, not he, was the one acting thick.

She went out quietly, leaving the door slightly cracked so she could listen.

"I'm sure you'll feel better in no time," she heard James say.

"I'd feel better if you'd sit beside me."

"I cannot imagine how that could help," James said. But apparently he did sit down, because the next thing he said was, "There. Do you feel better?"

"No, not yet," Amanda said and paused. And then she added, "Why don't you kiss me to make me feel better?"

A shocked silence followed. Juliana was shocked, too. She'd never dreamed Amanda had it in her! But then the silence continued, and Juliana realized it wasn't a shocked silence. It was the silence that resulted when two people were kissing instead of talking.

Amanda's boldness had *worked*.

Well, of course it had worked. Hadn't Juliana said it would?

But although she should be celebrating her plan's success, she didn't feel any better. In fact, she felt worse. She felt *underhanded*. She felt like she'd betrayed someone she'd come to think of as a friend.

"I don't think that would be a good idea," James finally said.

Juliana couldn't figure out what he meant by that, exactly, but her despair lifted. She released a breath she hadn't realized she'd been holding. He hadn't kissed Amanda. Not yet, anyway. She sagged against the door in relief.

Or rather, she *thumped* against the door in relief. And then it opened, and she all but fell into the library.

James caught her by her shoulders and grinned. "I thought you were Lady Billingsgate."

Of course he had. She'd said she was going to fetch Lady Billingsgate, after all. A mistake, she now realized, because of course James wouldn't kiss Amanda while expecting their hostess to show up at any moment.

That was why he'd said it wouldn't be a good idea.

But his hands felt warm on her shoulders, and she couldn't be sorry she'd made the mistake. She didn't want to trick James. She hadn't wanted to from the first. She was furious with herself for allowing Amanda to talk her into it.

"I'll fetch Lady Billingsgate," he said, "while *you* sit with Lady Amanda." And then he left, taking his warm hands with him.

Juliana made her way to the sofa and collapsed beside her friend.

Poor Amanda was shaking. "I did it," she said. "I forced myself to do it. And it didn't work!"

"I'm glad it didn't work. It was unethical to begin with. We mustn't try it again." It had made her feel too guilty. In fact, she *still* felt guilty. She wondered if she'd ever be able to look at James again without feeling a pang of guilt.

"But why didn't it work? I did everything you said, but he wouldn't kiss me."

That had been Juliana's fault, but she wouldn't admit it to Amanda. Besides, Amanda was equally to blame. If she had shown any warmth towards him—*him*, not his antiquities—before tonight, he wouldn't have been able to keep his hands off her, no matter who might see. After all, he'd wrapped his arms around Juliana in a museum crowded with people, and he wasn't even courting her!

Carefully, she said, "Maybe he wouldn't kiss you because you haven't allowed him to kiss you before."

"He never *tried* before," Amanda said. "He isn't a particularly warm person."

Juliana nearly dissolved into laughter. Not only was Amanda's judgement false and absurd, but she could scarcely believe she was hearing her, of all people, complain someone *else* wasn't warm.

Especially James. Why, James was the warmest fellow she knew. "You need to act more warmly towards *him*. You have to make him believe you want him."

"I *do* want him. I cannot marry Lord Malmsey! And our wedding is only two weeks away! I must tell Lord Stafford about my engagement."

"You cannot. He's too honorable to compromise you on purpose."

"Then how on earth am I to get him to compromise me at all?"

"You need to let him kiss you, and I don't mean as part of a plot. One kiss will lead to another, and eventually you'll be discovered. Society is a nosy lot, in case you haven't noticed."

"That sounds like a plot," Amanda pointed out.

"It isn't." All right, maybe it was. But it wasn't the same sort of plot as the one they'd tried tonight. Corinna had said that a kiss made all the difference. Once Amanda and James kissed, they'd both want to kiss some more, and the rest would happen naturally.

Surely there would be no reason to feel guilty about that.

"Lady Amanda!" Lady Billingsgate exclaimed, rushing in. "Are you unwell? Before Lord Stafford left, he told me you'd taken ill."

So James had left. Juliana wouldn't have to face him tonight after the way she'd betrayed their friendship. That was a relief, she thought as Amanda explained to Lady Billingsgate that she was quite recovered, thank you.

So why did it feel more like a disappointment?

THIRTY-TWO

RICHMOND MAIDS OF HONOUR

Mix Curd with Butter and add 4 yolks of Eggs beaten with a glass of Brandy, half a cup of Sugar, fine white Breadcrumbs with some ground Almonds and a little Nutmeg. To this put the juice of one Lemon and the grated yellow of 2. Press puff paste into your tins and fill and bake.

These small, rich cheesecakes are from a recipe said to have been in the family since Queen Elizabeth's (my namesake's) time. They will melt anyone. Excellent for begging forgiveness.

—Elizabeth, Countess of Greystone, 1728

THE NEXT morning dawned unusually bright and sunny, which should have made Juliana feel cheerful. But instead she still felt guilty.

It being Sunday, she attended St. George's Hanover Square Church, where the sermon was all about honesty, which made her feel even more guilty. So guilty that afterward she baked some Richmond Maids of Honour and asked Griffin to take her to Stafford House.

"Why?" he asked.

A perfectly reasonable question, but one she didn't want to answer. She was too ashamed of her actions to admit them to her brother.

"I just want to ask Lord Stafford if he'd like me to volunteer next week at the Institute," she said. That wasn't quite a lie, since she'd been wondering when he might need her again. "I forgot to ask him last night." With all that had gone on at the ball, she really *had* forgotten.

"You could send him a note," Griffin suggested.

"Just take me, will you?"

"Very well." Griffin shook his head in that mystified, brotherly way of his. "I cannot imagine why a note won't do, but I'll take you."

"Thank you," she said.

When he was sitting across from her in the carriage, he stretched out his legs and steepled his fingers. "How is your romance with Castleton proceeding?"

She fiddled with the platter on her lap, feeling shy about talking of such things to her brother. "He says he's falling in love with me, but he hasn't kissed me yet."

"He's a gentleman," Griffin said, looking not at all unpleased. "He shouldn't kiss you before you're wed. Or engaged at the very least."

Trust a brother to think that. She considered telling him Corinna believed a lady should kiss some frogs so she'll know when she's met her prince, but thought better of it. There was no point in getting Corinna in trouble, and besides, she was beginning to think her sister was right. If James and Amanda had already become close, perhaps the plan would have succeeded and they'd be engaged by now.

Not that she wished for *that,* mind you. She felt guilty enough as it was.

"The duke would agree with you," she said instead, in what she hoped was a neutral tone.

"I'm certain he'll ask for your hand soon." Griffin awkwardly patted her knee. "I'll have a talk with him in my stables."

"Pardon?" What did his stables have to do with anything?

"Never mind. We've arrived." The carriage halted in St. James's Place, and Griffin began to climb out after her.

"Wait here," she said.

"Why?"

"Just wait, will you? I cannot stay long—I have ladies coming to sew at two o'clock." All of her projects were beginning to make her feel a bit frazzled. "It won't take me but a minute to ask one simple question."

"Very well," he said, again shaking his head in that mystified, brotherly way. He plopped back onto the seat.

She banged the knocker, and the door was opened by the same crimson-liveried footman who had welcomed her last week. Through the window at the back of the entrance hall, Lady Stafford waved from the courtyard garden, then hurried inside to meet her. "How are you, my dear? I didn't expect to see you until your sewing party this afternoon. What do you have there?"

Juliana handed her the platter. "Some Richmond Maids of Honour for Lord Stafford. And for you, too, of course."

"They smell divine."

"I've come to ask Lord Stafford a quick question. Is he at home?"

"He's upstairs in his study, spending this beautiful day going over the Institute's books." Shaking her head in a fond, motherly way, she started toward the staircase. "Follow me, if you will."

It was quite the most elegant staircase Juliana had ever seen. The metal balustrade was painted to look like festooned drapery. Above her head, a segmented barrel ceiling gave the impression of a classical temple interior with garlands swagged between Roman pilasters.

She assumed Lady Stafford was leading her toward the study, but instead she walked her through an impressive library and into the most splendid room Juliana had ever seen. If she had been a fortune-hunting sort of girl, the very sight of it would have made her want to marry James. It put the gorgeous Palm Room below it to shame.

She'd never seen so much gilt in her life. It dazzled the eye. Fancy gilt columns supported a gilt ceiling. Between all the gleaming gilt, the walls were covered with painted scenes.

"We call this the Painted Room," Lady Stafford said. "Marriage is the theme."

Juliana nearly swooned over the frieze painted on the chimneypiece.

"Beautiful, isn't it?" Lady Stafford set the platter of cheesecakes on a gilt-legged marble-topped table. "It's a copy of the celebrated *Aldobrandini Wedding*, a Roman fresco excavated in the early seventeenth century and exhibited in the Vatican."

"It's exquisite," Juliana breathed. The theme of marriage continued all around the room. Above a pier glass, a circular panel displayed a painting of another Roman wedding. Other panels depicted music, drinking, and dancing. There were paintings of Cupid and Venus. Nymphs danced on the ceiling, lovers courted on the walls, and a frieze of rose wreaths and garlands of flowers went all around the cornice.

The whole mood was festive and carefree.

"Isn't marriage wonderful?" Lady Stafford said. "Please have a seat. I'll send in my son."

Juliana perched herself on one of four green silk sofas with gilt arms carved to look like winged lions. She folded her hands in her lap. She crossed her feet and uncrossed them. She rose and circled the room.

The winged lion sofas had six matching chairs, and she was heading for one of them when James walked in.

"Here," she said, grabbing the platter. "I brought these cheesecakes for you."

He took them, looking as mystified as Griffin. But not at all brotherly.

Not only was he without a coat or cravat and his shirt was unbuttoned at the neck again, but he'd rolled up his cuffs, too. A good six inches of his forearms were bare—strong-looking fore-arms, lightly sprinkled with dark hair.

"What are you doing here, Juliana?"

She jerked her gaze up to his face. There was no sense putting it off. "I came to apologize. Won't you have one of the cheese-cakes? The recipe is said to have been in my family since Queen Elizabeth's time."

He set down the platter. "Apologize for what?"

He wasn't going to eat any Richmond Maids of Honour. She prayed he'd forgive her without their magic. "For plotting with Lady Amanda to trick you into compromising her," she confessed in a rush. "In the library last night. I was hoping you would kiss her, and then I'd bring Lady Billingsgate to witness Lady Amanda's disgrace, so her father would be forced to assent to your marriage." She drew a shaky breath. "Can you forgive me?"

"That's—"

He had no more words, it seemed.

He turned away and sat abruptly on a sofa. He ran his hands through his dark, disheveled hair. He sprang back to his feet and walked a few paces away from her, his fists clenched.

Finally he turned back to her. She quailed. She'd known he would disapprove, but she hadn't expected him to look quite so severe. And so hurt. "Why would you do that?" he asked.

"Amanda doesn't believe her father will accept your suit. He isn't a very nice man."

"Surely he isn't an idiot." He unclenched his fists, but only to cross his half-bare arms. "I'm excellent husband material."

He certainly had a fine opinion of himself—though it wasn't unjustified, Juliana reminded herself. A man of James's wealth and status was a superb catch. "I'm sorry I went behind your back," she said, "but why are you so upset? However devious the means, the outcome would have been positive. You'd have found yourself married to the girl you love. Unless…"

An awful thought suddenly occurred to her.

She'd assumed that since he was still courting Amanda, he must have fallen in love with her. But what if he hadn't? What if her scheming had resulted in James being forced to marry a girl he didn't love?

"Do you not love Lady Amanda yet?" She held her breath, waiting for the answer.

"No," he said, looking quite sure. Not to mention appalled. It was the answer she'd dreaded.

So why did she feel relieved?

"Maybe you're in love with her, but you don't know it," she suggested. "Maybe you don't know what love feels like." It was a reasonable theory, certainly. She'd been wondering the same, after all.

But now he looked annoyed. "I know what love feels like, Juliana."

That was surprising news. "You've been in love before?"

"Yes. With my wife."

She couldn't have been more shocked if he'd punched her in the stomach. In fact, it felt like he *had* punched her in the stomach. She gasped for breath. "You have a wife?"

"I *had* a wife," he corrected. "Her name was Anne. She died in childbirth, along with our baby. More than a year ago."

"Dear heavens." The pain in Juliana's middle became an ache in her chest. She sank onto a chair. "I didn't know. I'm sorry. I'm sorry for everything."

Wearily, he lowered himself onto a chair of his own. He no longer looked angry or annoyed; he just looked sad. "I forgive you." His voice was hollow. "What you did was still dreadful, but I know your heart was in the right place. I forgive you as long as you promise not to try it ever again."

"Thank you," she whispered, not quite listening. She was thinking about his wife. He'd loved a wife, and she'd carried their baby, and they'd both died. It was utterly heartbreaking. Juliana couldn't bear it. She felt like curling up in her bed and crying for a week.

Then she realized what he'd said. "I won't try it again. I promise. And a Chase promise is never broken. That's been our family motto for centuries." Biting her lip, she grasped the two lion heads on her chair as though they could lend her their strength. "James, I'm so sorry you lost your family."

"You've lost family, too," he said.

"But not a child. It must be hardest to lose a child."

He nodded. "I didn't even get to meet him."

Her heart broke all over again. For his family, for him. She knew grief, knew how much it hurt, knew it took a long while to resume living life fully. And he'd lost not only a child, but a wife as well. It would take him time to recover, to allow himself to love another.

And like a ninny, she'd been putting pressure on him, pushing him toward Amanda.

She hadn't realized.

He needed more time. He'd said wonderful things about Amanda, and he wouldn't still be courting her if he didn't feel something. The potential existed. But he needed more time to fall in love with her.

A pity he had only two weeks.

Thirteen days, actually. Twelve days if he didn't see Amanda again until tomorrow. She couldn't let him wait any longer than that, or he might lose her.

She couldn't let him suffer yet another loss.

"Do you ever think," she said carefully, "about having more children?"

"My dear mother thinks about it for me," he said with a hint of his normal good humor.

"James…"

"Yes, I want more children." He paused and looked away, his voice going lower, quieter. "Even though I'll never fall in love again, someday I'll have to remarry."

How could he say such a thing? "You cannot marry without falling in love."

"People do it all the time," he said, looking back to her. "There are many reasons people marry besides love. Wealth, ambition, position, security, duty, honor. And to have children."

She changed tack. "How can you possibly know you'll never fall in love again?"

"I just do," he said flatly. "Falling in love would mean betraying Anne, and that isn't going to happen." He sighed, rubbing his forehead. "I could never marry someone I disliked, but certainly I could marry a friend. I could have children with a friend."

Juliana sighed, too. He seemed at peace with the idea, but…

Wealth, ambition, position, security, duty, honor…to have children. Those were sad reasons to wed, in her opinion—and old reasons as well. Her parents had married for such reasons. Today, in these modern times, most people her age preferred love matches.

Except…maybe Amanda.

Lord Stafford and I suit well, she remembered Amanda saying. *We're compatible. Maybe my father was right—maybe there are more important considerations than love.*

At the time, she'd worried that Amanda had decided to marry James for all the wrong reasons. But maybe the two were even better matched than she'd thought. Marriage would give them both what they wanted. Children for James, and a young, compatible husband for Amanda.

"Juliana?" James said. "What are you thinking?"

Still sad for him, she forced a smile. "I'm thinking that the two of us practiced going on outings during your lessons, but you've still had no outings with Lady Amanda."

"You want me to take Lady Amanda riding in Hyde Park? Or to the Egyptian Hall?"

"Not exactly." If James and Amanda were to become fast friends—fast enough to marry in less than two weeks—he'd need to take her someplace more idyllic. "I was thinking Vauxhall Gardens would be perfect."

She'd never been to Vauxhall Gardens, but from what she'd heard, there was no atmosphere more suitable for fostering intimacy. The gardens were described as a paradise of lush paths with many private corners, and at night they were lit by hundreds of lanterns. It sounded lovely.

"Vauxhall Gardens?" James repeated skeptically. From what he'd heard, the gardens served mainly as a spot for unseemly romantic trysts. "I've never been to Vauxhall Gardens."

"Haven't you?" Juliana said. "It's a lovely place."

A lovely place, indeed—to steal a lady's virtue.

Or a kiss.

Hmm. An intriguing thought. While James had no interest in stealing a kiss from Lady Amanda, he suspected he might rather enjoy the gardens with Juliana on his arm.

Getting her there, however, might be a trick to rival hers.

Now that he knew what Juliana was capable of, he wouldn't make the mistake of underestimating her again. Although he'd realized meddling was in her blood—one didn't have to know her more than a few minutes to be sure of *that*—he was still feeling somewhat dazed by her confession. Dazed and a little bit panicked. The fact that she was willing to resort to trickery in order to "help" her friends find love was nearly as terrifying as how close her plan had come to succeeding.

Not that he'd been tempted for even an instant to accept Lady Amanda's advances. But if they'd been discovered in the library at the wrong moment, it might have looked very bad for them both.

Meanwhile, he could only conclude that his own attempts with Juliana were falling pathetically short, or else she wouldn't be so eager to trap him into marrying her prissy friend. He'd have to redouble his efforts if he wanted to kiss her and make sure she didn't ruin her life by marrying that turd Castleton.

"I wouldn't know where to take Lady Amanda in Vauxhall Gardens," he told her, rolling his sleeves up one more turn. "Perhaps *you* should come with me instead the first time, to show me the good places."

"I don't know if that's necessary…" Juliana's gaze was fastened on his arms. "…though I suppose it never hurts to be prepared." Her eyes skipped back up to his face. "The gardens are closed on Sundays. Shall we make it tomorrow night?"

"Parliament is in session on Mondays—"

"Could you not take even *one* night away from the House of Lords?"

Perhaps he could. Since he wasn't getting anywhere with his bill, perhaps he should focus on Juliana instead. For a day, at least. Or a night.

"Very well," he said.

"Good." She rose. "I must return home before the guests arrive for my sewing party."

He nodded and led her toward the door. "I'll come by for you at seven o'clock tomorrow."

"I'll see that Aunt Frances is ready," she said as they walked through the library.

He groaned inwardly. The last thing he needed was Juliana's chaperone hovering over them. "Do you suppose Lord Malmsey would like to accompany your aunt?"

"I'm sure he would." She went lightly down the stairs, her renewed good cheer lifting James's spirits. She was adorable. A treasure, as his mother would say. "That's a splendid idea," she said.

Yes, it was. The two of them were certain to go off on their own, which in turn would leave James alone with Juliana. The plan was sounding better and better.

"Until tomorrow, then," he said. His butler opened the front door, revealing Griffin outside pacing around the Cainewood carriage.

"Until tomorrow," Juliana echoed, starting toward her brother. "Wait," she said, turning back. "I forgot to ask if you'd like me to volunteer this week at the Institute."

She would come again without her aunt, James thought. If he failed to kiss her at Vauxhall, maybe he could get her alone in one of the treatment rooms. "Absolutely," he told her with a smile. "How about Friday?"

"Friday will be fine." Returning his smile, she headed toward the carriage.

The butler shut the door behind her, but not before James heard Griffin's impatient huff. "Why in blazes did it take you so long to ask the man one simple question?"

THIRTY-THREE

*D*ARK WAS falling.

Juliana had arrived at Vauxhall Gardens with James, Aunt Frances, and Lord Malmsey at about eight o'clock Monday night, while the sun was still gracing the summer sky. It was a fine July evening, perhaps a bit chillier than usual, but without the slightest hint of rain. The pleasure gardens had proved as lovely as she'd heard, spacious and laid out in delightful walks, bordered with high hedges and towering trees, and paved with gravel that crunched beneath their shoes.

For the first half hour they'd strolled, finding something charming around every corner. Pavilions, grottoes, temples and cascades, porticos, colonnades and rotundas. Here was a striking pillar, there a wonderful statue, in the distance a series of large, picturesque murals. Throngs of visitors promenaded, showing off their finest clothing, their rowdy laughter and whispered endearments filling the night air.

Now, with the sun sinking low, they were seated at a table for four by the building that housed the orchestra, a structure that struck Juliana as Moorish or perhaps Gothic—she couldn't decide which, but regardless, it was magnificent. Its second story was open in the front so the musicians were visible inside.

While they listened to a concert of popular songs and compositions, they enjoyed a light supper of cold meats and bread and cheese accompanied by French claret. Aunt Frances was astounded at the high cost of their small portions.

"My word," she said disapprovingly, "this Vauxhall ham is sliced so thin one could read a newspaper through it!"

Lord Malmsey laughed and motioned to a serving girl to order more. "Would you like some cheesecake, too, my dear?"

"It cannot be as good as Juliana's," James said, shooting her a grin.

So he *had* enjoyed her Richmond Maids of Honour. Feeling inordinately pleased, Juliana smiled back.

As the musicians played the last notes of a piece by Handel, a piercing whistle split the night. "What's that?" she asked.

Lord Malmsey cocked his balding head. "Have you never been here before, Lady Juliana?"

She was about to tell him she hadn't, but then she remembered James didn't know that. "Not at night," she said instead.

The fib only reminded her that she had no excuse for being here with James. She hadn't a clue what stray impulse had compelled her to accept his invitation, when he should be escorting Amanda tonight. The two of them needed to spend more time together if he was to decide to marry her before her scheduled wedding in twelve days' time.

"Just watch, then," Lord Malmsey said.

And she stopped musing, sucking in a breath as a thousand oil lamps came to life, lit by myriad servants touching matches to their wicks in the same instant. The effect was nothing short of sensational, bathing the gardens in a warm glow that must have been visible for miles around.

"Enchanting!" her aunt exclaimed.

Lord Malmsey cocked his head again. "Have *you* never been here at night, either?"

"I've never been here at all," Aunt Frances said.

Shy, retiring Aunt Frances had missed out on a lot, Juliana

thought as they finished their supper, but that was about to change. She'd never been happier to see one of her projects prove a success.

"Shall we walk again?" Lord Malmsey asked, rising from the table. "The gardens feel like a different place among the lanterns."

"A lovely idea." Frances rose, too, and pulled on her gloves.

Juliana reached for her own but found her lap empty. "Where are my gloves?" She was sure she'd placed them there when she took them off for supper—it was a lifelong habit, after all. She checked the ground on either side of her chair. "I cannot find them."

"How odd." Shifting his gaze to Lord Malmsey, James waved a hand toward the beckoning paths. "You two go on ahead. I'll help Lady Juliana find her gloves, and then we'll catch up to you."

As Frances and Lord Malmsey walked off, Juliana leaned to peek below the table. "I cannot imagine where they might have gone." She rose and looked under her chair. "They seem to have disappeared."

"Perhaps they're in my pocket," James said. "Right beside mine."

She looked up at him, startled. "How would they get there?"

He shrugged one shoulder, a corner of his mouth turning up in a half smile. "How indeed?"

She laughed. "Give them to me."

"I think not. I think you'll need to get them for yourself."

She eyed his striped silk waistcoat, his dark tailcoat, his crisp white trousers. She didn't know which of his pockets he'd hidden her gloves in, but she wasn't about to slip her hands into his clothing to find out. She laughed again. "James…"

He took her bare hand in his. "Your aunt and Lord Malmsey will get too far ahead if we don't go after them. Come along."

The paths seemed jollier now that it was dark, the company enlivened with mirth and good humor. Music drifted from the orchestra through the trees. Seemingly suspended everywhere, the lamps looked like little illuminated balls glowing every color of the rainbow. Some were arranged in lines or arches, others grouped to represent the starry heavens.

Juliana thought Vauxhall Gardens was the most magical place she'd ever been. Her heart felt light, and her hand felt warm in James's. She knew she shouldn't allow him to hold it, but just then she didn't care about proprieties. Ahead of them on the path, Aunt Frances leaned close to Lord Malmsey, oblivious to her charge as usual.

When they caught up to the older couple, who had stopped by a tinkling fountain, Juliana pulled her hand free.

"Look!" Aunt Frances pointed overhead. "It's Madame Saqui!"

Wearing a dazzling dress decorated with tinsel, spangles, and plumes, the celebrated tightrope walker seemed to dance on air as she ascended a rope attached to a sixty-foot mast. Beneath her dress, her legs were muscled like a circus strongman's. Her balance was impeccable, her steps graceful and seemingly timed to the orchestra's lilting music.

"It looks like a ballet, doesn't it?" Juliana said.

"A ballet for two," James replied as the dancer's husband mounted a second rope beside hers. "I've heard they earn a hundred guineas per week."

She slanted him a teasing smile. "A sum you'd like to see spent on smallpox vaccinations, no doubt."

He laughed. "Entertaining enchanting ladies is also a worthy cause."

She felt a peculiar lurch at the implication that he might find her enchanting, although she knew quite well he was speaking of the company in general. They watched for a few minutes in breathless silence as the couple dipped and swayed, seemingly unconcerned they might plunge to their deaths. At the top, Madame Saqui performed an agile turn and saluted her husband as she passed him on her way down. When she reached the bottom, she sank into a theatrical curtsy and swept up a little girl, settling her small slippered feet on the tightrope.

"She cannot be more than four years old!" Juliana gasped at the sight of the child climbing the rope toward the stars. She covered her face with her hands. "I cannot watch."

"She's their daughter." James slipped an arm around her waist. "Performance is in her blood," he said, drawing her against himself.

She dropped her hands, glancing to see if her aunt had noticed James's bold move.

Her chaperone was no longer beside her.

"Aunt Frances?" She looked around. "Where is Aunt Frances?"

"She went off with Lord Malmsey," James said, waggling his eyebrows suggestively and making her giggle. "Shall we resume our walk?"

As he drew her down a darkened lane, still holding her quite close, she was struck again, as she had been at the Egyptian Hall, by how well they fit together. He smelled of starch and soap and spice. He matched his longer gait to her shorter one, and it seemed the night was warmer, the gardens more lush and fragrant. Tall trees towered on both sides, their silhouettes dark against the lantern-hazed sky.

"When will you bring Lady Amanda here?" she asked.

"Hmm," he said noncommittally, turning into a tiny secluded pocket garden.

It had a stone bench and a single lantern, so it wasn't quite dark. But it was dim, with high hedges all around. She heard a couple walk by, gravel crunching beneath their feet. No one peeked in through the narrow opening.

James released her and walked over to the bench, she assumed to sit down. But he didn't. Instead, he slid off his tail-coat and draped it over the seat. "Do you think this would be a good spot to bring Lady Amanda?" he asked.

"Maybe." James would surely feel intimate with her in this

cozy, hidden location. And she with him. They'd become close friends, and then they'd marry and have children. "I mean, yes," she decided. "This would be an excellent place to bring Lady Amanda."

"I thought so." His long fingers worked at the knot in his cravat. "What do you expect I should do with Lady Amanda when we're here?"

Juliana didn't know what to say, so she didn't say anything. She just watched him pull the cravat from around his neck, slowly and steadily, until it came off entirely and dangled from his fingers. "Why are you undressing?" she finally asked.

"I'm overwarm." His intense dark gaze was fastened on her in that way that made her wonder if he could read her mind. "Well? Have you no suggestions for Lady Amanda and me?" He released the cravat, and it fluttered to the bench. "Do you think perhaps I should kiss her?"

She swallowed hard. "Maybe."

"I thought so." He eased open the top button of his shirt. And the second button. "I think we should practice."

Her gaze was glued to the little V of skin where his shirt was unbuttoned. "Practice?"

"Yes, practice." He raised a wrist and unbuttoned a cuff. "You and me. Before I try it with Lady Amanda."

"You want to kiss me?"

He nodded, beckoning.

She felt another curious lurch. He wanted to kiss her. Just for practice, but still…

James wanted to kiss *her*. The last unkissed girl in England.

She wasn't supposed to kiss James—she was supposed to kiss the duke. But the duke had made it clear he wouldn't kiss her until they were married. He was so very, very proper. And Aunt Frances thought a kiss no great sin, and Corinna had told her she should kiss a few frogs so she'd know when she'd met her prince.

Not that James was a frog. He was…well, she didn't know

what he was, precisely. A friend, she supposed. A friend who was rolling up his cuffs, revealing his golden, rather muscular forearms.

And unbuttoning the buttons that ran down the front of his waistcoat.

Faith, if she didn't kiss him soon, he'd end up stark naked in the middle of Vauxhall Gardens.

"Very well," he said as the waistcoat flapped open. He wore a crisp white shirt underneath. "If you're not going to come to me, I will have to go to you."

And he did. He walked right up to her. She backed up, and he followed. She moved until her back was against a tall, fragrant hedge, and he followed until he was all but against her. Until there was only a hairsbreadth between them, until his scent overwhelmed her, until she could see the golden flecks in his brown eyes and feel his breath upon her face. She tingled all over, every inch of her skin feeling suddenly more alive.

He settled his hands on her shoulders. "May I kiss you?"

She couldn't say *yes* and she couldn't say *no*. But she lifted her face to his, holding her breath, waiting, her heart pounding and her eyes drifting shut.

His hands drew her closer, raising her on tiptoe, until his lips just grazed hers. The sensation was so faint and so fleeting she wasn't sure it had really happened.

"May I?" he asked again in a whisper.

"Oh, yes," she whispered back.

And his mouth settled on hers.

It felt unlike anything she'd ever imagined. His lips were firm and warm and *moving* against hers. He was so tall she had to tilt her head as far back as it would go. She felt his large, heavy hands slide from her shoulders—one to cradle the back of her head, the other to grasp the small of her back—and nearly lift her clear off her feet to press her still closer, full against his body. Her knees buckled, but it didn't matter because he was holding her up…

And then he set her down, steadying her before he broke the kiss.

The kiss? She'd just been kissed—finally.

Hallelujah!

Her heart still pounding, she opened her eyes. The first thing she saw was his mouth, which was suddenly fascinating now that she knew what it felt like. The lower lip was fuller than the top one, she noted. Between his lips and his straight nose, a faint shadow of dark stubble looked dashing and masculine. And higher still, his eyes looked like warm, melty pools of chocolate flecked with gold.

James was *gorgeous*.

She'd known he was handsome, of course. She'd told Amanda as much, many times. But his handsomeness had been just a fact like so many others. James was handsome. Corinna was a good painter. Griffin had been in the cavalry. All facts.

But now…

She looked at James. Really looked at him, seemingly for the first time. How could she have ever overlooked him? Faith, he was beautiful. And he stared at her just as boldly as she was examining him. She liked that.

She had to kiss him again. She reached up to him—

"Juliana!" It was Aunt Frances, her voice distant but recognizable. "Juliana, where are you?"

"Drat!" Juliana leapt away from James, the distance allowing her head to clear. He was standing there with half of his clothing unbuttoned. Aunt Frances was about to find them, and he was just standing there, unbuttoned.

"Dress yourself!" she hissed.

His fingers moved to the buttons of his waistcoat and began fastening them. Leisurely.

"Juliana!" her aunt called again.

She ran to the pocket garden's entrance and looked out onto the path. Aunt Frances was nowhere to be seen.

She turned back. "Hurry," she told James. "It's only a matter of time until she finds us."

Unrolling one of his sleeves, he shrugged and sauntered back to the bench, where his cravat lay atop his tailcoat in a jumbled pile. "Do I kiss better than Castleton?"

"I haven't kissed Castleton. He's too—"

"Stuffy?" he provided, looking all too pleased.

"He's not stuffy! He's just—"

"A prig."

"He's not a prig! He's proper and reserved, which is more than I can say for you."

He grinned. "That's more than I can say for you as well. Which is a compliment, mind you—"

"Juliana!" Lord Malmsey's voice joined her aunt's this time. "Juliana!"

She peeked outside again. Still clear. Her heart pounding, now from panic instead of excitement, she stalked over to James. He was buttoning his shirt so slowly it made her want to scream. "Hurry, will you?" She swept up his cravat, intending to throw it at him, but an enormous *boom* sounded overhead and she shrieked in alarm.

"Easy." The cravat drifted to the grass while James wrapped her in his arms. "It's just fireworks." Another *boom* exploded in the sky, accompanied by flashes of red and blue and white. "Your aunt will stop and watch," he said soothingly.

Knowing he was right, she pulled away and sat on the bench to watch the fireworks. But she wasn't soothed, nor did she feel at ease. Not even after he'd retrieved the cravat and awkwardly knotted it and donned his tailcoat and buttoned it up. Her heart was still pounding, and her stomach felt queer.

Great, fiery streaks of light burst in the heavens, and all around she heard "ooh!" and "ahh!" from all the people in Vauxhall Gardens, but all she could think was thank heaven and earth and everything else that she hadn't been caught kissing James while half of his clothing was unbuttoned. They'd have had to marry.

And she couldn't marry James. She just couldn't.

I'll never fall in love again, she remembered him saying. *But certainly I could marry a friend. I could have children with a friend.*

The duke was falling in love with her, but James never would. He'd only kissed her because they were friends and he needed a wife to give him children.

But Juliana couldn't be that wife. He had to marry Amanda, else Amanda would have to marry Lord Malmsey, who would have to give up Aunt Frances—and all three of them would be devastated.

She could never let James kiss her again.

THIRTY-FOUR

"**G**OODNESS GRACIOUS,**"** Lady Frances said, giggling like a schoolgirl, "when you both went missing for so long, I didn't know whether to summon the authorities or my nephew!"

Seated beside her in the carriage, Lord Malmsey chuckled. "It wasn't *so* very long, my dear."

Juliana laughed, too, though it was more of a nervous titter. "Summon Griffin, Aunty? Whatever for?"

"To make you and Lord Stafford marry, of course!"

Juliana blanched.

But as the last of Vauxhall Gardens' lanterns faded from view, James only smiled.

There were two reasons he smiled. Firstly, he was in a fine mood. Or not just a fine mood, but a splendid mood. A brilliant mood. A glorious, magnificent—

Anyway, he felt good. Because kissing Juliana had been so much better than he'd ever imagined. Gloriously, magnificently better. And now that he'd experienced kissing her, he was looking forward to moving on with the rest of his life.

That was, he was looking forward to spending the rest of his life kissing her.

And that was the second reason he was smiling: because the idea of being caught in a compromising position with Juliana, and thus being forced to marry her, didn't trouble him at all. Not one bit.

Not after that kiss. That kiss hadn't just been magnificent. It had been a revelation.

Some part of him had obviously already known the truth. It was the part that had driven him to unbutton so many buttons in the garden. And urged him not to button them back up in any hurry. And, after the fireworks, when he and Juliana had "miraculously" found their way back to their chaperones, it was the part of him that felt disappointed they *hadn't* been caught.

But he was still shocked to realize he'd fallen in love.

Until the kiss, he hadn't been able to admit that, not even to himself, because it would be a betrayal of Anne.

Except…it wasn't.

He'd fallen in love with Juliana, and it wasn't a betrayal at all.

He'd expected to feel appalled. Or guilty. Or disbelieving.

But he wasn't any of those things. He was in love. And he couldn't disbelieve it any more than he could disbelieve he had two hands and two feet.

Juliana smoothed her yellow dress. "We were only watching the fireworks, Aunty. Besides, you know I'm going to marry the Duke of Castleton."

On hearing that, irritation nearly punctured James's fine mood—but not quite, because *he was in love!*

He'd never thought this could happen.

Or maybe he'd been in too much denial to allow himself to think it could happen.

Maybe.

It was a possibility.

He was willing to admit to that.

But if he *had* thought such a thing—if he'd considered that someday, somehow he could fall in love with another girl without desecrating Anne's memory—he'd thought it could only happen after Anne somehow granted him permission.

Exactly *how* he could receive permission from a dead girl wasn't something he'd really considered. Maybe he could have gone to her grave and talked to her—he'd read such scenarios in books. Or maybe she could have come to him in a dream—he'd read that in books, too. Or maybe she could have sent him a sign; maybe he could have just seen something—something seemingly insignificant—and somehow known what it meant.

But none of that had happened. Because he didn't *need* Anne's permission. Because his love for Juliana had nothing to do with Anne.

Nothing.

Loving Juliana didn't diminish the love he'd had for Anne. It didn't mean he wouldn't always cherish the memories of their time together. He didn't love Juliana more than he'd loved Anne or less than he'd loved Anne.

He loved her differently.

She was a different girl, and he loved her for different reasons. Which made sense, because he was different now, too. This new love wasn't better or worse, or deeper or shallower. It was just *different*.

And it was exactly what he needed to make him feel whole again.

Unfortunately, it seemed Juliana's evening hadn't been *quite* as revelatory as James's. She still seemed bent on marrying that turd Castleton. The one who wanted her only because she came with a horse.

But James knew she'd felt something when he'd kissed her. He'd seen it written all over her face.

The carriage rolled to a stop in front of Cainewood's town house.

"Thank you," Lord Malmsey said as he stepped out.

"It was a lovely evening," Lady Frances said and stepped out, too.

Juliana didn't say anything as she stepped out to follow them. But before the footman could close the carriage door, she turned back to face James. "When are you going to take Lady Amanda to Vauxhall Gardens?"

He didn't want to take Lady Amanda to Vauxhall Gardens. He didn't want to take her anywhere. He'd *never* wanted to take her anywhere.

But he especially didn't want to take her to Vauxhall Gardens, the place where he'd had his first kiss with Juliana.

"Never," he said. "I didn't enjoy Vauxhall Gardens much."

"Didn't you?" She narrowed her eyes as though she didn't believe him. Which was hardly surprising, since in reality he'd enjoyed himself immensely. "Well," she said, "then where shall you take her?"

He wanted to say *nowhere*, but he couldn't. Because then he'd have no excuse to see Juliana. She was involved with the stuffy duke, which meant she wouldn't accept an invitation from James unless it was for the sake of Lady Amanda.

That wasn't such a terrible thing, he consoled himself. He and Juliana were becoming friends, and he liked the idea of getting to know her as a friend first. There was plenty of time to make her fall in love with him. If he continued feigning interest in Lady Amanda, he could keep up the "lessons" with Juliana, find occasional opportunities to touch her or kiss her, and slowly ease into their courtship.

He could afford to be patient. He was just getting used to the fact that he was in love with her. There was no reason to rush right into things.

"I'll take Lady Amanda wherever you'd like," he said. "Except Vauxhall Gardens. As long as you come along, too."

"I cannot come along!"

"You can if you're with Castleton." It galled him to say that, but he saw no other choice. No other way to get Juliana to spend time with him.

Well, he'd see her on Friday at the Institute. But that was four days away. Entirely too long.

"If we go somewhere I've never been," he told her, "I'll need you there to provide guidance."

She mulled that over for a moment, and then she said, "Very well," just as he'd expected. He'd known he could appeal to her meddling nature. She'd probably never in her life come to believe he was capable of fending for himself, but he could live with that.

In fact, he looked forward to living with that. He liked having her look after him. It was both touching and a never-ending source of amusement, one of her most endearing quirks.

"I think we should go see the new Battle of Waterloo panorama in Leicester Square tomorrow," she said. "I've heard it's very romantic."

Having witnessed war himself—albeit briefly—James didn't think it was very romantic, and he had never heard the term *romantic* attached to the Leicester Square Panorama building, either. But he had heard it was dark, and he supposed darkness could lead to romance, and while he was well aware that Juliana expected him to find romance with Lady Amanda while she found romance with that turd Castleton, he knew *that* wouldn't happen, so her false expectations didn't dampen his spirits in the slightest.

"I believe it closes at four," he said, "so I shall return to fetch you and Lady Amanda at one o'clock."

"And Aunt Frances," she reminded him.

"And Lady Frances. Invite Lord Malmsey, too, will you?" he said, reaching into his pocket for her gloves. "Here you are, l— lady." He cleared his throat. "That is, Lady Juliana."

He'd almost called her *love*.

He'd best be more careful; he wanted to get closer to Juliana, not scare her away.

"Thank you," she said, taking them and going into the house.

James was still in a fine mood as his carriage continued on to

Stafford House. Once there, he remained in a fine mood as he searched the morning room and the music room and the Palm Room for his mother. He took the stairs two at a time, still in a fine mood when he finally found her in her sitting room, reading a Minerva Press novel.

He'd never seen his mother read a Minerva Press novel. They were torrid romances, and he was startled to see her reading such a thing, but that didn't affect his fine mood.

"Yes, James?" she said, shutting it quickly and setting it upside down on the table beside her. "How was your evening?"

"It was pleasant," he said, perhaps the greatest understatement of his life. "I want to renovate my bedroom."

"You cannot change that room. It was designed by Henry Holland!"

"I don't care who designed it. Brown and plum are too somber."

Mother loved redecorating, but James's father had never let her touch Stafford House, so she'd had to content herself with overhauling their manor house in the countryside. James had known she wouldn't argue long. Clearly excited, she rose, belted her dressing gown more tightly, and walked over to sit at her feminine writing desk.

"What colors would you like, then?" she asked, dipping her quill in the inkwell.

"Red," he decided.

"Your favorite color. I should have guessed." She scribbled. "Any other requests?"

"And yellow. Red and yellow." He'd noticed Juliana often wore yellow, but he wouldn't explain that to his mother. The last thing he needed was her figuring out he'd finally decided to remarry.

"We'll do stripes," she said, still scribbling. "Wide red and yellow stripes on the walls above the wainscoting."

"I want the wainscoting gone. It's dark wood, and I don't want anything dark in the room."

She frowned, then brightened. "We'll paint the wainscoting white, then. Bright white enamel. And use narrower stripes on the upholstery. But solid red bedclothing, I think. Perhaps with yellow pillows."

"Fine." Henry Holland's design had used floral fabrics, so stripes sounded perfect. As different as could be. "And get rid of that monstrous old-fashioned bed, will you?"

"It's been in the family since the sixteenth century."

"It looks it."

"Nine Stafford earls were born in that bed—"

"I want something modern. Without a canopy or stifling curtains."

She looked up. And then she gazed at him for a very long moment. He wondered if she'd made the connection, if she'd realized that the bed, the curtains—all of it—held too many memories.

"Very well," she finally said. "If you insist, we'll move it to a guest room."

THIRTY-FIVE

"**I**T'S THE rheumatism, I fear," Lady Avonleigh said the next afternoon.

"It's dreadful," Lady Balmforth added. "The two of us ache every morning."

When James had fetched Juliana and the others for their outing, he'd explained that he needed to stop by his aunts' house on their way to Leicester Square. Seated in his aunts' drawing room on a peach sofa, Juliana watched him walk them toward a large picture window.

"I'm afraid some morning stiffness is to be expected at your age," he said sympathetically. He lifted Lady Balmforth's narrow hand and examined it in the window's light.

"Don't you need to use your quizzing glass?" she asked.

"Not for this. I see no evidence of swelling, and your joints don't look reddened or feel overly warm. If the achiness wears off before noon, that's a good sign." He flexed her elbow. "Does this hurt?"

"He's patient," Amanda said quietly, sitting beside Juliana.

"Yes, he is," she whispered back, lifting an embroidery hoop one of James's aunts had left on the table. It wasn't a simple sampler but an amazingly detailed scene—a cottage in the woods with animals among the trees. "Isn't this exquisite?" It had a faint smell she couldn't quite identify. She sniffed curiously, then coughed and quickly lowered the hoop. Gardenias and camphor. Ick.

"I wish he'd be a little more *imp*atient," Amanda whined. "We're going to be late."

"There's no need to worry. The rotunda doesn't close until four."

"But the duke will be waiting."

"Not for so very long." Juliana raised a half-finished crewelwork seat cover and ran her fingers over the pattern, a veritable field of flowers. This one was mercifully unscented. "Lord Stafford's aunts are very talented."

"Lord Stafford is on his knees," Amanda said. "That cannot be good for his injury."

James was crouched on the floor, obligingly examining Lady Avonleigh's plump ankles. Juliana didn't think about his injury much—it didn't seem to stop him from doing anything, so she couldn't see where it mattered. But apparently it mattered to Amanda.

"There's nothing Lord Stafford won't do for someone he cares for," Juliana told her, returning the crewelwork to the table. "You're lucky to have someone so wonderful courting you." Honestly, it was a bit annoying that Amanda didn't seem to realize how truly lucky she was. "It's nice of you to be concerned for him, though. Just remember to let him kiss you."

"What if he doesn't try?"

"He'll try. I've heard parts of the rotunda are quite dark." James would take advantage of the darkness—Juliana knew this from experience.

"What if I don't like kissing him?"

Poor Amanda seemed even more afraid of kissing than before. The failed trick must have traumatized her. "You'll love kissing him," Juliana assured her. Another thing she knew from experience. In fact, just thinking about that particular experience made her stomach feel all queer again.

Why was that?

Her puzzlement must have shown on her face, because the next thing she knew, James was standing over her, looking concerned. "Is something wrong?"

"No, not at all," she assured him—and herself. "Are you finished?"

"I've prescribed hot, damp towels for my aunts' aches. I'm certain they shall be fine."

She rose and walked over to where his aunts sat while their maids obligingly applied the towels. "I hope you'll both be feeling better soon."

"Oh, we shall," Lady Balmforth said as her maid wrapped one of her wrists. "Our James always knows what to do. I'm sure we'll feel better by the time Cornelia comes to fetch us in an hour. We're going to Gillow's to look at some new furniture for her house."

"Your needlework is lovely. I'm having a little sewing party tomorrow afternoon, to make some baby clothes for the Foundling Hospital. Would either of you be interested in joining me?"

"Cornelia told us about your sewing parties," Lady Avonleigh exclaimed, appearing better already. The odd gardenias-and-camphor scent was hers. "They sound delightful, my dear. I should love to attend."

Lady Balmforth clasped her hands together so enthusiastically she lost a towel in the process. "I should love to attend, too."

"Thank you so much. Shall I send my brother's carriage at one o'clock?"

"Oh, no," Lady Avonleigh said. "We have our own carriage, and John Coachman has much too much time on his hands."

"He naps," Lady Balmforth added. "Even more often than we do."

Juliana noticed James and Amanda both inching toward the door. "Excellent," she said before going after them. "I live at forty-four Berkeley Square, and I very much look forward to seeing you."

"That was rather presumptuous," Amanda said as they walked out to James's carriage where Aunt Frances and Lord Malmsey were waiting.

"I disagree," James said. "I think it was kind. My aunts were thrilled to be invited."

Juliana smiled. "They're very sweet."

"And very healthy," he said dryly. "Such a pity they don't know it."

"They just need something else to occupy their minds. That's why I invited them to my party—well, besides the fact that I do need their help. And I'm thinking I should introduce them to a few more charming gentlemen."

"I don't believe either of them is interested in gentlemen, charming or not."

"Have they never been wed?"

"Oh, yes. Aunt Bedelia was married four times."

"Four!" Amanda exclaimed.

"A baron, two viscounts, and an earl. They all died," he added, shaking his head as a footman opened the carriage door. "Poor, sweet lady."

Juliana made a concerned noise that turned into a gasp. Inside James's opulent carriage, her aunt was *kissing* Lord Malmsey!

"Gracious me!" Amanda cried, clearly scandalized. Not because she cared that Lord Malmsey was courting Aunt Frances, Juliana thought—after all, Amanda had given him permission to court other women. No, Amanda would have been scandalized to see *any* two people kissing. She was scared to death of kissing.

The couple jerked apart. A flush rushed up Aunt Frances's

neck and spread to her cheeks. Not a delicate flush, either—it was more like a bright red flood.

But she kept her composure. "Are your aunts feeling better?" she asked James, folding her hands in her lap.

"Remarkably." He handed Amanda in first, then Juliana before himself. She left space for him in the middle, but it seemed there wasn't enough, because he ended up squished against her. "To the Leicester Square Panorama," he instructed and settled back.

They all rode in silence for a few awkward moments. James felt very warm against Juliana. Her stomach was feeling even more queer. "Lord Stafford was telling us his aunt Bedelia has been married four times," she told her aunt.

"Oh, my," Aunt Frances said.

After a few more awkward moments, Juliana looked up to James. "Were there no children?"

"None that lived. And Aunt Aurelia's life has been even more tragic."

"How many husbands did *she* have?" Amanda asked in a tone that Juliana found rather judgmental.

James didn't seem to notice, however. "Only one, the Earl of Avonleigh. But their children failed to bring her happiness. Her eldest daughter eloped with a cousin, prompting her husband to disown the girl. Aurelia never heard from her again and learned she'd died a number of years later. Her middle child, a son, drank too much and accidentally drowned. And her youngest, another daughter, ended her own life soon after marrying. She jumped off the London Bridge, taking her unborn child with her."

"Oh, my," Aunt Frances said again.

"Aunt Aurelia's husband died soon thereafter. A 'visitation from God' was the coroner's official verdict, but I expect his spirit was broken."

"I don't doubt that," Lord Malmsey said.

Juliana nodded, her heart twisting in sympathy. "It's a wonder your poor aunt survived. She must be a strong lady."

"She is. They both are. But it's a shame they have no children or grandchildren to dote upon."

"They have you," she pointed out.

"I know, and I adore them. I admire their pluck." The carriage came to a halt. "I just wish they had someone else to pluck at once in a while."

The door opened to Leicester Square and a huge round building. Over a rather nondescript entrance, a fancy marquee said PANORAMA. Before it stood the duke.

Juliana was relieved to see he didn't look annoyed. On the other hand, he didn't look glad, either. He looked the way he usually did: detached and rather blank. His pale blue eyes calm, his expression neutral.

Everyone clambered out of the carriage. "Good afternoon, my dear," the duke said to her. "I was very pleased to receive your invitation."

He might try *looking* pleased, Juliana thought.

After everyone else exchanged greetings, the gentlemen bought tickets at the box office and they all proceeded inside. A long, narrow, dimly lit corridor stretched ahead, and it got even darker when the door shut behind them.

Amanda shrieked. Juliana rolled her eyes.

"There now," a voice said, soothing Amanda. "Take my arm."

It was the duke, not James.

James took Juliana's arm instead. Even in the dark she knew it was James, because he smelled like starch and spice instead of eau de cologne. And because her stomach felt even queerer.

"You should be escorting Lady Amanda," she whispered as they all groped their way down the hall, laughing and feeling their way along the walls.

"She'll be fine," he said.

Of course Amanda would be fine. There was nothing dangerous about a darkened, closed-in corridor. It wasn't scary

—in fact, it was rather fun. However, while the duke was very kind to soothe Amanda, James could hardly kiss her while she was with the duke. And that was the whole reason they'd come.

By the time they reached the end of the corridor, Juliana's eyes had adjusted to the low light and she could see somewhat. A tall staircase spiraled up. And up. And up. The light in the stairwell grew a little brighter as they went.

"My knees hurt," Amanda complained halfway up. "Can we please stop and rest?"

"Of course we can," the duke said.

Propelled by James, Juliana passed them and kept going.

Behind her, Aunt Frances giggled. "I cannot remember the last time I turned in so many circles!"

Indeed, Juliana felt like a blindfolded child being spun around as part of a game. It was a bit disorienting. She held on to James, noticing he seemed to be limping a little more than usual. Maybe Amanda had been right that he shouldn't have been kneeling.

Suddenly the staircase ended, and they emerged to find themselves transported to another time and place. Like magic, they'd gone from Leicester Square to Belgium in a matter of minutes.

Feeling like she was still spinning, Juliana wormed her way through the crowd and gripped the platform's rail. All around her, above and below, a battlefield stretched miles into the distance.

"Amazing," James breathed behind her.

It was overwhelming. She knew the panorama was only a gigantic painting, but everything in the rotunda was designed to trick the eyes. Indirect illumination, provided by narrow skylights beneath the edge of the domed ceiling, made it look like outdoors at dusk. Far below, a three-dimensional terrain stretched from under the platform up to the walls, filled with lifelike vegetation, objects, and figures that blended into the picture, making everything seem real.

And all around, the Battle of Waterloo raged.

Chaos reigned. Cavalrymen charged on horses with bayoneted infantry at their backs. Officers gave orders, soldiers aided the fallen, smoke rose from cannons in a stand of trees. The ground was low in places, muddy in others, fenced and open, brown and green, flat and rough and everything in between. Fields that should have been smooth were littered with the fallen and wounded, the contents of their knapsacks strewn all over. As far as the eye could see, men scrambled and fought, their guns and swords flashing in the glistening haze made by spent artillery.

When Juliana finally felt steady enough to release the rail, she edged sideways around the platform, working her way through the other milling spectators. It seemed they were all standing in a pavilion on the top of a small hill in the center of the battle. The soldiers looked wet, dirty, and blue with cold. She could have sworn she saw a mounted officer raise a hat to signal an attack. A shiver ran down her spine.

"I feel seasick," Aunt Frances said from somewhere close on the platform.

"Hold on to me," Lord Malmsey said. "You have delicate nerves, my love."

His love? Blinking in the twilight, Juliana tore her gaze from the panorama and turned toward the voices.

But the couple had disappeared.

THIRTY-SIX

"WHERE'S MY aunt?" Juliana cried. "And Lord Malmsey?"

James curved an arm around her, pulling her close. "We'll find them later," he said, his low voice seeming to vibrate right through her.

"Where are the duke and Lady Amanda?"

"Does it matter?"

"Yes!" Amanda was supposed to be the one here with James in the dark, not Juliana. Especially since having his arm around her made her stomach feel queerer than ever.

She swayed.

"Are you seasick, too?" he asked.

"No." She was just dizzy. From listening to his resonant, chocolatey voice. And thinking about kissing him. She couldn't kiss him again. If she was going to kiss anyone, it should be the duke.

But the duke didn't want to kiss her until they were married, and in any case, he was with Amanda. In fact, Amanda had probably latched on to him knowing he wouldn't kiss her.

If a girl feared being kissed, the duke was a much safer bet than James.

"Do you see them?" she asked James, trying to peer around him.

He drew her toward the staircase. "Maybe they've gone downstairs. I think we should go and see."

They walked all the way down, around and around, which hardly helped her dizziness. But the others were nowhere to be found. At the bottom it was darker, and they retraced their steps down the corridor, laughingly feeling their way along the walls again. James, Juliana could tell even in the darkness, was definitely limping more than usual. Reaching the end, they opened the door and looked out into Leicester Square.

She blinked in the bright sunshine. There was no sign of her aunt or Amanda or the other gentlemen. "They must still be upstairs," she said.

"They must." A family was approaching the door, so James drew her back inside to let them pass.

The children giggled when the door closed behind them and the corridor plunged into darkness. "Don't run!" the parents cautioned as they all made their way toward the staircase.

The little ones' yelps and giggles as they bumped each other and the walls echoed around the corridor, but still, when James took Juliana's hand and began to follow them, she could *hear* his uneven gait.

"Your leg is hurting you, isn't it?"

She felt rather than saw him shrug. "It was a tall staircase. I'm fine."

The scores of steps hadn't occurred to her when she'd suggested today's outing. Unlike Amanda, she never really thought about James's limp at all. He never mentioned it, and it was usually so slight. "Does it hurt very often?"

"Only when it's cold and rainy."

"Faith." She gripped his arm with her other hand, dragging him to a stop. "It must hurt *all* the time this year."

He laughed. "It's not that painful. The limb is stiffer than I'd like, but the sensation is just a dull ache. Nothing to merit your concern. In an odd way I actually appreciate the discomfort—it reminds me how fortunate I am to still have the leg."

"When did it happen? And how?"

"Peninsular War. Took a ball right below the knee." The giggles grew fainter as, at the other end of the corridor, the family started up the staircase. "The army surgeons wanted to amputate, but one managed to save it instead."

"I'm glad," Juliana murmured, thinking he was stoic and brave.

Amanda had no idea how lucky she was.

The family's footsteps faded away, and James continued down the corridor. "I felt incredibly grateful to the man. Since I could no longer march with the army, I needed another profession, and—"

"*That's* why you became a doctor," she interrupted softly.

"Have you still been puzzling over that?" he wondered with a low laugh as they neared the steps. "Yes, that's why I entered medical school. Eventually, though, I chose to become a physician instead of a surgeon. I decided I'd rather work with stethoscopes than saws."

Distracted by a horrifying vision of a bloody surgeon's saw, Juliana took a while to notice that instead of starting up the staircase, he'd drawn her around and underneath it.

"What are you doing?" she asked, rubbing her stomach.

"People will bump into us if we wait in the corridor. We'll wait here instead."

It was very dark under the steps, and James would take advantage of the dark. She'd told Amanda as much, hadn't she, because she knew his ways firsthand. "I think we should go back upstairs," she said before he could claim he needed more kissing practice.

"If we wait here," he argued, "your aunt and the others will surely come down."

"Aunt Frances won't be able to see us under here." Especially considering she was probably busy kissing Lord Malmsey. Bold men had a tendency to take advantage of the dark, and while Lord Malmsey might have started out rather shy, he was obviously getting bolder by the minute. Already today he'd been bold enough to kiss Aunt Frances in James's carriage and call her *my love.*

Juliana hadn't understood the queer feeling in her stomach—but all of a sudden, she did.

Lord Malmsey had called Aunt Frances *my love.*

Juliana wanted someone to call *her* his love.

She wanted *James* to call her his love.

Because she loved James, and she wanted him to love her back.

But that would never happen.

"I don't know what to do," she said.

And then clamped her mouth shut, because she had no idea what to say next. She didn't *want* to love him. She wanted to love the duke. But she loved James instead, because James was warm and affectionate and charitable and everything else the duke wasn't. It didn't matter anymore that James was too tall and had dark hair and a profession. He was brave and stoic. They fit perfectly together, and he was gorgeous, and as for his profession, well, he was trying to rid the world of the horror of smallpox, and whatever could be wrong with that?

But she couldn't marry James, because he would never love her. She'd be unhappy all her days, just like her poor mother.

And the duke needed her, and he was very kind, and he was sending her flowers and falling in love with her. James belonged with Amanda. They shared interests that Juliana didn't. They filled each other's needs.

Juliana's stomach didn't just feel queer anymore—it *hurt.* And she wished she'd never opened her mouth, because she couldn't possibly tell any of this to James.

Fortunately, he interpreted *I don't know what to do* in an entirely different context. "It doesn't make much sense to walk all the way up again only to turn around and come back down." Edging her even deeper under the steps, he traced his finger in a shivery line down her jaw. "Don't worry about whether your aunt will see us. I'll watch for her and the others. And while we're waiting, we can practice kissing."

She'd known he would say that, hadn't she? And she knew she should refuse. But she also knew she shouldn't make him walk up all those stairs again when his leg was already paining him.

"You don't need to practice kissing," she told him with no small amount of conviction. James had been married before, after all—not that he'd bothered to mention that fact when she'd first suggested the wooing lessons. He'd *had* practice. The way he kissed, a girl would have to be daft to think he needed practice.

His finger lingered at her chin, tracing shivery little circles. At the far end of the corridor, the door opened, admitting more people and light, enough light that Juliana could see the gold flecks in James's chocolate eyes.

The door shut, plunging the corridor back into darkness as the people made their way to the stairwell. The light had dazzled Juliana's eyes, and now she couldn't see a thing.

"It's been a long time since I've kissed anyone," said James's disembodied voice.

"It's been less than twenty-four hours."

"But before that, it was a long time."

His finger trailed down her throat, slowly. She hoped he couldn't feel her shaking. At least he couldn't see it. "You're not going to unbutton, are you?"

His laugh was quick, low, and pleased. "No, not here." His finger traced her collarbones, lightly. "Practice with me, will you?" he murmured.

She couldn't breathe. And she could hear people coming down the staircase.

"They cannot see us," he whispered, the words coming from just overhead. He'd moved even closer, and now his finger trailed its way back to her chin and tilted it up. "Will you?"

She whispered, "Yes." She couldn't help it. She'd allow just one kiss. Or maybe two.

She lost count.

The kisses were soft at first, trailing over her lips and jaw and throat, just as his finger had. She shivered and held on to him, lack of sight making her even more aware of sensations and sounds. Footsteps went up and down the stairs overhead while he slowly, lightly, retraced his path, each little spot of heat making her insides coil tighter in anticipation. And when his lips finally returned to hers, she threw her arms around his neck and kissed him as deeply as she knew how, wanting to kiss him forever, wanting him to make her forget that she shouldn't be wanting him at all.

"Juliana, are you down here?"

James pulled away. "Is that you, Lady Frances?" He whirled around and started down the corridor, while Juliana tried to catch her breath. Her pulse was racing, her head swimming. And she was suddenly cold. She hadn't even realized she was warm.

More footsteps sounded on the stairs, growing closer. Juliana stepped into the corridor just as four dark forms made it to the bottom. "There you all are!" she said.

At the other end, James opened the door, admitting a shaft of light. "We were looking for you."

"*We* were looking for *you*," Frances said, blinking madly. Well, it was dim, and she wasn't wearing her spectacles. "Lady Amanda wishes to return home."

"I was dizzy up there," Amanda said.

Juliana had felt a little dizzy up there, too, but she felt much more dizzy now. Dizzy and confused. She followed the others out into Leicester Square. Her knees felt shaky.

Her stomach was hurting again.

James would never love her. He needed to kiss Amanda and marry her, or everything would be ruined.

"Where should we go now?" she asked.

"Parliament," the duke said.

James pulled out his pocket watch, opened it, and snapped it shut. "Good gracious, it's nearly four o'clock." Indeed, people were starting to stream out of the Panorama. "The two of us should definitely go to Parliament."

How in heaven's name was she supposed to get James to kiss Amanda and decide to marry her if he was always in Parliament? "I've a sewing party from one o'clock until three tomorrow, but how about if we go somewhere in the late afternoon or the evening? The House of Lords doesn't meet on Wednesdays."

"We can go to Almack's," Amanda suggested.

"No," James said at the same time Juliana said, "I think not."

She wondered why he didn't want to attend Almack's, but it didn't really signify, because Almack's was a bad idea. Aunt Frances might be rather blind these days, but the lady patronesses who ran the gathering had vision sharper than tacks. It was too risky for James to kiss Amanda there. "How about Vauxhall Gardens?" she suggested instead.

"I adore Vauxhall Gardens," Aunt Frances gushed. "Especially at night."

"Only ladies of easy virtue go to Vauxhall Gardens at night," Amanda said, either not realizing or not caring that she'd just insulted Aunt Frances. "I enjoy gardens, but I'd prefer to visit somewhere more respectable."

"How about Chelsea Physic Garden, then?" James asked.

"Chelsea Physic Garden?" Juliana had never heard of the place. "Where is it?"

"In Chelsea, I presume," the duke said dryly.

Juliana shot him a peeved glance before turning back to James. "Is it very exciting?"

"It's very peaceful. I think Lady Amanda would like it. Only physicians and apothecaries can gain entrance, but I'm allowed to invite guests. And I could have my cook prepare a picnic supper."

"It sounds perfect," the duke said. "Shall we say five o'clock? Now I think we should be off."

THIRTY-SEVEN

*J*AMES'S AUNTS had proved to be even better seamstresses than Rachael and her sisters. Better and faster. As Juliana sat stitching like mad while her guests chatted, she tried to convince herself that, with Lady Avonleigh's and Lady Balmforth's help, she could successfully finish making all the baby clothes before her deadline a week from Saturday.

At the end of Monday's party, she'd had a hundred and twenty-one completed pieces and needed only a hundred and nineteen more. Well, perhaps the word *only* was a bit optimistic, especially considering most of the finished pieces were simple blankets and clouts. But it had been the first time the number of items completed exceeded the number of items still unmade, which seemed a milestone of sorts.

Counting today's sewing party, which was just getting underway, she had six left to go. Which meant if all twelve of her guests were willing to attend every time, she'd need them to finish…

Her head hurt. "Emily, how much is a hundred and nineteen divided by six?"

"Miss Emily isn't here," Lady Mabel wheezed.

Oh, that was right. Emily had finished cutting, and she still refused to sew, and she'd been busy lately anyway for some reason or another. Which meant Juliana had eleven ladies—well, twelve if she counted herself—and needed—

"Nineteen and five-sixths," Elizabeth said, interrupting her thoughts.

"Pardon?"

"One hundred nineteen divided by six is nineteen and five-sixths."

"You did that without paper?"

Elizabeth shrugged.

"My younger daughter was like that," Lady Avonleigh said. "She could do any calculation in her head."

"Our mother was good at arithmetic, too," Rachael said. "I expect Elizabeth inherited that ability from her."

"Brains do tend to run in families." Lady Stafford smiled toward Juliana. "Take my James, for instance. He's just as bright as Aurelia's daughter, who was his cousin."

"Much older cousin," Lady Balmforth pointed out.

"Yes. If she had lived, the poor dear, she'd have been a grand-mother by now, I expect—unlike my James, who is currently of marriageable age." Lady Stafford shot another smile to Juliana. "I was noticing at my dinner party, Lady Juliana, that the Duke of Castleton seems a mite reserved for a young lady of your enthusiasm."

"Yes, the duke surely is reserved," Juliana said distractedly, trying to figure out if they could make nineteen and five-sixths items at each party. "But that's only to be expected, considering his lonely childhood. Did you know he was born in this house? His cruel uncle and aunt sold it and made him move. The thought of it quite breaks my heart."

Seated beside Juliana, Rachael nudged her and leaned close to her ear. "I think Lady Stafford is hoping you'll marry her son."

Juliana wished things were different so she could. In fact, she wished so hard it made her grit her teeth. "Brilliant observation," she said tightly under her breath, "but much as I like Lady Stafford, her son doesn't love me. I'm marrying the duke. He's very nice and he needs me."

"I should think you'd rather have a husband who *wants* you," Rachael whispered.

"He does want me. He told me he's falling in love with me. He sends me roses. He dances with me at every event."

"From about three feet away."

It wasn't the duke's fault he was physically undemonstrative. He'd never known anything else. That was why he needed her.

Juliana's stomach hurt. She turned away and raised her voice. "I cannot thank you enough for coming, Lady Avonleigh and Lady Balmforth. You're both excellent seamstresses."

"Our mother taught us both to sew," Lady Balmforth said, "along with Cornelia, of course."

Lady Avonleigh nodded. "Cornelia and Bedelia didn't have daughters, but I followed tradition and taught mine to sew. My younger daughter was quite artistic and especially good with a needle."

Juliana and Rachael turned toward Lady Stafford expectantly. She didn't disappoint them. "My son is good with a needle, too. He does excellent sutures."

The cousins shared a smile, but Juliana's faded. "Do you think that together we can finish nineteen and five-sixths items this afternoon?"

"Twenty," Elizabeth said. "It's close enough to call it twenty."

"Of course. Do you think we can finish twenty? Twelve of us?"

"Of course," Corinna echoed. "We did twenty-three on Monday, remember? Without Ladies A and B."

Ladies A and B smiled, their needles flashing.

"Those were all clouts," Juliana said. "Not frocks, coats, caps, and the like, which are more complicated and take much longer."

Alexandra rubbed her belly, even though it still looked flat.

"We can finish twenty pieces, even if they're more difficult," she said soothingly. "We'll just stay later, until we're done."

"We can't," Amanda said. "Juliana and your aunt and I are leaving at five to go to Chelsea Physic Garden, and we'll need time to ready ourselves first."

"Chelsea Physic Garden?" Claire looked up from the little frock she was sewing. "What's that?"

"Some garden for doctors," Juliana said. "James thinks Amanda will like it."

Rachael tied off a thread. "You call him James?"

"Lord Stafford," Juliana gritted out, "said Chelsea Physic Garden is very peaceful."

"My son knows exactly what women enjoy," Lady Stafford said. "He's taken me to the garden in Chelsea, and it's lovely."

Reaching for a spool, Rachael leaned closer to Juliana. "So tell me about *James*," she whispered.

"There's nothing to tell," Juliana said. "And we must stop whispering. It's not polite."

"You're right," Rachael said louder as she threaded her needle. "I've been wondering," she said to the company in general, "whether it's a good idea to marry a gentleman expecting him to change."

Elizabeth's eyes widened. "Whom are you thinking of marrying?"

"No one in particular. It's just a hypothetical question."

"No," Corinna said flatly. "You cannot change people. If you marry someone expecting to change him, you'll be disappointed."

"Not necessarily," Juliana disagreed. "People change all the time. Look at Amanda."

Amanda blushed.

"Amanda *wanted* to change," Corinna argued. "That's very different from expecting a change in someone who's happy with himself."

Claire nodded. "Just think, Juliana. How would you feel if

someone married you expecting *you* to change? Or even hoping you would change? Wouldn't you prefer a husband who likes you just the way you are, without wishing you were different?"

"We're not talking about me," Juliana snapped. "It was Rachael asking the question."

But she knew they *were* talking about her. Or at least they could be. She was planning to marry the duke expecting him to change, and she knew the duke would probably hope she would change, too.

Whereas James liked her just the way she was. But only as a friend—he would never love her. He might like kissing her, but he'd never love her.

And he had to marry Amanda, or else three other people's lives would be ruined.

Her stomach had never hurt so badly in her life.

THIRTY-EIGHT

*A*S JAMES WAS leaving that evening, his mother walked into Stafford House. "How did your day go, dear?"

"Very well." Pausing in the entrance hall, he shifted the picnic basket he was carrying. "I wasn't shorthanded today, so I was able to stop by Gillow's to see the bedroom furniture you and your sisters picked out. It looks fine."

"Good. I chose the fabrics this morning, and I have a painter coming by later this week. This is all coming together very quickly."

"Excellent," he told her. "I truly appreciate your help. Did your sisters enjoy today's sewing party?"

"Very much. They're looking forward to another one tomorrow." She reached up to smooth his hair, making him feel about six years old again. "I was surprised to learn this afternoon that you're going to the Physic Garden rather than Almack's."

He shrugged. "Lady Juliana and Lady Amanda said they'd prefer to visit the garden."

"You've been spending a lot of time with your lovely young ladies."

"They're not my ladies, Mother." He hoped Juliana was

getting closer to becoming his lady—their outing to the Panorama had been encouraging—but she wasn't his lady yet.

"Are you going to marry one of them?"

He leveled his gaze on her. "Are you going to marry Lord Cavanaugh?"

She blinked. "I'm not prepared to say. At the moment I'm just enjoying his company."

"Exactly." He bent to kiss her on the cheek. "Enjoy Almack's, will you?"

He whistled as he went out the door, whistled as his carriage made its way to Berkeley Square. Things were looking up. He might have just managed to get his mother off his back, and in any case, an hour from now he'd be kissing Juliana.

He stopped whistling out loud when his guests joined him in the carriage, of course, but he was still whistling in his head. And toying with the deck of playing cards he'd slipped into his pocket. It was nearly six o'clock by the time they reached Chelsea and alighted from the carriage on Swan Walk.

"Good evening," he said to the guard at the garden's entrance.

"Good evening, Lord Stafford." The man swung open the gate set into the old redbrick wall. "Sunset is at quarter to nine."

"The garden closes at sunset," James told his party. "Is Wheeler here?" he asked the guard.

"Not tonight. He left at four."

"Oh, that's a pity," James said, although it wasn't a pity at all. In fact, it was exactly what he was hoping to hear.

"Who is Wheeler?" Juliana asked as they walked in.

"Thomas Wheeler is the Physic Garden's Demonstrator. He explains the uses of the medicinal plants to visitors. I can do that, though." He led them along a tree-lined path to the center of the garden. "Would you all like a tour, or would you prefer to dine first?"

"I'm famished," Castleton said. "We can look at plants later."

James suspected the fellow didn't want to look at plants at

all, which suited his plans just fine. He chose a grassy spot by the rockery and laid out a large blanket before opening the basket his cook had prepared. The duke and Lady Amanda hung back while James opened a bottle of wine and Juliana and her aunt unpacked cold chicken, bread, and cheese.

"I don't sit on the ground," Castleton said stuffily, taking his supper to a nearby bench.

What a turd, James thought for the umpteenth time.

Lady Amanda breathed a sigh of relief. "Neither do I," she said and joined the turd.

"You should sit by her," Juliana whispered.

"There's no more room on the bench," James whispered back. Actually, there *would* have been room on the bench if the two of them weren't sitting primly spaced apart from each other. But it was just as well, since he didn't want to sit with Lady Amanda anyway.

"No one else seems to be here," Lady Frances observed, happily settling close by Lord Malmsey on the blanket. "This place is so peaceful and enchanting."

Juliana pulled off her gloves as she sat down by them. "Corinna would love to come here and paint."

"I can obtain a ticket for her entrance," James said. He took glasses of wine to the turd and his companion, then lowered himself to the blanket by Juliana.

"What is the purpose of the garden?" Lord Malmsey asked.

James swallowed a mouthful of bread before speaking. "Doctors and apothecaries can visit to take cuttings of medicinal plants. But mostly it's used for educational and training purposes. Medical and apothecary students visit as part of their studies."

Juliana waved a chicken leg toward a white alabaster statue of a man holding a scroll, dressed in a fancy robe and a full, old-fashioned wig. "Who's that?"

"Dr. Hans Sloane, a former president of the Royal College of Physicians. In the late sixteen hundreds, he visited Jamaica and brought back a cinchona tree, having learned that the bark could be used to make quinine to treat malaria. He bought the garden later, when the Society of Apothecaries was at risk of losing it. He leased it back to them for only five pounds a year—they still pay the same price now."

"What an unusual rock garden," Lady Frances said, squinting toward it since she wasn't wearing her spectacles.

"The oldest in all of England, or so I've been told. It was built as a habitat for foreign plants that grow best in rocky soil. The white stones are from the Tower of London, the black from a volcano in Iceland, and that giant-clam shell is said to have been brought to England by Captain Cook."

"You seem to know everything," Juliana said, smiling over the rim of her wineglass. "We don't need a demonstrator, do we, Amanda?" She turned toward the bench. "Amanda?"

Amanda was gone. As was the turd.

"Where did they go?" Juliana asked.

"I don't know," Lady Frances mused. She turned to Lord Malmsey. "Theodore, would you help me look for them?"

"With pleasure, my dear." Belying their age, the two rose agilely to their feet, and Lord Malmsey tucked Lady Frances's hand in the crook of his arm. "Shall we, my love?"

Juliana shook her golden head as she watched them walk off. "I cannot believe it," she said when they were out of earshot.

James drained the rest of his wine and started packing up the remains of their dinner. "You cannot believe what?"

She frowned up at him. "I cannot believe Aunt Frances asked Lord Malmsey to go off alone with her. She's always been so shy. And I cannot believe everyone left us again."

Her eyes looked greenish, which was no surprise to James. After many hours of observation and analysis, he had finally puzzled out the mystery of Juliana's changeable irises: They were more blue when she was happy or excited, more green when she was worried or cross. Right now it wasn't hard to tell that she was rather distressed.

But the distress was a good sign. It wouldn't be long now before she figured out she didn't belong with Castleton. And if the evening went as planned, James would be turning her eyes back to blue before long.

"Everyone will be back soon," he said. "Lady Frances and Lord Malmsey will find the others."

"They aren't looking for them. They're off somewhere kissing."

"Really?" he said, reaching a hand to help her rise. "I guess we should go look for Castleton and Lady Amanda ourselves, then."

"Yes, we should," she said. "You're supposed to be with Lady Amanda."

Having seen where her friend and the turd had gone, James led Juliana along a path in the opposite direction, which, happily, was the direction he wanted to take her anyway. Trees lined both sides of the meandering gravel walkway, their leaves fluttering overhead. The sun was dropping toward the horizon, making the walled garden shady and romantic.

The ambiance couldn't have been better.

"I don't see them," Juliana said after they wandered a few minutes in companionable silence. "I cannot imagine where they might have disappeared to."

"Me, neither," James said, taking her hand. She'd left her gloves on the blanket, and her fingers felt warm in his, especially compared to the air. Juliana was wearing another dress made of thin, fine fabric, and with the sun setting, it was getting a bit chilly. "Maybe they're in the greenhouse," he suggested, leading her off the path. "They might have gone inside to warm up."

"It *is* warm in here," she said when they entered. Due to the abundance of glass, it was nearly as bright inside as out.

"I understand this was the first heated greenhouse in all of England," he told her. "Maybe the first in the whole world." He led her between the rows of plants toward the back wall. "Dr. Sloane wrote about the clever design of this greenhouse back in

1684. There are ovens beneath the floor." Stopping before a door marked PRIVATE, he reached for the knob.

"What are you doing?" she asked. "I don't think we're supposed to go in there."

"Maybe Castleton is in there with Lady Amanda."

"I think not." Still holding his hand, she pulled him away from the door. "Amanda would *never* go into a room alone with him. She's *much* too reserved for that."

"She was in a room alone with me," he reminded her. "Lord Billingsgate's library. She even tried to kiss me."

Her cheeks turned pink. "That's because she wants to marry you."

He reached again for the knob. "Maybe your aunt and Lord Malmsey are in there," he suggested, "kissing."

She pulled on his hand again. "I don't think—" she began, and then she gave a little yelp when he opened the door.

Smiling, he stepped inside. "They're not in here. Come in and see, lo—"

Bother. He'd almost called her *love* again.

Luckily, she was so concerned about trespassing, she didn't notice. After peeking her head in, she breathed a sigh of relief. "We're not supposed to be in here, James. The door is marked private."

"It's Thomas Wheeler's office," he said with a shrug. "The Demonstrator who went home earlier. He's a friend; he wouldn't mind." Actually, he *might* mind. But he'd never find out. James tugged on her hand. "Come on."

It was a tiny cubby, with a compact desk against the inside wall and a small round wooden table with two chairs in the center. "The table is for demonstrations," he explained. The exterior wall was glass, of course, it being part of the greenhouse. But trees grew so closely all around that no one could possibly see in, though plenty of light filtered in through the leaves and the glass ceiling overhead.

He shut the door, shutting them in together.

She whirled to face him, dropping his hand. "What are you doing, James?"

He reached into his pocket and pulled out the deck of cards. "Since we can't seem to find our companions, I remembered I wanted you to teach me to play casino," he said casually. "It's cold out there and warm in here, so I thought it might be nice to sit a while and play cards."

She eyed him warily, her gaze now blue-green. "Maybe for a minute."

"Excellent." He sat and waved her toward the second chair. After she sat, he slid his chair around the table and up against hers.

Taking the cards, she frowned. "You're supposed to sit across from me."

"I will after I learn. Right now I need to see your cards."

"Very well." When she shuffled the cards, he could feel the vibrations. They were that close. She dealt out four cards to each of them and four more faceup on the table, then put the rest aside. "Pick up your hand," she instructed, "and see if any of your cards match the ones on the table." Then she proceeded to explain all the rules, none of which he bothered listening to, since he already knew how to play casino.

As she talked and moved the cards around, he breathed in her sunshine-and-flowers scent and admired the light bouncing off her wheaten hair. He let his shoulder brush against her arm and watched her eyes turn a little bluer.

"Are you listening, James? Did you get all of that?"

"Of course." It was a simple game, really. At least for him. He and his brother had kept a running score for years, and he'd always stayed miles ahead. "I think I'm ready to play now."

"All right." She gathered the cards and began reshuffling them. "You can move to the other side of the table."

"I'd rather stay here for the first couple of hands. In case I need your help. By the way, what shall we wager?"

"Wager? We don't need to wager."

"I never play games without a wager. A wager makes it so much more interesting and fun."

"I suppose I'm not surprised. I heard about how Griffin lost thirty guineas to you playing chess." She stopped shuffling and slanted him a sideways glance. "But I didn't bring any money."

"We'll wager something else, then," he said blithely.

"Like what?" She looked wary again. But her eyes weren't turning green. They were staying blue.

"How about buttons?" he suggested.

"Buttons? We didn't bring buttons."

"We have buttons on our clothes. When one of us loses, he or she can unbutton a button."

THIRTY-NINE

JULIANA WAS scandalized. In fact, she couldn't remember ever being *more* scandalized.

Who ever heard of wagering buttons? The mere concept seemed wicked. How dare James suggest such a thing! If he ever suggested it to Amanda, she'd faint dead away.

That's why Juliana had to agree to the wager.

She had to teach James a lesson. And she certainly would—after all, since he didn't know how to play the game and had been daydreaming while she'd explained the rules, he was sure to lose. And cocky as he was, losing would mortify him. Then he'd know this sort of tactic could easily backfire, and he wouldn't try it with Amanda and make the poor girl faint.

"All right," she said, "we'll wager buttons."

James looked surprised and quite pleased. His fingers went immediately to his neckcloth, working the knot.

"What are you doing?" she asked.

"Exposing my buttons. Go ahead and deal." He peeled off his tailcoat and tossed it on the desk.

She dealt. They picked up their cards. James fanned his out and smiled. "I go first—is that right?" She nodded, and he plucked a king from his hand and used it to claim the king on the table. "Aha," he said. "You have to unbutton a button."

"You haven't won yet!" she protested. "That was just a single trick." Anyone could win a trick; the real skill was winning the whole game. "Were you not listening, James? We have to play until all the cards are gone, and then we add up the points, and whoever has the most points wins. *Then* somebody unbuttons a button."

She'd almost said *then you unbutton a button*, but she'd stopped herself in time. Of course she was going to win, but it wouldn't do to sound smug about it.

"Oh, no," he said. "We don't have time for that. We've only a few minutes, remember? It's getting dark, and we'll have to leave. We're wagering a button for each trick."

"We are not! We're wagering a button for each game."

"We don't have time to play more than one game. And you agreed to the wager, Juliana. Unbutton a button."

"Honestly, this is ridiculous." With a huff, she reached behind her back and wrenched open a button. "There. Are you happy now? It's my turn." It was only beginner's luck—she wouldn't let him win any more tricks. She took an eight out of her hand and claimed a seven and an ace with it, smirking because an ace was worth an extra point. "I took a trick," she said. "Unbutton."

James didn't seem at all reluctant to undo the top button on his shirt. He pulled a ten from his hand and took the ten of diamonds, which was worth *two* extra points. "I think you should unbutton two buttons," he said with a smirk of his own.

"I think not." She was surprised he even remembered the ten was a special card. Had he been paying more attention than she'd realized? "Each trick is worth one button only. Otherwise, you'd have had to unbutton twice when I took the ace."

He flicked open another of his buttons. "There, now I've unbuttoned twice for your ace. And you owe me *three* buttons for the ten."

"I cannot reach that many of my buttons," she said petulantly. This was not going at *all* according to plan.

He smirked again. "You poor thing. I'll get them for you." And he reached behind her back and unbuttoned three of her buttons.

She felt her cheeks blaze. She had a chemise on beneath her dress, so it wasn't like he could see any bare skin. And he wasn't looking, anyway. But she still felt ridiculous or scandalous or both.

"Really, James, this is very childish." She was so distracted she hardly knew what cards she was playing—which only made things worse. James's next trick was worth another extra point. He grinned. "Two buttons."

"How did you—?" And that's when it dawned on her. She gasped in outrage. "You already knew how to play casino, didn't you?"

His grin widened as he reached to undo two more of her buttons. "I never said I didn't."

"You asked me to teach you!"

"Exactly. But I never said I didn't know how to play." His eyes twinkled as he watched her discard. "Too bad you couldn't take a trick," he drawled. "I, on the other hand..." He took another trick with his final card. "I believe you owe me a button."

"You deceived me," she complained. "After you got cross with me for deceiving you."

He raised a dark brow. "This is a card game. It's not at all the same as trying to deceive someone into a marriage."

He was right about that. Drat. Right enough to make her feel guilty. Right enough to make her drop *that* argument like a hot poker.

She snatched up the deck and began dealing the next round. "I don't have any more buttons on my dress."

"Hmm." He picked up his new cards and discarded a six. "Then I think you owe me a kiss instead."

"I do not." None of her new cards matched anything on the table. She had two aces in her hand and had to risk one if she wanted a chance to win both. She chose one and tossed it down. "It's your turn."

"An ace," he mused, "imagine that." He swept both it and the six up with a seven. "Two more points! That makes three kisses you owe me."

"I'm not kissing you."

All at once, his demeanor changed. He set his cards face-down and propped his chin on one hand, which brought his eye level down to hers. He was still smiling, but it was less teasing, and his eyes searched hers. "Don't you like kissing me?"

It sounded like he was really asking, like he wanted to hear her answer.

Her skin prickled, even though it was very warm in the greenhouse. "Um…" She had to say something. "I…don't know."

"I think you do." He didn't sound smug at all anymore; he sounded kind. And his voice was deeper now. He'd grown more serious. "I think you do know. And I think you *do* like kissing me." He scooted closer and skimmed his fingers over her cheek. "I think you want me to kiss you right now," he said in that low, chocolatey tone.

Faith. She wanted him to kiss her. And she wanted to kick herself for wanting him to kiss her. Especially after his deception—she knew she was playing right into his hands.

Suddenly she found her own hand reaching out to brush the little V of skin that was visible where he'd unbuttoned his measly two buttons.

His smile returning, he moved even closer. And closer still. He still had his chin propped so their faces were level. For once she wouldn't have to tilt her head all the way back to kiss him.

"May I kiss you now?" he asked.

Why was he asking? Why didn't he just go ahead and kiss

her? He'd done the same thing at Vauxhall Gardens and in the Panorama, asking her permission, making her agree.

She wished he'd just kiss her instead of asking, because she knew she should refuse, and she felt bad for being too weak to say *no*.

"May I?" he pressed. He was so close, there hardly seemed to be enough space to breathe. Or maybe it was just that *she* couldn't breathe. Nor could she open her mouth to speak. She wanted to say *yes*, but all she could manage was a tiny, almost imperceptible nod.

That was good enough for him.

His mouth crossed that last little space and proceeded to kiss her senseless. Her cards fluttered to the floor as he managed to maneuver her onto his lap. She sighed and leaned into him, feeling every part of her that was touching him—which was *many* parts, what with her being cradled in his lap like that— tingling, her nerves thrumming, her senses swirling. Loving it, loving *him*, she hooked an arm around his neck and kissed him and kissed him for she didn't know how long.

Finally they had to come up for air, and her head slowly cleared, and she began to realize where she was. On James's lap… in the heated greenhouse… in the garden he was *meant* to be enjoying with Amanda…

Faith, what had she done?

She'd let James kiss her again, that's what. And pull her onto his lap! The man who was supposed to be marrying her friend— no, the man who *had* to marry her friend, or Aunt Frances would be devastated.

She was appalled at herself. Absolutely, positively appalled.

"Juliana?" James whispered. When she met his gaze, he broke into a smile. "Your eyes are blue. Deep blue."

She didn't want him smiling at her. He needed to be smiling at Amanda. "Obviously it's getting too dark for you to see," she snapped. "My eyes are hazel."

He laughed. And then he kissed her again, and she let him, which made her feel better and worse all at the same time.

"It *is* getting dark," he finally admitted, sounding reluctant. "We need to go find the others before the garden's gates are locked."

She slid off his lap, and he turned her around and buttoned her dress. And tucked in her hair that had slipped from its pins. And buttoned his two buttons, shrugged into his tailcoat, and knotted his neckcloth in place, haphazardly as usual. And she reached to straighten it, unable to help herself, even though she knew she shouldn't. And she let him kiss her again, a little sweet kiss that made her heart skitter.

But surely his heart, she reminded herself, didn't skip a beat.

She had to remember he would never love her. No matter how much he liked kissing her, he'd never be more than her friend. He needed to become friends with Amanda instead.

She *really* couldn't let him kiss her again after this. Or touch her again. Ever.

He gathered the cards from the table and the floor, and then they left the greenhouse and went back to the middle of the garden where everyone else was waiting.

Aunt Frances had obviously been kissing Lord Malmsey; in the dim light of the setting sun, they both looked flushed and happy. Aunt Frances had finished packing up the basket, and Lord Malmsey had folded the blanket. He was holding it over his arm.

Naturally, the duke and Amanda had done nothing to help. The two of them were much too aristocratic to do servants' work. And of course they hadn't kissed, either. Neither of them was flushed. No doubt Amanda had gone off with the duke purposely, specifically to avoid any kissing.

So Juliana had been kissed instead. And she very much feared she looked flushed, though she was quite certain she didn't look happy.

Never again, she reminded herself fiercely.

"Where have you been?" Amanda asked. "David and I have been looking all over for you."

For a moment, Juliana felt puzzled, but then she remembered the duke's name was David. How could she have forgotten the name of the man she was planning to marry? And when had Amanda—proper, reserved Amanda—begun calling the duke by his given name? She was planning to marry James, and she was still calling *him* Lord Stafford.

Nothing was right tonight. Nothing. Nothing was going well. Nothing made any sense.

Her stomach hurt.

"We were playing cards," James explained, pulling the deck out of his pocket to prove it. "All of you went off, so we decided to go in the greenhouse where it was warm and play cards."

Nobody looked suspicious. Apparently it was a reasonable explanation. Nobody, after all—most especially nobody as innocent as Aunt Frances or Amanda—would think playing cards could possibly lead to kissing.

But although that was a relief, Juliana's stomach still hurt. She had to fix everything. Somehow, some way, she had to get James together with Amanda.

"I'm going to the Pevenseys' tomorrow night," she said as they all started walking toward the Stafford carriage. "For a musical evening. I hope you'll all want to come." What she would do when they got there, how she would get James together with Amanda, she hadn't a clue.

But getting them there would be a start.

"I would love to attend a musical evening," Aunt Frances said as she climbed in.

"I would love to attend, too," Lord Malmsey agreed, following her.

"So would I," Amanda said and climbed in next, sitting across from them.

Juliana climbed in herself, taking the opposite end of the seat from Amanda in order to leave space in the middle for James.

She gestured to the duke, indicating the spot across from her. "I hope you'll come, too."

"Much as I would be delighted to spend the evening with you, my dear, I think I should go to Parliament," he said as he took the place by Amanda.

How annoying. How absolutely annoying. He was supposed to sit across from her and leave the space by Amanda for James. "I should think you would prefer to attend a musical evening," she said rather peevishly.

"I abhor the Pevenseys' musical evenings," he said, not peevishly in the least. And then he smiled down at her apologetically, and she realized he wasn't sitting in the space by Amanda, he was sitting in the space by *her*. Rather close, as a matter of fact, so she probably shouldn't be so annoyed. Perhaps her warmth was already making him more affectionate. She scooted a little closer, so they'd be touching.

And that was when she realized she wasn't going to be a duchess.

She couldn't marry the duke.

They were touching, but she didn't feel a thing. She wasn't tingling anywhere. She couldn't even *imagine* sitting on his lap the way she had with James in the greenhouse. Now that she knew what love felt like, she knew she would never have those feelings for the duke.

She felt terrible. The duke was so nice, and he was falling in love with her, but she couldn't love him back. He'd suffered hurt and rejection throughout his childhood, and now she was going to reject him again. How could she tell him? How could she cast him aside so heartlessly?

And what about Griffin? Poor Griffin. He was going to be so disappointed; he was going to have to start looking for another husband for her. She obviously wouldn't be marrying this season—it would probably be another year at least. How was she going to tell Griffin?

James climbed in. "I abhor such musical evenings, too," he

said as a footman shut the door. He took the place across from her and settled back, his legs so long his knees touched hers. How annoying when she was immersed in trying to figure out a gentle way to break this distressing news to her brother and the duke.

James smiled at her as though he could tell she was annoyed. As though he found it amusing. "No man worth his salt would choose a musical evening over Parliament," he informed her.

"A Roman proverb!" Amanda exclaimed.

"It is not!" Juliana snapped.

"It is," Amanda said reasonably, sounding very bookish. "It alludes to the practice of paying Roman soldiers with rations of salt. Our English word *salary* comes from the Latin word *salarium*, which means salt money."

"She's right," the duke said. "*A man worth his salt* has been a proverb for centuries."

It was a very long ride home.

*L*ORD MALMSEY was the youngest man in attendance at the Pevenseys' musical evening.

"Where is everyone?" Amanda asked.

Actually, the Pevenseys' drawing room was teeming with people. But all of them—save Lord Malmsey and a few doddering old men—were female. Remembering the way James and the duke had reacted to her invitation last night, Juliana sighed. "I guess most gentlemen *would* prefer to sit through Parliament than an evening of music."

"Except for Lord Malmsey," Amanda said.

"If it weren't for my aunt, he'd probably be at Parliament, too." Indeed, Lord Malmsey had made a beeline for Aunt Frances the moment they'd walked in the door. The two of them were off in a corner, whispering, even now.

Whispering endearments, no doubt. Lord Malmsey was looking more and more besotted—and more anxious about his still-intact engagement—every day. Juliana wished more than ever that Lord Malmsey could call off the wedding, but wishing didn't change facts. It just wasn't possible, not if he ever wanted to show his face in society again.

Amanda clutched Juliana's arm. "I need to talk to you."

"About what?"

"My father," she said, looking even more miserable than Lord Malmsey.

If Aunt Frances knew Lord Malmsey was engaged, she'd look more miserable than both of them put together. Juliana's projects all seemed to be falling apart. She still hadn't figured out how to break the news to the duke or her brother. "What about your father?" she asked Amanda.

But before Amanda could answer, Lady Stafford waltzed up. "Good evening, Lady Juliana!" All smiles in contrast to everyone else, James's mother was accompanied by Lord Cavanaugh, who, while older than Lord Malmsey, at least wasn't in his dotage. "It's a pleasure to see you here."

"I adore music," Juliana said. "I was thrilled to receive Lady Pevensey's invitation."

"This is your first season, isn't it?" Lord Cavanaugh asked dryly.

"Oh, hush," Lady Stafford said. "It shall be an enchanting event." She turned back to Juliana. "Are you attending Lady Hartley's breakfast on Sunday?"

"I haven't decided. I'm supposed to have a sewing party."

"Oh, you must attend—it's the event of the season. Everyone will be there."

"Including your sisters?"

"Without a doubt. I must tell you, my sisters are thoroughly enjoying your sewing parties. They haven't called on my son for an examination in two entire days."

"I have only four sewing parties left before the baby clothes are due." Three if she went to Lady Hartley's breakfast, which she might as well do if no one would be available to sew with her anyway. "I told Lord Stafford his aunts would have less time to ponder their health if they had gentlemen courting them, but he claimed they wouldn't be interested."

Lady Stafford flashed Lord Cavanaugh, who was courting her, a fond smile. "My sisters are older and set in their ways."

"I think they're just bored and need something to do. Something to get them out of their house after my sewing project is complete."

"Perhaps you're right, dear. They've been helping me renovate one of Stafford House's bedrooms, but that will be finished soon, too. I cannot imagine what else could be found to occupy them afterwards. They won't hear of redecorating their own house."

Standing on the temporary stage she'd had erected in her drawing room, Lady Pevensey clapped her hands. "If you'll all take your seats, we're ready to begin!"

"I shall think about your sisters," Juliana promised Lady Stafford before turning to find a seat. "There must be something they could do."

Aunt Frances and Lord Malmsey had seated themselves in the last row, so she headed toward the front in order to give them some privacy. After this afternoon's party, she had a hundred and fifty-seven baby items completed, which meant she needed eighty-three more. That hadn't seemed an impossible task, with four parties remaining—slightly more than twenty items per party. Perfectly reasonable, especially if she made a few by herself in between. But with only three parties…

"We need to talk." As she slid onto a first-row chair, Amanda grabbed her arm. "We cannot talk up here, right in front of the musicians."

Juliana didn't want to talk; she wanted to listen. She normally spent hours on her harp, but lately all her projects had left her scant time for playing. But Amanda looked panicked. "Very well," Juliana said, walking around to take a chair in a middle row. "What do you need to tell me about your father?"

Amanda took the chair beside her. "I've received word that he'll be arriving in three days. Early Sunday evening." She clutched her hands together in her lap, perhaps to keep them from shaking. "He's coming to see to the final details of my wedding."

Juliana reached over to squeeze her friend's white-knuckled fingers. "We still have time—"

"No, we don't! It's scheduled for a week from Saturday, and—"

"Ladies and gentlemen," Lady Pevensey announced, "I'm honored to introduce our first guest musicians. Miss Harriet Kent will perform Mozart's Sonata in C Major on the pianoforte, accompanied by her sister, Miss Hillary Kent, on the violin."

The room fell silent while the Kent sisters minced their way to the stage.

"A week from Saturday," Amanda repeated, "and—"

"Shh!" someone hissed behind them.

Juliana folded her hands in her own lap. "Wait," she whispered to Amanda.

Her friend waited, as tense as the younger Miss Kent's bowstrings. When the lively notes of the first movement filled the air, she wasted no time before resuming their conversation in a lower tone. "My wedding is a week from Saturday. My time is running out. I need James to compromise me—I must try again to trick him."

"You must not!"

"Shh!" someone else hissed.

"You must not," Juliana repeated in a whisper. "That would be unethical and dishonest. We shouldn't have tried it the first time, and I won't try it again."

"We have no choice!"

"Shh!"

"Shh!"

"Shh!"

Juliana twisted in her chair to glance behind her. Several people were glaring. All women. A couple of the aging men were already nodding off. "Hush," she murmured, turning back to Amanda. "Of course you have a choice. You can choose to act warmly towards James. Once you become friends, he'll propose to you and agree to the compromise."

She was beginning to think it would never happen. Or maybe she was beginning to *hope* it would never happen. Because James would certainly kiss Amanda if he proposed to her, and even though Juliana couldn't marry him, the thought of James kissing anyone else made her stomach hurt.

She leaned closer. "I have an idea," she whispered in desperation. She knew her friend wouldn't like it, but she'd feel much better about abandoning the duke if she could offer a replacement, and Amanda didn't seem to want to kiss James anyway. "Would you like to marry the duke?"

"No!" Amanda looked horrified. "I told you I would never marry a by-blow!"

Whispers broke out behind them, and a few more people hissed *"Shh!"*

Juliana wished Amanda hadn't said *by-blow* quite so loud. "Whyever do you keep going off with the duke, then?" she pressed. "Why have you begun calling him David?"

"Well, he's very nice. I think we're becoming friends. But there's a big difference between a friend and a husband."

Didn't Juliana know it.

She was disappointed but not surprised. She'd known Amanda kept going off with the duke only to avoid kissing James. "Maybe you should choose another man," she suggested. Plenty of gentlemen were still asking Amanda to dance at every ball. "At the Teddington ball on Saturday—"

"I want Lord Stafford. Besides, there isn't enough time to choose another man and expect him to propose."

"We have a little more than a week—"

"No, we don't. My father will be here Sunday, and knowing him he probably won't let me out of the house after that."

Drat. That did rather complicate matters. It seemed Juliana would have to see to it that James kissed Amanda—and not as part of a plot—before Sunday.

She would have to get them alone together. Truly alone. It was the only solution. James seemed more interested in pursuing

Juliana's friendship than Amanda's, so she couldn't count on him to take the initiative. And Amanda's fear of intimacy was obviously making her cling to anyone she instinctively felt would *never* try to kiss her—such as the duke—so she couldn't be counted on, either. If Juliana wanted James and Amanda to kiss, she would have to make sure there was no one else around for either of them to cling to, *and* she would have to make sure they were alone long enough to become friends.

But if Juliana could manage all that, everything else would work itself out. Once they were friends, James would warm up to Amanda. And once he kissed her, Amanda's cool exterior would melt—having experienced James's kisses herself, Juliana was confident of that. After all, *she'd* nearly got herself compromised by James on several occasions, and she didn't even *want* to marry the fellow!

And once all that was taken care of, the rest would fall into place, and everyone would end up married to the right person. Except for Juliana herself.

Her stomach hurt like the very dickens.

But how to get James and Amanda to go somewhere alone? She couldn't imagine. Amanda wouldn't agree to an outing without a chaperone, but perhaps Juliana could plan another group outing and then claim Aunt Frances felt ill. And she felt ill. And the duke felt ill.

Oh, bother, that would never work.

It felt like there was a dagger lodged in her stomach.

She'd figure out something tomorrow. Right after she figured out how she would finish eighty-three more items of baby clothes with only three sewing parties instead of four.

"Are you all right?" Amanda asked.

"Shh!"

Amanda lowered her voice. "Why are you clutching your middle?"

Juliana unfolded her arms and tried to draw a calming breath. She was nearing the end of her rope, she feared. One more tiny hiccup and she'd find herself curled up on Lady Pevensey's exquisite Turkey carpet.

"I'm fine," she gritted out, ignoring another chorus of *Shh!* "Just fine."

But although she normally loved music and the Misses Kent were more than proficient performers, Mozart didn't give her any enjoyment tonight. And neither did the Handel or Beethoven that came after.

She should have stayed home. She needed to sew. Even more important, she needed to discourage James's attentions so he'd turn to Amanda instead. And for *that*, she needed a few hours in the kitchen.

It was time to bring out her secret weapon: Miss Rebecca Chase's lemon slices.

FORTY-ONE

LEMON SLICES

Take a measure of Butter and one of Sugar and mix them together with the grated rinde of two Lemons. Put in two Eggs and then Flower, a spoon of leavening, and a little Milk. Put in a loaf tin and Bake until it rises and turns golde. Make holes with a skewer and pour in the juice of two Lemons. Leave the cake until colde and then turn from the tin and cut it into slices.

The sour lemons will turn a man sour to your charms. I thwarted my grandmother's matchmaking scheme twice by serving these slices to the dratted suitors.

—Miss Rebecca Chase, 1695

FOR FIVE DAYS—ever since she'd come to his house and offered to volunteer—James had been thinking about getting Juliana alone in one of the Institute's treatment rooms.

He'd barely listened to a word of yesterday's Parliament session. Overnight, his dreams had been full of sunshine and flowers and thin dresses. This morning, as he'd shaved and dressed, he'd let his mind roam free among various fantasy scenarios. In his favorite scenario, after a great deal of kissing, Juliana confessed her love for James, and then they both mounted Velocity and rode him over to Castleton's house to deliver in person the joyous news of their engagement.

All right, that one wasn't *entirely* plausible.

Especially since, as it turned out, fate was conspiring against him today.

Juliana rushed in as the clock struck one. Juggling two baskets while she folded her umbrella, she made her way through the crowded reception room. "I'm sorry, but I cannot stay long. I've instructed the driver to come back in three hours. I've much too much sewing to do." She paused and blinked. "What are you doing behind the counter?"

"Playing assistant while I interview for a new one," he said, frowning at her dress. For no good reason he could imagine, she was wearing a rather plain garment made of some sort of thick material—wool?—and had filled in her neckline with a froufrou scarf. Most displeasing.

"Another assistant has left?" She came around to join him and set down her baskets. "Again?"

"Unfortunately, yes. Somehow, another one found herself with child." He shook his head. "I don't understand it. It's an epidemic."

"I suppose you gave her fifty pounds?"

"Yes. She was much relieved, but now I need to find someone new. What did you bring me?" he asked, lifting the doily that covered one of the baskets.

"Fabric." Laughing at the look on his face, she pulled out a handful of white material and waved it under his nose. "Would you care for some? Appetizing, isn't it?"

He gave her a wry smile. "I thought maybe you'd made some sweets."

"I don't have time to bake. I barely have time to breathe." She sighed and delved into the second basket. "But I baked anyway. Have a lemon slice." After he took one, she shooed him toward the back. "Go vaccinate some of these people before even more show up, or else they'll have to stand out in the rain. I'll take over here, and I'll let you know if anyone promising comes in to apply for the position."

James went, finding the lemon slice delicious but grumbling all the way nonetheless. He'd never resented having too many patients before—the more people who agreed to be immunized, after all, the sooner smallpox would become a thing of the past. But just now, it wasn't sniffling children he most wanted to see in his treatment rooms. It was Juliana.

Without a stupid scarf covering her up to her chin.

Between sewing baby clothes, Juliana proved a model of efficiency, but he and the other physician could vaccinate only so fast. Nearly three hours passed before the number of patients dwindled enough so that everyone waiting had a seat. When Dr. Payton left and two more doctors arrived for the second shift, James heaved a sigh of relief and joined Juliana behind the counter.

There was a little crease between her brows, and though her gaze flicked to meet his for a moment, it was soon back on the task in her hands. Her shoulders looked stiff and hunched. He stepped behind her to massage them, finding her muscles tense and knotted.

"Come into the back with me," he murmured. "I'll make you feel better."

"I cannot. The carriage will be here any minute, and until then I must keep sewing." Though her needle stabs seemed frantic and rather random, she was getting the job done. "Besides, we really shouldn't be alone, James. You know what will happen."

Of course he knew what would happen. He would kiss her, and she would like it, which would eventually lead to better things. Though he knew it was only a matter of time before she realized that she, not prissy Lady Amanda, belonged with him, he was beginning to get impatient.

He kept rubbing her shoulders, firmly but tenderly,

wondering why her taut muscles refused to relax. "Just for a minute," he wheedled. "Nothing will happen in just a minute."

In two or three minutes, however...

"Your afternoon assistant has yet to arrive," she said without looking up. "We cannot leave all these people out here unsupervised."

She was right about that. He sighed and planted a kiss on the top of her head, not caring if the patients saw. "No luck finding a new assistant?"

"Have another lemon slice, will you?"

He didn't take one, because he didn't want to let go of her to do so. Her slight shoulders felt good in his hands, though their stiffness wasn't easing, which was worrisome. "I'm not hungry," he said.

Now *she* sighed. "Your last assistant sent in a friend, but I didn't think you should hire her."

"Why not? Could the woman not read?"

She bit off the end of a thread and leaned away from him to reach into her basket for a spool, sighing again when he leaned with her. "Yes, she could read. But I feared she'd find herself with child before long."

His fingers stilled. *"What?"*

"You heard me." She pulled off a length of thread. "You've lost two assistants due to pregnancy already. Why do you think that is?"

Actually, he'd lost four assistants to pregnancy, not two—but he wasn't about to admit that now. "Something in the water?" he speculated.

"Your generosity," she declared. "You're too nice, James."

"Pardon?" He released her shoulders and walked around to face her. "How on earth can a person be too nice?"

"When your niceness allows others to take advantage of you," she said, her fingers not faltering for an instant. "I'd lay odds that last girl sent her friend here with a promise of fifty pounds."

James's jaw dropped. "You think they're getting pregnant on purpose?"

"Or they were never pregnant at all." She stuck the end of the thread in her mouth to wet it.

He leaned on the counter, shaking his head in disbelief. "It sounds far-fetched to me. But even if you're right, what am I to do? I suppose I could consider only male applicants, but that seems rather—"

"Certainly not! I think you need to find someone older, more responsible. Someone you can trust."

"Most older women aren't seeking work. They're busy raising families."

"I mean *much* older women." Having threaded the needle, she looked up, and he found himself lost in her greenish eyes. "Like your aunts."

He blinked. "My aunts?"

"Excuse me," she said, turning away to hand a number to a woman waiting by the counter with two children.

"You're number forty-two," she told the woman. "I'll call you when it's your turn."

She turned back to him, meeting his gaze again, looking like she wanted to say something. But she didn't. Her eyes went even greener. She swallowed slowly and lowered her gaze to her lap, wrapping her arms about her middle. She looked frail.

The chatter of the waiting patients grew louder in the silence that stretched between them.

He whipped out a hand and plucked the scarf from her front.

"Hey!" She snatched it back. "Whyever did you do that?"

"You're not acting like Juliana. And you don't *look* like Juliana—not with that silly scarf or whatever it's called."

"It's a fichu," she informed him primly, stuffing it back into place.

Juliana was never prim. Or so tense and distant. And, most of all, she definitely wasn't frail. He reached to skim his knuckles along her chin. She didn't react. "What's wrong, Juliana?"

Her jaw set. "Nothing."

"You're working too hard. You're exhausted."

She reached into one of the baskets and handed him a lemon slice. "Eat this, please."

"I'm not hungry."

"Eat it," she demanded in a distinctly un-Juliana-like way. Her gaze flicked to the door, where a footman in Chase livery had just entered. She waved to him, looking relieved. "My carriage is here. But your aunts are bored. They need something to do."

"They're both countesses, in case you've forgotten. They're not looking for employment."

"And I'm not suggesting you pay them. Your mother told me they're enjoying my sewing parties, and even more significant, they've stopped calling on you to examine them. But I've only three more parties, and then they'll be bored again and back to their tricks. Unless they help you instead." She shoved the fabric, needle, and thread into the other basket. "They won't think of it as employment or work, you see; they'll consider it an act of charity. And if they're busy helping here, they won't have time to fret about their health."

It was brilliant. In one fell swoop, Juliana might have solved both his problems, giving his aunts something to do and providing him with permanent, reliable assistants.

Apparently Juliana's meddling wasn't *always* an inconvenience.

"How do you do it?" he asked. "How do you figure out what people need and put two and two together? Why *are* you so good at what you do?"

She shrugged. "I just pay attention."

It couldn't be that simple. "What if my aunts don't want to be assistants?"

"They'll be thrilled at the very suggestion," she promised with supreme confidence. "Shall I ask them for you?"

"I can ask them. I'll stop by on my way to Parliament. Thank you, Juliana," he said, reaching to touch her arm. When she flinched, a shock of hurt rattled him. "What is it? What's wrong?"

"You were right—I'm exhausted. And overwhelmed. And the dratted lemon slices aren't working."

"Pardon?" He looked down to the uneaten slice in his hand and back up, horrified to see tears flooding her eyes. "What do lemon slices have to do with anything?"

"Nothing," she muttered. "I'm sorry." She inched around the counter and headed toward the door. "Eat the lemon slices, will you? All of them. I'll see you at the Teddington ball tomorrow. I must go home and sew."

FORTY-TWO

ON SATURDAY evening, Griffin watched Juliana scan the Teddingtons' ballroom. "Where's Lord Stafford?" she asked.

"Shouldn't you be looking for Castleton?"

"He's in the card room, gambling away his fortune."

Griffin wondered why she sounded so disapproving. "Castleton isn't an inveterate gambler. He plays only to amuse himself."

She shrugged. "He only ever does anything to amuse himself."

"And you find this objectionable?" He narrowed his gaze. "Since when?" She was supposed to be in love with the fellow! Unless...he was suddenly seized by an alarming notion. "Do you not want to marry him anymore?"

She looked away. "He needs me."

"I should hope you'd want to marry someone because *you* need *him*."

She cocked her head at him. "Rachael says people should marry because they want each other, not need each other. It's remarkable how all the unwedded people I know are so very wise in the ways of marriage," she added dryly.

Griffin ignored that. "Has Castleton kissed you yet?"

"Would you want to hear about it if he did?"

He supposed he didn't; there was little more uncomfortable than envisioning one's sister in a romantic embrace. However, he knew Juliana well enough to know she wouldn't hesitate to give him the details in all their cringe-inducing glory, so he had to figure her response meant the duke hadn't kissed her yet.

He'd meant to have a talk with Castleton the next time he came to call on Juliana, but the fellow hadn't been coming around lately. "I think I'll go play cards," he told his sister.

"Just don't lose thirty guineas."

Wherever had *that* caustic comment come from? he wondered as he made his way to the card room. He rarely gambled, and never for high stakes.

Castleton was playing whist. "Yes?" he asked when Griffin walked up.

"I heard from my stableman yesterday. Velocity has been running well. You still want him, don't you?"

He shifted, tossing a card on the table without meeting Griffin's gaze. "Very much."

"Excellent. You might try kissing my sister."

Griffin turned to go and ran smack dab into Rachael, who was wearing a dress the same sky blue color as her eyes. She looked like she might have a slight cold—red nose, glassy eyes—though it didn't dampen her appeal.

But for once, he wasn't flustered by Rachael's sultriness; he was too busy panicking over what she might have heard.

"What are you doing here?" he asked through clenched teeth.

"At the ball or in the card room? My sisters dragged me to the ball. And I followed you in here." She glanced around at all the people uneasily. "I have something I'd like to ask you. In private."

He relaxed. It seemed she hadn't overheard his conversation with the duke. "Let's find Lord Teddington's library."

"All right." She walked beside him from the room. "What

does Velocity have to do with the Duke of Castleton kissing your sister?"

Blast it.

He hesitated, but another explanation wasn't springing to mind. "Ah, yes, well...I promised him Velocity if he married her."

"You promised him a *horse* for marrying Juliana?" Her glassy eyes looked incredulous. "How could you do that, Griffin?"

He looked away, turning down a corridor he hoped would lead to the library. "She wants to marry him. I want to see her happy."

"How happy do you expect she'll be when she finds out her husband married her for a horse?"

He peeked in an open door to see a music room. "Whyever would she find that out?"

"Perhaps because I told her?"

"You wouldn't." He turned to her. "Tell me you wouldn't."

"I'm not sure I shouldn't."

"Rachael, please tell me you won't say anything. It would only hurt her feelings."

"You should have thought of that before you made the offer." She stared at him for a moment while he shifted uncomfortably. "All right. I won't tell her. Unless she ends up engaged to his grace, at which point I think it will be in her best interests to know, whether it hurts her feelings or not."

"Thank you," he said, not sure he was actually all that thankful, since the duke and his sister would likely be engaged quite soon. But maybe not. And at least Rachael wasn't running to Juliana just yet.

They tried the next room, but it turned out to be a small family dining chamber. "Whatever made you think of offering a horse for your sister?" she asked, continuing down the corridor.

He shrugged. "It seemed like a good idea at the time. Perhaps I was a bit foxed."

"Well, then it's a good thing you're not often drunk." She

stopped before another open door. "Ah, the library." Taking a deep breath, she entered and walked over to a long leather sofa. She turned and sat carefully, folding her hands in her lap. "A few weeks ago you suggested I try to find my father. I was wondering how you'd propose I do that. Seeing as he's dead, I mean."

Griffin frowned, noting a trace of anguish beneath her businesslike tone. Leaving the door open, he joined her on the sofa. "He might not be dead."

"In the letter I found, Mama referred to herself as a widow."

"The letter could have been deliberately misleading," Griffin pointed out, and then, seeing hope leap into her eyes, hurriedly added, "although it probably wasn't. But in either case, I may be able to help you discover his identity."

"How?" She coughed, then sniffled. "Mama left no other letters that mentioned anything about an earlier marriage. Her parents died young, and after her sister died when I was but a child, she had no family left. She never even had any close friends other than your folks—Mama always kept to herself, do you remember?" She shook her head. "I wouldn't know where to start."

"Her things? Did she keep nothing to remind her of her previous husband?"

"Nothing at all. I went through everything when I cleaned out her rooms to ready them for Noah."

Noah, Rachael's younger brother, had recently come of age and taken responsibility for the earldom—a responsibility Rachael had borne on her own since the tender age of seventeen. She was intelligent and competent. If she'd found nothing, there was likely nothing to find.

But now that she was willing to pursue the subject, Griffin didn't want to give up so easily. "Perhaps you missed something. Or saw something but didn't recognize it as a clue."

She looked dubious. "There was nothing, Griffin."

"Would it hurt to look again?" If he could judge by her

expression, it very well might. "I'll go through your mother's things with you," he offered. "I might notice something you missed."

She pulled a handkerchief from her sleeve and dabbed at her nose. "All of Mama's things are at Greystone," she said on a sigh, referring to her family's country estate. "Perhaps we can go through them at Christmas."

As much as Rachael clearly wished to put this off, he wasn't willing to see her misery last until Christmas. It was so against her nature. "Christmas is six months away—"

"I'll think about it," she said, standing suddenly. "I'm not feeling well. I'm going home."

FORTY-THREE

*A*UNTS AURELIA and Bedelia had been thrilled when James asked them if they might help out at the Institute. They'd arrived at New Hope to be trained first thing after breakfast Saturday morning and taken to their tasks with great enthusiasm, running the reception room with astounding precision. James had been able to vaccinate more patients in a day than he usually did in three.

At four o'clock, before his aunts departed to ready themselves for the Teddington ball, he'd penciled their names on his schedule, careful to make sure their assigned shifts wouldn't overlap and run him ragged. Then he'd gone home to change, decided to lie down and rest his feet for just a moment, and awakened four hours later.

By the time he dressed and left, it was past ten o'clock. He arrived at the ball very late and a little moody. When Occlestone happened upon him just inside the entrance and made a snide remark, James nearly walked right back outside again. But he wanted to tell Juliana how well things had gone at the Institute today.

Unfortunately, Lady Amanda buttonholed him before he got the chance.

He hadn't even been announced yet—he'd only just handed his things to the footman manning the cloakroom—when she approached him, wringing her hands. "Lord Stafford, where have you been? One of Lady Teddington's guests is terribly ill."

Absurdly, he noticed she wasn't wearing gloves. And she looked quite distressed. She was usually so cool and aloof. Whose illness could she possibly be so concerned over? She seemed to have no close friends, except for—

"Is it Juliana?" he asked, his heart suddenly beating double time.

"No. Let me show you to her." Bypassing the ballroom, she hurried him down a corridor.

"It's another lady, then? What's wrong with her?"

"I don't know." She turned into a room and spun to face him so fast he nearly collided with her. "Kiss me," she said, and then, throwing her arms around him, she pressed her lips to his.

He went rigid as a corpse, stunned and disoriented and horrified and *why was this strange girl attached to his mouth?*

He pushed her away. "What in blazes do you think you're doing?" His wits were slowly returning, but with them came additional confusing emotions. He felt guilty for shoving her, especially because she'd almost toppled over, and he also felt bad for wiping his mouth with the back of his hand, which had been quite rude and unnecessary, but he hadn't been able to help himself.

But the most confusing feeling of all was nothing. He'd never before kissed a girl and felt *nothing*. Or at least, nothing pleasant. Nothing besides a face mashed against his own.

"What was I *doing*? I was kissing you!" she wailed, and now he felt even worse, because she looked just as horrified as he felt. "Have you fallen in love with me yet?"

"*What?*"

"Juliana said that after I'd kissed you, you'd fall in love with me. Have you?"

"No!" He shook his head emphatically. Lady Amanda was a

lovely girl, even more lovely now that she was finally showing some spirit. Her cheeks were flushed prettily and her blue-gray eyes were flashing.

But he loved a girl with hazel eyes.

"Where is Juliana?" He glanced around. "Good gracious, this is the ladies' retiring room." The room was strewn with reticules and other feminine belongings. Screens in two corners most likely hid chamber pots—but he wasn't about to make his way over and find out. "It's a miracle no one else is in here. Someone could appear any minute."

"I know."

"Ladies tend to visit in bunches. Any number of guests could have seen us kissing!"

"I know."

"You know? You *know*?" He grabbed her by an arm and took a step back, and then another, and another, until they'd returned to the momentarily deserted but very public corridor. "Have you any idea what could have happened had we been caught?"

"What I was hoping would happen?"

"What you were hoping…" Bile rose in his throat. Slowly, through clenched teeth, he said, "You and Juliana planned to trick me again, didn't you? That meddling little—" He broke off, coughing, choking on fury.

Was it just yesterday he'd decided her meddling could be helpful? Well, to blazes with that!

"She didn't meddle," Lady Amanda said, her eyes flooding. "It was my idea this time. All my idea. She refused to help me. She said it would be unethical."

"Blasted right it is!" What was it with ladies crying around him lately? Yesterday Juliana, and now Lady Amanda. Had all the girls he knew formed a pact to watch him squirm?

A tear overflowed and ran down her cheek. "Why can't you just agree to kiss me, then? You want to, don't you? You've been courting me for weeks."

"I most certainly have…"

Not. He'd meant to say *not.* But he couldn't get the word out. Good gracious, he abruptly realized, he *had* been courting her for weeks. Or at least it must have seemed that way to her. He'd sent gifts and asked her to dance and—

Suddenly he needed to sit down. But there were no chairs in the corridor, and he seemed to have lost the strength to propel himself to another location. He leaned against the wall instead. "Well, that is…"

How could he explain it? Although she and Juliana had certainly been wrong to trick him, what he'd done was just as bad, wasn't it? He'd misled Lady Amanda to achieve his own ends with another girl. There was no excuse for such behavior —all he could think was that she so rarely showed her feelings, perhaps he'd forgotten she had any. Which was despicable of him. How could he have been so thoughtless and cruel?

"I'm sorry, Lady Amanda," he said, "I—"

"My father will be home tomorrow evening," she interrupted in clipped tones, clearly impatient with his half-baked efforts to explain himself. "He may not let me out of the house again before my wedding. However will I escape marrying Lord Malmsey then?"

"Escape…what?" He blinked. "Your wedding? I don't understand. What on earth makes you think Lord Malmsey would marry you? He's in love with Lady Frances."

"Well, he offered for my hand before he *met* Lady Frances. And my father is going to make us marry, unless—"

"You're *engaged*?" he interrupted. "To Lord Malmsey?"

All the time Juliana had been trying to match him with Lady Amanda, the girl had been engaged?

"We're to be wed a week from today. And the only way I can get out of it is if I'm caught with another gentleman." She grabbed both his hands. Painfully reserved Lady Amanda grabbed his hands, and she wasn't even wearing gloves. She was *that* desperate. "Could you please just cooperate?"

He knew he should. He knew it was only right to make amends for his actions by following through. But he couldn't.

He just couldn't.

Two chattering guests entered the corridor, heading for the ladies' retiring room. He pulled his hands from Lady Amanda's and lowered his voice. "I cannot," he said. "I'm sorry, but I cannot cooperate. I cannot marry you. I'm in love with another girl."

He fled back to the cloakroom before guilt could get the better of him. He couldn't decide whether he was more furious with Lady Amanda for trying to trick him again, Juliana for trying to match him with someone who was engaged, or himself for misleading them both. All he knew for sure was that he wanted to go home.

"James!" he heard as he passed the ballroom.

He turned to see Juliana, a cautious smile on her face.

Cautious? Juliana? Was she in another strange mood?

"How did it go with your aunts?"

"Fine," he said shortly.

Her smile disappeared. "Is something wrong?"

"Your friend tried to trick me again. Your *engaged* friend."

"Oh." Her face went white. "Faith. I can explain—"

"I'm sure you can, since you always have a plan to fix every-thing. But I don't want to hear it tonight. I'm going home."

Still deathly pale, she hesitated a moment.

She hesitated. Juliana hesitated. Confident, self-assured Juliana.

"All right," she said at last. "Can we discuss this tomorrow at Lady Hartley's breakfast?"

"I don't think so. I have more important things to do than attend a silly breakfast." The Institute would be closed since it was Sunday, but perhaps he'd work on the account books. Or clip his nails. Anything would be better than wasting half the day smiling at people he didn't care about. He'd never attended garden parties or balls by his own choice—he put up with them only to placate his mother and, more recently, to see Juliana.

But he didn't want to see Juliana. Or rather, to have her see him. To face her in a tent full of nosy spectators.

Right now he couldn't even face himself.

FORTY-FOUR

AFTER JAMES left, Juliana returned to the ballroom, furious and intending to find Amanda.

Before she had a chance, Amanda found her.

"Whom?" the older girl asked, tears spilling from her red-rimmed eyes. "Whom is Lord Stafford in love with?"

"I told you not to try to trick him again! And why on earth did you tell him you're engaged?" People were gawking at them, so Juliana hurried her to a corner of the ballroom. "Now he'll never agree—" She stopped short, finally registering Amanda's question. "What makes you think Lord Stafford is in love with anyone?"

"He told me! I kissed him, and then—"

"You *kissed* him?" A stab of jealousy took Juliana by surprise. Or, all right, to be honest, she wasn't surprised. But it certainly felt bad and very wrong. "What did he do then?"

"He pushed me away. You said he would fall in love with me, but he pushed me away!"

The jealousy faded as quickly as it had flared, replaced instead by elation. Wild, intoxicating elation. Juliana had never felt more buffeted by volatile emotions, and she'd have never thought she could feel so euphoric while her friend was clearly so wretched. But she couldn't seem to control it. Amanda had kissed James, and he'd reacted by pushing her away.

She must be a terrible, heartless friend, because she wanted to scream with joy.

"I asked him if he'd just cooperate," Amanda continued with a pathetic sniffle, "and compromise me so my father would have to let me marry him. But he said he couldn't, because he's in love with another girl." She heaved another prolonged, woebegone sniff. "Who is it?"

"I don't know," Juliana said. It wasn't a lie. She had her suspicions, but she didn't *know*.

James had claimed he would never fall in love with anyone. He'd never admitted to having any sort of loving feelings for Juliana. He'd never called her *love* or even *dear*. He'd never sent her flowers. And he'd seemed very cross with her tonight.

"I don't know," she repeated, looking away.

Because although she didn't know, she couldn't help hoping…

Her gaze wandered the ballroom, past Lord Malmsey dancing with Aunt Frances. Had her meddling doomed them both to despair? Even if James *did* love her and eventually forgave her, how could she ever be with him knowing their happiness came at the expense of other people she cared for?

And then there was the duke…

Having at last emerged from the card room, he stood gazing at her, a heated look in his eyes. He'd never looked at her like that before. Not even close. Just her luck, now that she'd decided she couldn't marry him, he'd finally decided he wanted her.

Amanda shifted uneasily beside her. "Why is David looking at me like that?"

"Like what?" Juliana asked. Then she blinked. And stared.

Faith, the duke wasn't looking at her at all! Let alone looking at her *like that*. He was looking at Amanda. *Like that.*

Could the duke love Amanda? *Amanda?*

Well, why not? she thought, glancing back and forth between

them. After all, they were two peas in a pod. Two perfectly round, blemishless peas, with about as much passion between them as one would expect from a pair of legumes.

No, that wasn't quite true. After all, at the moment the duke certainly had something in his eyes that looked like passion, and Amanda's eyes were shining with some powerful emotion, too. Perhaps their sort of passion was simply different from Juliana's —and James's. Not better or worse. Just different.

Honestly, the duke and Amanda were ideal for each other. He related better to her than he ever had to Juliana. Amanda's cold upbringing had matched his own, after all. The two of them could understand each other. Support each other.

She turned back to face Amanda. "It's a shame you won't marry a by-blow, because that would solve everything."

Amanda bit her lip. "I might marry a by-blow if the by-blow was the duke," she said meekly.

Juliana gasped. "Are my ears deceiving me? Did you just say you would marry the duke?"

"I was wrong." Instead of looking down at her feet as she used to, Amanda met Juliana's eyes. "He's not to blame for his parents' mistakes, and he's kind and a good person."

"Then whyever did you say *no* at Lady Pevensey's musical evening? With such vehemence, no less?"

"You want to marry him yourself. You've been trying so hard to help me. The last thing I want to do is repay you by stealing your suitor. You're such a good friend."

"You're a good friend, too." Juliana took Amanda's hands. "I don't want to marry the duke. I want you to have him instead. Wait here," she added, squeezing Amanda's fingers before she released them. "I'm going to make it happen."

As she walked toward the duke, Juliana couldn't help noticing that his blond, pristine handsomeness matched Amanda's pale beauty precisely.

She came to a stop before him. "You're not in love with me," she said. Although he'd claimed he was falling in love with her, it was a statement, not a question. "You're in love with Lady Amanda."

"I hold her in some affection."

Juliana supposed that was reserved-speak for *love*. In any case, it was the best she would get out of the duke, and it would be enough to satisfy Amanda.

"Would you like to marry her?" she asked.

He didn't hesitate. "Very much. Even though she doesn't come with a horse."

"Pardon?"

"Never mind. I would definitely like to marry her. Unfortunately, I understand she's engaged to another."

"She told you that?" Juliana asked. But obviously, Amanda had. While Juliana and James were kissing, Amanda and the duke must have been talking. "We can fix her engagement," she said. "But first you need to ask her for her hand."

The duke nodded gravely.

"It might help to tell her how you feel," she advised as she walked him toward Amanda, thinking him the sort of young man to forget that. "You may want to exaggerate a bit."

After delivering him to her friend, she backed away and watched from afar as he and Amanda conducted a conversation that looked more like a business discussion than a proposal. In the end, when Amanda nodded, he leaned forward and kissed her on the cheek.

It seemed an auspicious beginning. Maybe after a year or two they'd progress to kissing on the lips.

The negotiations complete, they summoned Juliana. In the course of the next half hour, the three of them came up with a plan. After church tomorrow, they would all attend Lady Hartley's breakfast party, where, at precisely three o'clock, Amanda would be caught in the library with the duke, her dress unbuttoned down the back.

Amanda blanched when Juliana suggested the last bit, but they all agreed it was necessary to assure her ruin. By the time

Amanda's father arrived that evening, her compromise would be a fait accompli. He would have to allow her to marry the duke.

"Will you ask Lord Stafford to help 'discover' us?" Amanda asked.

"No. He told me he won't be attending." Juliana thanked goodness for that, because he'd never approve of their plot. "But I'm sure plenty of other people will come running when I call, so there's no need for him to be involved."

With any luck, James would never hear about what happened at all.

And after all was said and done, if she was fortunate enough to learn he loved her, she would never—never ever—meddle again.

IN HIS STUDY at Stafford House the next day, James pushed aside his paperwork and sighed.

Sometime during the sleepless night, the hot fury had cooled to a solid lump in his chest. Mother had the sniffles. He'd passed the morning in a haze, hoping she'd decide she was well enough to leave for Lady Hartley's breakfast. When she finally did, he'd sat down at his desk, added the same column of numbers three times, and come up with three different answers.

He couldn't concentrate. He still couldn't wrap his mind around the fact that Juliana had been hiding Amanda's engagement from him ever since they'd met. He'd thought he knew her.

But then again, he'd thought he knew himself, too. And when it came right down to it, his disappointment in himself was much harder to swallow.

True, Juliana had made a mess of things. But she was a meddler, and he'd known that all along. Sometimes her scheming worked—with his aunts, for example—and sometimes it didn't.

Everyone made mistakes, and as bad as her actions had been, his own had been no better. He was hardly in a position to judge. They'd both been playing games. Her games may have *nearly* forced him into an unwanted marriage, but his had *actually* hurt a real person's feelings.

And he loved Juliana nonetheless. He loved every scheming, meddling inch of her.

And he, for one, was done playing games.

Decision made, he pushed back from the desk, summoned his valet, and went to his newly renovated bedroom to change. The red-and-yellow-striped bedroom he hoped to share with Juliana.

It was time to buy her roses.

ONLY THE CREAM of society held "breakfasts" in the afternoon.

Beneath a tent in Lady Hartley's garden, the breakfast was well underway when James arrived just before three o'clock. As he scanned the several hundred seated guests, searching for Juliana, Occlestone rose from a nearby table.

"You owe some lady an apology, Stafford?"

James glanced down to the flowers he held, a dozen red roses. "Something like that." In his carriage between the florist's shop and Lady Hartley's, he'd unwrapped and nervously dethorned them. Now, rewrapped in the crumpled paper, they didn't look like much.

"I missed you in the House of Lords this week. Or rather, I didn't miss you."

"I was there Thursday," James said mildly, still searching the crowd. He had more important things to do than bicker with Occlestone.

"Oh, yes, you were there Thursday. How could I have forgotten your feeble argument in favor of returning the Elgin Marbles to Greece?"

"It's a matter of morality," James snapped. "We have no right—"

"Where on earth is my daughter?" another voice cut in.

Grateful for the interruption, James turned, then blinked at the stranger's stern demeanor. "And your daughter is…?"

"Lady Amanda Wolverston," Occlestone answered for the stranger, clapping the man on the shoulder. "Good to see you at long last, Wolverston. What has it been, two years? Three? Parliament has sorely missed your voice of reason."

While Lady Amanda's father muttered something about excavating antiquities on his property, James looked him over. He was rather short, with fair hair and beady, pale blue eyes. His mouth was compressed and turned downward, and deep lines on either side made it clear frowning was his habitual expression.

He looked exceedingly unpleasant. Poor Lady Amanda.

A flash of yellow caught James's eye. Juliana, leaving the tent. "Excuse me," he said quickly and moved to follow her.

He reached the garden just in time to see her enter the house. Wondering what reason she could have for going into a house during a garden party, he crossed the threshold just in time to see her reach the other end of what seemed a long corridor. From there, best he could tell, she turned and stole into a room.

He hurried after her, composing apologies in his head, desperate words spilling from his brain in a rhythm that matched the pounding of his feet.

Juliana, I shouldn't have judged—

Juliana, please listen—

Juliana, I love you—

Reaching the end of the corridor, he opened what he hoped was the right door and stepped into a library. As he quietly shut the door behind him, his mouth fell open.

Evidently it had been the right door. Between two deep red velvet curtains, Juliana stood facing a window, a dark silhouette against the light. Her dress was unbuttoned all down her back, and her sleeves had slipped down her arms.

"Juliana," he whispered.

She turned and stepped forward, her hair glinting the palest blond.

It wasn't Juliana.

"Lord Stafford!" Lady Amanda's cheeks flushed bright red. She jerked her dress back up on her shoulders, but not before he glimpsed an oddly shaped birthmark near her cleavage. "What are you doing here?"

"What are *you* doing here?" he asked. Had he entered the wrong room? Where was Juliana? "Why are you undressed?"

"I—I'm just—"

She was clutching the top of her dress for dear life, unwilling to let go in order to button it. James stalked across the room to help her.

The door opened and closed again. "What are *you* doing here?" the Duke of Castleton asked in his annoyingly stuffy manner.

The turd. "Buttoning the lady's dress," James spat. "What are you doing here?" The paper-wrapped roses tucked under one arm, his fingers awkwardly buttoned as quickly as possible.

But not quickly enough. Before he was anywhere near finishing—before Castleton could even open his mouth to answer James's question—the door flew open once more, and a flood of people poured in.

Led by Occlestone.

"How dare you preach morality in the House of Lords, Stafford!"

James's fingers fell from Lady Amanda's buttons, and the roses fell, too. He scooped them up. "This isn't what it looks like."

Occlestone's snout went into the air. He'd never looked more like swine. "I doubt the lady's father will agree."

"My father is here?" Lady Amanda squealed.

"Lord Wolverston is looking for you. I shall fetch him forthwith."

"Please don't," she said quickly, but Occlestone was already gone.

The onlookers turned as one to watch him go, then broke out in excited whispers.

"Gracious me." Lady Amanda sounded even more wooden than normal, which must have been how she expressed panic. Slowly she turned to face James, her eyes dull. "What an unpleasant man."

James grimaced. He hadn't missed the smirk on his rival's face. Occlestone was relishing this little nugget of revenge.

Which might turn out to be far more than little.

Lady Amanda's gaze surveyed the whispering crowd. "What are we going to do?" she asked urgently.

"Nothing. There is nothing we can do." His instincts said to run. But escape was impossible. Alerted by Occlestone, Lady Hartley's guests were arriving in droves, filling the doorway, cramming the room. He could only be grateful his mother and aunts weren't among them. So far, anyway. Hopefully they'd all come down with the sniffles and gone home.

A long velvet curtain swished behind him, and he turned, shocked to see Juliana step from behind it. "What on earth is going on here?" he asked.

Her gaze swept the fascinated bystanders, then settled on him as though they were the only ones there. "I'm so sorry." She *did* look sorry. Devastated, in fact. Not that that did any good. "We'd planned for Lady Amanda to be discovered with the duke."

James swung to Castleton in disbelief. "You were party to this? You willingly—"

"Yes," Castleton interrupted stiffly, but before he could explain anything, more people streamed into the room—Mother and her sisters among them, blast it—as Lord Wolverston arrived with a roar of displeasure.

"Stafford, you will pay for this!"

James's stomach sank. He'd never been formally introduced

to Amanda's father—in fact, he'd never even laid eyes on the man until a few minutes earlier. But he wasn't surprised to find that Wolverston knew his name. Occlestone would have supplied him with all the lurid details as he fetched him to the scene of the crime.

James should have run.

Although he was no taller than Lady Amanda, Lord Wolverston was commanding in his fury. "You will wed my daughter in place of Lord Malmsey. Next Saturday, as planned."

A buzz filled the room. Gasps of surprise and astonished whispers. It seemed Lady Amanda's betrothal had been a well-kept secret.

"No!" she cried. "This is all a mistake!"

Her father turned to her, his jaw clenched. "A serious mistake indeed, young lady." He swung back to James. "I'll expect you at Wolverston House Saturday at noon, with a special license."

James's gaze flicked to his horrified mother before he nodded. There was nothing else he could do. Having been witnessed buttoning Lady Amanda's dress at an event attended by half of the *ton*, he had no choice but to comply or lose all honor.

"What if Baron Malmsey still wants her?" someone shouted over the babble. "Will you deprive him of his betrothed bride?"

"I would *never* go back on my word." Lord Wolverston craned his neck, searching the crowd. "Malmsey!" he bellowed. "Do you still wish to wed my disgraced daughter?"

Someone pushed Lord Malmsey forward. "I—I—" he sputtered. A meek man to begin with, he seemed to have shrunk into himself. "I—"

"The baron doesn't want her," Wolverston said.

Well, of course he didn't. He wanted Lady Frances.

"She must wed the earl," Wolverston concluded, suddenly sounding less furious. In fact, if the man were capable of such a thing, he might have grinned.

"Please, Father!" Lady Amanda begged. "This isn't fair! Father, you must listen! You must reconsider—"

"There will be no reconsidering." Lord Wolverston grabbed her by the arm, making her wince. "We're leaving."

"Please, Father!" she wailed as he dragged her through the crush. "Pleeeease!"

It was a wail James feared he would hear the rest of his life.

Literally.

FORTY-SIX

$\mathcal{A}$S LADY Hartley's guests followed the Wolverstons from the room like rats following a piper—except in this case they were mesmerized by Amanda's heart-wrenching pleas —Juliana watched Lady Stafford push through them in the other direction.

"James!" she cried, throwing her arms around him.

He held her for a few seconds, but then extricated himself. "Please go, Mother. Take Aunt Aurelia and Aunt Bedelia back to the tent. I'll talk to you in a few minutes."

She looked to her sisters, who were standing there open-mouthed, and back to him. "But, James—"

"Please. I need to talk to Lady Juliana."

As Lady Stafford and her sisters reluctantly departed, leaving James and Juliana alone, he turned to her.

She felt like she hadn't breathed in the last five minutes.

And like she might never breathe again.

She thought she should cry, but she felt numb. She didn't know what to say. She didn't know what she *could* say. All the words seemed to have been sucked right out of her.

"I'm sorry," she whispered. It was all she could manage.

James only nodded.

She'd never seen him look so pale, so stricken. Not even when he'd been deathly afraid of Emily's snake. The very sight of him in that state made anger rise in her, which finally loosened her tongue.

"Lord Occlestone should be shot."

"Others followed us in here as well," he said wearily. "Lady Amanda's father would have found out one way or another. Occlestone is a lout, but he isn't to blame for this."

"I know. *I'm* to blame. But I'll fix it."

She *had* to fix it.

James's lips quirked to form something that might have been a sad smile. "You cannot fix everything, Juliana. But the fact that you never stop trying…well…it's one of the many things that made me fall in love with you."

There was no way she could live with herself if he had to marry Amanda. "I can fix this, and I will," she reiterated. "I have to." And then she froze. "One of the many things that made you…what?" She held her breath again, but for an entirely different reason, and then her gaze dropped to his hand. And her breath whooshed out of her. "You brought roses."

He glanced down, as though he'd forgotten he was holding them. "They're a bit worse for the wear."

They *did* look a tad bedraggled. "But they're red roses."

"There aren't many of them. I couldn't easily carry more than a dozen. Not two dozen like we ordered for Lady Amanda, and compared to what Lord Malmsey sent to your aunt—"

"They're *red* roses." He wasn't handing them to her. "Are they for me?"

Abruptly, he held them out. "Who else could they possibly be for? For what other girl would I dethorn red roses? I must've nicked myself twenty times."

"You said you would never fall in love again." She grabbed the flowers and held them tight to her chest, the paper crinkling, their sweet scent wafting to her nose. "Oh, James. I love you, too, you know."

She launched herself into his arms, and he held her close, the bouquet crushed between them. And then the tears that wouldn't fall finally did, because really, it was just too much.

And too late.

He'd brought her red roses. She'd been hoping he loved her, hoping for it harder than she'd ever hoped for anything before. But now that she knew he did, her meddling had ruined everything.

She was going to fix it, but for now she couldn't stop weeping.

"Hush," he murmured while her tears wet his waistcoat. And, "hush," while they soaked through to his shirt. And finally, "Do you know what I hate even more than snakes?"

She shook her head, rubbing her nose in the damp warmth.

He put a finger under her chin and lifted it, until her eyes were forced to meet his. "A girl's tears," he said. "I swear, love, they make me feel more helpless than anything."

"I'm sorry," she said, and she was. Sorry for crying, and sorry that made him unhappy. But mostly sorry James loved her and she loved him and everything was ruined.

"Hush," he said one last time, and then he lowered his head and kissed her, a small soft kiss. And another one. And yet another, but it wasn't soft, it was crushing instead.

Juliana stopped crying, partly because she didn't want to upset him anymore, but mostly because kissing him felt so right. She wrapped her arms around his neck, and leaned into him, and threaded her fingers into his dark, tangled hair. Everything was wrong, but James—tangles and all—was heartbreakingly right.

She was in love.

She'd never been so happy and so sad all at once.

"I'll fix this," she said when they finally broke apart. "We have five days before Saturday."

He smoothed her hair back from her face. "Five short days."

"Five and a half," she whispered, inhaling his scent, starch and spice mixed with roses. She held him tighter, wishing she didn't have to let go.

But she did have to. At least for now.

"Five and a half," she repeated.

It would have to be enough.

FORTY-SEVEN

THE NEXT DAY, Juliana paced around the drawing room while she waited for her guests to arrive for her one o'clock sewing party.

"I cannot concentrate." Seated at her easel, Corinna dabbed a bit of gray on the underside of a cloud. "I know you're going to make me sew all afternoon, so for now, will you please sit down?"

Juliana sat and stabbed her needle in and out of a little white nightshirt. For about a minute. Then she rose and began moving again, the nightshirt dangling from her clenched fingers. "There must be some way to fix this. It's disastrous for everyone involved."

"Aunt Frances doesn't think it's a disaster," Corinna pointed out.

That much was true. Although their aunt had been shocked to learn Lord Malmsey was engaged, he'd managed to talk his way back into her good graces before Juliana even had a chance to help. In fact, last evening she'd returned to the tent in Lady Hartley's garden to find him proposing on bended knee—a proposal Aunt Frances had joyfully accepted.

But the fact that the two of them were thrilled hardly mitigated the disaster that had befallen everyone else.

She and James were devastated. The duke was devastated. No doubt Amanda was devastated, too, although Juliana hadn't seen her since last night. Lord Wolverston had taken his daughter straight home—proclaiming loudly, according to several eyewitnesses, that she wouldn't be seen again in public before her wedding. Juliana had received an apologetic note from Amanda this morning, explaining that she wouldn't be able to attend any more of her sewing parties and her Aunt Mabel wouldn't be there, either.

Apparently having been less than impressed with his sister's chaperoning—or rather, her lack thereof—Lord Wolverston had given poor Mabel such a lecture that she'd gone straight to bed with the asthma and expected to remain there for the week.

Out in the foyer, the knocker banged on the door. A few moments later, Adamson came into the drawing room with two letters for Juliana.

"Thank you," she said, breaking the seal on the first one and scanning the short message. "Drat!"

"What is it?" Corinna asked.

"Rachael cannot come today. She has a cold." She opened the second letter, her eyes widening as she read the words. "Double drat!"

"What now?"

"James's aunts are ill, too. And his mother. How in heaven's name am I going to make twenty-five items of baby clothes today with only you and Alexandra, Claire and Elizabeth, and Aunt Frances?"

Working feverishly in every free moment, Juliana had managed to complete seven garments on her own between her last sewing party and today, but she still needed to collect seventy-six pieces of baby clothes during just three more parties. That was more than twenty-five per party, and today she would have six fewer sewers contributing.

"In the scheme of things," Corinna said, "I should think those baby clothes are the least of your troubles."

"You're right." Ordering herself to stay composed and keep things in perspective, Juliana plopped down on the sofa and resumed sewing. Her gaze went to the bedraggled red roses sitting in a vase on the mantel. They looked nearly as droopy as she felt. "James's forced betrothal to Amanda is much more distressing."

"Perhaps Lord Wolverston has calmed down by now," Corinna suggested. "Maybe if Amanda explains that it was all a misunderstanding, he'll reconsider."

"I don't think so. For all his bluster, he was clearly delighted to see her catch an earl instead of a lowly baron." Juliana's needle dropped from her fingers. "That's it!"

"What's it?" Corinna tilted her head, perusing her work in progress.

"If the Duke of Castleton offers to marry Amanda instead of James—"

"Her father would refuse, wouldn't he?" She dabbed at the cloud some more. "Isn't that why you plotted her compromise in the first place?"

"But everything's different now. Lord Wolverston wouldn't be breaking his word or breaching a contract. At this point, he only wants to see his ruined daughter wed and off his hands, and after all, if an earl is better than a baron, surely a duke is better still." It was so obvious, Juliana wanted to kick herself for not realizing right away. All this worry could have been avoided. "Why on earth would he refuse?"

Corinna shrugged and dipped her brush. "Your logic seems sound, but Amanda seems to think her father is unreasonable."

"I'll bake some wafers, then, just in case." According to the wafer recipe in the family cookbook, they were reputed to have a handy calming effect. "But I cannot imagine why he would refuse."

"Well, then, I'm certain he won't. You always know best, after all."

Since Juliana obviously *didn't* always know best—as proven by last night's disaster—she found her sister's sarcasm needling. But she was sure Lord Wolverston wouldn't refuse. The man would have to be an idiot to reject a duke as a son-in-law.

Five minutes later, Juliana was on Amanda's doorstep, explaining her new plan. "Why on earth would your father refuse?" she concluded.

"I cannot imagine." Amanda's eyes had been dull with despair, but now they shone with hope. "I wish he were home so we could ask him right now."

"The duke must be with us, in any case. Your father is a stickler, after all, so the duke will need to formally request your hand. And Lord Stafford should be in attendance as well, to confirm he agrees with the proposed solution. When will your father be home?"

"I'm not privy to his schedule. But he usually insists on dining at precisely six o'clock."

"Perfect. I'll send a footman with notes to summon Lord Stafford and the duke, and we'll all be here at half past six."

"He won't take callers in the middle of dinner."

"Do you know for certain he'll stay home afterwards?"

Amanda shook her head.

"Then inform your butler beforehand that we're expected. That way he won't go to your father to ask his permission." Juliana started down the steps, then turned. "Oh, bother. I'm sure Lord Stafford is at the Institute, but I have no idea where to send a note that will reach the duke."

"He'll be at his club," Amanda said, "playing cards."

"Which club?"

"White's, of course."

"Of course," Juliana echoed, vaguely surprised she hadn't known the answer herself. After all, she'd been planning to marry the duke up until a few days ago.

It seemed she'd never really known him at all.

"Are you sure you're not upset that David loves me?" Amanda asked suddenly. "I know you wanted to be the duchess."

"Of course I'm not upset. The two of you belong together." Juliana truly believed that, although she did wonder if Amanda wouldn't eventually come to resent her husband's distant, chilly nature. "Um…if I told you I'm the girl James loves, would you be upset about that?"

"Gracious me," Amanda said, "you can have him. The fellow's colder than a Gunter's ice."

FORTY-EIGHT

WAFERS

Rub Butter into Flour with some small amount of Salt. To this put Cream and Honey and roll out until very thin. Cut into small rounds and put them in your oven and eat them hot or cold.

A very simple treat, these have a calming effect. My grandmother used to serve them to my grandfather to make him reasonable.

—Anne, Marchioness of Cainewood, 1764

*E*VEN WITH A flurry of activity, Juliana's afternoon had passed excruciatingly slowly. Despite the heroic efforts of her five guests, her sewing party had added only eight items to her stockpile, well short of the twenty-five she'd been hoping for. But she hadn't been able to prolong the gathering past her usual four o'clock stopping time, knowing the gentlemen would be arriving at quarter past six.

She'd shooed everyone out of the house and hurried to the kitchen to make the wafers. When they came out of the oven, she donned her most virtuous dress—a white one—and applied just enough cosmetics to look fresh and innocent. Then she paced around the drawing room until Corinna grew irritated enough to set down her paintbrush and summon their maid to accompany her for a walk.

Juliana hadn't *meant* to drive her sister away from the house. But all the same, she couldn't help feeling pleased that she'd be able to explain her plan to James and the duke without enduring Corinna's usual sarcastic asides.

James arrived first. She hurried him into the drawing room, giving him the details as they went.

"Then Lady Amanda can marry the duke," she concluded, "which will leave you free to—" She clamped her mouth shut. While James had proclaimed his love, he hadn't made an offer of marriage. "Why on earth would Lady Amanda's father refuse?" she added instead.

"I don't know." He glanced toward the open door, then shrugged and drew her into his arms. "But I pray he won't, because Lady Amanda *isn't* the girl I hope to wed."

She laid her head against his chest, savoring his warmth, knowing she was the girl he hoped to wed. But still wishing he'd said it aloud.

All the same, she was sure she'd get her proposal soon enough. "Lord Wolverston won't refuse," she said firmly. "He'd be an idiot to reject a duke as a son-in-law."

"My confident Juliana." James tilted her chin up, and she found herself melting into his intense chocolate gaze. Something fluttered in her middle as he placed a lingering kiss on her lips, skimming his hands down her sides to find hers, lacing their fingers together and squeezing tight. There was something different about their kisses now that they'd admitted to loving each other, something possessive and meaningful.

Something she knew she'd never feel with anyone else.

"Ahem." They broke apart to find the duke standing in the doorway. "Your note said you have a plan?"

Though she blushed wildly, she kept one of James's hands laced with hers. "Yes," she said and quickly explained, finishing with "Why on earth would Lady Amanda's father refuse you for a son-in-law?"

"He shouldn't," the duke said stiffly, his reproachful gaze on their clasped hands. "He'd have to be dumber than a box of hair to do that."

FORTY-NINE

JULIANA AND Castleton were both sure Lord Wolverston wasn't stupid enough to reject a duke. And James had silently agreed with them—until they arrived in the man's dining room and he greeted them with all the warmth of an icicle.

"I don't recall issuing dinner invitations."

Lady Amanda set down her fork. "They're not here for dinner, Father."

"Excellent. Then I'm certain they'll have the good manners to leave."

"No, they won't." In all the weeks James had spent in Lady Amanda's company, he'd never seen her look so resolute. "The Duke of Castleton has something to ask you, Father."

"I don't choose to listen." Wolverston leisurely drained his wineglass before setting it down. "Hastings, see these people to the door," he said and began to rise.

"No!" Amanda jumped from her chair and pushed him back down. "You will sit here and listen."

He gazed at his suddenly assertive daughter as though she'd grown a second head. "Since when—"

"Lord Wolverston," Juliana interrupted, holding forth her

basket. "If you're finished with your dinner, would you care for a sweet? I baked wafers this afternoon."

He stared at *her* as though she had *three* heads. "Ladies shouldn't stoop to the level of kitchen maids."

An awkward silence filled the room. Even stuffy Castleton seemed to object to Wolverston's stuffiness. James hoped the turd wasn't reconsidering whether to accept this man as his father-in-law.

James sure would be.

But the duke stepped forward. "My lord," he said formally, "I assure you that my wife—my *duchess*—will never step foot in a kitchen. I would like to request the honor of your daughter's hand in marriage."

"My daughter is marrying Stafford," Wolverston replied stiffly. "This Saturday." He rose again. "Now I expect you all to leave before I have to see that you're thrown out."

"Father!" Tears sprang to Lady Amanda's blue-gray eyes. "The Duke of Castleton is proposing marriage. A *duke*, Father! Surely you cannot refuse him!"

"I can, and I will." He looked to Castleton. "When next I see you at White's—this evening or another time—we shall pretend this interview never occurred," he said and turned to leave.

"No, we shall not." Castleton strode around the table and stood blocking the man's way to the door. "I wish to wed your daughter, and she wishes to wed me. If you've a valid reason to object, I want to hear it."

"You don't want to hear it." Wolverston's expression had shifted to something resembling stone. Only less expressive.

"I *demand* to hear it," the duke insisted through gritted teeth, his hands clenching and unclenching reflexively.

James was impressed—the turd looked downright impassioned!—and also concerned that this new, impassioned duke might actually try to strangle their host.

But Wolverston didn't seem a bit concerned. "Very well, then, Castleton," he said, his words as calm and emotionless as his stony face. "I once had a liaison with your mother. Twenty-nine years ago, to be precise. I think it likely you're my son."

Juliana dropped her basket.

"I expect you'll find that a valid objection to your marrying my daughter," Wolverston added flatly. Then he pushed past the duke and left, without so much as glancing back.

Another awkward silence reigned.

"The wafers were supposed to make him reasonable," Juliana finally whispered. "He didn't eat them."

"They wouldn't have made a difference." James wrapped an arm around her shoulders—an arm that felt heavy as lead.

He glanced from her stunned face to the others. Castleton no longer looked impassioned; instead, he looked drained, empty, flimsy. Lady Amanda had crumpled. In the shocked silence that had followed her father's confession, she'd folded back onto her chair and lowered her head to her lap.

She was saying something now, but her skirts muffled the words.

"What was that?" James asked.

She lifted her head slightly. "I said…I cannot marry my brother."

"He said it's *likely* I'm his son," Castleton pointed out. "Which implies I might not be." But he sounded as dispirited as she.

"You and Amanda's father are both blond and blue-eyed," Juliana observed in an equally despondent tone.

There was no need for anyone to point out that Lady Amanda had blue eyes and blond hair as well. Or that it was common knowledge the duke's natural father hadn't been the late Duke of Castleton.

He shifted uneasily. "Hair and eye color are hardly proof of paternity," he mumbled without an ounce of conviction.

But it was more than coloring. Now that the connection had been suggested, James realized Castleton looked much more like Wolverston than the man's daughter did. It was something in the line of the jaw, something in the tilt of the head, something in the length of the nose. Something about the stiff carriage and the short stature.

Something twisted in James's gut.

"It can't be proven one way or the other," Juliana said. "But the thought of you two marrying now…" Swallowing hard, she put a hand to her middle. "It makes me feel slightly ill."

"It makes me feel *very* ill," Lady Amanda muttered into her lap. She slowly sat all the way up, looking very ill indeed. Avoiding Castleton's eyes, she gazed unfocused at James. "We shall have to marry—"

"There's still Lord Malmsey," Juliana cut in, making James's heart sink. She was grasping at straws, and broken ones at that.

She was out of ideas.

James took both her hands in his. "No, love. You know Lord Malmsey has already offered for Lady Frances. You wouldn't want to see him ripped from your aunt's side, would you?"

She shook her head, tears glazing her suddenly green eyes.

He pulled her close, knowing it would be for the last time. Much as he hated tears, he wanted to cry with her. He *would* cry with her if he could.

But he felt dead inside. Sinking and twisted and dead.

There was no way out. He had to marry Lady Amanda.

He had to marry Lady Amanda.

He had to marry Lady Amanda.

No matter how many times he repeated the fact to himself, it seemed impossible to believe.

Impossible to accept.

But he had to.

He released Juliana slowly, reluctantly, thinking it was the hardest thing he'd ever had to do.

"I'll be back Saturday at noon," he told Lady Amanda, and went out.

FIFTY

CHOCOLATE CREAM

Take a Quart of Cream, a Pint of white Wine, and a little Juice of Lemon; sweeten it very well,

lay in a sprig of Rosemary, grate some Chocolate, and mix all together; stir them over the Fire

till it is thick, and pour it into your cups.

Chill your cups in ice before serving. A delicious cure for melancholy.

—Belinda, Marchioness of Cainewood, 1792

"**W**HY ARE YOU so sad, Lady Juliana?"

"I'm not sad, Emily." *Sad* was much too mild a word to describe how Juliana felt the next day. "You're doing very well. Keep mixing."

The little girl looked up from the cast-iron stove in the Chase family's basement kitchen. "You *look* sad." Stirring with one hand, she stroked the snake draped over her shoulders with the other. "Herman, don't you think Lady Juliana looks sad?"

Juliana broke a brick of chocolate with unnecessary force, thinking Herman might as well go ahead and answer. A talking reptile wouldn't be half as astonishing as Lord Wolverston's revelation last night.

And James's reaction to it.

He'd left. He'd held her for a moment, but then he'd left. He'd apparently come to the conclusion that he had to marry Amanda, and accepted it, and just…left.

By all appearances, he had no interest in discussing the situation. He'd said he'd be back on Saturday. He'd made up his mind, and she probably wouldn't even see him again until he was married.

If then.

She sighed and began grating chocolate into the triple batch of cream and sugar that Emily was stirring in the pot. "I haven't seen you in quite a few days, Emily."

"A new family moved in across the square. Lord and Lady Lambourne. And they have three children. Three *girl* children."

Another surprise. Juliana usually knew everything that went on in Mayfair. Evidently she'd been slightly preoccupied of late. "What are the girls' names, then?"

"Jane, Susan, and Kate. Susan is just my age."

"That must be lovely for you." She kept grating. "And what do the Lambourne girls think of Herman?"

"Oh, they find him bang up to the mark," Emily said enthusiastically.

The Lambourne girls must have taught her some new slang. Usually Juliana would have smiled at hearing it. But she was too dejected.

And too irked with their new neighbors' acceptance of Herman. It threatened Juliana's efforts to civilize Emily.

The child stirred faster. "You're putting an awful lot of chocolate in, aren't you?"

"One can never have too much chocolate," Juliana said.

So what if she'd added twice as much as the recipe called for? She *needed* chocolate. Her mother had always said it was supposed to cure melancholy, and she'd never been more melancholy in her life.

But in this case she feared it wouldn't be enough. Especially since the chocolate reminded her of James and his beautiful, chocolatey eyes…

Oh, hang it. How was she supposed to feel better when the love of her life was marrying another girl? When four people's happiness had been ruined? When it was *all her fault*?

Emily had stopped stirring. "You're crying," she said. "You *are* sad."

"I guess I am." Setting down the chocolate and the grater, she forced a smile. "I think we're finished here."

"What's wrong, Lady Juliana?"

What *wasn't* wrong? She couldn't marry James. She'd doomed him to a dreadful future with a wife he'd never love, a future full of chess and antiquities and very little else. She was exhausted and overwhelmed—she hadn't slept last night at all—and somehow, some way—God only knew how, and apparently He wasn't telling—she had to produce sixty-two items of baby clothes in the next four days.

"What's wrong?" She could barely push the words through her tight throat. "Everything, it seems."

"Is it about Lord Stafford?"

She blinked. "What makes you think that?"

The little girl rolled her big gray eyes. "It's obvious you like him. I've known that for ages. And he likes you."

Apparently the truth had been obvious to an eight-year-old but not to herself. At least she was a precocious eight-year-old. "Well, he doesn't seem to want to see me right now."

"Then you must go see him. You have to talk to him. You cannot just stand around and mope. You have to *do* something, Lady Juliana."

Faith, Emily was right. Juliana had never before just stood by and let things happen, and she couldn't imagine what had made her start now. Melancholy, she supposed. But she couldn't allow melancholy to rule her.

Thank goodness she was making chocolate cream.

"Oh, you dear, dear child." She dashed the tears off her

cheeks and wrapped Emily in a hug. "I'm supposed to be helping you, but you're helping me instead."

"Are you going to go see Lord Stafford now?"

"Not right now. I sent notes asking all the ladies to come sew today even though I've never held any parties on a Tuesday before. They'll be here in less than an hour, and I cannot get to the Institute and back in that short time." Drat, James would be at Parliament by the time her sewing session was finished. "I shall have to go see him tomorrow. You'll stay for the sewing party, won't you?"

"Is there any more cutting to be done?"

"No. The cutting is all finished."

"Then I'm going to play with Jane, Susan, and Kate." When Juliana opened her mouth to protest, Emily held up one of her small hands—the one that wasn't stroking her snake. "You don't really want me to sew, do you? I'm sure to end up bleeding."

No, Juliana didn't want Emily to bleed. The mere thought made her feel sick. And the last thing she needed now was to spew a stomachful of chocolate over a stack of her hard-won baby clothes.

"Go ahead and play with the Lambourne girls. You have my blessing."

"Can I eat some chocolate cream before I leave?"

"I need to put it on ice first to make it cold. I'll bring you some tomorrow."

Emily helped her transfer the sweet pudding into three dozen cups before she left to visit her friends across the square. After that, Juliana had just enough time to steal upstairs to her bedroom and wash her blotchy face before her guests arrived. She brushed on a little powder and went down to seat herself in the drawing room. As she picked up her sewing and Corinna kept painting without comment, she congratulated herself on how calm and composed she must seem.

Rachael was still ill, and now Claire and Elizabeth were, too.

As were Lady Stafford and Lady Balmforth. Lady Avonleigh was feeling better, though, and she arrived first.

"Oh, my dear," she cried, "I'm *so* sorry." And she rushed across the room to enfold Juliana in her arms.

Juliana rose from the sofa and let herself be comforted by James's aunt. Except the embrace wasn't comforting. The harder Lady A hugged her, the harder she had to fight to keep the tears from falling again.

"I wanted you to marry my nephew," Lady A murmured, tears in her voice, too. "I wanted you to be my niece."

"I wanted you to be my aunt. I wanted Lady Stafford to be my mother." It seemed forever since she'd had a mother, and Juliana knew no one more motherly than Lady Stafford. She shuddered in Lady A's arms, inhaling camphor and gardenias. "There has to be *something* we can do."

"Our James doesn't believe there's anything to be done. But if anyone can think of something, it's you, my dear." Lady Avonleigh pulled back and wiped the moisture from Juliana's cheeks with gentle fingers. "You keep thinking, and I will, too."

"Thank you," Juliana said wanly.

She was about to say something more, but then Aunt Frances came downstairs, and Alexandra arrived, and Corinna reluctantly abandoned her painting and came over to join them all and sew. And the talk turned to Aunt Frances's pending marriage and Alexandra's burgeoning belly. Not that Alexandra's belly was actually protruding yet, but she kept rubbing the thing as though she could feel the baby inside, which made Juliana insanely jealous.

Yes, jealous. She could admit it. Not that she wanted a baby this instant, but the way things were going it seemed like she might *never* have one of her own! And she *so* adored babies—not only were they darling, but they needed help with everything, which suited Juliana just perfectly.

And now *Aunt Frances* was talking about having a baby. In her forties! It made Juliana wonder if she'd have to wait till her forties to have a baby. But all the talk around her was happy talk, so she forced another smile and kept sewing, because they all had been kind enough to help her make baby clothes, and there was nothing more she wanted than for everyone to be happy.

She rang for chocolate cream, but eating it didn't seem to help. The conversation flowed around her. Lady A got up and wandered over to Corinna's easel, admiring her latest painting. "Very impressive, my dear."

"Thank you," Corinna said.

Alexandra smiled as she plied her needle. "Did you know Corinna is going to submit a painting to the Royal Academy next year?"

"Several," Corinna corrected. "I'm hoping one will be accepted for the Summer Exhibition."

"Really?" Lady A mused. "I did tell you my younger daughter was artistic, yes? Though it seemed unlikely, she always hoped to see one of her paintings in the Summer Exhibition, too. But her real dream was to be elected to the Royal Academy."

"That's my dream as well," Corinna said. "I know it won't be a simple matter, but I'm planning to work hard for the honor."

The older woman measured her for a moment, then returned to sit beside her. "I want to help you," she announced. "My daughter never attained her dream—I'd like to see you attain yours."

Aunt Frances knotted and snipped off a thread. "How can you help her?"

"I don't know, but I'll do whatever I can." Lady A picked up the little cap she was making and smiled at Juliana. "You're good at coming up with ideas. If you wouldn't mind helping, maybe together we can see that your sister becomes the next female member of the Academy."

That would be wonderful for Corinna. And of course Juliana wouldn't mind helping. She needed another project. It would be a lengthy project—it would take many years—but keeping busy would make it easier to bear her and James's despair.

Well, not really. But she'd find a solution for their despair soon. She would talk to James tomorrow.

Oh, drat—she was *not* going to cry.

FIFTY-ONE

THERE WERE different ways of dealing with the blows life randomly chucked at people. James's method—perfected during the years he mourned his brother, father, wife, and newborn child—was to bury himself in work.

Since Sunday he'd been living in a blur—a dark, painful, all too familiar haze. The haze had lifted briefly on Monday, when it had seemed Juliana's plan might succeed. But since learning the truth about Castleton's birth, the darkness had closed in again.

James couldn't say that what he faced now was worse than coping with death. Of course it wasn't worse. But it didn't seem better, either. It was different.

Death was final. One mourned, one grieved, one eventually moved on. But what he faced now…it wasn't final—it was *forever*. It was a life sentence. It seemed so arbitrary, so accidental, so unfair.

And so wretchedly inescapable.

And so he worked. Because it seemed there was nothing else he could do.

He knew what he couldn't do. He couldn't leave an innocent young woman to suffer a lifetime of disgrace. He couldn't condemn himself to a future devoid of all honor. He couldn't abandon his principles and run off to be with Juliana.

No matter how tempting that sounded.

Which was: *very* tempting.

But he could work. He couldn't help himself, and he couldn't help Juliana. But there were other people he could help. Right now, that was the only thing that seemed to make sense.

One thing James knew—probably the thing he knew best—was how to bury himself in his work to the exclusion of everything else. To the exclusion of everything painful. And so on Tuesday he'd risen at dawn and spent the entire day at the Institute. And the entire evening in Parliament. And then he'd gone back to the Institute and stayed there until the wee hours, finding things to do, until he could go home and fall into bed and get up and start all over again.

Today he'd risen at dawn and returned to the Institute, even though he had two physicians scheduled and wasn't really needed. There was no Parliament tonight, so he'd stay here until the wee hours, finding things to do, until he could go home and fall into bed and get up and start all over again.

He'd do the same tomorrow and Friday. Saturday would be a little different—there would be an interlude in the middle for his wedding. But then he'd come back here to the Institute and repeat the pattern again.

It wasn't a totally unbearable life. At least he had a purpose. And he was keeping himself so busy he didn't have time to think. Thinking threatened his mental health, and the busyness was a sort of medicine—a medicinal ointment he could smear all over everything to subdue his emotional ailments.

The medicine, sadly, was an imperfect cure. As the Bible said —Ecclesiastes, if he remembered right—"Dead flies cause the ointment of the apothecary to send forth a stinking savor." Despite countless Sundays in church, he'd never quite understood what "stinking savor" was supposed to mean. But to put it another way, in simpler words, there was a fly in the ointment.

And the fly was a girl.

Girls always—always, always—wanted to talk. Not the superficial talk of gentlemen—talk of news and the weather and horses—which didn't make one think. Gentlemen's talk could substitute for busyness. But ladies' talk was different. Because ladies didn't just talk.

Ladies wanted to *discuss* things. And discussions required him to think. Which in turn sent forth that stinking savor he was trying so hard to avoid.

If only he could avoid girls entirely.

Unfortunately, that was impossible, since approximately half the world's population was female. There was his mother, always wanting to discuss things. There were his assistants, always wanting to discuss things. The stinking savor was everywhere, trying to make him think, bombarding him with stinking thoughts.

Since Aurelia was his only healthy relation, she was this morning's assistant and therefore his current threat.

"There must be something that can be done, James, something we haven't considered."

"There's nothing, Aunty. Would you hand me that box of sugar sticks?"

"Certainly." She reached to the shelves behind the counter. "But there must be something," she said, handing him the box. "We need to talk."

"I've got an Institute to run. I don't have time for talk."

"We'll have to talk later, then. I've promised to help Lady Juliana sew this afternoon, and then I was planning to stay home and nurse Bedelia this evening. But I suppose I can sneak out and meet you at Almack's."

"I won't be attending Almack's." If there was a place in London where the stinking savor was most prevalent, it had to be Almack's. And why should he *have* to go, anyway? Abstaining from the marriage mart was the only possible benefit he could derive from this forced marriage, so he meant to take full advantage of it.

Blast it, his impending wedding was the worst thought of all. He wasn't even really having a discussion, and yet Aurelia was making him think stinking thoughts.

Gritting his teeth, he turned from the counter. "Fifty-two! Follow me, please." A young mother rose with her three little daughters. Four more talking girls. He led them to a treatment room as quickly as possible.

He walked another set of patients to the door and brought more patients to the room they'd just vacated. He restocked sugar sticks in all three treatment rooms. He unwrapped lancets and other supplies. He scribbled in his account books and revised next week's schedule. He returned to the reception room to fetch more patients.

"You're not needed here," Aurelia said. "You're not leaving me anything to do."

"Just keep handing out numbers. And smiling at patients. They appreciate the reassurance."

"You should go home, James. You've got dark circles under your eyes. Before you need a physician yourself, you should go home and rest."

Home? Where Mother was languishing in her sickbed waiting to *discuss* things? "I think not." The door opened, and two people went out past another person waiting to come in. "Here comes another patient. You can give her a number." In fact, maybe he'd do that himself. Handing out numbers didn't require one to think. Turning away, he reached over the counter for one of the worn paper squares.

"You're number sixty-seven," he said as he turned back. "I'll call you when...Juliana..."

His voice trailed off, sinking along with his heart.

"James." Walking closer, she offered him a tentative smile, a sad smile, a smile that made his heart keep sinking until it fell clear down to his toes. "We need to talk."

Oh, no. "Have you thought of a solution?"

"Not yet. We need to think together. We need to discuss—"

"There's nothing to discuss. Nothing will come of it, Juliana. What's the point?" It would make him think. It would make him think stinking thoughts.

"Can we go somewhere private?"

"I don't want to talk."

"Please, James." Her eyes were green, deep green, green and pleading. "Please, let's just go to a treatment room."

"James," Aurelia said softly, "your patients are staring. Take her to a treatment room."

Girls. If only he could avoid girls. "The treatment rooms are all in use."

"Take her to your office, then," Aurelia pressed.

"Don't you think that would be improper?" he asked his aunt, and to Juliana he added, "Don't you think Lady Frances would disapprove?"

"Bosh," they said in unison.

"We've been together in private before," Juliana reminded him, no doubt referring to not only a treatment room here at the Institute but also a secluded, lantern-lit pocket garden, a secret hideaway under a staircase, a warm cubby inside a greenhouse. "I didn't hear you protest then."

He hadn't needed to avoid thinking then.

"It's not as though you're likely to ravish her," Aurelia pointed out. "You're marrying another girl."

There it was. That word *marrying*. A stinking thought. And he wasn't even having a discussion.

He gave up. "Very well," he said, "but there's nothing to discuss."

He hurried Juliana into the back, determined to avoid a discussion. There was only one way he knew of to do that. One way to avoid stinking thoughts.

He led her into his office, shut the door, and yanked her up against him.

It wasn't a gentle kiss. It was a frustrated, disillusioned, furious and pent-up kiss. It was a kiss full of hurt and regret and every bad feeling that had been haunting him.

But Juliana's arms went around him, and she felt warm and sweet and thrumming with energy. She tasted like chocolate and smelled like sunshine. She was everything that was good and bright. Everything he'd been missing.

He didn't think; he just felt. He just felt Juliana, and she felt impossibly alive. He wanted her more than he wanted life, needed her more than he needed to breathe.

"Juliana," he choked out.

She pulled back. "We cannot do this."

"We cannot *not* do this." He brushed silky strands of hair from her troubled eyes.

"You're right, but it's wrong," she said. "We must talk—there must be a way—"

"We cannot change anything. We cannot talk, not without touching, and we cannot touch, because that's wrong, and—" He swore beneath his breath. "This is why I didn't want to see you until after Saturday."

"You were right." He heard tears in her voice. "I cannot see you again until after you're—"

"Don't say it." He couldn't stand that word *married*. After he was married, he'd never kiss her again.

"I'll go home," she said, shaking. "I have to make fifty-two more items of baby clothes by the day after tomorrow." Her voice wobbled. "Your mother is still ill, and so are Lady Balmforth and Rachael and Claire and Elizabeth." Her tone rose in pitch. "That leaves only Alexandra and Lady Avonleigh to help me, Corinna, and Frances, and of all of us, your aunt is the only decent seamstress."

"You're going to kill yourself, Juliana. You cannot sew in the state you're in. The Foundling Hospital can make do with a few less clothes."

"I promised. A Chase promise is never broken—have I ever

told you that before, James? It's been our family motto for centuries. I have to make fifty-two items of baby clothes, even though I'll never get to have a baby."

"Why would you think that?" He pulled her close and felt her tears dampen his shirt. "You'll have a baby with someone else."

"I don't want a baby with someone else," she whispered.

"You say that now, but you will." Someone else would love her. Someone else would make her his.

Those were among the most stinking thoughts he'd ever had, ever.

And now he couldn't stop thinking them.

FIFTY-TWO

FOR TWO DAYS, Juliana had done little but sew baby clothes morning, noon, and night, but she *still* needed to complete thirty-three more pieces by the end of the day.

She didn't know how she was going to do it. Her sisters and Aunt Frances were sewing almost as much as she was, but none of them were very speedy or talented. Lady Avonleigh had helped them all morning, but James had needed her this afternoon at the Institute. And everyone else was still ill. Recovering —and thank heavens for that—but not yet strong enough to spend hours plying a needle.

Her fingers ached. Her vision was blurring. And she didn't have bad eyes.

"You're crying," Alexandra said sympathetically.

"I'm not. I think I must be catching everyone's sniffles."

"In your eyes?" Corinna asked.

Alexandra nudged her. "I think Juliana needs chocolate."

"I'm not hungry." Juliana hadn't felt much like eating the past couple of days, not even chocolate. "There are still cups of chocolate cream left, if you want some," she said, and that was when she remembered. "Oh, drat."

Aunt Frances looked up. "What's wrong, dear?"

Other than a dearth of baby clothes and the love of her life marrying another girl tomorrow? "I promised Emily I'd bring her chocolate cream. Three days ago."

"Take her some, then," Aunt Frances said. "The fresh air will do you good."

She couldn't spare the time. Could she? "Maybe I will," she decided. It would take but a few minutes. She set down her sewing, fetched two cups from the kitchen, and walked next door to knock on the Nevilles' door.

Their gaunt butler answered. "Yes?"

"I've come to call on Miss Neville."

"I fear Miss Neville isn't available."

"Is she playing with the Lambourne girls?" The fresh air *did* feel wonderful. Maybe she'd fetch three more cups and walk across the square to introduce herself. It would take only a few more minutes—a few more minutes she wouldn't have to be sewing.

"I'm afraid not, Lady Juliana." The old butler looked mournful. "The poor child is in bed."

"In bed?" It was four o'clock in the afternoon, and Emily wasn't one for napping. "Is she ill?"

"Not yet, but she will be. The Lambourne girls came down with smallpox today."

"Smallpox!" Her heart suddenly beat double time. "Has Miss Neville not been vaccinated?"

He shrugged his thin shoulders. "I'm only the butler, my lady."

"I'd like to visit with her, if you please."

The butler, who was pock-scarred himself, eyed her smooth, unmarked skin. "She may be contag—"

"I've been variolated, so I cannot catch smallpox. Please show me to Miss Neville."

Juliana heard Emily's sobs before she even entered the room. In her bed, the little girl was buried beneath a mountain of blankets. A fire blazed on the hearth, and the windows were closed and draped, making the chamber dim and stiflingly hot. The air smelled slightly of vomit.

And a man held Emily's arm over a small bowl with her blood dripping into it.

Juliana gulped convulsively. Her mouth felt dry, her breath came short, and her stomach clenched, making her fear she might vomit next. It was silly, and it was stupid, but she couldn't help herself.

Forcing herself to focus on Emily's tear-streaked face, she moved closer. "Faith, what is going on here?"

"The doctor is hurting me!" Emily wailed. "I want Herman!"

Her heart pounding, Juliana set the chocolate cream on the bedside table and smoothed Emily's hair back from her brow, seeing no sign of pocks. "Surely she hasn't fallen ill already?"

"Not yet," the doctor said. "I'm preparing her for the disease."

"Preparing her? I think not."

"She must be purged and bled and blistered. The procedures will help her body withstand the infection."

"They will not!" James didn't believe such things. "They will only weaken her." Juliana's gaze jerked back to the bowl of red fluid, and her head swam. She quickly looked away, but not before noticing the doctor's hands appeared none too clean. James wouldn't approve of that, either. He thought cleanliness helped prevent infection. "Please leave. Bandage Miss Neville's arm and—"

"Lord Neville sent for me—"

"Well, *I'm* sending you away!" Where was Lord Neville, anyway? Did he have any idea what this man was doing to his daughter?

"You have no authority—"

"I have every authority," Juliana lied. She squared her shoulders. "I'm Lady Neville, and I order you to unhand my step-daughter and leave at once."

She could hardly believe those words had come out of her mouth. And even more than that, she could hardly believe the doctor believed her.

But he did.

"Pardon me, my lady. My apologies." He set down the bowl and dug in his bag, removing a cloth. "I assumed you were naught but a visitor," he explained hurriedly as he pressed it to the cut he'd made in Emily's arm.

"That will teach you to make assumptions," Juliana said haughtily, moving to hold the cloth in place. "Hush, Emily," she soothed. "You're going to be fine." At least she hoped Emily would be fine. She had no idea whether the girl might come down with smallpox, but she was certain *this* doctor's services weren't helping. "You may send a bill to Lord Neville," she instructed him, "but I'll thank you to leave now."

She kept herself busy tying the bandage while the doctor quickly gathered his things and left.

"I want Herman," Emily said as soon as he cleared the door. She struggled up to a sitting position and motioned toward a terrarium in the corner. "G-get me Herman. P-please."

Juliana walked over to the glass box, sighing as she reached in to lift the snake. She'd never actually touched him before. But Herman felt drier and warmer than she'd expected, and she smiled to see the child relax as he settled around her neck.

"Th-thank you," Emily breathed. Her sobs had diminished to shuddering sniffles. "I c-cannot believe that doctor be-believed you were my mother."

"Stepmother," Juliana said dryly. "And I cannot believe it, either."

"I don't want to get smallpox, Lady Juliana."

"Of course not, sweetheart," Juliana said soothingly, squeezing Emily's good hand. "We're going to get you a better doctor, one who knows how to make you well without hurting you."

She had no idea if there *was* any way to make Emily well—

but she wasn't about to mention that to the terrified little girl. Juliana had an awful feeling there was nothing to be done other than pray. But there was someone who would know for sure. Someone who knew more about smallpox than anyone else in London.

"I'm going to send for Lord Stafford," she said, rising from the bed. They'd agreed not to see each other until after tomorrow, but really, she had no choice. Emily's health was at stake—maybe even Emily's life. "Wait here while I write a note and give it to one of your father's footmen." She started out the door. "No, make that one of my brother's footmen," she amended. The Neville staff was so old, it would be tomorrow before one of them managed to shuffle to the Institute and back. And besides, she needed to run next door in any case, because they'd be wondering what was keeping her so long.

A few minutes later, she returned and peeled all the blankets off Emily. She banked the fire and drew back the curtains and opened the window. Gritting her teeth, she took the little bowl of blood and dumped it into the bushes outside, then rinsed it with water from Emily's washstand and dumped that out, too. When all that was finished, her heart calmed a little and her stomach felt much better. She dragged a chair to Emily's bedside, found a book, and read aloud for more than an hour until James arrived.

When the butler showed him to the room, he paused in the doorway and looked at her. Just looked at her, like he was drinking her in.

"Juliana," he said softly. He looked tired and disheveled, his hair tousled and his neckcloth askew. He'd probably donned that and his tailcoat in his carriage on the way from the Institute.

Her insides squeezed at the sight of him. "I know we said we wouldn't..."

She drifted off, noticing his gaze had shifted to Emily. And Herman. A moment ago his heart had been in his eyes, but now those eyes were glazed, and he looked very much like she'd felt when she'd seen Emily's blood. Like his pulse was thready and his stomach was in knots.

Which was very probably the case.

"Emily," she said carefully, rising from her chair, "you need to give Herman back to me now. I'm going to put him in his box until Lord Stafford is finished."

"No!" Emily clutched the olive green reptile. "I want to keep him."

"Emily—"

"The other doctor took him, and then he hurt me. I want to keep Herman!"

"Emily—"

"It's all right," James said, looking pale as paper. "She can keep him." He drew a deep breath and looked back to Juliana. "Your note said she was ailing?" His gaze flicked to Emily's bandage and back again. "Did she hurt her arm?"

"Not exactly. The other doctor bled her. She's been exposed to smallpox, and—"

"Where? When?" He didn't hesitate to approach the bed. But his hand was gripping the handle of his leather bag so tightly his knuckles had turned white. "Tell me what you know."

"She's been playing all week with three girls who came down with smallpox today."

"How do you know it's smallpox? Do they have spots, or only a fever?"

"Spots," Emily said. "But Susan told me she was hot the day before."

He nodded. On the opposite side of the bed from Juliana, he set his bag down on Emily's night table. "Do you feel hot?"

"No. Not now. I did before, but Lady Juliana took all the blankets off of me."

"The other doctor had her under seven of the things," Juliana explained disgustedly.

"Idiot." James leaned closer to Emily and reached toward her, flinching before he placed a hand on her forehead. "No fever," he reported, quickly pulling back from the girl and her snake. "That's a good sign. Smallpox usually isn't contagious for the first week or two after exposure, but one can never be certain."

"If it's a good sign," Juliana said cautiously, "does that mean you can do something to prevent her getting it?"

"Maybe." He opened his bag and drew out items she'd seen at the Institute. "Very possibly. Vaccination within three days of exposure will usually completely prevent it. Between four and seven days, vaccination still offers a chance of protection, and at the very least should modify the severity of the disease. Has she already been vaccinated?"

"I don't know," Juliana said. "The butler doesn't know, and Lord Neville isn't here."

"The doctor sent him to the apothecary," Emily said. "To get more purg—purg—"

"Purgative," James supplied.

"Lovely," Juliana muttered. "Do you think it's been less than three days since she was exposed? Since the Lambourne girls became contagious?"

"We don't know," he said. "It would be better if Emily's friends hadn't developed spots. But then I suppose we wouldn't be certain it was smallpox, so..." He shrugged and lifted the quizzing glass that dangled from the chain around his neck. "Open your mouth, sweetheart," he said, bending closer to Emily.

He held his breath as he examined her, his jaw clenched tight. Knowing Herman must be scaring him to death, Juliana held her breath, too. Maybe it was a bit silly to be afraid of a harmless snake, but not any sillier than to feel ill at the sight of blood. She marveled at his self-control, his determination, his bravery. His knowledge. His skill. His perfectly formed lips...

She gave her head a little shake to clear it.

Amanda had better appreciate having such a wonderful husband, she thought fiercely.

When he straightened, they both blew out a breath. "What were you looking for?" she asked.

"Small red spots on her tongue and in her mouth. Pocks usually show up there first, although I wouldn't expect to see any this early, before the fever. In any case, she has none."

"That's good, right?"

He nodded and visibly steeled himself before leaning close again to unfasten the buttons that went down the front of Emily's nightgown. Herman was draped on either side of the placket, and his fingers trembled a little. Regardless, Juliana had never seen anyone unbutton anything so quickly.

"I want to check the rest of her body. Spots most likely wouldn't appear there yet if she's contracted smallpox, but we can hope her friends actually have some other disease that presents differently—"

He snatched his hands back and froze, staring.

At first Juliana thought he'd been bitten by the snake. Then she realized he wasn't staring at Herman, but at Emily's chest.

Or, to be more precise, at an odd, fleur-de-lis shaped birth-mark on Emily's chest.

He frowned and murmured, "I think I've seen a birthmark like this before."

Emily nodded. "My father has one, too. All the Nevilles have one. In exactly the same place."

"Oh," James said. Still staring down at the fleur-de-lis, he frowned again. "But I've never seen your father's chest."

"Yes, you did," Juliana reminded him. "At Lady Hammer-smithe's ball, remember? Lord Neville was choking, and you saved his life."

"I removed his neckcloth but not his shirt. I only loosened a couple of buttons. I never saw—"

He blinked. And gasped.

"What?" Juliana asked.

His gaze flew to meet hers. "I never saw Lord Neville's birth-mark, but the day I was caught with Lady Am—" He broke off, glancing toward Emily and back again. "With your unbuttoned friend," he revised.

Then he paused before concluding, very slowly, "I saw that birthmark on *her*."

Faith, he was right! Juliana suddenly remembered it herself—a fleur-de-lis revealed by Amanda's drooping neckline. She must have seen it from her hiding place behind the curtain that day.

No, she couldn't have seen it. She'd been at entirely the wrong angle.

But she *had* seen that birthmark on Amanda. Hadn't she?

Her brain felt fuzzy, but she knew she'd seen it. She closed her eyes and pictured it…in her very own bedroom, the night she'd presented the "new" Amanda to society, when she was dressing for Lady Hammersmithe's ball.

And that meant…

Something hovered in the back of Juliana's mind. Something significant. Across the bed from James, she followed his gaze down to Emily. If all the Nevilles had that birthmark, and Amanda had that birthmark…

Then Amanda was Lord Neville's daughter, not Lord Wolverston's.

And that meant…

"Oh, faith," she breathed.

*J*AMES'S EYES met Juliana's, and they both sucked in their breaths. She was obviously struggling just as hard as James to keep her mouth shut, to keep from blurting out everything in front of little Emily.

The girl's father arrived, purgative in hand—muttering about hiring some servants young enough to run errands—and James asked him if his daughter had ever been vaccinated. Neville looked confused by his presence, but he answered readily enough.

The answer was no, which James found rather irksome.

To everyone's relief, the purgative was put aside. Emily whimpered while James explained the vaccination procedure, but in the end she bore it well. A tiny incision, a little dip into the wound using an ivory lancet tipped with cowpox virus, and a swiftly applied bandage. It all went very quickly, even though James didn't have a sugar stick. In fact, he couldn't remember ever vaccinating anyone faster.

Herman might have had something to do with that.

Now they could only wait. The incubation period for smallpox generally ran seven to fourteen days, but occasionally went as long as seventeen. Emily had most likely been exposed two or three days earlier, which meant it would be at least two weeks before they knew for certain whether she was out of the woods.

But the odds were well in her favor. And for now Emily was healthy and happily spooning up chocolate cream.

It was nearly seven o'clock by the time all was said and done and James and Juliana left the Neville house. As soon as the door closed behind them, she turned to him on the doorstep. "Will she really be all right?"

"I cannot make any promises, but I think so. She may not get smallpox at all, and if she does, it should be a very light case."

Even a light case of smallpox could be arduous, but at least it wouldn't be fatal. And in any event, what would be would be. James had done all he could, and the matter was in God's hands now.

And he and Juliana had pressing matters of their own to discuss—yes, he was ready to *discuss*.

He was ready to think.

"Lady Amanda isn't Castleton's sister," he said, taking one of Juliana's hands.

"I know. I figured that out." She squeezed his fingers, looking more lively than he'd seen her in days. "Isn't it marvelous?"

"She might not think so," he said cautiously. "Such a strait-laced girl might be upset to learn she's another man's daughter. Even a much nicer one."

"She'll cope with it. She'll have to. And the best part of it is, you won't have to marry her when there's no good reason for her not to marry the duke." She seemed to be holding her breath. "You won't, will you?"

Much as he wanted to make her that promise, he couldn't. Not yet. "Wolverston may still insist—"

"He can withhold Amanda's dowry and inheritance, but he cannot make her say 'I will.'" Sounding very sure of herself— well, she *was* Juliana—she finally released her breath. "Amanda won't need her father's—or rather, Lord Wolverston's—money if she's wed to the duke."

"The duke may not agree."

"He wants her. I think he'll agree. Let's find him and ask him now." She started down the steps, then stopped and turned back to him. "Oh, drat. We can't." Her newly recovered enthusiasm disappeared, replaced by blind panic. "I still have to make thirty-three pieces of baby clothes before tomorrow morning."

"No, you don't."

"Yes, I do! Perhaps the others made three or four items in the past couple of hours, but that still leaves—"

"You don't have to make any more baby clothes, Juliana." He smiled and kissed the puzzled little lines between her brows. Then he tugged on her hand, drawing her down the steps and across the pavement, back to her own house. "Look," he said, stopping in front of the large window that fronted number forty-four's drawing room.

On the other side of the glass, Corinna leisurely painted, her face a mask of concentration. Behind her, Lady Frances stood with her back to the window, gesturing or perhaps explaining something. On the far side of *her*, a dozen young women were perched on the drawing room's chairs and sofas, hunched over the needlework in their hands.

Juliana turned to him, bewildered. "Who are they?"

"My former assistants and a few neighborhood girls they managed to scare up. Common-born girls may not all learn to read and write, but they do know how to sew."

She blinked. "How did they get here?"

"Aunt Aurelia gave me the idea. She came into the institute today, telling such stories. Poor Lady Juliana is sewing her fingers to the bone, dear Lady Juliana will never finish in time." He shrugged. "So I called in a favor."

"A favor?"

He nodded. "Before you summoned me to Emily's house. The girls were quite happy to oblige."

"Faith." Her eyes shone with disbelief and gratitude and something else that was even better. "Have I told you I love you?" she whispered through an obviously tight throat.

He squeezed her hand. "Yes, but do feel free to tell me again."

"I love you." She bit her lip. "And thank you. Thank you from the bottom of my heart." She squeezed his hand back. "I must go help them now, but—"

"No. Oh, no. You're much too exhausted, and we have much more important things to do."

"James—"

"Go inside if you must, tell them Emily is all right and you've been invited to Stafford House for dinner."

"Aunt Frances might be oblivious, but she's not stupid. She knows your mother is too ill to host a dinner party."

"*I'm* hosting you. We'll go to my house for dinner as soon as we've talked to Castleton. Your aunt is needed here to supervise, and this is no time to fret about proprieties, Juliana. I'm starved."

He dropped a soft kiss on her lips and sent her on her way. It started raining while he waited impatiently on the doorstep.

Everything was still up in the air.

When she came back out, they dashed to his carriage together.

"They've made twenty-one items of baby clothes already," she reported. "With only twelve to go, they really don't need me." Being Juliana, of course she already had a plan. "The House of Lords is in session. You'll have to go in alone to fetch the duke, but then you should bring him out to the carriage so we can talk to him together."

James sent an outrider to Stafford House to get his cook started on dinner, and told his driver to head for Parliament.

Unfortunately, Castleton wasn't at Parliament.

He wasn't at his Grosvenor Square town house.

And he wasn't at White's, which was the final place Juliana could think to check.

It was rather annoying. Just now—when all their futures were at stake—*now* the duke had decided to be unpredictable?

They left notes at the last two locations, explaining all they'd learned and requesting that Castleton notify them of his intentions as soon as possible. Then they went to Stafford House to wait, because there was nothing else they could do.

Dinner was ready when they arrived, and the table was set for two, one plate at either end of the oval table that seated six. "I'm not hungry," Juliana said.

"You're worn out. We both are. We should try to eat at least a little."

He moved the dishes at the far end to the spot around the curve from his. And then they sat. Because there was nothing else to do.

James wasn't hungry anymore, either. He'd lost his appetite. Everything was *still* so up in the air. They both picked at their food, alternating between silence and spurts of forced conversation through three courses.

There was nothing else to do.

"Maybe we should go look for the duke again," Juliana suggested when they finished an hour later and James was pouring port.

He set down the bottle and handed her a glass. "Where?" he asked, taking a rather large swallow from his own glass.

"I'm not sure. But there's nothing else to do." She looked at the glass in her hand. "I've never had port."

"It's strong but sweet," he said. "Try it."

She took a tiny sip and then another one, hoping it might steady her a little. "I like it."

Just then, a red-liveried footman walked in. "My lord." He set a letter on the corner of the table, gave a smart bow, and left.

It was a single sheet of heavy, cream-colored paper, folded in thirds and secured with a large red seal. James and Juliana stared at it for a moment, as though they were both afraid to touch it.

"The stationery is from White's," he finally said, pushing it toward her.

"It's from the duke." Her hand shook as she lifted it. "It has to be."

"Open it."

She turned it over, her eyes green and apprehensive. "It's addressed to you."

Obviously she felt it was his right to read it first, but James suspected she'd snatch it from his hands if he tried. "Open it," he repeated.

She nodded and broke the seal, slowly unfolding the single page. Before she even finished scanning it, she let out a little shriek and launched herself onto his lap, the letter landing on the floor as she wrapped her arms around him and held tight.

So tight he could barely breathe. "What does it say?" he choked out, unsure whether she was crying from happiness or despair. Her only answer was a sob. He leaned awkwardly with her attached to him and picked up the letter. He turned it over, anxiety impaling his chest.

Lord Stafford,

I wish to wed Lady Amanda Wolverston with or without her dowry. No horse will be necessary, either. I would appreciate the assistance of yourself and Lady Juliana in explaining the matter, which I expect Lady Amanda will wish to verify with Lord Neville. To that end, I shall present myself at Cainewood's home at ten o'clock tomorrow morning, unless I hear from you otherwise.

Yours sincerely,
Castleton

The pain in James's chest eased as he dragged in two lungsful of the most delicious air he'd ever breathed.

Perhaps Castleton wasn't such a turd, after all.

Everything was going to work out.

It was a blasted miracle.

"No horse." Juliana sniffled into his shoulder. "He said that once before. What on earth could he possibly mean?"

He supposed it couldn't hurt to tell her now. "Your brother promised the duke a horse named Velocity as part of your dowry if he'd marry you."

She raised her head. "You've got to be jesting. A *horse*?"

James shrugged. "I believe Griffin was rather foxed when he made the offer."

"That idiot."

"Griffin? Or the horse?"

"Griffin, of course. Velocity is a very intelligent horse."

He laughed and kissed her. "Do you expect *I* will get Velocity when I marry you?"

"It would serve Griffin right if you insist on it. Although I didn't realize you cared for racehorses."

"I don't, particularly. But the sale of such a fine animal would pay for a lot of vaccinations. I expect Castleton would bid mightily—what?" Juliana had pulled back enough to stare at him, tears streaming down her cheeks again. "What could be wrong now?"

"Was that a proposal?"

He blinked. "I suppose so. But it wasn't a very good one, was it?" He rose and set her on the chair, then dropped to one knee. "Ouch."

"Try your good knee," she said with a watery laugh.

He did. Carefully. And then he took both her hands in his. "Juliana, my love…would you do me the very great honor of becoming my wife?"

"Yes!" She launched herself at him again, with such force he fell back onto the floor, which, thankfully, was carpeted, since he banged his head so hard he saw stars. "I'm sorry," she said, crawling over him. "Are you hurt?"

"Not in the least." His head ached like the dickens, but he

didn't care. "Are you?"

"No. I know you hate it when ladies cry, but I can't seem to stop."

"It's all right," he assured her, "as long as you're crying from happiness." Watching a fat drop fall from her chin to his neck-cloth, he added, "You *are* happy?"

"Oh, yes!" she bawled and leaned down to kiss him.

It was a very wet kiss.

"Lord Stafford? Is everything all right?"

Juliana jumped up, and James turned his head to the side to see his housekeeper standing over him. "Ah…very much so, Mrs. Hampton." He pushed himself to sit and ran a hand through his hair. "We were just, um, going upstairs. Yes. We're going to drink our port in the Painted Room."

"Very well, my lord. Shall I have something brought to you?"

"Nothing. Nothing at all." Scrambling to his feet, he collected both their glasses. "We'll just go up now."

"Should you need anything, do let me know," Mrs. Hampton said. And just stood there. Staring.

"Of course. We're going up now." Handing Juliana a glass, he gestured with the other in a way he hoped looked suave and dignified. "Shall we?"

$\mathcal{A}$T THE TOP of the elegant staircase, James didn't walk Juliana through the library and into the gorgeous room with the lion head chairs. Instead, he took her the opposite direction.

"Um, James? Isn't the Painted Room the one with all the marriage scenes? The one where I gave you the Richmond Maids of Honour and…"

She trailed off, thinking it might not be the best idea to remind him why she'd come that day: to apologize for tricking him. Because she'd wanted him to marry her friend, and she hadn't known he'd lost his wife and child. Her face heated just thinking about that day and the events that had led to her apology. How dreadfully naive and foolish she'd been!

Thankfully, he didn't seem to notice the awkward pause. "I thought I'd show you another room—mine, to be precise— though it will be *ours* very soon," he said all in a rush.

She slanted him a curious glance. Was it her imagination, or did he sound a bit nervous?

He stopped by an open door. "Close your eyes," he said, "and wait here."

The room beyond was so dark she couldn't see anything anyway. "Why do I have to close my eyes?"

"Just do it," he said. "Humor me, please."

So she did. She closed her eyes and waited, holding her glass of port. She heard some rustling, a dull thud, and finally a whoosh that she guessed was a fire coming to life. And then she waited a little longer, listening to him walk around, doing who knew what, until finally he came back to her and placed a quick kiss on her lips, making her smile. "All right," he said, "You can open your eyes."

So she did. He was so tall he blocked her entire view. "I cannot see past you."

Appearing to be holding his breath, he nodded and stepped aside. "What do you think?"

Beyond him, the room now glistened with light. On the tables, atop a bureau, on the nightstands, candles flickered. At least a dozen, or maybe more.

"It's splendid," she breathed. His bedroom looked nothing like the rest of the house; there was nary a hint of gilt and nothing ancient or ornamental. The furniture was all matched, modern Hepplewhite, the height of fashion, carved of light satinwood in lines that were gracefully curved and distinctive. The red and yellow fabrics looked silky and sumptuous. Even the walls were covered with silk, wide stripes above fresh, enameled white wainscoting. Arranged before a white-manteled fireplace—the fireplace he'd lit on this cold, rainy night—sat a love seat and two plush chairs, upholstered with narrower stripes.

And then there was the bed. Covered in solid red damask and heaped with plump yellow pillows, it had slender, towering posts and positively dominated the room.

"It's the most beautiful bedroom I've ever seen."

Releasing his breath, he bent to press a warm kiss to the top of her head, a kiss so adoring it made her sigh. "I'm so glad you like it."

She turned and gazed up at him. "Everything looks brand-new."

"It is. I had it redecorated especially for you. For us. My favorite color is red, and you do like yellow, don't you?"

Her free hand smoothed her yellow skirts. "It's my favorite color," she said slowly, and took a sip of port to cover her confusion. "But how…I mean…faith, however did you redecorate it so *fast*?"

"I've known for weeks that I wanted to marry you." His low, chocolatey voice seemed to vibrate right through her. "I'm only sorry it took me so long to tell you. We could have avoided so much agony."

Oh, drat. Tears were springing to her eyes yet again. Honestly, she was turning into a veritable waterworks. "I should have realized," she admitted, swallowing a lump in her throat. "But I was so sure you'd never love me. I was so set on marrying the duke and having you marry Amanda to save her from Lord Malmsey."

"We both made mistakes, love. But everything's going to be fixed now."

Yes, they'd both made mistakes. She wasn't perfect; nobody was. She was human like everyone else, and the past few weeks had proved it.

It was disappointing in a way, but in another way she knew it had always been inevitable. And she was so, so thankful that everything was being put to rights. "I don't think I've ever, ever been so happy." Her heart was swelling so much she feared it might burst. "I can hardly wait to share this room with you."

He pulled her close and cupped her chin in his free hand. And then he kissed her. Her senses spun, and it definitely wasn't from the wine.

He drew away, a mischievous smile curving his lips. "Come explore your new bedroom, then. Mrs. Hampton won't interrupt us here." He grabbed her free hand and began pulling her across the threshold.

"What?" He couldn't mean to share the room with her *now!* "Forget Mrs. Hampton—your mother is in the house!"

"Yes, and she's ill and no doubt sleeping soundly, and her bedroom is way down the hall." When she planted her feet and stopped their forward progress, he reversed direction and tugged her back into the corridor. "See? That very last door. She won't hear a thing."

Juliana wondered just what sort of *thing* he had in mind.

She blushed furiously and took another gulp of port.

It *was* a very long corridor, she had to concede. She'd noticed a door inside James's bedroom, which probably led to a sitting room or a dressing room. Or both. Doubtless his study was on the other side of those, and then his mother's dressing room before her bedroom, and maybe a sitting room for her besides. And perhaps some guest rooms in between. Stafford House was enormous.

But all of that was beside the point. "We cannot be alone in this room with your mother sleeping down the hall. Or even if your mother wasn't home. Not before we're married. It's not the thing, James—it's highly improper."

"You've never worried about being improper before. As you pointed out yourself just recently, we've been in private together more than once." He spoke in a low tone, his voice taking on that chocolatey quality. "At Vauxhall, and the Panorama, and the Physic Garden..."

She blushed again, remembering all those times. Remembering the greenhouse in Chelsea especially, when she'd sat on his lap. Remembering how he'd made her feel. "But we weren't in your bedroom."

"Does the fact that it's a bedroom really make a difference?"

"Well, yes. In those other places we only kissed. In bedrooms..." She flushed even hotter, which was quite vexing—normally this sort of talk didn't make her bat an eyelash. But something about discussing this in view of James's gigantic bed made her feel shy.

"Is *that* what you think?" He gave her an odd look. "I do only want to kiss! For goodness' sake, Juliana, I'm still technically engaged to someone else."

"Oh. Right." Now she felt mortified. Apparently, James had a more virtuous mind than she, and *he* had been *married* before. In a small voice she said, "I suppose that's fine, then." She took a deep breath and walked into the room.

"I just want us to be alone where we won't be interrupted," he said, shutting the door behind them. He joined her where she was admiring a lovely inlaid table.

She smiled up at him. "I want that, too."

He returned the smile, and, taking her wineglass, set it beside his on the table. "Do you trust me?" he asked.

"Of course."

He was edging closer, making her pulse leap. "Can I kiss you now?" he asked.

Why couldn't he just kiss her? Why did he always have to ask?

He tucked the loose strands of hair away from her face. "I swear, right now I want to kiss you more than I want to breathe. Can I?"

Why did he make it her decision as much as his, make it so she couldn't claim he'd ever taken advantage, not even to herself?

Why, why, *why*?

But she knew why. It was because he was honorable. Because he was the best person she'd ever known. Because he was everything she'd ever wanted all along, even before she'd known herself enough to know it.

She loved him. She'd loved him since before she'd known what love was. And he was waiting. Waiting to hear she wanted him just as much as he wanted her. And if anyone deserved to know she wanted him with all of her heart, it was James.

"Yes," she said clearly, meeting his gaze. "Yes, please. Please kiss me."

And he did. He drew her close and kissed her, a kiss so warm that she submerged herself in it completely, sunk into it like a hot spring. It barely registered when he walked her over to the love seat and they dropped onto it together, she'd plunged so deep. Her senses seemed entangled, so that she knew there was heat and spice and wine and and chocolate but she didn't know which she was seeing, smelling, touching, tasting. But it didn't matter—all of it was James. He kissed her, and kissed her, and kissed her. She was so immersed in him, it felt like hours before she realized there were words floating back and forth across her mind…

I'm still engaged to someone else.

She sprung to her feet and backed up several wobbly, disoriented steps, breathing hard.

"Juliana? "

"This is wrong. We need to stop."

"Juliana—"

"James? Are you home?"

It was his mother, out in the corridor. Juliana choked, coughed, covered her mouth.

"James, is that you?"

"Blast it," he gritted out and climbed to his feet. It was quite a climb, given how tall he was, and how squashy the love seat was.

"James?" His mother knocked on the door.

"I'm coming, Mother." He tramped to the door and opened it just enough to slip through—so his mother wouldn't see Juliana inside, thank goodness—and shut it behind him.

And then Juliana sank back down on the squashy, still-warm love seat, catching her breath, listening to their conversation.

"Oh, James, I thought I heard you. How are you feeling, dear?"

"Tired. I was sleeping."

"In your clothes? Poor dear." There was a pause, during which Juliana imagined Lady Stafford ruffling James's hair, even though he was much too old to have his hair ruffled. "I'm so sorry about everything that's happened. I so wanted you to marry Juliana."

"I know." She heard James sigh. "It may still happen."

"What do you mean?" Lady Stafford sounded very excited. "What do you mean, it may still happen?"

"I'm very tired, Mother, and I don't want to explain it now. Can we talk about this in the morning? How are *you* feeling?"

"Better. Much better. I think I'll be able to attend your wedding tomorrow."

"I'm hoping there won't *be* a wedding." His voice was getting fainter. "Let me take you back to bed. We'll talk in the morning."

"I really don't want to wait until morning to hear this, James," Juliana heard very faintly.

And then she heard nothing. He must have been walking his mother back to bed. It took him a very long time to return, and at first Juliana figured that was because it was a very long corridor, but when he took even longer, she figured he was probably explaining everything to his mother. Lady Stafford was rather persistent, after all. Most mothers were. Juliana figured she'd probably be a rather persistent mother herself.

If she ever got to *be* a mother.

What if everything didn't work out?

At last James hurried back into the room and shut the door behind him. He headed straight toward her and pulled her up from the love seat.

"What are you doing?" she asked.

He wrapped his arms around her. "Getting back to kissing you."

"We cannot kiss, James. We especially cannot kiss alone in your bedroom."

"*What?*" He pulled back and stared at her. "Whyever not? I thought you wanted—"

"What if everything doesn't work out?"

"What do you mean, what if everything doesn't work out?"

"I heard you tell your mother it *may* still happen. And you're *hoping* there won't be a wedding tomorrow."

His hands dropped, then rose again to take her by the shoulders. "I was just trying to get her back to bed. I didn't want to stop and explain everything. I didn't want to have a *discussion*. I wanted to get back to you."

She shook her head stubbornly. "What if everything doesn't work out? We shouldn't be kissing in your bedroom if you're going to marry Amanda."

Now his hands rose to cup her cheeks. "I'm not going to marry Lady Amanda. You read Castleton's note. Everyone is in agreement."

"Her father isn't."

"He isn't even her father!"

"That doesn't signify. He's legally her guardian. He might have another objection."

Looking defeated, James let go of her and plopped down on a chair. "What could he possibly come up with now? Who could he possibly claim slept with whom in order to make Lady Amanda and Castleton's marriage impossible?"

"I don't know. All I know is we all thought he couldn't possibly have a valid objection before, and it turned out he did. So it could happen again. Or someone else could have an objection. We don't know, James. We have to wait."

He let out an exasperated groan. "As soon as we straighten everything out, we'll be wed tomorrow. I was planning to get married tomorrow, anyway."

Despite her frustration, despite everything, she couldn't help laughing. "Don't be ridiculous. We cannot get married tomorrow."

"Why not? It was simple to get the special license to wed Lady Amanda—all it took was money. I can get another license with your name on it tomorrow with no trouble at all."

"We need more than a license, James. I need a wedding dress. And we have to deal with the whole mess regarding Amanda's parentage tomorrow, and I have to deliver the baby clothes. The Governors are expecting me at the Foundling Hospital tomorrow afternoon, with two hundred and forty items."

Thank heavens they were finished. The women James had hired had only needed to make twelve more. Everything was going to work out.

In that quarter, at least.

"All right," he said dourly. "We'll get married the Saturday after that. If we go out in the corridor, can I kiss you one more time?"

She shouldn't allow it, not even in the corridor. But she couldn't deny him, and after all, they'd certainly kissed already. "Yes," she said, "you can kiss me in the corridor. And then we need to go let Amanda know what's happening."

He opened the door and drew her into the empty corridor and kissed her, and all the while, all the time she had her arms around his neck and was kissing him, she was crossing her fingers and hoping everything would work out.

FIFTY-FIVE

AND SO IT WAS that James arrived at Lady Amanda's house on the day Lord Wolverston had commanded, but a full twelve hours before the man expected him. Also not according to plan, he didn't arrive by the front door.

"I think her bedroom is right there," Juliana whispered, peering up from the back garden. "That window with the pale blue drapes."

It was on the second floor. James eyed the wall, which was plain stucco with no footholds in sight. He bent down to gather some pebbles.

"What are you doing?"

"Getting Lady Amanda's attention." He tossed one, and the little *clink* sounded like it carried for miles.

She winced. "You're going to wake someone."

"Mmm-hmm. That's the whole idea." *Clink.*

"I thought you would scale the building."

Clink. "Sorry to disappoint you"—*clink*—"but you're marrying a physician, not a sportsman." *Clink, clink.* "I already have one bad knee."

"I'm marrying a physician," Juliana echoed as though she couldn't quite believe it.

James also thought it was too amazing to quite believe. Especially since several people involved didn't know what was happening yet. Especially because someone might make an objection. That was the reason she'd insisted they couldn't kiss in his bedroom, wasn't it? And she hadn't been exactly wrong.

Not that he was happy about the situation.

"James."

"Hmm?" *Clink.*

Before he could toss another pebble, she caught his hand. "I love you."

He turned and smiled down at her. The rain had stopped, and the sky had cleared, and the low light of the full moon gleamed off all her beautiful, straight hair that had slipped from its pins while they'd kissed in his bedroom. Her hair that was a million different colors of blond and brown. She reached her free hand to touch his cheek—she was probably feeling the slight roughness, late as it was—and as he bent his head, her lips parted slightly—

"Whatever is happening out there?"

James and Juliana jerked apart.

Lady Amanda had opened her window. "Lord Stafford? What are you doing with Lady Juliana?" She sounded reproachful.

And he could hardly blame her. They were still technically engaged, after all.

"We came to wake you," he said.

They quickly explained their discovery, while Lady Amanda's eyes got wider and wider. At the end, Juliana sighed sympathetically. "I do hope you're not terribly distressed to learn you're...well..."

"A by-blow?" Lady Amanda supplied shakily. "I shouldn't be distressed, should I? After all, the man I love is a by-blow, too."

"Faith," Juliana exclaimed with a soft laugh. "You've surely had a change of heart. Meet us at my house at ten o'clock. The duke will be waiting, and we'll all go next door to Lord Neville and verify the truth."

"My father won't let me out of the house at ten. He's expecting me to marry at noon."

"He's not your father," Juliana reminded her. "You have no obligation to obey him. I'm sure you can find a way out."

"I cannot—"

"Tell Lord Wolverston you're dressing for the wedding," she said out loud, and then softly under her breath, "Honestly, do I have to plan everything?" She sighed and raised her voice again. "I'll make sure there's a ladder from your window down to here. I'll have one of my brother's footmen deliver it."

"I cannot climb through a window!"

"Then use the servants' exit. Either way, I'll expect you at my house at ten o'clock."

Muttering, Lady Amanda shut the window in question, and Juliana turned and looked at James for a moment. She raised her hands and placed them on his shoulders. "I was going to kiss you before Amanda opened the window," she said softly.

Actually, he'd been going to kiss *her*, but he didn't think it would be a good idea to argue. Especially when she was looking at him like that, with her eyes so very blue. Even with only the moonlight, he could tell they were blue.

"It's going to work out," she declared. "Can I kiss you now?"

"Yes," he said, and Juliana kissed him. After all the weeks he'd spent trying to tempt her into letting him kiss her, she kissed him. She kissed him as they walked back to the street, stumbling and kissing along the side of the house. And as they walked down the street, ignoring a carriage that rumbled by. And when they got to her doorstep, she still kept kissing him.

Finally, James pulled back with a low laugh. "You're wearing out my lips."

She pulled his head down and kissed him again, a quick, joyous kiss.

"I'm never going to last until next Saturday," he said. "I need macaroons for extra energy."

"Oh," she said with a sigh, and then, "You know what, James? I don't want there to be any more secrets between us."

"I agree," he said. "No secrets, and no lies."

"I *never* lie," she said, sounding a little defensive. "Well, I did lie to that dratted doctor, but I never lie unless it's absolutely unavoidable. I don't want any lies, either, and no half-truths." She drew a deep breath. "The macaroons don't really give one extra energy," she confessed in a rush.

"Oh, really?" He snickered.

"Did you snicker at me? Me, the girl you want to marry?"

Well, maybe he had, but only because he found her little superstitions so charming. He wasn't superstitious at all, and he couldn't quite believe anyone would think macaroons could give one extra energy. Or do anything else, either, other than taste delicious.

"I didn't snicker," he said, although that meant he was already telling her a half-truth.

He'd been married before, so he knew some half-truths were part of a harmonious relationship. But he wouldn't tell her a half-truth unless it was absolutely unavoidable.

"All right," she said, and then, in a lower tone, "I actually baked them to make you…*amorous*."

"Oh, really?" he repeated, but he didn't snicker. There was no way macaroons could make one amorous, either. But he loved that she thought they did. "You're a treasure, Juliana," he told her, hoping she'd bake him macaroons many, many times in the years to come.

Hoping very hard.

And then he kissed her again and left, and went home and spent the rest of the night with his fingers crossed, even though he wasn't superstitious.

FIFTY-SIX

*I*N THE END, Amanda was the one who objected.

Shaking like a leaf, she arrived at Juliana's house at quarter past ten. "What took you so long?" Juliana asked. "You were supposed to be here at ten. You only live down the street."

"It was this dress." She brushed at enormous, voluminous white skirts that were at least twenty years out of fashion. Faith, they were so wide there had to be hoops under them. "Have you ever tried to climb down a ladder in a dress this big?"

"Why are you wearing it?"

Amanda looked at her like she'd lost her mind. "It's my grandmother's wedding dress. It's a tradition in my family to wear it."

Fifty years out of fashion, then. The skirts were actually somewhat yellowed, not pure white. "You're not getting married today, Amanda. That's the whole point of going to talk to Lord Neville."

"After I told my father I was getting dressed for my wedding, I couldn't very well not do that, could I?" she said primly. She looked to the duke. "Besides, we're getting married today, aren't we?"

"Not today," the duke said in his stiff way. "A ducal wedding generally requires some months of preparation."

"If you love a girl," James said scornfully, "I should think you'd want to marry her as soon as possible."

Juliana thought she heard him mutter "what a turd" under his breath, but surely he wouldn't say that. Not about a duke. And then she worried for a moment that the duke would blurt out that he didn't love Amanda, but only held her in some affection, which could ruin everything.

But thankfully that didn't happen. They all walked next door to Lord Neville's house, and James banged the knocker.

The gaunt butler answered. "Yes?"

"We've come to call on Lord Neville," Juliana said.

The old fellow's eyes widened when he spotted Amanda in a wedding dress that his own bride could have worn fifty years ago, assuming he'd ever married, which he probably hadn't since most people required their butlers to remain bachelors. But he was a mannerly sort of butler, so he didn't say anything. About that, anyway. "Wait in the drawing room, if you please," he said instead, "and I shall see if Lord Neville is at home."

Viscount Neville was at home, of course. He spent his evenings gambling at his club, which meant he was never out and about very early. In fact, he came downstairs looking a bit rumpled, as though perhaps his valet had needed to drag him out of bed.

Juliana could see right off that he was Amanda's father. Amanda fit in age between Emily's two brothers, the one who was married and the other one who was away at Cambridge most of the year. Lord Neville was blond and gray-eyed like both of his daughters, and tall like both of his daughters, too. And as he seemed to overindulge in everything, Juliana wasn't surprised to learn that he'd had a dalliance with Amanda's mother.

Or at least not as surprised as she'd have been a few weeks ago. It seemed she lived on a very promiscuous street. Besides

Lord Neville's affair with Amanda's mother, Lord Wolverston had carried on with the late Duchess of Castleton when she'd lived in Juliana's house.

It was a good thing she'd be moving to St. James's Place soon.

Assuming everything worked out, that was. She really couldn't wait any longer to find out.

No one was saying anything, and, in fact, Viscount Neville seemed a little mystified to find all these people in his house. He seemed especially fascinated by Amanda in her ancient wedding dress. Juliana was dying to resolve everything, so she figured she might as well just spit it out. "Lord Neville, are you Lady Amanda's father? She has a fleur-de-lis birthmark in the same place as you and Emily."

Amanda gasped and blushed wildly, and Juliana was sorry to embarrass her, because she knew Amanda considered that private. But she figured it was better to come out and say it than to wait and have Lord Neville ask to see it, which would have been even more embarrassing for Amanda.

"I've been wondering about that," Lord Neville said slowly, "for eighteen years. Please, let me explain."

Lord Neville had been between wives when Amanda was conceived. He'd been very much in love with Lady Amanda's mother, but Lord Wolverston had refused her the divorce she wanted. Unfortunately, it had been—and still was—impossible for a woman to divorce a man, although a man could divorce his wife if she'd been unfaithful. Lord Neville and Lady Wolverston weren't precisely sure that the child she was carrying was the viscount's, so they'd been planning to wait to see if the baby had the Neville birthmark, and if that proved to be true, they'd planned to use it as leverage to press for the divorce. Wolverston wasn't the sort of man who could stomach people knowing he'd been cuckolded, especially if they'd had the proof to show all of society. His honor meant everything to him. He put his reputation before everyone else's happiness.

"Well, *that's* certainly the truth," Juliana muttered.

"I'm so sorry, my dear," Lord Neville said to Amanda. Her face had gone rather white, and she was looking at him. Just looking at him. He began moving toward her. "I was devastated when your mother died giving birth and Lord Wolverston refused to let me even see you. He wasn't a very nice man."

"He still isn't," Juliana said.

"I never knew for sure whether you were my daughter," Lord Neville continued, still inching toward Amanda. Who was still just looking at him. "I hoped you were, but there was no way to find out. As you grew, I would see you sometimes, and I thought more than once about asking you if you had the birthmark. But you seemed a very reserved young lady, and I feared such a question would shock you clear down to your toes."

"It would have," Juliana said.

Lord Neville was standing right in front of Amanda now. "I also feared Lord Wolverston might treat you harshly, suspecting you might not carry his blood in your veins—"

"He did," Juliana interrupted.

Lord Neville hung his head. "I'm so sorry."

Amanda suddenly came to life. She *was* a very reserved young lady, so she didn't jump into Lord Neville's arms like Juliana might have done, but she finally opened her mouth.

"Don't be sorry," she said. "I understand. And I'm so glad you're my father instead of Lord Wolverston."

Lord Neville did gather her into his arms then, embracing her tightly. Amanda's arms went around him, too, although they appeared rather reluctant and loose.

"I'm glad that's settled," the duke declared. "Now we can start planning our wedding for next summer."

And *that's* when Amanda objected.

She released Lord Neville—heaven forbid she should stay improperly close to a man, even a man she'd just discovered was her father—and turned to the duke. "I object to that plan," she said, and then she added scornfully, "If you love me, I should think you'd want to marry me as soon as possible."

Evidently, the duke had no answer to that, since he just stood there with his mouth open.

Amanda lifted her chin. "I'm wearing my grandmother's wedding dress. I think we should elope right now to Gretna Green."

"That wouldn't be very ducal," he finally said, "or at all proper."

Amanda raised her chin higher. "I don't care," she said. "I'm tired of being proper. I want to marry you now."

And then she gave him *the look*. She glanced down, bowing her head a little to display her lashes against her cheeks. Then she swept her eyelids up, gazed at the duke full on again, and slowly—very slowly—curved her lips in an alluring smile.

The duke didn't fall at her feet. But he did sigh and say, "Very well, then."

Juliana was shocked. Positively shocked. When *she'd* tried that on the duke, he hadn't reacted at all.

Obviously she'd been right that he and Amanda were ideal for each other.

James's arm stole around Juliana's waist, in front of everyone. He pulled her against his side, where she fit perfectly. "Everything worked out," he murmured in her ear, a low, chocolatey murmur that made her shiver.

Though everything had indeed worked out, it was just too sensational for Juliana to quite believe. Wasn't there someone who could still make an objection? Someone who could still ruin everything? "What about Lord Wolverston?" she asked Amanda, crossing her fingers.

"He's not my father," Amanda reminded her, flashing a smile at Lord Neville. "I have no obligation to obey him. And I couldn't care a fig about him *or* my inheritance. David is all I need."

Juliana was bursting with pride. She'd taught Amanda well.

And Juliana could uncross her fingers now. Come to that, she could throw her arms around her new—official—fiancé, too!

She promptly did, crying, "Oh, James, I'm sure I've never, ever been so happy!" And then, her heart swelling so much she feared it might burst, she kissed him in front of everyone.

"Ahem."

She broke apart from James to find both the duke and Amanda gaping at them, looking extremely reproachful. But Juliana couldn't bring herself to care. She only laughed.

Though she *had* learned a lesson about trying to change people. And she had a declaration.

"I'm never going to meddle again," she said.

James snickered, and everyone else laughed.

FIFTY-SEVEN

"THANK YOU very much," one of the Foundling Hospital's Governors said in the Committee Room that afternoon. "Our next reception day is the second Saturday in August."

"The tenth?" Juliana asked.

"Yes," another Governor confirmed. "We very much appreciate you donating the baby clothes, my dear."

James held his tongue until they were outside in the Hospital's courtyard. But he couldn't contain himself any longer than that. "I cannot believe you committed to making more baby clothes! You're exhausted and overwhelmed!"

"How can I deny these poor children anything I'm able to give?" Juliana gestured to all the girls exercising in their matching uniforms. "If, due to my donation, only one more baby can be accommodated, only one more mother restored to work and a life of virtue, it will be entirely worth it."

Apparently seeing he wasn't convinced, she moved closer and reached up to put her hands on his shoulders. Sunshine and flowers washed over him.

"I know what I'm getting into this time," she said. "I can pace myself better. Last time I started with just one party a week, but now I know—"

"You're not having any more sewing parties," he interrupted. "We'll hire people to make the baby clothes."

"Much as I love you for saving me yesterday, this shouldn't be your responsibility."

"Who said anything about *my* responsibility? I've already found you plenty of seamstresses. I trust you can handle the rest."

She laughed. "Are you sure they'd want the work? Those fifty pounds you gave each of them ought to last awhile." She shook her head. "Do you realize that's enough to cover a family's expenses for two years? You're too nice, James. You're too generous."

He could never be too nice or too generous to her. She deserved everything he could give her and more. She was a treasure. She was exactly what he needed.

He didn't know how he was going to wait until next Saturday.

"Besides," she went on, "don't you want to save your money to pay for more smallpox vaccinations?"

"Have I ever told you that you're a treasure?" Was there another girl anywhere as concerned for everyone but herself? "I don't have enough money to rid the world of smallpox single-handedly, but I can do my part here in London and still afford to support other causes. And buy you beautiful dresses and anything else you ever want." He flashed her a grin. "I'm not a pauper, you know."

"I know. You set your table with gold spoons."

"They're sterling plated in gold," he informed her.

"I figured that out." She sighed. "Are you sure you don't want me to make baby clothes?"

She wasn't particularly good at it, and there wasn't another lady of the *ton* who would willingly do such mundane work. But then, no other aristocratic ladies he knew set foot in the kitchen, either. Juliana was different, and that was why he loved her.

He smiled down at her, loving her more than he'd ever thought possible, wanting her more than he wanted his own life. The next seven days were going to be the longest of his life.

"Of course I want you to make baby clothes," he told her. "For *our* babies."

And he watched her eyes turn blue before he kissed her.

FIFTY-EIGHT

Saturday, August 10
Cainewood Castle

IN RECENT WEEKS, when Juliana had dreamed of walking down the aisle, she'd often pictured the duke.

But she'd never imagined Amanda would be on the gentleman's arm.

As she turned to face her guests after the ceremony in her family's ancient chapel, she glimpsed their two pale, beautiful faces in the crowd. And the truth dawned on her: her real life was so much better than anything she could dream up.

Even with a snake accompanying the flower girl.

Emily had never come down with smallpox—thanks to James—and the Lambourne girls had recovered, too. Since Amanda and the duke had returned from Gretna Green, Juliana had sometimes seen them holding hands, and she was beginning to trust that one day they'd pluck up the courage to make a child together—assuming at least one of them knew how the unseemly deed was done. And miracle of miracles, Aunt Frances and Lord Malmsey had *already* started a child. Last month,

Juliana had returned from delivering the baby clothes to find the two of them waiting in the drawing room with a minister and a special license. Two weeks later, Frances had missed her monthly.

Everyone was happy.

Except for James.

She could feel the tension in his arm as they walked back up the aisle. He'd been so frustrated when Frances, his aunts, and his mother had all insisted on having a full month to plan this wedding, and even more frustrated to find that the preparations had proved so consuming—and all the women in his life suddenly so vigilant—that the two of them had found it impossible to steal even a moment of private time.

Well, she'd been frustrated, too, of course. But after all, she planned on marrying only once. She'd needed a wedding dress, and she'd wanted everything to be perfect.

And it was.

Still and all, being always together yet always under observation had been terribly difficult for them both, and she'd found herself relieved a couple of weeks ago when Parliament adjourned, meaning the season ended and everyone dispersed to their estates in the countryside. James had stayed in London to help his mother move in with her two sisters, and the four of them had arrived here only last night.

As they emerged from the chapel into Cainewood's quadrangle, James ran his hand down all the little covered buttons on the back of her beautiful white wedding dress. "There. We're married. Can we be alone now?"

She laughed. "We cannot abandon our guests two minutes after the ceremony, James."

There hadn't been time to plan a large wedding—it would have taken much longer than a month for that—but everyone she cared about was here. Her gaze skimmed the clipped green lawn that sat in the middle of the castle's towering four stories of living quarters. There, in the shadows of the crenelated walls, stood her sisters. Corinna's eyes shone as she laid a hand on Alexandra's blue-silk-covered middle, which was protruding a little bit now. Beside them, Tristan beamed at his wife.

People Juliana had grown up with were scattered over the grounds, a contingent from Berkeley Square by the tumbledown keep, a few countryside neighbors walking the battlements. James's friends and associates were here, too. Claire and Elizabeth were sharing a confidence—hmm, Juliana would have to wheedle it out of Claire later—and their tall, handsome brother Noah was chatting with James's aunts.

There was Lady Stafford—finally Juliana's mother-in-law—leaning much closer to Lord Cavanaugh than was strictly proper. There were the duke and Amanda, holding hands again and talking to Lord Neville and Emily. There was Lady Mabel, who wasn't wheezing out here in the countryside. There, standing in the untamed, ankle-high vegetation way over in the old tilting yard, were Lord Malmsey and Aunt Frances—

"James? May I borrow your quizzing glass?"

Dressed formally as he was, he had it in a pocket instead of hanging from a chain around his neck. When he pulled it out and handed it to her, she raised it to her left eye.

"Aunt Frances is wearing her spectacles!"

"Lord Malmsey doesn't seem to mind," James observed as they watched the older couple steal a kiss. "They do say love is blind."

"Who says it?" she asked, handing him back the quizzing glass. "Please don't tell me it's a Roman proverb."

His low laugh vibrated right through her. "I believe I heard it at the theater. *Romeo and Juliet*, if I'm not mistaken. I'm not all that bookish, you know. I mostly prefer newspapers and novels."

So did she. And she loved the theater. They *did* have common interests. With a happy sigh, she looked back out over the scene, noticing Rachael standing off by herself, watching Griffin mount the steps to the great hall.

James slipped the quizzing glass into his pocket and pulled

something else out instead. Something that sparkled in the afternoon sun. "A little something to remember this day," he said with a smile.

"I have my ring," she pointed out. She twirled the plain gold band—a Stafford heirloom that she'd instantly adored—around her finger. "And I have you, which is the best thing of all."

"And now you have this." He held up the pendant, a white gold heart encrusted with diamonds.

Her breath caught at the sight of it.

James moved closer to fasten the delicate chain around her neck. "It's been at least five minutes," he murmured by her ear. "Can we abandon them now?"

"No," she said with another laugh, touching the gorgeous pendant where it was framed in her neckline. "I need to mingle with our guests."

With a finger on her chin, he lifted her face. Her heart squeezed in her chest and suddenly, she felt breathless.

"I'll give you an hour," he warned softly against her lips. "But not a minute more." Then he quickly kissed her and sent her off.

~

G RIFFIN SCANNED the great hall one final time, pleased with what he saw.

The chamber hadn't looked this good since the ball he'd thrown last year in hopes of wrangling a husband for Alexandra. The enormous Gobelin tapestries on either end of the hall had been cleaned and rehung, their vibrant colors defying their age. Beneath the old hammerbeam roof, the ancient planked floor gleamed with polish. Servants were busy lighting the torches mounted between each of the arched stained-glass windows, and soon the huge chamber would be ablaze with light. Up in the minstrel's gallery, the musicians were tuning their instruments.

In a matter of minutes, the hall would be filled with music and dancing, laughter and glittering guests. He hoped it would be a night Juliana would remember forever. There was nothing he wanted more than to see his sisters happy.

Thank goodness he had only one more left to marry off.

"Griffin," came a nearby voice. A low, sultry voice.

He turned to see its owner, finding her standing there in a red dress that skimmed her every curve. Most of her hair was done up in a sophisticated style, leaving just a few loose chestnut tendrils to fall in soft waves around her face. She even *smelled* good. A heady, floral scent wafted toward him, making him take an uneasy step back.

Since she'd sidestepped his offer of help last month, he hadn't seen her. Juliana hadn't hosted any more sewing parties, and he hadn't attended any more balls. He'd been wrapped up in the business of Parliament, followed by some mild problems here on the estate. All the accursed responsibilities he'd found thrust on him along with the unwanted title had kept him too busy for any socializing.

Which had been fine by him. He hadn't clenched his teeth in five whole weeks.

"What do you want, Rachael?"

She blinked, no doubt taken aback by his unintended harshness. But she recovered her composure quickly. "If your offer is still open, then yes, I'd like your help going through my mother's things."

He smiled, softening. "Before Christmas?"

She drew a deep breath and nodded. "How about next week?"

FIFTY-NINE

FIVE HOURS later, James found himself confronted by the most daunting column of buttons he'd ever seen.

During the last month—seemingly the longest month of his life—he'd imagined this night a hundred times, if not a thousand. And up until now, it had gone more or less as he'd planned.

He'd closed them both into this room—the Gold Chamber, Juliana had called it—and proceeded to kiss her senseless while faint snatches of romantic music drifted in from the great hall far down the corridor.

He'd been quite proud of himself, really, because he'd been determined to take his time. If anyone deserved a wedding night that was slow and tender and sweet, a wedding night she'd remember forever, it was his treasured Juliana. And so far, despite the fact that he'd been all but shaking with anticipation, he'd managed to go slowly.

But then he turned her around and saw all those tiny, fabric-covered buttons.

"What in heaven's name possessed you to order a dress with so many buttons?" he muttered through gritted teeth, more frustrated than he remembered ever being—ever. If he continued as planned, if he continued going slowly, unbuttoning this blasted dress was going to take *all night*. "There must be at least a hundred buttons."

Juliana laughed, a low, wicked laugh that rippled across every nerve in his body. "I thought you liked buttons, James," she chided softly over her shoulder. "For some reason, I've come to believe you like buttons. I instructed the seamstress to put so many buttons on my dress because I had the impression you'd enjoy unbuttoning all of them."

And he did, in a sense. Slowly he swept the hair off the nape of her neck, slowly he placed a soft kiss on the sensitive, warm bit of skin above her top button. An adoring kiss, drawing in her scent, that irresistible scent of flowers and sunshine and Juliana. And then slowly he began unbuttoning the buttons, the never-ending column of buttons. And in a sense, he did enjoy it. But in another sense, the agony of anticipation seemed to be more, much more, than any fellow should have to bear.

It didn't take all night, but it took much, much longer than he wanted. Going slowly proved to be much, much harder than he'd hoped. Juliana sighed, and she caught her breath, and each of her sweet little sounds seemed to crawl into him and lodge someplace in his heart. It seemed forever by the time he managed to unbutton all the buttons. It seemed longer than the longest month of his life.

After all the waiting, after all the torturous unbuttoning of buttons, he finally stood back, for what seemed like one everlasting moment, the first time he saw Juliana just as she was, in all her glory.

And she *was* glorious.

It was a moment he'd always remember, a scene forever imprinted in his mind.

True to its name, the Gold Room was decked out with gilt furniture, all the walls and the four-poster bed draped with heavy golden fabrics. Everything seemed to shimmer. Juliana's skin seemed to shimmer, beckoning him. Juliana's eyes shimmered, a deep, deep blue gleam that entranced him. Her hair seemed to shimmer. No sooner had they entered the Gold Room than he'd released it from its pins, and now all the shining straight tresses were shimmering over her shoulders, glittering in the golden light.

"Your chest *is* all ridged like the centaur's," she whispered, sounding fascinated.

"What?" he whispered back, and then, "Never mind." With a low laugh, he went to kiss her. He didn't ask her this time. He knew what her answer would be, and he didn't want to hear any more words.

He wanted only to hear her soft sighs as he finally made her his.

Juliana had dreamed of this night, but nothing had ever seemed so beautiful, nothing had ever felt so right. Nothing had ever felt so perfect as the two of them together.

Now that all the waiting she'd endured these past months—waiting to meet the right gentleman, to make certain she'd fallen in love, to be truly alone with James—was over, she could finally say with certainty: Love *was* worth waiting for.

Of course it was. Hadn't she always said so?

But still and all, as James kissed her, his lips a warm promise on hers, she couldn't help being thankful that she'd never have to wait again.

AUTHOR'S NOTE

∾

DEAR READER,

In April 1815, Mount Tambora erupted on the Indonesian island of Sumbawa, sending more ash into the air than any volcano in the last ten thousand years. Over the next year, the dust rose into the upper atmosphere and spread slowly across the planet, obscuring the sunlight to such an extent that extreme weather conditions prevailed in places halfway around the world. The growing season was plagued by a series of devastating cold waves that destroyed crops, greatly reducing the food supply and causing widespread famine. Snow fell in June, and 1816 came to be known as "The Year Without a Summer."

The people of the time hadn't the knowledge of our modern meteorologists, so they didn't know why the weather was so cold. Countless absurd theories were proposed, including those expounded by the guests at the balls in *Juliana*. Although some people did indeed blame Benjamin Franklin's lightning rods, had Franklin still been alive, he might have guessed the real reason. During a similar cold spell in 1784 caused by the great eruption of Mount Asama in Japan, Franklin wrote of a "constant fog over all Europe and a great part of North America," speculating that the dust he observed in the sky might be due to volcanic explosions or the breakup of meteorites.

In James's time, smallpox was sometimes called the Speckled Monster. Throughout recorded history, it killed ten percent of the population. As a youngster, before being variolated (intentionally infected with smallpox as a preventative measure), Edward Jenner was "prepared" by being starved, purged, and bled, and afterward he was locked in a stable with other ailing boys until the disease had run its course. All in all, it was an experience he would never forget—one that later inspired him to experiment and discover that immunization with cowpox prevented smallpox.

In 1801, after he pioneered vaccination, Jenner issued a pamphlet that ended with these words: "…the annihilation of the Small Pox, the most dreadful scourge of the human species, must be the final result of this practice." Unfortunately, almost 180 years went by before his prophecy came to pass.

In *Juliana*, James was too optimistic in hoping smallpox vaccinations would soon be made compulsory. England didn't pass such a law until 1853, and the World Health Organization (WHO) didn't launch its campaign to conquer smallpox until 1967. At that time, there were fifteen million cases of smallpox each year. The WHO's plan was to vaccinate everyone everywhere. Teams of vaccinators traveled the world to the remotest of communities.

The last documented case of smallpox occurred just eight years later, in 1975. After an anxious period of watching for new cases, in 1980 the WHO formally declared, "Smallpox is Dead!" Jenner's dream had come true: The most feared disease of all time had been eradicated.

The Foundling Hospital was established in 1739 by Captain Thomas Coram, a childless shipwright concerned about the plight of unwanted babies in London. In his time, seventy-four percent of the poor children born in London died before they turned five, and the death rate for children put in workhouses was more than ninety percent. In contrast, the Foundling Hospital's mortality rate was under thirty percent. If that sounds high, remember that smallpox, measles, tuberculosis (consumption), and other diseases were endemic during this period. Most people did not reach old age.

In 1740, artist William Hogarth, an early Governor of the Hospital, donated the first painting to the Hospital and encouraged other artists to follow his example—and thus England's first public art gallery was born. When the wealthy came to see the art or attend concerts given by another Governor, George Frideric Handel, they were encouraged to make charitable donations. Although there's no written record of anyone donating anything besides money, we like to think that the Governors would have been open to an idea like Juliana's.

By 1954, the year the Hospital closed, it had served more than 27,000 children. Today you can visit the Foundling Museum in London, which is on the site of the original Hospital and contains artifacts as well as the art collection, displayed in fully restored interiors.

Most of the homes in our books are inspired by real places you can see. Stafford House, James's home in St. James's Place, is based on Spencer House, one of the great architectural landmarks of London. Built in the eighteenth century by John, 1st Earl Spencer (an ancestor of Diana, Princess of Wales), it was immediately recognized as a building of major importance. Should you ever find yourself in London, we highly recommend a visit. Its exquisite rooms have all been restored, and you will see many of the antiquities Amanda admired in this book. Spencer House is open to the public every Sunday except during January and August.

The Chases' town house at 44 Berkeley Square has been described as "the finest terrace house of London." It was designed in 1742 by William Kent for Lady Isabella Finch. Unfortunately, you cannot visit, because the building is currently being used as a private club. But if you go to Berkeley Square, you can see it from the outside—look for the blue door.

Cainewood Castle, Griffin's home where Juliana and James married, is loosely modeled on Arundel Castle in West Sussex. It has been home to the Dukes of Norfolk and their family, the Fitzalan-Howards, since 1243, save for a short period during the Civil War. Although the family still resides there, portions of their magnificent home are open to visitors Sundays through Fridays from April to October.

I hope you enjoyed *Juliana*! Next up is *Corinna*, which is not only Corinna's story, but Griffin and Rachael's, too! Please read on for an excerpt as well as more bonus material!

Always,

Lauren Royal

Though Lady Corinna Chase is more interested in pursuing her art than finding a husband, she can't help but take notice of the handsome Irishman who's moved in next door. When she discovers her new neighbor isn't who he says he is, will she expose him, or find herself drawn into the hoax?

The British Museum, London
April 1817

"WE WANT TO see the Rosetta Stone," two impatient voices chorused.

For the third time.

"Just a few more minutes," Lady Corinna Chase promised her sisters, her gaze focused on her sketchbook.

"A few is three," Alexandra, the oldest, pointed out.

"Or maybe five," added Juliana, the middle sister.

"But certainly not thirty," Alexandra went on. "You said 'a few more minutes' half an hour ago."

"And half an hour before that," Juliana put in.

Corinna was used to ignoring her sisters' chatter, but the squeak of wheels threatened her concentration. Alexandra was rolling a perambulator back and forth in hopes of soothing Harold, her infant son. Though ladies generally didn't make a habit of carting their babies around town—most aristocratic mothers happily left their children in the care of wet nurses and nannies—Alexandra had insisted on buying one of the newfangled contraptions, because she rarely let little Harry out of her sight.

Squeak. Squeak. Squeak. "How can you gaze at statues for so long?"

"I'm not gazing. I'm sketching." Corinna drew another line, following the curve of the marble figure's muscled thigh. "And as you see, this is not a statue, it's a panel. Part of a frieze from the famous Parthenon in Greece, to be exact. And more importantly, the figures carved on it are anatomically correct."

Which was the reason she'd come, of course. The reason she'd been willing to drag herself out of bed at a preposterous hour to come see the Elgin Marbles. Corinna wanted nothing more than to study human anatomy so she could improve her skills in portraiture. Unfortunately, the anatomy classes at the Royal Academy of Arts were entirely forbidden to girls.

Entirely.

Forbidden.

It was infuriating. Corinna's fondest wish was to be elected to the Royal Academy, an honor no woman had attained since 1768. Though she harbored no illusions of accomplishing this goal at the tender age of seventeen—for one thing, Academicians were required to be at least twenty-four years old— earning a nomination was a long, involved process, and she hoped to take her first step within a matter of weeks, by getting one of her paintings accepted for the Royal Academy's Summer Exhibition.

That was something girls *did* accomplish on a regular basis, although not usually with portraits. Proper ladies painted only landscapes and still lifes—painting people was considered unseemly. But Corinna's heart lay in portraiture. As she'd grown older, she'd found herself more and more drawn to the human figure, fascinated by the challenge of capturing a personality on canvas.

But how was she supposed to paint people accurately if she wasn't allowed to attend anatomy classes?

"We cannot stay much longer," Juliana said. "I need to make sure everything's in place for Cornelia's wedding." Cornelia, Juliana's mother-in-law, was marrying Lord Cavanaugh at her home later that evening. "And I want to see the Rosetta Stone," she added for the fourth time.

"So go see it."

"And I want to see the gems and minerals," Alexandra said. "And the jeweled—"

"Go see it all. Go see every rock in the museum." Corinna flipped a page, refocusing on the nude form of the gorgeous Greek god before her. "I'll be right here."

"That would take an hour or more." *Squeak. Squeak.* "We cannot leave you here in the Elgin Gallery alone."

"I'm not alone. There are people everywhere." Too many people, constantly jostling her and blocking her view.

"The Rosetta Stone is in the main building."

"It's perfectly proper for two married ladies to cross the museum grounds together." Unlike Corinna, who was a bit of a free spirit, her sisters seemed always concerned with being proper. "I knew I should have brought Aunt Frances along instead. She's more patient than either of you."

"She's also nine months gone with child," Alexandra retorted. She sighed. "We'll be back in an hour."

"Make that two or three," Corinna muttered as they left. Hearing the pram *squeak-squeak* away, she smiled. She and the Greek god were alone at last.

Holy Hannah, he was magnificent.

If only she could find a young man who looked like *this*, she'd have nothing left to wish for.

Not that she had the slightest intention of wedding anytime soon, much to her brother's displeasure. Griffin wanted nothing more than to marry her off, to have her—his last unwed sister— out of his house and off of his hands. To make her someone else's responsibility.

To that end, he'd been dragging Corinna to balls and to Almack's and to every other social event on the calendar, for the express purpose of hurling her at every eligible gentleman he could find. The season had only been underway a few weeks, and already she was grumbling more than Juliana had all last year.

Griffin really *did* take all the fun out of it.

True, she was fond of dancing, and she also liked gentlemen, of course. Especially the ones who'd managed to get her alone, behind a potted palm in a ballroom or in a dark corner on a terrace, for a stolen kiss. But those had been few and far between this year—her brother was a much more vigilant chaperone than dear, oblivious Aunt Frances.

Artists were supposed to be creatures of passion, were they not? Well, Corinna's life seemed to be sorely lacking in passion. After the shattering consecutive deaths of her father, mother, and eldest brother kept her hidden away in mourning through much of her adolescence, she'd emerged a fresh-faced sixteen-year-old eagerly anticipating her first season. Anticipating glamour, gaiety, novelty, intrigue, and most of all, passion. And when she'd finally made it to London, finally come out in society, finally experienced her first kiss, it had all been…

Rather pleasant.

But that was all.

So excuse her if she was in no great hurry to put aside her grand, exhilarating, ambitious artistic dreams in favor of the *rather pleasant* pastime of finding love.

Especially since, now that Corinna was seventeen and the last unmarried sister, Griffin was making it *rather annoying*.

Catching her lower lip between her teeth, she was using her pencil to shade the fascinating muscles on the god's toned bare chest when something caught her eye. Glancing up, she spotted two young gentlemen heading in her direction. Not an unusual sight—the gallery was crowded with people—but something about these gentlemen held her interest. Actually, it was just one of the gentlemen. The taller one.

The one who bore a striking resemblance to the Greek god she'd been sketching.

Flipping to a new page, she started sketching him instead. Quickly, before he disappeared from view.

His angular, sculpted face was framed by crisp black hair that grew long at the back of his neck. His eyes were the greenest she'd ever seen. Sadly, he was somewhat more clothed than the marble gods, but having sketched quite a few of them, she fancied she could imagine what he looked like beneath his smart but conservative trousers, waistcoat, and tailcoat. Her pencil outlined broad shoulders—

She froze midsketch as the two gentlemen walked right up to her.

"Good afternoon," the shorter one said.

Like his taller companion, he was dark-haired and green-eyed and good-looking. And he was much more fashionably dressed. But all in all, she decided, not nearly of the same godly caliber.

Still, she felt flustered. She wasn't accustomed to handsome young men introducing themselves. Good manners dictated they ask permission of a young lady's chaperone, who would then provide the introduction.

Of course, Corinna's chaperones were currently off who knows where, looking at rocks.

"Good afternoon," she returned guardedly. "Mr....?"

"Delaney," he drawled. "Sean Delaney, at your service. And this," he added, indicating the taller man, "is my good friend, Mr. John Hamilton. Having noticed you sketching, he wished to greet a fellow artist. You've heard of him, I presume?"

Had she heard of him? Corinna's sketchbook and pencil fell to the floor. *Everyone* had heard of John Hamilton, the young renowned and reclusive painter of landscapes.

She turned to him, positively stunned. Her Greek god was John Hamilton—John Hamilton!—and he wanted to meet her. *Her*, Corinna Chase, possibly the most *un*renowned artist in all of London.

"Mr. Hamilton," she gushed, "I cannot tell you how much I admire—"

"Please stop," he interrupted, bending to scoop up her fallen supplies. He straightened and, with a roll of his gorgeous green eyes toward Mr. Delaney, handed the items to her. "I'm sorry, but

I'm not John Hamilton." His lilting voice was distracting. The melodic Irish accent didn't quite mesh with the Greek physique. "I'm Sean Delaney. And I'm afraid my brother-in-law here—the *real* John Hamilton—has a horrible sense of humor."

"Now, Hamilton." The other fellow dolefully shook his head. "There's no need to hide your identity from this charming young lady."

"It's *your* identity, and you feel the need to hide it from everyone." The Irishman drew a line in the air that traced his companion from head to toe. "You'll note he's the one dressed with artistic flair," he pointed out to Corinna before brushing at his own plain black clothes. "I'm merely a common man of business."

"Please forgive Mr. Hamilton." Mr. Delaney—or perhaps he was Mr. Hamilton—raised a brow toward Corinna. "He's much too self-effacing."

"Blarney!" the Greek god shot back. "You're a dunce, Hamilton."

Corinna felt like a tennis ball bouncing back and forth between two players. She didn't know which one to believe. But since she didn't expect to see either of them ever again, she figured it didn't signify.

While they'd volleyed, she'd regained her senses enough to recall that Mr. Hamilton was a member of the committee that chose artwork for the Summer Exhibition. *That* was what truly mattered.

She clutched her art supplies to her chest. "I'm an oil painter myself," she told both of them, praying one really was John Hamilton. "I'm here sketching the marbles to learn anatomy so I can improve my technique for portraits. It's my fondest hope that one of my canvases will be selected for this year's Summer Exhibition."

"I'm certain Mr. Hamilton will vote for it," the shorter one assured her gravely.

"I will not." The Greek god's fists were clenched, and his

Irish lilt came through gritted teeth. "I mean, he won't. Or perhaps he will, but I'm *not* Hamilton."

"Pshaw." His friend waved a smooth, graceful hand. "He's—"

"Corinna!" She looked away to see her sisters and the pram squeaking their way toward her. "I'm sorry we took so long," Alexandra said. "Are you finished yet?"

Corinna beckoned them eagerly, certain Juliana would discern which fellow was John Hamilton. An inveterate meddler, Juliana could ferret out any secret. "I'd be pleased for you to meet Mr. Hamilton," she said, turning back to the gentlemen.

They were gone.

Lifting sweet little Harry from the pram, Alexandra frowned. "Mr. Hamilton?"

"The landscapist, John Hamilton. He was just here." Corinna scanned the crowded gallery, to no avail. "He's gorgeous. Or perhaps it's his friend who's gorgeous, or his brother-in-law—"

"Whatever are you on about? Everyone knows John Hamilton never appears in public." Looking sympathetic, Juliana touched her arm. "I think we should go. I must get home well before my mother-in-law's wedding, and in any case, you've clearly been sketching too long."

~

AVAILABLE NOW!
Learn more about *Corinna* at
www.DevonAndLaurenRoyal.com

ENTER FOR A CHANCE TO WIN
a sterling silver replica of the pendant James gives Juliana in this book!*

Visit the Contest page on Lauren & Devon's website
at www.LaurenandDevonRoyal.com
and answer a question to be
entered in the monthly drawing.

No purchase necessary. See complete rules on the site.

*Please note: Depending on when you enter, the prize may be another piece of jewelry associated with one of Lauren & Devon's books. The authors reserve the right to discontinue this promotion at any time.

LAUREN ROYAL decided to become a writer in the third grade, after winning a "Why My Mother is the Greatest" essay contest. Now she's a *New York Times* and *USA Today* bestselling author of humorous historical romance novels. Lauren lives in Southern California with her family and their constantly shedding cat. She still thinks her mother is the greatest.

DEVON ROYAL is the daughter of romance novelist Lauren Royal. After attending film school, she wrote an award-winning TV comedy pilot and worked in digital video production before turning her focus to fiction writing. Devon lives in Southern California with her husband and son. She also thinks her mother is the greatest.

ACKNOWLEDGMENTS

~

OUR HEARTFELT THANKS:

To Katarina Grant, curatorial assistant at the Foundling Museum in London, for invaluable research into the history of donations to the Foundling Hospital.

To our teenage family members Alex and Bella Royal, for graciously beta reading our sweet and clean books for us.

To all the honorary Chase cousins in our Chase Family Readers Group, for their enthusiastic support.

And, as ever, to all of our readers, who are constantly sending us letters that bring smiles to our days and send us back to our MacBooks to write more.

Thank you, everyone!

CONTACT INFORMATION

~

Newsletter

littl.ink/News

Facebook Readers Group

facebook.com/groups/ChaseFamilyReaders

Website

www.DevonAndLaurenRoyal.com

Email

royall.ink/Email